CAROLINA CONNECTIONS ROMANTIC COMEDY COLLECTION: BOOKS 1 & 2

The Fix & The Spark

SYLVIE STEWART

Rolling Hearts Press

COPYRIGHT

In accordance with the U.S. Copyright Act of 1976, the scanning, uploading, and electronic sharing of any part of this book without the permission of the publisher constitute unlawful piracy and theft of the author's intellectual property. If you would like to use material from the book (other than brief quotations for review purposes), prior written permission must be obtained by the author who can be contacted at sylvie@sylviestewartauthor.com. Thank you for your support of the author's rights.

This book is a work of fiction. Names, characters, places, and incidents are products of the author's imagination or are used fictitiously. Any resemblance to actual persons, living or dead, events, or locales is entirely coincidental.

Copyright © 2019 by Sylvie Stewart
Edited by Heather Mann

ISBN: 978-1947853-23-2

ALSO BY SYLVIE STEWART

The Carolina Connection Series:

The Lucky One *(Carolina Connections Book 3)*

The Game *(Carolina Connections Book 4)*

The Way You Are *(Carolina Connections Book 5)*

The Runaround *(Carolina Connections Book 6)*

The Nerd Next Door *(Carolina Kisses, Book 1)*

Then Again

Happy New You

Game Changer

About That

Full-On Clinger

* * *

Between a Rock and a Royal *(Kings of Carolina, Book 1*

Blue Bloods and Backroads *(Kings of Carolina,* Book 2)

THE FIX: A SINGLE MOM ROMCOM

by Sylvie Stewart

COPYRIGHT

fix (fiks)

noun - informal. a position from which it is difficult to escape; a predicament.

verb - to repair; mend.

- Dictionary.com

verb - to unbreak shit

- Sylvie Stewart

Chapter One

PANTS? WHO NEEDS PANTS?

*L*ANEY

I awoke to a foot in my mouth.

No, not the old feeling of having said something horribly inappropriate that you immediately wish you could un-say, but an actual foot. *In my mouth.*

"Ung guh!" I spat. To say this was a disturbing way to begin one's day would be a gross understatement—emphasis on the *gross*. "What in the … ugh." My head dropped back to the pillow as comprehension dawned. Rocco's size twelve with those cute little toes lay on the pillow next to my face, along with a small puddle of drool. I took in his sleeping form, passed out upside down in nothing but his Ninja Turtle underwear.

"We can't keep doing this, dude," I whispered to myself. My little exhibitionist, having contorted himself into some kind of inverted nocturnal backbend, had spent the night in my bed—yet again. Being awakened by small naked body parts was starting to mess with my head. Not to mention, who knew where those little feet had been? Oh, wait, I did. *Blech.*

Completely unprepared to get up for the day, I snuggled back into my favorite dogwood printed sheets and stared up at the ceiling. I was discovering that moving to a strange new house was rough on a kid. Hell, it was rough on me and I was twenty years older than him. All things considered though, Rocco had been a real trouper since leaving the only house he'd known at my parents' and moving into the cute fixer-upper we now call home. But there were obviously still some kinks to work out—case in point, my rude wake-up call.

When my parents first brought up the possibility of their out-of-state move, I don't think I had ever seen them so edgy. There was lots of hand-wringing and "um, well, you know" before I had demanded they just spit it out—I was halfway convinced one or both of them were dying of Ebola or something equally horrifying.

I'd been feeling increasingly uncomfortable for leaning on them so heavily since the little stick had turned blue, so it was almost a relief to have the decision to get a place of my own taken out of my hands. Turns out while I had feared our moving out would hurt my parents' feelings, they had been afraid I'd fall to pieces without them. One come-to-Jesus conversation later and my mom was accepting a new position at the University of Richmond in Virginia while I was on the phone with a realtor.

The truth is, early on, I would never have survived a day of motherhood without the undying, and most importantly, non-judgmental support of my family and my best friend—as well as the financial, if not physical, support of Rocco's dad. But it was past time for me to pull my big girl panties up and I knew it. All the support I'd received had allowed me to finish my associate's degree and get a job which, while not being entirely stimulating, allowed me to take care of my kid and me. As far as single moms went, my situation was the dream, and I knew it.

Turns out there is something remarkably satisfying about holding ownership of the place where you lay your head at night, and our new house was adorable. It had bright white siding—after a power-washing from my dad—and black shutters that were mostly on straight. And it was topped off by a cheery bright red front door. The house was a ranch and it was a bit older, but it had three bedrooms, two baths, and a fenced-in backyard for Rocco and the dog I was sure we would eventually get. It was close (but not *too* close) to the stores and restaurants, and the street was nice and quiet. I loved it and I was proud of our new home, even if it did have some drawbacks—leaky faucets, a few uneven floors, and *maybe* a few more major problems. But that was okay. All of that could be fixed with time and a little help from my idiot younger brother. I hoped.

On the condition that he would help with the repairs and renovating, I had agreed to let him stay with Rocco and me. It was a win-win—my faucets wouldn't drip, and my brother wouldn't be homeless, considering that his previous residence had also been my parents' house. Even he had to admit that, at twenty-two, following your parents to a new state in order to live in their basement was borderline Jay and Silent Bob. And besides, all his drinking buddies were here in Greensboro so there was that …

So now the house was ours and we were making it into a home. What I didn't know before moving was that a new house breathes differently than your old one. It has its own voices and creaky bones to creep you right the hell out if you're not used to them. And we were definitely not used to them—thus the previous month of waking up to Professor Underwear crowding my sleep space in an entertaining array of positions.

It was past time to get out of bed so I laid my hand on Rocco's bare foot and pressed a soft kiss to his head. I inhaled the unique "boy" scent of sweat and the outdoors, trying not to wake him. The floor squeaked under my feet, and out in the hall I tried in vain to avoid the cockeyed floorboard that's entire existence was centered around mocking my lack of coordination. One stubbed toe and several curses later I reached the kitchen and went straight to the vintage avocado-colored fridge for my morning coffee. Okay, what I actually mean is Diet Coke. *Don't look at me like that. There are plenty of people who don't like coffee. And some of them are even over the age of thirteen.*

One could say I am *not* a morning person. As in, I may be borderline vampire. All these people who wake up at the crack of dawn to enjoy a leisurely pot of coffee and read the paper completely baffle me. And don't get me started on those five-a.m. gym weirdos. In my world, no sane person ever wakes up a minute earlier than it takes to frantically throw things together and arrive at the day's destination a mere hair's breadth from being tardy. And usually looking like their five-year-old styled their outfit. And hair.

Armed with my caffeine, I made my way into the laundry room —okay, "room" may be a tad generous, technically it's more of a laundry "closet"—to see if I had somehow managed to wash and dry appropriate clothes to dress Rocco for daycare and me for work in a somewhat presentable fashion. Luckily, the dress code at

Brach Technologies, where I log my 40 hours a week, is pretty laid back. I can usually get away with pants and a blouse or even a nice t-shirt if I throw a sweater over it. Comfort is key if I'm going to sit in a cube all day being hypnotized by my monitor, so my work wardrobe receives almost zero effort from me—much to my best gal pal's horror.

On the complete opposite end of the spectrum, my best friend, Fiona, puts together outfits in a manner I can only describe as "crafting." Copious amounts of thought, skill, and passion are involved when Fiona gets dressed in the morning. Remember the character Cher in *Clueless*? Now you're getting the picture.

Last Tuesday I rendered Fiona completely speechless (a miraculous feat in itself) when she'd picked me up from work and spied the pair of Skechers I was wearing. *What?! They're comfortable! And they were the dressy-ish kind anyway, so suck it!*

The moment my Skecher-shod foot had hit the floorboard of her Prius, Fiona's mouth dropped open, her head tilted back, and she crossed herself, all while doing some kind of deep breathing thing. I had already settled in the passenger seat so there was no escaping the drama. May as well get comfortable, so I pulled my brunette mess of hair into a sloppy ponytail with the hair tie I always keep on one wrist. Let her rant about that one too.

"Dear Saint Jimmy, she knows not what she does. I swear," she muttered to the roof of the car.

"Um, I know who you're talking to and I'm pretty sure he's still alive and well and no doubt creating more toe crushers as we sit here."

"Of course he's not dead!" Fiona's head snapped to me.

Oh, it looked like *Exorcist* Fiona was coming out to play.

"I just wanted to apologize in case he's listening," she whispered before clearing her scowl and finally gracing me with her cheery customary Fiona smile. "So, aside from the fact that you clearly got dressed in the dark this morning, how was work?"

Letting her dig slide like I always do, I tapped my index finger to the side of my mouth in feigned thought. "Let's see, ten being a complete lobotomy and one being menstrual cramps, I'd give it a six. Annette brought doughnuts," I explained.

"Mmmm," Fiona mused while pulling carefully out of the parking lot, both of us silent for a moment, contemplating the sheer yumminess that is a perfect doughnut.

"Oh!" she brought her head around suddenly, startling the bejesus out of me. "You'll never guess who I saw on my Starbucks run this morning! For once I know something before you do," she taunted in a sing-song voice before prattling on and gesticulating like a varsity cheerleader with the semester's hottest gossip. "And don't let me forget to tell you about the party we're invited to this weekend—a *wellspring* of man candy, I promise you. God, I need to get laid." Her head tilted back before she straightened again, perhaps remembering she was supposed to be driving. "Anyway, about the coffee thing, I was running late because Gary kept reminding me about needing his half-caff extra, *extra* hot, as if that's actually a thing, so I had to wait forever for the poor barista to get it right and I was just turning around when—" she stopped abruptly. "I forgot. Where am I taking you? Pete's or the other place?"

My seven-year-old Corolla had kindly held onto the last fragments of its bald tires just long enough for me to save for the new ones, thus my chauffeured ride to the body shop. "Pete's. He gave me a better deal on the tires and said he'd try to fix my door dent for free," I replied. *Is there anything more depressing than blowing $300 on tires?*

She looked at me out of the corners of her Gucci-sunglass-covered eyes. "Yeah, and I'm sure it had nothing to do with Thelma and Louise bobbing around under his nose when he gave you the estimate." Her chin raise saluted my "girls." "Did he manage to bring his eyes anywhere above chin level at any point in the negotiation?"

I chose to ignore her little joke at the expense of my rack. If I've told her once I've told her a thousand times, you don't get to have big boobs without having big *other stuff* to go along with it. Mother Nature has some sense of justice, after all. "So, continue with this big news," I redirected her, pulling my drugstore sunglasses from my purse.

Fiona has what I like to call an "Oh look, something shiny!" level of distractibility. Her habit of losing track of thoughts and taking little verbal strolls during conversation can be a tad confusing. Listening to her tell a story is like picking your way through a vocal minefield. But since she's my best friend, I choose to find it charming. As do most people, actually. That's just Fiona—a charming little verbal-diarrhea-spewing pixie with a gorgeous heart-shaped face and wispy blond hair. She is also the most cheerful and positive person I know, and although she occasionally has a temper and definitely has a dirty mind, everyone loves Fiona. Most people would like to carry her around in their pocket like one of those celebrity purse dogs, but infinitely better. However, she's mine and I will never give her back.

"Oh, right," Fiona said. "So, Starbucks … anyway, the barista hands me Gary's coffee but it's the wrong one and I turn around to tell her mine is the venti black one, not the tiny grande with cream … although why Gary doesn't like a little cream, I don't know."

Something else about Fiona? She has a mouth on her, no doubt, but she also has this uncanny knack for saying things that sound overtly sexual (at least to those of us with dirty minds, so, yeah, pretty much everyone I know), but are in fact completely innocent. And she doesn't seem to know she does it, therefore making it all the more hi-*lar*-ious, especially coming out of that angelic face. It's so bad that my idiot brother and his equally idiotic best friend have a running bet where the first one to get turned on by something Fiona unwittingly says owes the other five dollars on the spot.

"… and I practically run smack into Gavin," I heard her say.

Speak of the devil. Literally. My idiot brother, Gavin.

"Gavin? *My* Gavin? My idiot brother, Gavin? What in the poop was Gavin doing at Starbucks? He doesn't have enough money for a Starbucks coffee. He doesn't have enough money for a complimentary coffee!"

"Well, I know, but give him a break," she chided and then grimaced. "And you've got to stop saying 'poop' so much, Laney. It's kind of nasty."

I waved her off with my hand. "I know, I know, it's disgusting, but I'm trying not to say 'fuck' anymore and Rocco won't stop with all the 'poop, fart, and butt-crack' talk so it's invaded my vocabulary without my permission—like osmosis or something. Forget about that," I shooed. "What about Gavin? You know, he's been acting shady lately, the little bastard, and I know he's up to something that's going to end up costing me either money or pride, and I can't afford either." I rubbed my freckled cheeks, a habit I have whenever I get stressed or nervous.

"No!" Fiona cried excitedly. "That's just it! He was interviewing for a *job*!"

My hands dropped. "Shut your face! At Starbucks?!"

"No, of course not." She waved a dismissive hand. "He'd have to shower for that."

"And wear a shirt," I replied, taking in this revelation.

"And pants," Fiona finished thoughtfully.

Hmm. The source of Rocco's "underwear only" policy was becoming evident.

"So where was he interviewing then?" I asked.

"At some construction company with an office next door to Starbucks. He said something about the company renovating the Harris Teeter on Friendly by my dry cleaners. Not that you would know what a dry cleaner is, my fashion-impaired friend." She gave a little giggle. Why was I friends with her again? "But I digress … apparently the company is growing really big and they need some new muscle to push it hard on a couple new jobs."

I snickered only momentarily at her inadvertent dirty remark, too distracted by the notion that my beloved ignoramus may actually be growing up and attempting to take on responsibility. *Wow*. I might cry.

This brings me back to my laundry room at 7:15 in the morning where I was sifting through clothes while trying not to spill my Diet Coke. Rocco's wardrobe was a snap: shorts, t-shirt, socks, sneakers. *Bam*. I'm not one of those moms who dress their kid like a tiny grown up in collared shirts and pleated pants with belts and Top-Siders. He's not executing a business deal—he's going to preschool. Where he will most likely get paint in his hair, will most definitely get boogers (hopefully his own) on his shirt, and will quite possibly pee his pants. Shorts and a t-shirt work fine for that.

Aha! I finally uncovered a slightly wrinkled, white eyelet button down for myself that I could pair with my low-rise black pants, kickass silver-studded belt and some comfy ballet flats. Clothes in hand, it was time for me to wake up my little streaker.

Halfway back to the master bedroom, I heard music. Billy Idol, to be precise, his plea to "ride the pony" coming from the extra bedroom where Gavin had been squatting for the last few weeks. The song was abruptly silenced (*thank you*) with what sounded like a cellphone hitting a wall. That was odd. Gavin had the same sleeping-in gene I did so why would– *Yes!* I remembered now— today was Gavin's first day of work! I squeed to myself and executed some super cool dance moves. I may soon be able to afford the $7 bottle of wine. Not that I could tell the difference, but whatever. The morning was already looking brighter.

With Rocco, now fully dressed, settled in at my shabby-chic kitchen table munching on his bowl of Cocoa Krispies—sans milk, of course—there was *still* no sign of Gavin. It had been twenty minutes. Further inspection back in the hall revealed a closed door and a muffled snore.

"Knock, knock." I rapped as I pushed open the door. "I figured I should rattle your cage since eighties rock doesn't seem to be doing the—*Oh God! Put it away!*" I slapped my hand over my eyes so hard I could practically feel the shiner forming, the vision of Gavin's pale white ass cheeks burning a hole through the back of my skull. The only thing keeping the vomit down was the fortunate fact that he was on his stomach instead of his back.

"Guhfmm … what?" came the drowsy male snuffle from the bed, accompanied by a rustling of sheets.

Still shielding my eyes, I whispered-yelled, "Get your hairy ass covered!" I did not want to alert Rocco to any possible distraction involving his favorite person and unfortunate role model.

"Hey, it's not hairy," Gavin protested with a yawn. "You're just jealous cuz mine's perfect and yours is, well, you know."

I turned to face the hall again and lowered my hand. "You can't be late on your first day, Gav. And for God's sake, put on some pants—there's a minor in this house and there is no way to un-see that whole mess you've got goin' on, Billy Idol." Careful not to glance in his direction, I made a vague circular motion with my finger and hurried away to finish getting myself ready for the day.

I returned to the kitchen with five minutes to spare. Gavin, thankfully now clothed in faded jeans and an old concert t-shirt, was leaning against the counter with his own bowl of Cocoa Krispies raised to chin level. He spooned a bite into his mouth and focused on his nephew.

"But why doesn't she like ponies?" Rocco's puzzled expression passed between his uncle and me, his lisp making "ponies" come out as "poneeth." His brown eyes crinkled in confusion while his thick dark hair tilted to the side along with his head. "Ponies are awesome."

Gavin pointed his now empty spoon at Rocco. "I don't think it's that she doesn't *like* ponies, Rock—it's just that it's been too long since she's *ridden* a pony," he said, chuckling to himself at his oh-so-lame joke and giving me a sidelong glance in repressed merriment.

"Ha ha," I responded and then gestured for Rocco to give me his empty bowl and cup from the table. "Your Uncle Gavin needs to quit with the livestock stories and get going to his new job," I told Rocco. "And we need to get a move on, dude, or we're gonna be late for school. Go grab your shoes." I tossed the dirty dishes in the sink for later.

Rocco dashed to the side door to retrieve his sneakers and I turned to face my brother. "Seriously, Gavin, good luck today," I stretched onto my tiptoes to give him an unexpected peck on his scruffy cheek. "Knock 'em dead!"

"Yeah, yeah," he replied self-consciously, running a hand through his unruly mass of dark brown hair—hair that I noted had clearly not been washed on this day. *Baby steps*, I told myself.

We both knew this job was a big deal—a turning point of sorts, I hoped—but not wanting to make him feel more uncomfortable than necessary, I threw a small wave over my shoulder, picked up my lunch bag along with Rocco's backpack, and escorted my kid out the door.

"Yeah, good luck, Uncle Gavin!" Rocco hollered as he hopped down the garage steps toward the car. "Maybe if you do a good job we can go on a pony ride this weekend!" As the door closed behind me, I caught a brief glimpse of the cereal spewing from Gavin's surprised mouth and onto my linoleum floor.

One guess as to who'd be cleaning that up later.

Poop!

Chapter Two

IF IT'S GOOD ENOUGH FOR A CAVEMAN...

NATE

"I think that about covers it," said the nurse, handing over the discharge papers. "Any other questions?" Her pleasant smile passed over my mother, sister, and me, finally coming to rest on my father who was perched on the side of the hospital bed.

"I think we've got it from here." My mother breathed in deeply and released it in a resigned sigh. "Plenty of rest, no alcohol, healthy diet, and no stress—easy enough." She tried for a small smile with limited success, although it was unclear whom she was trying to reassure, us or the nurse. Nothing about this mess was easy.

My father spoke up from his seat on the bed. "Are you sure about this whole *no red meat* thing?" His hand swept up to point a finger at me as if this had all been my idea. "What the hell do you think cavemen ate, bean sprouts? No! I'll tell you what they ate—

meat! And then when they were done with that, you know what they ate for dessert? More meat! And you think they weren't stressed? Of course they were; they were being chased by lions and wooly mammoths and who the hell knows what else as soon as they set foot outside the cave. Talk about stressful." His finger made sure to single out each occupant of the room before his tirade settled.

Bailey stepped forward. "Props to your cavemen brethren and all, Dad, but you're forgetting one *tiny*, important detail," my younger sister interjected, crossing her arms. "They all lived to the ripe old age of twenty and were about four feet tall."

"I'll leave you all to it. Feel better, Mr. Murphy!" The nurse retreated to the hall. I didn't blame her.

It was time to wrap this shit show up. "All right, Dad, let's get the hell out of here and get you home." I put my arm around my mom's shoulder and gave her a squeeze. She leaned into me with a hesitant smile.

"It's about damn time," my dad grumbled.

I couldn't blame him for his less than chipper mood. If I'd had my chest cracked open days earlier and had to endure a week of bland hospital food and plastic sheets, my disposition would be pretty damn sour too. Is there anyone on earth who *doesn't* hate hospitals?

In truth, seeing my old man lying on the bed with his body stuck full of tubes and wires when I'd arrived last week had really done a number on me. His normally robust presence had been completely absent and a frail and extremely, well, *mortal* looking figure had taken my dad's place. The shock of it was extraordinary. After that, it had taken very little time for my brain to catch up with my gut. Priorities automatically began to shift in my mind, and decisions that were once complicated and difficult became simple and quite inevitable. I was home, and I was here to stay.

* * *

"Soooo," Bailey began once she and I were seated at the dining table in my parents' home, the same home we'd both grown up in just outside of Greensboro. The topic at hand? The family business. "What the hell do we do now?"

I brought my hands together on the tabletop as I took in the familiar surroundings, my mom's small touches noticeable throughout—the Lladro statues lining the sideboard, the dried flowers arranged among the dishes in the china hutch, and a few of Bailey's paintings hung carefully on the opposite wall. I brought my eyes back to my sister and narrowed them at her. "Not so fast, Bay. I've been here a week—don't think you're dumping this whole thing on me as if I have all the answers. I don't know what the hell I'm doing and you can't play your little 'Oh, I'm such a right brain person so I couldn't possibly do anything so uncreative and logical' game. I'll drag you with me kicking and screaming if I have to."

"Oh, shut up, you pompous turd!" She slapped at my arm. "Have I complained yet? I'm more than prepared to jump in. I just don't know where to start. Dad oversees everything, and I mean *everything*. Nothing is outside the scope of his domain." She sighed and propped her chin up with her hand. "It's just a bit overwhelming."

Bailey and I had spent the last few days running back and forth between our dad's office and the hospital; we were anxious, over-whelmed, and pretty fucking exhausted.

So even though Bailey is usually a pain in the ass, I regretted my earlier tone and started over. "Okay, I'm sorry. I guess I thought you'd have a better idea than I would of the best course of action here. I've been out of the day-to-day picture for a couple years now and you've been working steadily with him so I guess I just assumed." I shrugged.

"Yeah, but I'm the design person. I can put together an interior with my eyes closed, but all the administrative and construction crap is not in my wheelhouse, Nate. I'll help where I can but ..." She offered a super fake smile and lifted her hands up in the air. Classic Bailey—trying to be cute.

"Have I reminded you yet today that you were a mistake?" I asked, because I'm her brother and it's my job.

"Nate, I could eat a bowl of alphabet soup and crap out a better insult than that."

I laughed. "Okay, that was a good one."

"I know—I've been storing them up since you've been away. I've missed you, you big asshat." She pushed my shoulder. "And I'll do my best to help wherever I can. Deal?"

"Deal." I pushed her right back and she fell off her chair. "Oops."

I knew she was right and the bulk of the responsibility would have to fall to me. I'd been working in construction in one aspect or another since I was sixteen and could legally enter a job site. Even before that, I had spent many childhood afternoons on the trailer floor of whatever site my dad was working at the time. I built some pretty stellar houses and skyscrapers and, well, superhero hideouts, using Legos or blocks or whatever else I had on hand.

My dad's company, Built by Murphy, was founded by his father and was the family's pride and joy. It was also a legacy my dad made no secret he wished to hand down to his two kids when the time came. Unfortunately, none of us had anticipated that time coming so soon, or so abruptly. Not that any of us were under the illusion that Riordan Murphy would quietly submit to the laid-back life of a retiree just because he had a major heart attack. But he would certainly be taking a step back—or several steps if my mom had anything to say about it. In light of that, someone had to take a step forward, and it looked like I was the only man for the job.

Construction is tough. There's a reason most movie scenes involving construction sites occur during smoke breaks or lunch breaks. It's hard to glamorize dirt and concrete dust, let alone try to carry on a conversation through the deafening buzzes and whirs of heavy equipment and power tools. Hard hats and hard work make you sweat and they exhaust you by the end of the day. But then you wipe your filthy face with your even filthier shirt and stand back to take in your work. And *that's* when the magic happens, at least for me. The bones of a future house, or the foundation of a parking structure, or even a whole damn building stand before you. And you know that *you* built that. *You* helped lay that floor, *you* smoothed that concrete, *you* hung that drywall. Your accomplishment is tangible. And, sure, most days you forget to stand back— you're exhausted and ready to hit the shower or grab a beer, or you have some crappy errand to run. But on the days that you remember, there's no feeling like it.

I wasn't reluctant to adopt the actual construction aspect of the company—never had been—but as I'd seen with my dad, the guy who runs the show doesn't wield a hammer. He spends half his time in meetings and the other half putting out fires. This holds little interest for me and is the main reason I left town a few years back. I didn't want to get sucked into the *business* of doing construction. I wanted to do my job, do it well, and at the end of the day just leave it there and get on with whatever the rest of the evening held for me. Taking his work home with him and strategizing to grow a company is what landed my dad in open heart surgery at the age of sixty. No thanks. But what choice did I have?

It all came down to one thing—family. And worse yet, fucking Irish family.

* * *

"Come on in," I beckoned to the kid.

It was the following Monday and I was starting my day at an apartment building we were putting up on the north side of town. I'd spent the weekend at the office and at the company's various worksites with Bailey, still trying to get up to speed. We had a few new crew members starting this week and it looked like the first one had arrived.

So maybe "kid" wasn't exactly the right word for the guy standing at the open doorway. He was probably early twenties, and I had only just turned thirty-one myself. But from the looks of his work history that Bailey had passed on to me, I couldn't think of what else to call him. There was hardly a thing there. What in the hell had this guy been doing since high school?

He stepped toward me in the site trailer, hands in the front pockets of his jeans, a tentative expression clear on his face. He was fairly tall, probably only an inch or two shorter than my 6'2" and I suppose he looked strong enough. Bailey did mention the stellar character references she'd gotten from a couple of the guy's former baseball coaches, I think. At any rate, something made her give him a shot, so I figured I'd just go with it. The kid didn't know shit about construction, that was clear, but that didn't bother me per se. At this point, I just needed all the extra hands I could get, and as long as we kept a close eye on him, he could learn a lot of what he needed to know on the job. Nothing like trial by fire.

"Monroe, right?" I asked him.

"Yeah, that's me. Gavin Monroe."

"Nate Murphy." I stuck out my hand.

He took it and gave it a firm shake. "Nice to meet you. And, uh, thanks for the job. You won't be disappointed."

"Well, I guess that remains to be seen, Gavin." His Adam's apple bobbed but he held my eyes. This could work out fine after all. "Follow me and I'll show you around. You'll have to pardon me—I'm still trying to get up to speed on all these open projects, but I'm assuming my sister told you all about that when she interviewed you?"

"Yeah, she did. I hope your dad's doing better."

"He's hanging in there, thanks." I handed the kid a hard hat as I donned my own by the door of the trailer. "You bring a pair of work gloves with you?"

"No, sir." The uncertain look was back.

"We'll find you a pair." I took a step down the stairs. "I'm assuming those boots are steel toed." It wasn't a question.

"Yes, sir."

"All right, come on, I'll introduce you to Mark. He's the foreman on this job and he'll get you squared away. Not sure if you'll stay on this site or not but we'll play it by ear." I strode toward the closest building, not waiting to see if the kid followed. "And cut the 'sir' crap!" I raised my voice over the buzz of a power saw. "You work hard and do your job and save the manners for your mom."

THE BUT SANDWICH

LANEY

"Soooo hungry," Gavin whined like the little baby he is. He was stretched out on the sofa with his hands cradling his stomach and his sweaty shirt sullying the upholstery.

"Why didn't you eat any lunch?" I asked from the kitchen where I was helping Rocco with his backpack. We'd just walked in the door a minute earlier and I was equal parts eager and anxious to hear about Gavin's first day.

"I did." Whine. "But they had me running around so much I burned that off by about one o'clock. I forgot how much sweat a human body can produce in a day."

Eww.

"I'm hungry too, Mommy," Rocco said as he pulled off his shoes and left them in the middle of the floor—right by the dried up, half-chewed Cocoa Krispies I'd forgotten about from this morning. Double eww.

"Okay, baby." I grabbed the paper towel roll from the counter and went to the sink to wet a few. "How does frozen pizza sound?" I called to the other room.

"Make it two, and no veggies!" came the response from Gavin.

"Yeah, no veggies!" Rocco echoed.

I smiled. I know I probably shouldn't. But when I didn't stop to think too hard about whether or not Gavin was the best influence on my son, I was so grateful that there was a man in his life on a consistent basis. One who would never flake out on him and suddenly find something better to do. Sometimes it even seemed that the similarity in their maturity levels was, in fact, the very glue that bonded them.

I admit that one of my fears when my mom and dad moved was that Rocco would be left with just me, and I would be depriving him of the opportunity to have loving and reliable men in his life. That was definitely a contributing factor in my decision to allow Gavin to move in with us.

My biggest fear has always been messing my kid up.

I just had to keep reminding myself that, in the battle for Rocco's well-being, a guy who loves him will beat out veggies every time.

As awesome as my kid is, he obviously did not just spontaneously appear in my womb one day—as if my ovaries were having a boring day and said, "Hey, you know what would be fun?" No, he was the result of numerous lime gelatin shots, a hot friend-of-a-friend musician visiting from California, and some extraordinarily bad judgment on everyone's part.

Dominic, Rocco's dad, is actually a nice guy and I have to give him some credit. After the initial, and expected, freak-out when I'd tracked him down by phone with the news every nineteen-year-old guy wants to hear—guess what? It's a boy!—he'd tried to step up the best way he knew how. It had been three months since the fateful deed in the back seat of a borrowed extended-cab truck (*I know—don't remind me*), and only three days since I'd finally stopped Linda Blair-ing my guts out with morning sickness. As I sat on my bed in my childhood room clutching my cellphone, we had discussed possible options—me moving to California, him moving to North Carolina—but in the end, it had just made sense for each of us to stay put. My family was here, and I was midway through my freshman year of college. His family was scattered, but he had just been accepted into a very prestigious music program, and while his family had quite a bit of money, we'd both known that him dropping out and moving across the country for his knocked-up one-night stand would not go over well.

As cringe-worthy as it sounds, we were complete strangers. And while neither of us wanted Dominic to be a stranger to his child, uprooting hadn't been the best plan. So I had stayed here and Dominic had flown out for the birth. And after a paternity test, which his family's lawyer had naturally insisted on, a reasonable arrangement for child support was agreed upon and we worked out visitation. Dominic, even now, didn't make much money, but with his family's resources he made sure we got what we needed financially.

And he does love his son—I know this. But I don't know if he'll ever love anyone more than he loves his music, and that's not what I want for Rocco in a full-time dad.

Now Dominic flies out to take Rocco for a few weeks every year between breaks in his busy touring schedule. And we all forge ahead. But at night when I lie in bed and rehash all the parenting decisions I could have handled differently that day—not to mention all the calories I shouldn't have eaten and all the chores I should have completed—I often wish to the bottom of my soul that our story of mother and son had begun differently. That instead of a duo, we were some incredible kick-ass trio.

I set the oven to preheat and attempted to ease into a group discussion so I could covertly interrogate Gavin about his job. I began with Rocco. "So, Rock, did you and your new friends do anything fun at school today?"

"Nah." He twitched his little nose.

"What do you mean, 'nah'? You were there all day."

Another change since we'd branched out on our own, Rocco was attending a new school—otherwise known as daycare—for the full day instead of the half day of preschool we'd done while living with my parents. Once I'd pushed past the guilt, I could appreciate that this was actually a positive change for him. He'd spent the majority of his time around adults before, and it was high time he made some friends his own age.

I moved to the half wall between the kitchen and the living room to find Rocco mimicking his uncle as he lay in my favorite cushy armchair, hand to his gut and head thrown back.

"I dunno," was his complete response.

"Well, what did you do all day?"

"Don't 'member." He shrugged and twitched his nose again.

Well, how do you respond to that? I guessed it was time to move on to the next topic.

"Okay. How about you, Uncle Gavin? Did you do anything fun with your new friends today?"

Gavin's head came off the couch to fix me with narrowed eyes. "Am I allowed to say I don't remember either?" Taking in my look he said, "Yeah, I thought not. It was okay, I guess. They all treated me like the newbie, as expected. Most of the guys were okay, some of them were dicks—I mean, jerks." He glanced Rocco's way, but the little guy was unfazed. "It was mostly a lot of lifting things and holding this or that while somebody secured it."

"That doesn't sound so bad," I commented. "Where were you?"

"I was at some apartment complex off New Garden, but the boss said they might move me to the grocery store on Friendly or maybe even the commercial building going in at the end of our street. I told him I lived here so I think he might try to put me on that one, which would be cool."

"What commercial building?" I asked, unfamiliar with anything being built by our neighborhood.

"I don't know, some building they're putting up with rental spaces—right at the entrance."

That was odd. "There are houses on either side."

"Don't ask me—it's my first day. Nate said the houses were in foreclosure so they got the properties at a really good price. They're gonna tear them down and put something else up."

Apprehension speared my gut, but I pushed it aside. "So it sounds like you met a lot of people for your first day. That's good," I led.

"I guess."

What was it with guys? Would it kill them to share a little?

"Well, since Mom and Dad aren't here, someone has to say it.

I'm proud of you, Gav," I told him. "I know this isn't your dream job but I'm glad you're moving on."

His sudden frown had me regretting my last statement. *Stupid!*

He inhaled and then sighed. "It's no major league game, but whatever. It is what it is."

"What's a commercial building? Will it sell toys from the TV?" asked Rocco as the oven dinged—time to put in the pizzas.

"Uncle Gavin will explain." I turned back to the kitchen to make dinner for my guys. *Baby steps, Laney, baby steps.*

My phone rang an hour later. Gavin was busy holding a giggling Rocco upside-down in the living room and shaking him to get the pizza to reappear. I was adding dishes to the growing pile in the sink, telling myself I'd get to them later. The number on the caller ID was unfamiliar, but I pressed Accept.

"Hello?"

"Oh hi. Is this Laney Monroe?"

"Yes."

"This is Mellie Jordan from Cornerstone Daycare. How are you?"

Rocco's daycare teacher.

"Oh hi, Mellie! I'm good—how about you?" We exchanged pleasantries.

"I'm just fine, Laney. Listen, I'm sorry to bother you at home. I was hoping to catch you when you picked Rocco up this afternoon, but I think I just missed you. I wanted to touch base on a couple things—nothing's wrong, so don't worry," she reassured me.

"Okay, what's up?" I asked.

"Well, first of all, I wanted to tell you that we all *love* Rocco here. He is just such a sweet little guy."

My chest wanted to swell at this, but my motherly instincts were sensing a "but sandwich" on the horizon—*your kid is great, but he's pantsing all the other kids on the playground and we'll have to expel him, but did I tell you we really think he's great?*

"But," Mellie continued.

Here it comes.

"I'm just the teensiest bit concerned about him, socially speaking," Mellie said.

My hand that wasn't holding the phone went to my cheek and the rubbing began.

"He seems to spend most of his time playing by himself, and when we try to encourage him to join in with some of the other kids he says he doesn't want to," she continued.

Rub.

"I wouldn't mention it since he's new to the school and I know kids can be shy, but we just haven't seen any improvement yet—I catch him looking at what other kids are doing so I think he's interested, but he won't go that next step. Sometimes one of us teachers will play with him to get the ball rolling and he'll talk to us just fine. But not with the other kids."

Rub rub.

"I'm not trying to scare you or anything because this is probably something we'll look back on later and laugh about, but at his age, he really should be engaging in interactive play with other kids instead of parallel play we see with the younger ones. I wanted to ask, does he have friends in the neighborhood or from his old school he interacts with regularly? Am I just bothering you for nothing?" She laughed lightly.

Rub rub rub rub—*oh, Jesus Christ, somebody just bring me a loofah!*

"Um, hmm. Well, you see, Mellie, we just moved to a new neighborhood as well as the new school and we really haven't gotten a chance to meet too many people …" I trailed off.

"Oh, you poor thing—that *is* a lot of change all at once. Rocco probably just needs a few more weeks to get in the swing of things, then. Is he getting a chance to see any of his old friends?"

Crap. How did one explain this? *Of course my five-year-old has friends! There's his uncle who is great fun and is always offering to share his* Playboy *collection. Sure, his brain could probably be traded with an orangutan and nobody would notice, but who doesn't like monkeys, right? And then there are Rocco's grandparents! His grandma lets him help grade exams and tells him all sorts of interesting tidbits about late twentieth-century American history—what kid doesn't love to chat about Vietnam?! Let's not forget Grandpa either—he takes Rocco to the Farm and Fleet to talk to the three-fingered manager about riding mowers, because that guy is the one to ask about machines with sharp blades. And, sure, a couple of these besties just moved four hours away, but there's always Skype and everyone knows that is interactive as hell—nothing parallel in sight!*

Rub.

Yeah, that wasn't going to go over well. Time to fess up.

"The truth is, Mellie, what you're talking about has pretty much always been the case. He's not really been into kids his own age. He's an only child and has always seemed content to hang out with adults. I've tried not to worry about it before. I guess I just hoped it would resolve on its own." *How could I have missed this apparently huge red flag?*

"I understand. And, again, I don't want you to worry. But maybe we could try to help things along a little more. Why don't you ask him if there's a child in the class he would want to have a playdate with? Then you could arrange it at your house so Rocco would be more comfortable and see what happens from there," she suggested.

"That's a really good idea. I will definitely talk to him about it." I switched hands so the other cheek could get in on the action.

"Okay, good."

"And thank you for calling about this, Mellie. It's reassuring to know that you guys are looking out for the kids so carefully." I truly did appreciate it even if this particular phone call added one more turd on the shit sandwich that was my motherhood resumé.

"Of course. You have a great night, Laney, and we'll see you and Rocco tomorrow!" she finished brightly, proving once again that people who work in daycare are born with a different set of genes than the rest of us.

Chapter Four

KEEP CALM AND GO IRISH

NATE

"Lookin' good, old man!" I said to my father as he lounged in his favorite black leather recliner. This was the first time I'd seen him in regular clothes instead of pajamas since the heart attack, and I was relieved to see more color in his cheeks. It had been two weeks since my return to town and almost a week since I'd been back to my folks' house. Work was a shitstorm and I'd been doing my best not to bother my dad any more than necessary, but it was nearly impossible to decipher whatever organizational puzzle he worked by. Bailey and I were having a hell of a time keeping our heads above water. Not that we would ever tell *him* that.

Remote in hand, he paused the football game he was watching and turned to me with a hopeful expression. "For the love of God, please tell me you brought something to eat that doesn't taste like cardboard." It was no secret that my mom's cooking wasn't stellar on a good day, so I could only imagine what it tasted like with all the salt removed.

"Sorry." I held my hands up to show they were empty. "Mom only let me visit on the condition I brought nothing into the house that you might find even remotely edible. I got a TSA pat-down from her in the foyer."

"Eh, I figured as much." He settled back into the chair. "Distract me, then. Tell me what's going on at work. Did Mark get that permit squared away? I've got the number of that guy at the—"

"All taken care of," I interrupted.

"Yeah, but we'll be in deep shit if every 'i' isn't dotted on that one," he insisted.

"I know. Mark and Doug have both been a big help, and Bailey knows a lot more than she led us to believe, so we're handling it. I promise we'll keep you in the loop and let you know if we need help. I've already called you a dozen times with questions, and I may be permanently banned from the house if Mom catches us talking shop," I warned. "That was another condition for my visit. She should consider a stint with the Secret Service if this whole retirement thing doesn't work out. Was she such a ball-buster with her students? If so, I'm starting to worry about what may have actually been in all those homemade cookies they used to send home with her." That got a smile out of him.

"Your mother's a saint." He un-paused the game.

"Yeah, I know. What's the score? Are we winning?"

He gave me a disgusted look. "Of course we're winning. We're the Irish."

At halftime I went in search of my mom and some doctor-approved refreshments. She sat at the kitchen table swiping at her iPad.

"Hey, Mom."

She held up her hand as if to stop me while her eyes stayed on the tablet. "Nathan, don't even think about asking for a beer. Your dad cannot have alcohol no matter what kind of pathetic faces he tries to make."

I grinned and went over to kiss the top of her head. "I wouldn't dream of it," I reassured. "What are you reading?"

"Oh, just looking for some healthy recipe ideas. Nothing I've made so far has been a hit and I never realized how much sodium is in pre-packaged food. It's ridiculous!"

She shifted her attention my way and caught my eyes. "Sorry —enough of that. I want to hear about you. How are you, Nate? Are you and Bailey hanging in there?"

"By our fingernails, but yeah, we're doing fine. Don't worry."

"Anything I can do to help?" She tilted her blond head.

"Sure. You can get one of those stupid 'Hang in there' cat posters and give it to Bailey—it'll be hilarious to watch her try to be polite when she opens it." I smiled.

She slapped the back of my hand and scoffed, "Don't torture your sister."

"I'll consider it. I suppose it *would* free up some time in my schedule."

Her hand went to my arm more gently this time. "I know your dad can't say it yet, but you need to know that we both appreciate so much that you came home to take over." Okay, I guess it was time for the serious portion of the visit. "It's no secret that this wasn't your plan, at least not yet, so I wanted to say thank you again. I don't know what we would do without you." She started to tear up.

"Whoa, whoa—no need to get all mushy. You know I'm happy to do it. And besides, I'm not *really* taking over. Dad will be back when he's feeling better." She scowled at me so I hurried on, "I mean, I know it won't be full-time like before, but still."

My mother shifted in her chair. "I know. There is no way he'll give up the business completely, but you know your dad doesn't do things by half measure. I'm just afraid he'll gradually ramp things up until we're right back where we started, and we may not be so lucky next time." She had a point. "So that's why we need to use this recovery time to find him some hobbies."

Say what?

"The doctor said there are plenty of activities he can do that are great for keeping blood pressure down and can be quite engaging. I'm hoping if he becomes interested in something else he might not be so eager to dive back into the deep end."

"Like what?" I asked, picturing my dad playing croquet or painting tiny military figurines with a little brush and a monocle. Inside my head I chuckled—outside I was the picture of serious reflection.

"Oh, you know, putting together jigsaw puzzles or collecting coins or stamps. Or painting landscapes. There are all sorts of things." Her excitement was palpable.

Oh wow. This was going to be fun.

✳ ✳ ✳

"I've got one," Bailey howled. "We can get him some gardening clogs and a subscription to *Home and Garden*." Bailey and I were swapping new hobby ideas for Dad between fits of hilarity, picturing the ultra-masculine force of nature we knew as our father in an array of awkward scenarios. All of them included our mom cheering on the sidelines. So far the best one involved the Westminster Kennel Club and some dog trimming shears.

"You *cannot* tell Mom about this conversation," I reiterated, sitting across from her desk and trying to school my features.

"Duh, you shit head," came her clever response.

It was Monday morning and we were supposed to be going over some bid paperwork for an upcoming meeting with a potential client, but I could not resist sharing our mom's plan from the weekend.

"Oh," Bailey started, finally getting us back to business, "I forgot to tell you. Doug called with some potentially troublesome news about the foreclosure properties on Old Oak Ridge. It seems the neighbors are not taking too kindly to having a commercial property in their midst. In his words, 'Trouble is a-brewin'.'"

I waved her off. "Tell them to take it up with the zoning office. Everything is in order on our end. If they don't like it, tough. Tell them to move."

"No, dear brother of mine, *you* get to tell them all of that. Why do you think I'm telling you? You're going to be there anyway when the crew starts the tear down on Thursday so there's no need for little old me to butt in." She smiled sweetly.

"Thanks." I smiled back, a tad less sweetly.

✶ ✶ ✶

Meetings concluded for the day and all phone calls and e-mails returned, I finally walked in the door of my apartment just after eight o'clock. I had done a grocery run the night before so at least I knew there would be something to eat in the fridge. And beer, thank Christ. As anticipated, I had yet to get my hands dirty since I'd been back in town and it was making me irritable. I just needed a night to sit on the couch, watch some TV, and drink a beer.

Thankfully, I now *had* a couch, which hadn't been the case last week. I had chosen to rent a place until I found time to shop for a house or condo and settle in more permanently. My mother, of course, had offered my old room. Yeah, not gonna happen. And I would have considered staying temporarily with Bailey but then I remembered that she was *Bailey* and I concluded that my own place would be just fine.

Most of my furnishings and belongings were in storage back in Austin where I lived for the last two years. When I'd gotten the tearful call from my mom about my dad, I dropped everything and got on a plane. Luckily, a job I'd been working was just wrapping up, so I wasn't leaving a bunch of loose ends. But there was still two years' worth of my life I just left hanging.

Some of my buddies back there kindly offered to move my stuff into storage for me and I had to break my lease, but the land-lord liked me and was a big-time family man himself, so he hadn't penalized me like he could have. It didn't hurt that I'd helped him put a deck on his house last summer and his wife was always giving me cookies and stuff. We had a good relationship. In fact, I had several good relationships and a pretty sweet life in Austin. I was sad to leave.

After watching the game with my dad this past weekend, I had moved a couch and a few other old furnishings from their basement to my apartment. I figured it was enough to tide me over until I found a new place and could get my things from Austin moved permanently. Hopefully, once things calmed down a bit, I'd have time to search for a better place. This one was kind of a shithole, but it was cheap. And for the moment I was content with borrowed furniture, beer, and TV.

Halfway into my IPA and an episode of *Ice Road Truckers* my cellphone rang. I glanced at the screen.

Shit. Reagan.

I muted the TV and answered the call, "Hey Reagan, what's up?"

"Nate! Oh my God, it's so good to hear your voice!"

"Yeah, you too. What are you up to? How are things back in Hippie Haven?"

Her voice lost its initial excitement. "They suck without you, Nate. I miss you."

And that right there was what I'd been afraid of. It was the reason I'd avoided her calls for the past week, although I kept promising myself I'd call back when things lightened up. Reagan was a really nice girl. Honestly. And she made it clear she found me to be a nice guy too. But I suspected she also thought I was *the* guy. Reagan was sweet and pretty hot, she was definitely not *the* girl. Who even knew if any such girl was out there, but I knew for sure that Reagan was not it.

We met at a bar a few months before I'd moved away, and we'd been casually seeing each other since—*casual* being the key word. I was very upfront with her because the last thing any guy wants is girl drama. But then I started noticing some big fucking red flags. She left some of her things at my apartment, and when I mentioned them she tried to laugh it off. Then I heard one of her friends ask about her boyfriend and at first I thought, *oh shit, is some guy gonna jump me for banging his girl?* Until I realized they had been talking about me. I tried to back off and I even sat her down for a conversation about it, but nothing stuck. I'd been planning to break things off completely when my dad's heart attack hit and all hell broke loose.

"Aw, that's sweet." I didn't know how the hell else to respond. "Oh hey, I've been meaning to thank you for sending those boxes. You really didn't need to trouble yourself." She had evidently shown up at my place while my buddies were packing up my shit. She implied to them that I'd asked her to send some of my clothes and personal items, which I most definitely hadn't. She packed up a few boxes and sent them my way. It was nice to have some of my own stuff, no doubt, but the way in which I'd received it signaled nothing but trouble.

"Of course! I knew you'd want some of your stuff and I wanted to do something to feel like I was helping out. How is your dad?"

See? Really nice girl.

"He's doing a lot better, thanks."

"Oh good. So, listen, I was calling cuz I really wanted to hear your voice, but also because I was thinking of coming out to see you …"

Christ on a bike, there it was.

"Oh, Reagan, wow." *Why didn't I break things off before I left?* "Uh, that's really nice of you to think of me. The thing is … work is really crazy right now." *Just tell her the truth, asshole!* "I mean, I'm working all sorts of late hours and between that and checking on my folks … I don't think now is the best time," I finished lamely like the big fucking coward I am.

"Oh. Sure, I mean, I understand. It's just, you know, I was thinking I could maybe combine it with a trip to the beach too—you know, soak up some rays before the summer is completely over and all that," she tried again.

I started to sweat.

"I just don't think it's a great idea right now." *Or ever. Just say it—or ever.*

Silence.

"Okay, no big deal. It was just a thought!" she finally replied, her discomfort evident. "Well, you let me know if I can send anything else or if you need something."

"I will. Thanks for calling, Reagan. And for all your help. Really."

"No problem." Her voice was quiet. "Bye, Nate." She hung up.

God, I'm such a douchebag.

Chapter Five

WANTED: ONE PLAYDATE – WILLING TO BEG

*L*ANEY

Suffice it to say, my talk with Rocco regarding a potential playdate did not go well. In fact, it didn't even go at all. I waited a couple days after Mellie's phone call to broach the subject, and like a moron I'd chosen to do it as I was getting him ready for bed one night.

"What are you looking forward to doing at school tomorrow?" I opened with, helping him pull his pajama shirt over his head. Why we even bothered to put PJs on every night when they just ended up on the floor twenty minutes later, I don't know.

"I don't wanna go to school tomorrow." He frowned and twitched his nose.

"You don't? Why not?"

"I don't like school." His eyes started filling with tears and there was that nose twitch again. *What in the hell was that all about?*

"But school is fun," I tried. "You get to see your friends and play with toys and run around on the playground. You love all that stuff."

"I wanna stay home with you." He sniffled and I dabbed at his eyes with a tissue from the box by his bed.

"But, buddy, I won't be here. I have to go to work." *Kill me now.*

"Then I wanna stay with Uncle Gavin."

"Baby, Uncle Gavin has his new job, remember?"

"I miss Grandma and Grandpa!" Out came the full-fledged wail. "And I hate school! I'm not going anymore!"

Whose brilliant idea was it to do this at bedtime? It's like I was a damn rookie or something.

Since that had been an epic fail, I decided yesterday to send a quick e-mail to Mellie asking if she could suggest a good candidate for a playdate. I was surprised when I received a response almost immediately (again with these daycare teacher genes—the e-mail even had a winky smiley face emoji and an inspirational quote at the end of it).

Tucker Peterson, she'd suggested. I had my mark.

My alarm went off ten minutes earlier than usual in the morning and I managed to get Rocco to school several minutes early, thank you very much. A Tootsie Roll had provided sufficient motivation to get him in the car that much faster than usual. As every parent knows, bribery is an essential tool useful in preventing the explosion of one's head.

I stood by the classroom door, determined to find my target. I had a vague recollection in my mind of Tucker's mom from the first day I'd brought Rocco to school. If memory served, she had blond hair and was fairly tall and thin. *Aha, there she was! And there was Tucker at her side.*

Good God. Of all the rotten luck.

The child wore a polo shirt with the collar popped and, I kid you not, seersucker pants. Oh, I'm sorry, *slacks.*

What five-year-old even owns— Okay, don't judge, Laney. They are probably great people. Super, even. I gave myself an inner smack to the head and approached with a smile.

"Hi, are you Tucker's mom?" I did my best to gush.

She turned to me and smiled in return. "Yes, I am." *See? This was going well already.* "I'm sorry, I don't think we've met."

"I know. I'm Laney Monroe. My son, Rocco, just started here a few weeks ago." I gestured to my son who was—wait, what *was* he doing? He appeared to be cramming his entire body into his cubby. *Shit.* I quickly looked back to her, hoping she hadn't noticed my kid being, well, weird. No such luck.

"I'm Bess Peterson," she responded, a little less brightly than before, but she did extend her hand which I enthusiastically shook. Ugh. She did the limp-fish-partial-shake which made my very firm —and very normal—shake come off as trying way too hard. My left hand began its ascent to my cheek for a good rub but I stopped it, thank God, before things got even more awkward.

"It's so nice to meet you, Bess. Listen, I know you probably have to run, but I wanted to invite Tucker over for a playdate this weekend with Rocco." I glanced down at her son with a smile that was probably coming off as a little crazy at this point. But he wasn't paying attention to me. He was busy with a finger up his nose while the other hand played with his crotch. *See? Our kids have so much in common already!*

"Oh, that's really sweet of you to ask, but I think we're all booked up this weekend," she said, with what really did sound like genuine regret. All right, let's not give up yet.

"Oh, I understand. Things can get a bit crazy trying to cram everything in after the work week." I made some odd zinging sound—or maybe it was more of a whistle—either way, I was sounding like an absolute moron. I couldn't have stopped my hands from coming to my cheeks if you'd paid me a gazillion dollars. Still, obviously not satisfied with my current level of humiliation, I continued, "How about next weekend?"

"Gee, I—" She stopped and shooed Tucker toward his cubby—on the opposite end of the wall from Rocco's, mind you. "Have a good day, sweetie!" she called after him and then turned her smile back to me. "We usually seem to have lots of things scheduled on the weekends, but I'll check our calendar and get back to you. Sorry, I really do have to run. It was nice meeting you." And she was gone.

Note to self: arrange playdates via e-mail in the future.

Taking my own advice, I stopped in Mellie's office on the way out the door to get a list of e-mail addresses for a few more moms. Armed with new candidates, I drove to work mentally drafting my incredibly charming e-mails I would send over my lunch hour to secure a friend for Rocco.

* * *

By the following Monday it was evident that the moms at daycare were all big fat bitches. Okay, maybe that was a bit harsh. It's hard to accurately judge tone over e-mail, and I certainly hadn't emailed *every* daycare mom, but still. What were all these kids doing on the weekends that they couldn't squeeze in an hour or two to play? Was there some big Mensa convention I didn't know about? More likely, there was a giant sale at the mall on child-sized penny loafers and actual polo ponies. *Okay, that was a bit judgy.*

By the time I got the fifth rejection e-mail the picture was becoming clearer. All these kids had been in school together since they were in diapers. They had their little established playgroup and apparently the membership roster was all filled up. It was like *Heathers* for the nose-picker set.

I supposed I could try to reach out to some of the parents from Rocco's old school but that just seemed even more awkward. If he hadn't played with their kids when he had seen them every day, why would they want their kids to come over to play now?

Grrr!

My internal rant was interrupted by the sudden appearance of Annette's curly head over my cubicle wall. "I have the perfect guy for you," she announced. "I'm setting you up and I will not take no for an answer."

"Um, hello to you too."

Annette continued without acknowledging me, "His name is Alex and he's twenty-nine. He has a seven-year-old daughter— divorced—him, not his daughter. He just started at Dan's work and he is *really* cute. I made Dan grill him about his personal life and he is, quote, 'feeling like I'm ready to start dating again.' It's perfect, but I promised Dan I'd get your permission before giving him your number. Say yes." She pushed her glasses up on her nose and put on an overly bright smile while nodding her head and trying to get me to follow suit.

I guess I could use a distraction. What the hell.

"Fine."

* * *

Week two of Gavin's job and he was still employed—woohoo! We had just finished an early dinner and I was determined to get Rocco in the bathtub tonight if it killed me. It had been a couple days—all right, five days, *don't judge me*—since he'd bathed and he was getting ripe. In between showing Rocco mouthfuls of mashed potatoes at the dinner table, Gavin had shared a few details of his day.

In my mind it played out like a little show I called *Gavin Goes to Work*, such was my excitement about his new job. There was even a jaunty theme song—*I understand, I need a hobby*. My brother may be an idiot, but he was *my* idiot, and when it came down to it I just wanted him to be happy. It sounded like the job was going pretty well and his overall good mood boded *really* well.

I was just about to start the bath water when the doorbell chimed a painful warbling sound. One more item to add to the growing fixer-upper list.

"Gav!" I yelled to my brother. "Can you start Rocco's bath for me?" I headed for the front door.

On the front porch was a tow-headed boy who looked to be around Rocco's age, standing next to a smiling woman with auburn hair pulled back in a ponytail. The woman was tall, probably three inches taller than my 5'5", and she was dressed in black yoga pants and a dry-fit workout shirt in a bright fuchsia. The boy was holding a toy gun in one hand and a—hmm, was that a machete?—in the other. He smiled up at me with a gummy grin, his two front teeth missing.

"Hi there!" the woman greeted with a very thick Southern accent—not North Carolina thick, Texas thick. "I'm Charlotte Baker, your neighbor from just down the street." She pointed to her left. "This is my son, Aiden. We just wanted to introduce ourselves and welcome y'all to the neighborhood!"

"Do you like guns?" Aiden asked me.

"Hush," Charlotte said. "Sorry, his grandpa collects antique guns."

Understanding the world of young boys, I glossed right over it and put out my hand. "Hey, I'm Laney Monroe. It's nice to meet you. I have a five-year-old son so I'm familiar."

"Oh, that's great!" Charlotte shook my hand—no limp fish evident. "Did you hear that, Aiden?" Then back to me, "I'll bet they'd get along real well then. Aiden's six."

Ding ding ding! Was that the sound of a playdate calling?

"I'm sure they would," I returned, before briefly considering calling Rocco out for an introduction. The likelihood that he'd emerge from the hall naked stopped me, though, as it would prove a tad more awkward than NRA talk. "We'll have to arrange something." I made sure to keep my smile just this side of crazy. Sorry, lady, you're not getting off my porch without a commitment.

"Did you know that a samurai sword can cut a man's hand off in one swing?" asked Aiden.

Charlotte's plummeting comfort level was palpable. "What has your daddy been lettin' you watch on YouTube?"

Eyes on the prize, I let it slide like water off a duck's back.

"Whatever it is, I'm sure my brother has let Rocco watch worse. Boys will be boys and all that." Good grief I was laying it on thick.

"Oh, don't they just beat all?" she drawled. "I think I like you." She beamed at me, and God almighty did I beam right back. I think I liked her too.

We chatted a bit longer until she brought up the second reason for her visit.

"I wanted to ask if you've heard anything about this buildin' that's supposed to be goin' up by the entrance to the street." She pointed again in the direction of her house.

"Um, I think I may have heard something about that," I hedged, praying that Gavin was safely ensconced in the bathroom with Rocco and would not overhear.

"Some of the other parents and I have been lookin' into it a little and we're a bit concerned. Who knows what kinds of businesses are buildin' there. We don't want some bar openin' up so close to us, or anything really that'll mean a bunch of strangers hangin' around or loud noise at night. Not to mention the extra traffic on the street while our kids are out playin'."

I had to admit, some of the same thoughts had occurred to me since Gavin first brought it up last week. I'd just bought this house, and although I got a good deal because of the work it needed, I didn't want to watch its value go down. And of course I wanted to live in a safe neighborhood, especially with Rocco to consider.

"It's been difficult to get much information over the phone, so those of us who can make it were plannin' on goin' over there early Thursday mornin' to try and get some answers. That's when they're gonna start tearin' down the houses."

"Mmhm," I made a noncommittal noise.

"Anyway," She put her hand briefly on my arm. "It would be great if you could make it. I'm plannin' on headin' over around seven to try and catch them early, and I know a couple other people who are comin'." Her face brightened again. "Oh, hey, and we're also gonna have a little get-together this Saturday at our house with some of the other neighbors and their kids. You should come along and bring Rocco! The kids will probably just play on the X-box or run around the yard while we talk about some of the neighborhood stuff but it should be fun!"

Victory! My weekend playdate!

"That sounds great!" We exchanged phone numbers before she and Aiden went off with a wave.

"Soooo," I said, entering the bathroom where a very naked Rocco was splashing in the tub. "Guess who just scored you a playdate with some cool neighborhood kids and an X-box?" I crowed. "Me! That's who." I may have tried out a couple of my cool dance moves too. *Why hadn't I ever taken a hip-hop class?*

"Just, no," Gavin said from his perch on the closed toilet seat.

I loved most everything about my little house, but I had to admit the hall bathroom was a bit small. It had a tub/shower combo, a toilet, and a tiny pedestal sink. Unfortunately, both the toilet and the sink were pink. I'm a girl and even I was slightly offended.

"What's an X-box?" Rocco's dark head tilted back and his face got scrunchy.

"Trust me, kid. You want to play X-box," said Gavin. "It's an electronic game you can play with other kids. It's awesome—and you can usually kill stuff." Hopefully they wouldn't be playing *those* games—although since it was Aiden's game … yeah.

"What kids?" Rocco still didn't look sold on the idea. And there was the nose twitch again.

"Some of the other kids who live in our neighborhood. I just met one of them—his name is Aiden and he's six," I enthused.

Rocco's head tipped back down and he dive-bombed his privates with a plastic shark. I gave Gavin a side glance.

"Sounds fun, Rock. You should totally go," he offered before standing up. "Well, I'm out." And he left the overcrowded bathroom.

"Will I hafta talk to them?" Rocco asked, zooming the shark through the bath water.

"I guess. I mean, at least a little. Why wouldn't you want to?"

"Do I hafta play with them and stuff?" Another damn nose twitch.

"That's kind of the whole point, baby." *Someone please give me the code to my kid's brain.*

"Oh." Still with the shark. "Nah, I don't wanna go."

"I'm gonna be there too," I kept with the sales pitch. "The other grown-ups and I will be talking and doing adult stuff but I'll be right there the whole time."

"In the same room?" I got his eyes again, along with another twitch. *What are you so worried about, little man?*

"Probably in the next room but you can come see me whenever you want."

"Hmm." His tiny lips shifted to the side in thought. "I guess."

That was the best I was gonna get so it was time to move on. "All right, dude, let's get this hair washed and then I'll let you stay in for ten more minutes—but then you *have* to get out, no arguments." With the amount of time this kid liked to spend in the bathtub you'd think he was a beleaguered mother from a Calgon commercial.

Out in the hall, I stopped at Gavin's open door. He was standing barefooted by the dresser fiddling with his phone, still dressed in his dirty jeans and t-shirt from work, his shaggy brown hair matted from his hardhat.

"I don't get it. What kid doesn't want to go on a playdate? Didn't you always want to hang out and do boy stuff when you were his age? I was always hanging out with other kids, wasn't I?" I asked him. Maybe I was having some selective memory problems.

Without looking up from his phone he responded, "Sure, I guess." Ever the skilled conversationalist.

Rocco's voice floated from the bathroom, singing a made-up song about armpits. "Be honest, Gav. Is Rocco, I don't know, a bit *odd*?"

His head still tilted down to his phone, only his eyes lifted to mine. "Are we both hearing the same noises coming from the bathroom right now?"

Chapter Six

DEAR SUPERMAN: YOUR BROTHER'S A DICK

*L*ANEY

Thursday dawned bright, and I mean *bright*. A person was not meant to get up this early. I stumbled around my bedroom, having woken up without my little sleep buddy beside me for the first time since we'd moved. *Oh, sweet progress!* My alarm had gone off early because I wanted to get Rocco and myself ready for the day and still make it to meet Charlotte at the building site before rushing to school and work. This was going to be a three Diet Coke morning for sure and I needed my caffeine fix stat.

Last night, I had spent some time on the internet looking up nervous tics to see if Rocco's new nose twitching thing was something to worry about. Turns out yes and no. It seems these little tics are really common in young children, boys especially, and they tend to go away over time. Unfortunately, my research also revealed that the impetus for these kinds of tics was often a feeling of general stress. So, in a way, it told me what I already knew. *Ugh.*

After a quick shower and a rush-through of my usual hair and makeup routine, I tucked my hair behind my ears and called it good. Congratulating myself for setting out clothes the night before, I slipped on a pair of charcoal dress pants with a skinny red pinstripe and a V-neck sleeveless blouse the color of a poppy. I paired this with some very low heeled open-toed shoes in a matching color. Even Fiona would approve.

I went to wake Rocco but found his bed empty, firetruck sheets in a rumpled mess and pillow missing. After a search of the living room and kitchen I checked the only other possible place. Yep. There he was, snuggled up next to my brother, firetruck pillow cradling his head and all of Gavin's covers bundled around him. My brother lay next to him, curled in the fetal position with no covers but, thankfully, some boxer briefs to protect my eyes from the bleach bath they would have needed had things gone differently.

"Your son stole my covers," grumbled Gavin in a sleepy murmur.

I smiled—only because my kid is cute, not because I enjoy my brother's pain—and went over to the bed to get Rocco.

"Hey buddy." I rubbed up and down his back. "Time to wake up." His sleepy eyes blinked repeatedly as he rolled to his back and stretched his arms above his head. "Did you decide to hang with Uncle Gavin last night?"

"Yeah," he said around a yawn, "but he farts in his sleep."

Suddenly wide awake, Gavin interjected, "I do not!"

"Do too."

"Do not! And *you* steal all the covers!"

Again, why doesn't my son want to play with other five-year-olds? He clearly lives with one already so it should be a no-brainer.

"Okay, okay, let's get up and leave Uncle Gavin to himself." I urged Rocco out of bed.

"What time is it anyway?" Gavin asked.

"It's only ten after seven. I had to get up early because I have something to do before work." I walked toward his door.

"Crap. Too early," he muttered, but I suddenly had an idea.

"Hey, since you're already awake, would you mind getting Rocco ready and giving him some breakfast? What time do you leave for work?"

"I'm working at the site up the street this morning. I don't need to be there till eight. I was *going* to take advantage and sleep in," he said pointedly. "Why do you need me to take care of Rock? Where are you going?"

Hmm, how should I handle this one? I didn't really want to tell Gavin that I was going to help some neighbors give his new company a hard time, but I didn't want to lie either. "Remember that lady who came by the other day with her kid? She wanted me to help her out with something this morning. I'll be back in plenty of time for you to make it to work." Vague, let's stick with that.

"Okay, I guess. Just give me ten more minutes of snooze time, Rock, and I'll get you some breakfast." Gavin laid his head back on his pillow and covered his eyes with his arm.

Knowing that Rocco can't tell time and Gavin, like me, possesses no internal alarm clock, I set a buzzer for ten minutes and turned the TV on to cartoons. "When that buzzer goes off, go get Uncle Gavin and tell him it's time to wake up. If he doesn't get up tell him that I will erase all his college women's volleyball recordings from the DVR," I told Rocco as he settled in on the couch. I may as well have been talking to myself. I paused the show and tried to block his view. "Tell him your clothes are lying on my bed, okay? I just need to run up the street for a few minutes but I'll be back in time to take you to school." I got a nod but his eyes never left the TV. I un-paused it and hoped for the best.

Wanting to stay in Charlotte's good graces but get this over with as soon as possible, I grabbed my cellphone and slipped out the side door, heading quickly toward the sidewalk. As I approached the end of our block where it intersected with Old Oak Ridge Road, I spotted Charlotte and Aiden with a couple I didn't recognize and a toddler girl who appeared to belong to them. The man also held a sleeping baby in his arms, wrapped in a pink blanket. Aiden was poking at the ground with what I hoped was a plastic knife, and he had what appeared to be an arsenal of various other knives tucked into some kind of utility belt looped around his pants.

Behind the group I spied two yellow construction vehicles—don't ask me what they were called—and a flatbed truck loaded with two more. The truck's signage read "Built by Murphy" and there were three men huddled in conversation to the side of the large vehicle—the tallest of whom held a cellphone to his ear with one hand, the other hand gripping the back of his neck as he alternately barked into the phone and to the men beside him. *Tense much?*

Charlotte spotted me immediately. "Hey, Laney! So glad you made it!" She waved excitedly.

I couldn't help but respond to her friendliness with a smile. "Morning, Charlotte!"

"This is Darcy and Glen. They live across the street from me, and this is their daughter Haley and this cute little bundle is Mackenzie." She gestured enthusiastically to each person in turn. "This is Laney. She just moved into Missy Greene's old place. She has a son who's only a year younger than Aiden."

After introductions were made and pleasantries exchanged, Charlotte got down to business and pointed discreetly to the group of men by the truck. The one who had been on the phone a moment ago was now scowling and gesturing angrily at a clipboard held by one of the other men. "Okay, so from what I know, I think one of those guys is the owner of the construction company. I figured he'd be the one to talk to." She looked back down the street toward our houses. "I was hopin' we'd have a few more people, but it looks like it's just us for now."

Little Mackenzie chose that moment to awaken and start fussing. Glen began bobbing up and down doing the crying-baby-dance in what seemed to be a well-practiced routine. Charlotte looked at me. "Laney, you mind comin' over there with me?"

No, Charlotte, actually I think I'll just hang here with the baby and these people I don't know—you go on ahead—you see, my brother just started working for this company last week and it's the first real job he's ever had since he ruined his baseball career by being an idiot, and I kind of don't want to mess it up for him. But I'll be right here cheering you on. Go team!

"Sure."

There was absolutely no reason for these guys to think I even knew Gavin. I'd just keep my mouth shut and let Charlotte do all the talking. Piece of cake.

I followed Charlotte as she waved her hand in the air and walked toward the men, her auburn hair swinging and her hips sashaying in workout pants and a bright yellow fitted t-shirt. "Yoo-hoo. Gentlemen!" she called. I didn't know there were actual people who used the expression "yoo-hoo." I was loving this chick.

All three men turned in unison to the Southern firecracker that was Charlotte. The man on the left held the clipboard to his forehead in order to shield his eyes from the sun, and his handsome face broke into a wide grin at the sight of my neighbor.

Oh, I knew this guy. Well, not this particular guy, but his type was unmistakable. He was the guy at every party, every gym, every concert with the cock-sure smile who stood a bit too close and made allusions to his cock size within your first conversation. He was also the guy who found any and every excuse to take his shirt off—*oh, is it hot in here or is it just me?* Gag.

My eyes moved on and I have no idea how the man on the right reacted to us because, as my eyes moved from cocky guy, they caught on angry-cellphone-guy in the middle of the group and chose to stay there for a nice long rest. *Thank you very much,* said my lady bits.

This guy was tall, he was built, he had a square jaw that could cut you, and despite the sunglasses that hid his eyes and the scowl that said, "don't even think about talking to me," he had my belly dropping to the ground in an instant. His almost black hair was in need of a cut and it looked like he'd been running his hand through it for a week. There was just the right amount of stubble covering his perfect jaw—enough so he looked sexy and a bit rough but not sloppy. My knees felt a little wobbly.

Paging Superman, I think I found your long lost, scruffier, sexier, and broodier twin. It was at this point I patted myself on the back for not wearing high heels because if I had, I would surely be kissing the dirt right about now.

Charlotte, seemingly right at home in the presence of hot super-heroes, kept right on going without pause. "Hello there. My name is Charlotte Baker. I live just up the street." She was already upon them and I scurried a bit to catch up. Charlotte looked back toward me. "This is another neighbor, Laney Mon—"

"Laney!" I interrupted loudly and thrust my hand out toward cocky guy. "Just Laney is fine." I avoided Charlotte's quizzical look. *No last names needed here, guys—let's keep it casual.*

"Well, Laney," I got the smile and nod as cocky guy shook my hand. "Charlotte." He switched to hers, handsome smile ready to charm our panties off. "I'm Mark. It's a pleasure to meet you both. This here is Doug." Mark indicated the man on the right whom I hadn't had a chance yet to assess. Doug appeared to be in his late forties with blondish hair and the beginnings of a paunch. Face unreadable, he nodded in greeting but didn't offer his hand. "And this is Nate. He runs the show around here." Mark turned his thumb toward the man giving me high blood pressure. Nate, face *completely* readable, turned his scowl on Mark, not pleased to be thrown under the bus. Unfazed, Mark continued, "What can we help you ladies with today?"

"Well," Charlotte began, her charming smile returning his, "I'm assumin' you're the company puttin' up the new property?"

When that got no response she continued, "Yes, well, we have some questions we wanted to ask if that's all right."

Mark, still the only one of the three to speak, moved closer (*See? I told you*) and said, "Sure. Happy to help." At this point I think it was safe to assume he was envisioning Charlotte naked.

"We've been tryin' to find out exactly what kind of business is goin' to be movin' into the new property. Can you tell us that by any chance?"

"Well, Charlotte," Mark began, "we won't really know that until the property is completed and the spaces are rented out, but I can tell you that there will be a total of three rental spaces. There are a variety of businesses that could make use of the spaces, but until rental agreements are signed, I'm afraid I can't be more specific than that. Wouldn't you say, Nate?" he passed the issue off, his eyes still glued to my neighbor.

"Yes Mark, I would say," the hottie ground out in displeasure, his voice low and a bit gravelly, perfectly matching the whole sexy, scruffy thing he had going on there. "Let's cut to the chase, girls, what is it *precisely* that you're concerned about?" His eyes moved to us, his impatience unmistakable. Somebody had a crap sandwich for breakfast this morning.

"Um," Charlotte was beginning to hesitate, "you see, we all have kids and we don't want to see any … *unsavory* types comin' around the neighborhood. And, um, increased traffic might be an issue too …"

"I see," Nate snapped. "So you don't want us bringing creepy assholes around your kids, and the tenants should stay off your street. Got it. Can we get back to work now? We've got a crew showing up in twenty and a long list of shit to get done. You can head back to your little mommy-and-me troop." He tilted his chin toward Darcy, Glen, and the kids. "We'll take it from here."

With that, he turned around and headed toward the cab of the truck. And, dammit to hell, I couldn't help but take in the view from the back with a little bit of "bow-chicka-wow-wow" echoing in my head. Thoroughly disgusted with my girl parts for turning to the dark side, I returned my gaze to Charlotte.

Her jaw hung open and she looked like she might cry. A surge of protectiveness washed over me and (mostly) overruled my baser feelings. She was a nice person—she didn't deserve to be yelled at by that, that big fat sexy jerk! She was friendly and cared about her kid and invited strangers like us to her house for playdates and just wanted to keep everybody safe! Sure, her son may or may not be a future serial killer, but everyone has flaws. What right did this guy have to berate her for asking a simple question? No way, you rude, arrogant, insulting, too tight t-shirt wearing *dickhead*—Laney Monroe has a bone to pick with you.

"Hey!" I yelled out to his retreating, sexy-as-hell back. "Nate, or whatever the hell your name is! You get back here and apologize to her. That was totally uncalled for!" My fists found purchase on my hips and I prepared for a fight.

"I'm sorry," Mark, looking not so cocky anymore, tried to interject, but the bell had rung on his bout. It was time for the heavyweight round. I shot him a look that silenced him, so I knew my message had been received.

Nate was back. "Lady, I don't have time for this. Doug has already told your friend by phone to contact the zoning board if you all have a problem. They permitted us to put this building here and as long as we follow all the rules set out by them, the city, and the inspector—which we will—this is *not my problem!*" He brought his face closer and ripped off his sunglasses, revealing brilliant blue eyes that were frosted over with disdain. "Look, it will probably end up being a nice little salon so you and all your friends can sit and get your nails done and have a little gossip session where you can talk shit about me all you want. *I don't care.* Now, if it's all right with you, I think I'll get back to work."

"What in the hell is going on here?!" came a loud and very, *very* familiar voice from behind me.

Well, shit.

I looked over my shoulder to find Gavin looking completely perplexed and Rocco riding on his shoulders, both hands grasping Gavin's ears like handles. But even the sight of my two guys couldn't stop the raging storm brewing in response to this absolute prick in front of me. It was *on.*

Chapter Seven

GETTING CREATIVE

NATE

"I got this, Gav!" the ball of indignant fury in front of me called over her shoulder to—wait, wasn't that the new kid? *What was going on here?*

Why did I even bother getting out of bed this morning?

I should have known the day would be crap-tastic from the moment I woke up.

I'd accidentally left my phone, which doubles as my alarm clock, in the kitchen last night so I missed my alarm and, by default, my morning run. I need my morning run to clear my head and make a game plan for my day. I think better, feel better, and probably behave better if I get to run first thing.

And not only did I miss my alarm, I also missed half a dozen phone calls from work. The freaking siding we were supposed to install at the apartment project today had arrived late yesterday and nobody noticed until early this morning that it was the wrong kind.

Mark called first thing with that one. It was unclear if the error came from the manufacturer or from our end, which would make it even more complicated. But either way it left us with half a crew spending the day with their thumbs up their asses while we fell behind schedule and bled money. Not ideal.

I made a few more calls and we were able to shuffle some things around, but we were still going to be running behind until we got the right siding—and who the hell knew when that would be?

And behind all of that was the nagging fear that somebody would slip up and tell my father about it, which would bring on a whole new shitstorm coming from both him and my mom. Good Christ, I felt like chucking it all and catching the first flight back to Texas. This day was like screwing a skunk—it had hardly even started and I'd already had enough.

Mark, Doug, and I decided to touch base in person at the Old Oak Ridge site where Doug and I were planning on starting our day anyway. So, without time for coffee, breakfast, or my run, I'd taken the fastest shower known to man and headed over there. Suffice it to say, I was not in a receptive mood for any more bull-shit when I'd arrived.

Enter the amateur pageant queen and her friend. Her smoking, fuck-hot friend with glossy dark hair halfway down to her ass and intense gray eyes that lit my dick on fire. Not to mention the rest of the package. To say I'm a tits-and-ass kind of guy is like saying the Cookie Monster has a vague fondness for sweets. And, *goddamn*, did this girl have some T and A. She had a little bit of that Christina Hendricks thing from *Mad Men* going on. And she was serving up the attitude to go with it. Maybe Texas was a bad idea after all.

I knew I was being a total dick, and I'm sure my hot little friend and her red-headed neighbor didn't deserve it, but I couldn't help myself. The crew was almost there and I had just gotten off the phone with the siding company—they were estimating another two weeks before they could get the right order in. That was a shit-ton of money and time, and I didn't have the patience to deal with these neighborhood people who were wasting my time with shit that wasn't even going to be an issue for months, if ever. So I released the asshole on them.

Sue me and then get me a coffee.

But it looked like this girl was just getting started, and now I was finding out she was somehow involved with one of my crew? What the fuck was going on with this day?

Her eyes blazed into mine as she drew in a deep breath in preparation for whatever was about to come. It was impossible to ignore the rise of her perfect breasts, and I caught just a glimpse of black lace at the vee of her red shirt from my elevated vantage point. It almost made me want to be cooperative. Almost.

"Listen here, you misogynistic prick."

Contrary to everything I'm sure I was expected to feel at that point, my dick rose to attention ("You called?").

"You can't stand here making your half-assed assumptions and treating us like we're some brainless little fairies flitting around all day with nothing better to do than take a crap on you and your macho-man bullshit."

Yup, still sporting wood.

"We are all homeowners on this street who have a right to know what is happening in our neighborhood."

She wagged her index finger in my face and I wanted to bite it.

"We take the safety of our children and families very seriously, as well as the value of our homes in which we have invested our hard-earned money—"

God, she was in my face now and I could see the dark ring around her flinty gray irises. Would they be the same shade when she was under me?

"Money we've made doing *real work* the same way you do, and I will not stand here and let you treat us like we are somehow less than you and your precious crew while you wave all your big muscles around and beat your chest!"

Big muscles? Now we were getting somewhere.

"Now," she commanded, "you will apologize to Charlotte for jumping down her throat and you will address our concerns in a tone that smacks a little less of arrogant dickhead."

If I didn't get her out of here I was either gonna kiss her or drop down on my knees and beg her to marry me. I had to find an exit strategy—fast.

"What did you say your name was again?" I asked.

"Laney." Her right hand suddenly rose and cradled her cheek.

"Your full name."

She swallowed. "Laney Monroe."

"Monroe." I felt the name on my tongue and kept my eyes glued to hers. "She belong to you, kid?" I yelled out to Gavin just so I could watch her eyes light up with rage again. God, this girl was smoking.

"I don't *belong to him*!" Her hand dropped and her voice

exploded with indignation. "God, you really are an asshole, aren't you?"

There was no arguing with that one.

With that, she turned and I got to watch the show as her perfect ass strutted away toward Gavin and the kid on his shoulders.

"Come on, Charlotte. We're done here!" To me, she shouted, "This is *not* over!" And all three of them headed out. I continued to watch the show, noticing Gavin glancing worriedly back at me a few times. He appeared to be arguing with her. With *Laney*. I couldn't blame him—that was the most fun I'd had in weeks.

Ten minutes later, with most of the crew in attendance I saw Gavin Monroe approaching, this time without the little kid and the hot girl.

"Nate, I am so sorry," he began. "My sister can be a little hot-headed sometimes but I talked to her and I promise she won't be bothering you anymore, I swear—"

"That's your *sister*?" I cut him off.

"I know, right. She's a pain in the ass."

I just nodded, not sure Gavin would appreciate anything I had to say about his sister's ass. "Don't worry about it," I threw back at him. "Go see Doug. We've gotta get things moving here."

And I would definitely need to carve out a little time in my schedule for a rematch with one Laney Monroe.

* * *

"No, Mark, my dad won't want to collect electric trains as his new hobby. And if you like your nuts where they are you'll mind your own business and tell Bailey to keep her gaping pie-hole shut from now on." I said to the moron on the other end of the line. Mark and I were pretty good friends but sometimes I seriously questioned his level of common sense.

It was Friday evening and I was standing on Gavin Monroe's front porch, having gotten his address from his employee file and hoping to catch his sister at home. I had yet to ring the bell when Mark called and I'd picked it up assuming, who knows why, that he was calling about actual work. Turns out Bailey had let him in on the search for Riordan Murphy's new hobby and he couldn't resist getting in on the action.

"Why not? I could get him one of those train engineer hats." He guffawed.

"Two things, Mark. One, you do know that even with a bum heart my dad could beat you into the ground, right? And two, don't even think of letting him or my mother get the barest wind of this conversation. The goal is to lower his blood pressure, not elevate it. And, besides, Bailey and I are family so he can't kill us. Just think about where that leaves you."

"You're no fun, man. I'm calling Bailey to swap ideas instead," he complained.

See? No common sense. "You go right ahead, man, but don't come crying to me when he turns you into a eunuch. Later, Mark."

"Later." He hung up and I turned to ring the doorbell.

However, the door was already open.

"If you're looking for Gavin, he's not here. He's probably at Jake's shooting pool. You should try there—I hear it's a pretty male-dominated crowd—hardly a woman in sight, so you should feel right at home." Laney gave me a fake-ass smile and started to close the door but I stopped it with my foot. Her expression changed to a glare.

"Whoa, hold on there. I'm actually here to see you." She didn't try to break my foot right away so I continued, "I wanted to apologize."

Her look turned suspicious. "Apologize?"

"Yes. You were right. I was an asshole."

"And have you directed this apology to Charlotte as well?" One hand went to her hip.

Oooh, she was a sharp one. "I will as soon as you give me her address. Can I come in before the neighbors start calling the cops?"

After a few moments she opened the door a touch. "I guess. But you have to act like a normal person. I have company and my son is here." Ah, so the little kid was *her* son, not Gavin's. But she didn't have a ring, I'd noted earlier. Still, I reminded myself to tread carefully. She stepped aside and left the door open for me. I followed her into the house and closed the door behind me. The doorknob fell off into my hand. *Huh?* I looked at her questioningly. She looked at my hand.

"Oh crap," she said and grabbed the knob from me while pushing the door to rest in a position that was mostly closed.

"You're worried about my building threatening your kid's safety and your front door doesn't even close?" I couldn't resist.

Her hand shot to my mouth and covered it. "I thought you were here to apologize," she hissed.

I was too distracted by the effect her touch had on me to respond. Her warm hand stayed over my mouth a few seconds too long as her eyes rose to meet mine.

Could she feel that too? Apparently so, because the next

second her hand dropped like it had been burned, and then both of her hands went to her cheeks and started running up and down over the sweet little freckles I'd just noticed. *Sweet little freckles? What was I now, a girl?*

She turned her back and hurried from the entryway. I couldn't do anything but follow.

It turns out we were headed into the kitchen where a very petite blond woman stood at a stove that was older than dirt, stirring something in a pot. The little boy from yesterday, who I now knew was Laney's son, was sitting at a blue table with a pile of Legos in front of him. He wore a gray t-shirt with a yellow chick on it and the words "Chicks Dig Me." Just under the sleeve of the shirt I could see one of those stick-on tattoos but I couldn't tell what it was supposed to be. I liked this kid already. I could work with this.

"Nate, this is my friend Fiona and my son, Rocco." Laney did the introductions, one hand still holding her cheek.

Oh shit, a thought suddenly occurred to me. Were these women a couple and this was their son? I was usually so good at spotting signals and I could have sworn Laney was into me, even if she didn't want to be.

The woman named Fiona whirled around, clearly not expecting a strange man to appear in the kitchen. She looked me over and I can tell you she was not shy about her head-to-toe perusal. I was beginning to feel a little violated, she was so thorough. Okay, so totally straight—that was a relief.

"Fiona, Rocco, this is Gavin's boss, Nate Murphy. Rocco, say hello to Mr. Murphy," Laney gently directed.

"Nate. Nate's fine. How's it going, Rocco?" I waved to the kid.

"Nice tattoo. Did you get that in prison? I'll bet it kills with the ladies."

Crickets.

"Five-year-olds don't really get sarcasm," said Fiona, leaning toward me and offering her hand.

"Oh," I said stupidly as I took it. Fiona couldn't have been more than about 5'4" and she was wearing sky-high heels, so her actual height was probably closer to an even five feet. She had light blond hair and a tiny face to match her tiny body. She was cute in a spunky kind of way, but was a complete contrast to her bombshell of a friend.

"So, Nate, I hear you've been stirring up some trouble in the neighborhood," Fiona led with a wink.

"Oh no," Laney interjected, "none of that. Nate is just here to apologize for yesterday and then he's going to be on his way." She had lost her slightly frazzled demeanor and was back in command.

"No!" Fiona argued and looked beseechingly at me. "You have to stay for dinner. I'm making penne with a fabulous tomato cream sauce and meatballs for my main man over there." She tipped her head toward the table where Rocco still hadn't acknowledged my presence and was busy building a Lego structure. "You'll love it!"

While the two women silently communicated in a series of indecipherable facial expressions and hand gestures, I accepted the invitation before it could be revoked. "Sounds great!"

"Are you the man with the construction trucks?" Rocco spoke his first words to me ten minutes later. We were all seated at the hideous blue table over bowls of admittedly delicious pasta. Fiona could *cook*.

"I am," I said, thrilled to finally have something that might win the kid over. I needed all the help I could get. "You like construction trucks?"

"Yeah. Uncle Gavin took me to see them yesterday but we only stayed for a minute. My favorite is the backhoe." All of his "s" sounds came out as "th" sounds and I had to admit it was pretty damn cute.

"That is a good one." I nodded at him.

He twitched his nose and went back to his meatball. It seemed I was dismissed. So much for that.

As Fiona had been preparing the pasta earlier, I took the opportunity to explain to Laney that my tirade yesterday had been the result of things that had nothing to do with her or her friend. I did a bit of light groveling and she seemed to be receptive on the condition that I also apologize to Charlotte. I agreed and the matter was closed. Why she chose to bring it up again over our nice dinner, then, was beyond me. I was just hoping that the presence of Fiona and Rocco would help keep things friendly.

"So Nate, you really don't have any idea what kinds of businesses will rent the space?" She licked some pasta sauce from her top lip and I had trouble concentrating on her question for a minute.

"Uh, not really at this point, Laney. I mean, certain types of businesses couldn't be licensed on this particular property anyway. There are rules for required distances from churches, schools, and what-not, but I can't really help you out too much with anything concrete." I brought another forkful of the delicious pasta to my mouth.

"But you'll own the property, right, so technically you can decide whether or not to rent it out to specific people, right?"

Oh no, we were not going there tonight. We were having a nice meal, her friend seemed to like me well enough, and her kid had even spoken to me. I was not messing this up.

I finished chewing and wiped my lips with a napkin. "There's actually a lot more that goes into those kinds of decisions. Is there any more of that garlic bread, Fiona?"

"Sure thing, Nate." Fiona handed me the bread basket. "I'm sure Nate's company will do its best, *Laney*. They don't want trouble any more than you do, isn't that right, Nate?" Fiona smiled at me and then let her eyes shift to Laney.

"Right," I responded and then shoved a whole piece of bread in my mouth so I wouldn't have to say another word.

"But let's just speak in hypotheticals," Laney continued, undaunted. It was like she was *trying* to annoy me. What was I saying? Of course she was trying to annoy me. "You wouldn't rent the space to, say, a medical practice, would you?"

Genuinely confused, I forced the bread down my throat in a painful lump and responded in a tight voice, "What's wrong with a medical practice? You could walk Rocco to a doctor's appointment." I gestured to the kid.

"I don't wanna go to the doctor!" Rocco objected vehemently.

"Nobody's going to the doctor," Fiona soothed him.

"Yeah, and some junkie would break in at night and raid the drug cabinet. That happens more than you realize," Laney declared, hand waving in the air.

I turned my head to the left and then to the right, looking for what? I had no clue. "What are you, a true crime author?"

"What's a junkie?" Rocco chimed in at the same time.

Sensing, as I was, that this was going nowhere good, Fiona interjected, "Time for dessert!"

* * *

Thankfully, the rest of the evening went smoothly. Fiona was very chatty, Laney tolerated my presence, and Rocco even spoke another handful of words to me. Laney and I exchanged a few more heated looks, hers possibly fueled more by annoyance than lust, but I'd take what I could get at this point. I had yet to get her alone again, though, so when it was time to leave I was thrilled that Fiona led Rocco down the back hall and Laney was left to walk me to the door.

"So, thanks for dinner," I said.

"Thank Fiona. She invited you." Laney tried to glare at me but instead I got a reluctant smile. Damn, she was pretty. Tonight she had her hair up in a messy ponytail and she was wearing a black t-shirt and cut-off jeans, neither of which could hide her curves. I was dying to kiss her, but I figured she'd probably slap me at this point.

As we approached the door I remembered the damn doorknob. "Laney, you can't go to sleep with your door like this," I told her.

She waved me off. "I know. It keeps falling off, but I can fix it. At least temporarily—until Gavin gets to it." She opened the door and I had no choice but to step out onto the porch.

"No offense to your brother, Laney, but he doesn't know shit about fixing things from what I've seen so far."

That earned me a bigger smile. "We'll figure it out."

"You know, I did notice a couple things in your kitchen that could use some attention too, and I've been told I'm pretty handy …"

"Handy or handsy?"

"Funny."

"I thought so."

"I've got some free time this weekend. I'd be happy to come over tomorrow and fix a few things. Truthfully, I've been spending so much time on the phone and driving from place to place that I haven't actually held a tool in weeks—it's killing me."

Oddly, she seemed to be holding back a laugh at first and ducked her chin to her chest. But then she raised her head back up, schooling her expression and starting to shake her head.

"That would be awesome!" Fiona's head popped in from out of nowhere. "She'll see you tomorrow morning." The door closed in my face.

"I'll be here at nine. I'll bring coffee!" I yelled through the door before turning around and stepping off the porch.

"She doesn't drink coffee!" came the voice through the door.

I smiled. I'd have to get creative then.

Chapter Eight

BOOM!

LANEY

"Oh my God. When I turned around and saw that man I swear I ovulated on the spot. *Boom!* Instant fertility. They should give that guy out as a prescription—fertility clinics nationwide would fold overnight." Fiona looked at me dreamily and then switched to her mad face (which was ineffective on its best day). "Lucy, you got some 'splainin' to do—you did not accurately describe just how edible that guy is!" Her expression changed again as the wheels turned. "And did you see the way he was eye-fucking you across the table?" She fanned herself.

I put my hand over her mouth and looked over her shoulder. "Little ears, Fee!"

She peeled my hand off her face. "He's in the bathroom. I told him to brush his teeth so I could come back and eavesdrop."

"You know he's not brushing his teeth, right? He'll be back out here in three minutes wearing only his underwear and asking what he was supposed to be doing in there," I told her. "And Nate was not eye-fucking me! I can't believe you invited him over here tomorrow!" I whisper-yelled.

"Maybe I should open my own matchmaking business—it's coming back in style, you know. It could be Matched by Fiona." She motioned an imaginary sign in the air in front of her. "Kind of like Nate's company, Built by Murphy. It could be kind of a family thing." She gave a giggle.

"Fair warning—I may kill you. In the meantime, do I owe you a portion of my dowry now or will later be fine?"

"Later works for me."

* * *

A second dessert, one supervised round with the toothbrush, and three books later, Rocco was finally in bed and Fiona and I were relaxed on the couch with wine and girl talk.

"So, what happened to his dad?" Nate was still the topic at hand.

"Gavin said he had a heart attack a few weeks ago and Nate moved back to take over the family business until he recovers," I told her. "I heard Nate talking on the phone about trying to find relaxing things for his dad to do with his time. Sounds like a fairly long recovery."

"Oh my God," Fiona gushed and put a hand to her face as though I'd just handed her a puppy with a giant pink bow. "That is *so* sweet. He said he just moved back but I didn't know all of that. See? He's hot *and* he loves his family."

"Yeah, just what I've always wanted—a sexy man who loves

his family and hates women," I sniped. I was trying desperately to hold onto my mad but my resolve was fading. Evidently I was holding a puppy too, but mine had taken a roll in a pile of poo and still needed some work before it was as adorable as Fiona's.

Fiona swiped at my arm. "He doesn't hate women. So he was totally sexist yesterday—a real pig—but listen to *us*. We've been reducing him to a cut of brainless man meat for the last ten minutes! Face it—we *all* suck. But he apologized, didn't he? And he did seem genuinely interested in helping you." Her eyes sparked with a familiar shine. "And besides, did you see that ass? Like I said, '*Boom!*'" She did the fist-explosion thing.

"Stop. The last thing my ovaries need is encouragement to start sending out party invitations. Do I need to remind you what happened six years ago? And besides, you're missing an important point. *We* kept our sexist talk private—*he* broadcast his to all and sundry!"

"'*All and sundry?*' Are we in a Jane Austen novel now?" She set down her wine glass and sat upright on the couch. "I say, that gentleman's posterior looked positively fetching in those britches, don't you concur?"

I threw a couch pillow at her.

"Anyway," she continued. "It doesn't matter now because he's coming over tomorrow and there's nothing you can do about it. Can I come over and watch? I'll bring popcorn."

"Give me that pillow back. I need something to smother you with."

"Aww, I love you too, Laney."

A voice came from the kitchen. "There *is* a God. I think they're gonna kiss."

Fabulous, Gavin and his trusty side-kick were home.

"You know that's my sister, right?"

"She's not *my* sister," came the response from Brett, Gavin's best friend since high school. They both stood at the half wall watching us on the couch.

"Hi, Brett," Fiona and I chimed in unison. It's fun to play with dumb animals.

He may have whimpered a little while Gavin continued moving into the living room. "Who's coming over tomorrow?"

I arranged my face into what I hoped was an innocent look.

"Your hot new boss." Fiona threw my ass under the bus.

"No no no No NO," Gavin's voice escalated as he moved closer to me. "You promised me you were going to stay out of this! Jesus, Laney! You've spent the last two years nagging me to 'get over it' and I finally do exactly what you wanted and you start fucking it all up!"

"Be quiet! Rocco is sleeping!" I responded in only a slightly lower tone.

"*You* be quiet! I can't believe you! Call him back and tell him you made a terrible mistake and you and the mom squad are backing down for good. I actually like this job and I don't want to get fired before my first paycheck!"

"Get your damn feathers out of a twist, Donald Duck. Nobody's getting fired. I didn't even invite him over tomorrow. He invited himself."

"Well, technically I invited him." Fiona meekly raised her hand. We both ignored her.

"When exactly did this happen? How was it you and Nate were even talking to each other?"

"Listen, it's no big deal. He stopped by earlier to apologize for being a dick yesterday—" I held up my hand to keep him from interrupting. "And he noticed a few things that needed fixing so he offered to come by tomorrow to help out."

"Brett and I were going to fix things around here." His tone calmed slightly.

Fiona turned to Brett who had also entered the living room by that point. "I didn't know you were good with tools. How long has this been going on? I may need you to come over to my place and fix a few things."

Brett's upper lip appeared to be sweating.

"Since he was about thirteen, I think," Gavin said, all tension gone and a repressed smile replacing it. Hissy fit finished.

"Wow, that long?" Fiona replied.

"God*dammit*!" shouted Brett. He reached into his pocket and pulled out a wad of cash. He slapped a five-dollar bill into Gavin's already outstretched hand and stormed off to the kitchen. "Anybody want a beer?" he called out behind him.

* * *

If you haven't already guessed, I am in no way, shape, or form a "tidy" person. When I know company is coming over, I stuff everything in my bedroom or a closet. When I do laundry, only about thirty percent of it ever gets folded and finds its way to a dresser drawer. When I cook a meal, which I don't do as often as I should, I first need to wash the knife and cutting board because they are still sitting in the sink from last night's meal prep. Essentially, I was freaking the hell out the next morning in anticipation of Nate's arrival.

Expecting that he would probably want to check out the entire house, I was left with very few options for stashing my mess. Sure, he'd seen the kitchen and living room the night before, but I'd cleared those out before Fiona had arrived—although why I even bothered doing that for her anymore was beyond me. She was well aware of my cluttered and chaotic "decorating" style. When everyone was over last night, there had been no fewer than six pairs of Rocco's shoes crammed into the pantry, not to mention the unopened mail behind a potted plant and the giant pile of toys and clothes on my bed (or, more recently, my floor, since I'd shoved them all off before I went to sleep last night). So today I spent the entire morning alternately chugging Diet Coke and doing my best to make the house look like it didn't belong on an episode of *Hoarders*. A twinge of guilt almost penetrated when Rocco came out of his room and asked what was going on with his bed.

"I made it," I told him, assuming this was explanation enough.

"Huh?"

"You know, I tucked the sheets in the sides and arranged the comforter and pillow and stuff."

"I don't get it. They're just gonna get all pulled out when I go to bed tonight."

My kid was a genius.

"Exactly." I kissed him on the head just as the dying doorbell wailed.

Shit, poop, shit! I wasn't ready! I was all sweaty and I'm sure my hair was a disaster. I needed another shower after running around the house like an insane person. Well, too late now. Both hands rubbed at my cheeks.

Whatever. It wasn't like I wanted to impress him or anything. *Pshhh.*

I trailed Rocco to the front door like I was approaching my execution and watched him turn the finicky knob. And there, standing on my front porch, was my executioner—all six foot whatever of him in a threadbare t-shirt designed to render women speechless and send urgent signals right to their hoo-has. His shirt impeccably showcased his muscular chest and arms, and a pair of worn army green cargo pants showcased, well, all of *that.* And then there was the face, which looked even more flawless than it had yesterday, if that were possible—and next to the dazzlingly panty-melting smile sat one perfect dimple. The freaking puppy had had a full spa day. How the hell was I going to resist a fluffy puppy with not just a giant pink bow but a fucking dimple?

"Hey, Rocco. Laney." Nate pulled a box of Krispy Kreme doughnuts out from behind his back. Of course he did. My stomach joined my lady bits in celebration.

"Doughnuts!" Rocco squealed.

"Will this buy my entry?" Nate asked.

"Come on in, Nate." I stood aside and he handed the box of doughnuts to me. Hmm, apparently he didn't want any. He bent down and picked up a bag I hadn't noticed by his booted foot. I assumed it held his tools and supplies. He followed Rocco and me to the kitchen, closing the front door behind him.

"So you *did* fix it," he observed of the knob.

"Kind of." I twisted my mouth to the side, resigned to letting him have his way with my, um, house.

"I brought a replacement anyway. I hope you don't mind."

Rocco was already at the table stuffing his face with a doughnut, bits of glaze sticking to his cheeks and chin.

My kitchen was super cute, but I could see Nate's eyes assessing it the night before and I doubted he appreciated the awesomeness of my shabby chic table and my vintage fridge. I had to admit the linoleum needed to go, and in my dreams I'd get granite countertops and maybe even an island. But the kitchen as a whole was actually quite roomy, and nobody could argue against the big picture window that gave a primo view of the backyard. I'd dressed it in flowy white cotton curtains with turquoise tie-backs to match my table. I thought it looked amazing.

Rocco finished swallowing his last bite and spotted Nate's bag. "You got tools?"

"Sure do. I'm going to fix a few things for your mom. Maybe you can help me out." Nate leaned against the counter and crossed his arms over his chest. I checked my chin for drool.

Rocco looked to me and then back to Nate. "I don't know if I'd be comf-ter-ble with that." Nose twitch.

Nate looked a bit surprised and uncomfortable himself. I'm sure he had been anticipating drawing Rocco out with the offer of doughnuts and tools, but leave it to my kid to throw him for a loop.

"It's okay, buddy. You can do what you want," I told my son, knowing that pushing Rocco was never the best plan. "But can you thank Nate for the doughnuts and then go wash your hands and face in the bathroom?"

"Thank you for the doughnuts," he recited and then dashed off to the bathroom.

Nate and I stood facing each other in silence. He finally pushed off the counter and said, "So, you mind if I take a look around the place?"

"Help yourself. It's not big enough to require a tour so have at it." Fingers crossed he wouldn't open any closets.

He smiled for some reason and kept looking at me. Did I have something on my face? There was that dimple again and my lower belly started singing gospel hymns. He turned and headed for the hallway.

I craned my neck to watch him go far enough away before I pounced on the doughnut box and shoved half of a delicious treat in my mouth. Oh, yum.

A few minutes (and doughnuts) later, Nate returned. I discreetly ran a hand over my lips to hide any evidence and gave him my own smile. *Nothing to see here.*

He directed his thumb back toward the hall with an unreadable expression on his face. "Did you know your kid is in the bathroom singing about penises?"

Kill me now.

"Ah, 'The Wiener Song.' A perennial favorite." Gavin unexpectedly appeared behind Nate.

A bit startled, Nate turned to face him and then stuck out a hand. "Hey, Gavin. Good to see you, man." They exchanged macho pleasantries.

"Laney said you're gonna help her with a few things around the house. You don't really have to do that, man," Gavin told his boss.

"Oh, no, I'm happy to. I was telling your sister last night that I haven't gotten my hands dirty in weeks and I've got an itch for it." That wasn't precisely what he'd said. It seemed Fiona wasn't the only one dropping double entendre around here. *Oh please, you know you were thinking it too.*

"Okay, man, it's your funeral. I would stay and help you guys out but I'm supposed to meet my buddy at the gym." He hiked up his backpack over one shoulder. "Later." He passed by Nate, and before passing by me he discreetly pointed two fingers first to his eyes and then to mine. I flipped him off.

* * *

"What's that one for?" Despite his earlier reservations, it turned out Rocco could not resist the lure of power tools. As soon as the electric drill had uttered its first growl, Rocco was glued to Nate's side. I, on the other hand, was standing back but still enjoying the view and another Diet Coke.

"This is a Phillips head screwdriver." They were finishing installing the new knob and deadbolt on the front door. "You use it to screw in this kind of screw." He showed him the small screw in his hand.

"Can I hold it? What if you need to take a screw out? Do you use a different tool? Are there other ones named after people? There's a kid in my class named Philip."

Nate seemed a bit frazzled, no doubt trying to figure out how to answer four questions at once.

"I forgot to tell you." I approached. "Talking to Rocco is like attending a press conference. There will always be one more question."

He laughed and looked up from his position on the floor.

Damn, he was handsome. My hand itched to reach out and touch his hair.

"Redirection and distraction are your friends," I said. "And if all else fails, pulling a quarter out of his ear is a crowd-pleaser."

"Noted," he replied, still smiling, and went back to work on the door. "So, Laney, you never said last night—what is it you do for a living? I know you work in an office …"

"Oh, right." I leaned against the wall next to the front door. I suck at small talk. "You know those new chips on credit cards that protect all your information?"

"Sure. I heard everyone was switching over to those. You program those?"

"No. But you know how some credit card machines still make you swipe instead of using the chip? Well, there are companies whose job it is to convert all the machines so everyone has to use the chip. That's what my company does."

"And you somehow make that happen?" He lowered the screwdriver again.

Rocco, clearly bored by the interruption in the action, wandered down the hallway away from us, probably to disrobe or make up a new song about vaginas.

"No. But I write technical procedures for the people who devise the *actual* procedures to make that happen." *Oh God, could I possibly be any more boring?*

"So, you're like the woman behind the curtain." It was sweet how he was trying to make me sound more interesting than I am.

"More like I'm the woman who transforms geek-speak into normal-person-speak."

He finished with the screwing (*ha!*) and stood to face me so I had to look up. His lips were curved upward and there was that damn dimple. "Ah, so you're a translator. That probably comes in handy in many areas," he mused. "Perhaps you could use your skills to help me understand women."

"No can do." I shook my head, feeling a little light-headed at his closeness. "Our jobs as women are to exist as enigmas whose sole purpose is to render men absolutely perplexed. Help me understand men, though, and I may be able to crack a bit of the code for you." *Oh crap, was I flirting?*

"That's easy—give us food, sleep, and sex and we're good." His lips quirked again.

"I'll jot that down." Mine returned the favor.

"Just be sure you reference the original source in the bibliography."

"Rest assured, I wouldn't dream of attributing that little gem of wisdom to anyone else. You are a true savant, Nate. Has anyone ever told you that?" *Definitely flirting.* This conversation was too inane to be anything else than a prelude to sexy time.

"Has anyone ever told you that you have a smart mouth?"

Before I could respond he tugged me into his arms and kissed the hell out of said mouth.

Bring on the sexy time.

Chapter Nine

FISHING

NATE

Her lips were velvety, and she tasted of mint and soda. One of my hands lifted to her cheek and the smooth skin I found helped me understand why she seemed to spend so much time stroking it herself. I could spend an entire day just kissing and caressing her lips and face alone—okay, well I doubt I'd be able to stop myself there. As my other hand reached to tangle in her hair, I tested the seam of her lips with my tongue and she parted without further encouragement, granting entrance to my tongue so it could taste hers.

I could feel her body shaking a bit, out of nerves or excitement I didn't know and I couldn't have cared less at that moment. But her tongue eagerly dueled with mine as I turned her toward the wall and pinned her there. My thigh found its way between hers and I pressed. My cock stood at attention as I ground into her leg with the finesse of a fifteen-year-old.

This girl was driving me crazy. I couldn't stop myself from bringing a hand from her cheek down her side and resting with my thumb just under her breast. She made a little gasping sound as she pulled her mouth away slightly to draw in a breath before moving back in for more. One of her hands drove into the back of my hair while something cold pressed into the small of my back.

Huh? Before I could comprehend what it could be it was gone and a loud clank came from behind me. Laney came to attention abruptly as she pulled back from me, a surprised look overtaking her eyes. The rest of her face remained flushed and her lips swollen from our kisses. She couldn't pull back far since I still had her pinned to the wall, and her breasts rose and fell as they remained pressed into my chest. She tried to look around me but my height prevented it.

"What's wrong?" I ground out, focused on getting my mouth back on hers.

"Um." One hand came to her cheek and her eyes darted away from mine. "I think I spilled my soda on you."

I stepped back from her and, sure enough, the can lay on the ground in a small puddle, and a hand to the ass of my jeans revealed a large wet spot.

"This is so embarrassing," Laney mumbled, still leaning against the wall, both hands to her cheeks now.

I couldn't help but smile at her. "Totally worth it."

She returned my smile, hers a bit smaller, then disappearing completely. "Shit. Rocco." Her eyes darted to the hall entrance.

Mine followed but no one was there. I admit I had completely forgotten about the kid, my attention had been focused solely on

Laney and getting my hands on her. In retrospect, I suppose my timing could have been better.

"I'm so sorry," she began again and darted around me toward the kitchen. "Let me get some paper towels and try to clean you, I mean *this*, I mean *you know*—up." She came back with the paper towels and tore a few sheets off, thrusting the rest of the roll at me. I wouldn't have minded her trying to clean me up herself.

"If you want, I can lend you some of Gavin's jeans and run yours through the washer," she offered from the floor where she was bent wiping up the mess. I had to force my gaze from her perfect backside.

"No thanks. I'll be fine." No way was I borrowing her brother's clothes. Just, no. "I've got to get going in a little bit anyway. I'll just swing by my place and change there. It's not far."

"I didn't realize you lived close by." She rose from the floor.

I could see her hardened nipples through her shirt and I lost focus for a moment.

"Yeah, I've got a little apartment between here and New Garden. It's pretty crappy, really, but it's just temporary so I don't mind."

An indecipherable look crossed her face. "Well, at least let me feed you or get you something to drink before you go. I can't let you work for free." Her smile was mostly back, some of her discomfort had dissipated.

"I won't say no to a soda, but this time you can just hand it to me." I followed her to the kitchen.

"Haha." Her cheeks began to pink again. Damn, that look was good on her.

I wanted to see how else I could get her to turn pink.

"I've got Diet Coke and Mountain Dew." She reached into the refrigerator.

"Mountain Dew. I've had enough Diet Coke already today," I teased again.

"You take classes on how to be a smartass?" The sass was back.

I took the soda and smiled at her. She seemed to like that because she just stared back at me for a silent beat.

Rocco skipped into the kitchen, ending our little moment, and a double take confirmed that, while he still wore the shirt from earlier, his pants were missing.

Laney's hand covered her eyes and then she shook it off and smiled at me. "Did I neglect to tell you we have a pants-optional policy in our house?" She seemed to realize exactly what she'd said a moment too late and I couldn't help bursting into laughter.

"Good God." She covered her eyes again but then smiled and threw a dish towel at me. "Shut up."

"You shouldn't say 'shut up,' Mommy," said Rocco, opening the pantry door. *Squeak.*

"I know, baby, I'm sorry. Nate was being very naughty and I forgot. I'm going to make you some lunch so we can head over to that playdate soon, okay?"

The kid didn't respond. But I noticed his nose twitch again. Did he have a troublesome booger or something?

"That sounds like fun," I offered, leaning against the counter and opening my soda.

Still no response.

"I'll bet you've got lots of new friends in the neighborhood, huh?"

Just a shoulder shrug and a nose twitch. Should I get him a tissue?

"I'm gonna play Ninja Turtles." And he was gone.

"Was it something I said?" I asked Laney, who had her head in the refrigerator pulling out lunch fixings.

"No, not at all. He's just having a rough time making friends his own age, and there have been a lot of changes recently so he needs time to catch up."

"Oh." I was a bit relieved to not be the cause of any upset. I was also curious about these changes but didn't want to pry too much. "So, I assume moving here was a recent change." I hedged.

"Very," she confirmed, now at the counter making a PB&J. "Until a few weeks ago we lived with my parents, but they decided to move to Virginia and it was time anyway, you know." She rested the knife and looked up at me.

No, I didn't know, but it was sounding like the baby-daddy wasn't in the picture. I wanted to know more but I stayed silent, hoping she'd elaborate on her own.

"It was great having all the help with Rocco, especially when he was a baby, but five years is a long time and it's nice to be on our own now." She looked around the mismatched kitchen with a smile. "I love it here." Her eyes landed on mine and must have seen the skeptical look on my face. "Don't start!" She pointed the jelly knife at me. "It has its flaws but it's just quirky."

"Well, I'm happy to help with those 'quirks' if you'll let me come back next Saturday," I offered, hoping she'd accept. The memory of that scorching kiss was urging me to push for sooner than next weekend, but maybe I should tread lightly.

Fuck it. "In the meantime, you could let me take you out to dinner."

"Oh." she set the knife down and, yup, the hand went to her cheek. Why did I find that so fucking appealing? "I don't know, Nate. You're Gavin's boss and …"

"So, we'll leave him at home. He's a big boy and can get his own dinner." I tried to win her over with the smartass thing. That got a smile.

"Can I think about it?" she asked.

"I guess that's better than no. Let me give you my number so you can call me when you decide to say yes." Okay, a little cocky, but at least I'd get her number.

We exchanged numbers and she called Rocco in for lunch.

"You know, if you're so excited to hang out with me, you should come to this playdate with us," she said with a mischievous spark.

"Playdate?" I'm sure my expression was equal parts confused and apprehensive.

"Yeah." Her smirk was in full force. "The—what did you call it? Oh, right, the 'mommy-and-me troop' is getting together to strategize how to terrorize the big bad construction company."

My face completely fell. *Shit.*

"Oh, get that look off your face, Sparky. I'm just joking. You were getting too cocky and I had to knock you down a peg. I'm just going to tell them what you've told me so far, omitting the sarcasm of course, and explain that you'll do your best to keep us informed. I'll even try to convince them not to TP your trailer or leave flaming bags of dog poop on your steps. Happy?" Her smile was stunning. I had to get myself in check or I'd be hauling her off to her bedroom, kid or no kid.

Able to breathe normally again, I approached her and tugged on a stray lock of hair. "Not yet, but I'm getting there." Her cheeks colored again.

"Heh, dog poop!" Rocco chuckled from the table.

She lowered her face. "Let me walk you to the door."

I followed her after waving goodbye to Rocco.

"Wow! This works so well. I love it." Laney turned the new knob and swung the door open easily. "Thank you, Nate." She tilted her head to smile at me. Hell, if fixing her doorknob could inspire that look I could only imagine what other things could do.

We stood a bit awkwardly for a moment, looking at each other, both of us aware of how close Rocco was and how close we both were to saying, "screw it" and proceeding to, well, screw it. So I chose to bend down and kiss her cheek. "You're welcome. And don't forget to call me." She smiled but didn't respond so I turned around and stepped off the porch.

Halfway to my car she called out behind me, "Hey, Nate! Tell your dad to give fishing a try. It's relaxing while still being manly. And it involves both sharp things and motors—what's not to love?"

I did a half turn and pointed to her. "You just may have something there." I smiled. She certainly did have something.

Chapter Ten

WHEN IN DOUBT, CHOOSE BURGERS OVER SUSHI

*L*ANEY

Holy. Balls.

Nate Murphy has the power to make a woman forget her name. *How does he do that?* It's like his scruffy jaw and his dimple are my kryptonite. One moment we were having a nice little conversation and the next I had my tongue down his throat and was pouring my drink all over him. This was actually fortuitous since, in addition to forgetting my name, I had forgotten that my five-year-old was twenty feet away! I had been ready to tear my clothes off and beg him to take me right there by the front door. *What was wrong with me?*

Oh God, and then he asked me out!

Squee!

But not squee.

Shit.

There was Gavin's job and there was Rocco, and the last thing we needed was some guy who was only in town temporarily.

Ugh.

Not to mention it had been so long since my last date I'm pretty sure dinosaurs had still roamed the earth. I mean, a girl has needs and I'd been sort of satisfying them by myself for the most part. I'd dated a couple guys since Rocco was born, but nothing had stuck. And the fact I wasn't all that disappointed about it just went to show that those relationships were way wrong. But with the way I was reacting to Nate right from the start, I was pretty sure this guy had heartbreak written all over his too handsome, too freaking perfect face. And arms. And ass. Jesus, I was starting to sound like Fiona with all my scattered thoughts. *Get a grip, Laney.*

I had to set this incredibly sexy and tempting topic aside and focus on something else. Another date, in fact—the playdate. I peeled myself off the back of the door and headed back to Rocco. But I penciled in a good old-fashioned phone gab with Fiona on my mental calendar. I may have also penciled in a good old-fashioned fantasy session with my vibrator, but I'll never tell.

* * *

Charlotte's house was just as I'd imagined it to be—warm, comfortable, and wholly Southern. There were fresh flowers and sweet tea and, most importantly, welcoming hugs and greetings all around. Rocco suctioned himself to my leg but gradually loosened up as he saw some of the other kids organizing a few games. He eschewed the round of tag in the backyard—which, unsurprisingly, involved plastic knives and guns—and instead wandered over to check out the X-box battle that was launching in the next room. However, he made sure to maintain an open line of sight to me the entire time. I considered it a small win anyway.

Once I got a moment alone with Charlotte, I told her (mostly) about my visit with Nate on Friday and the information he'd shared. I explained to the best of my ability the cause of his rude behavior and told her he wanted to apologize to her. When I asked for her permission to pass on her number to him she graciously accepted, as I knew she would. It seemed all was already forgiven in her eyes and she turned them to me speculatively.

"So, do I sense a little chemistry goin' on here?"

"What? No, of course not!" I replied, totally unconvincing in my hasty denial.

She just smiled and raised her eyebrows. "Even if he was a class-A jerk, I'd have to be blind not to see the sparks lightin' up the air around you two." She was way too smug.

"Oh, shut up," I told her, and she just giggled. Damn her cute little ass.

My job was done. I'd shared my pertinent information, my kid was slightly engaged with others his own age, and I had a glass of real Texas sweet tea. *Ugh, why do people like this stuff?*

* * *

"Remind me. Why are you always over here when you could be out enjoying a totally awesome nightlife of hot guys and no responsibility?"

Instead of the phone call, Fiona had elected to come by my house for our girl gab. Seriously, she could be out doing anything she wanted at any time. She had money to party or go on vacations or buy out the entire SkyMall catalog—*hey, some of that stuff is cool*—but she chose to spend the majority of her time with me and my dysfunctional little family. To say she came from money was like saying Ghirardelli double fudge brownies were *kind of okay*. The bitch was loaded. Luckily, she was completely missing the "bitch" gene. She held rotating jobs mostly out of boredom and, I suspect, to generate stories to share with me when we got together. That's real friendship for you.

Truthfully, though, I don't think Fiona knew what she wanted to do with her life so it was easier to just keep busy and keep postponing life decisions. With her family's wealth, she didn't need to work if she didn't choose to.

In direct contrast to all the rich snob stereotypes, her parents were wonderful people who were in full support of any decisions Fiona made—and I mean *any* decisions. She could decide to move to some inner city to teach underprivileged kids, or tour Europe on a three-year luxury excursion, or tattoo her entire body and pose naked for a magazine spread. Nothing but love and acceptance would come her way. It was the simplest and most authentic relationship between parents and child I'd ever seen.

When Fiona was nine years old she'd received a death sentence in the form of an aggressive leukemia diagnosis. Through bottomless funds, prayers, and a wealth of medical miracles she had survived, and not only that, she'd thrived beyond basic remission and into adulthood as a healthy, happy, and wonderful person.

Sure, the aggressive treatments had resulted in her short stature and a slightly increased risk of developing a possible subsequent cancer during the course of her life, but she was our shining star.

Everyone who knew her and her sunny spirit reveled in it and called themselves lucky to know her.

Unfortunately for me, on this particular evening, the sunny spirit was hiding behind the complete exasperation in her expression.

"What?! It's just not a good idea. But believe me, I comprehend the sheer hotness of that man even more than you do. I swear there was a moment when he was kissing me that I thought I'd forgotten to put on underwear this morning."

She gave me a puzzled look. We both knew I was no commando girl. Not with my generous booty.

"I'd remembered all right—they had just spontaneously combusted under the force of his testosterone. Holy hell, he was that good!" I fanned myself at the memory.

We both giggled like idiots.

"Where are Rocco and Gavin?" she asked after we settled down.

"They went to the batting cages with Brett."

"Aww. That's so sweet."

Sometimes I forgot to appreciate the time Gavin spent with Rocco and the experiences he provided that a dad should be doing. It was time to lighten up on him.

"Yeah, unfortunately Rocco has a pretty un-athletic mother and a musician for a father so Gavin's dreams of living through Rocco may be dashed early on," I said.

Not to be deterred from the main topic of the evening, Fiona persisted, "So you're really not going to go out with Nate?"

"Ugh. Believe me, I'm totally tempted, but what happens when we get in a fight and Gavin gets stuck in the middle? Or, more likely, what happens when Rocco and I both fall in love with him and he takes off for his next adventure? Because he will, you know. As soon as his dad is back on his feet, he's gone. I can't do that to any of us. And even if, by some miracle, he decided to stay, why would he want to saddle himself with a single mom and a kid? I'm sure he's just looking for a fun distraction to pass the time and I'm not up for that." The feeling of sadness that overtook me was disproportionate to the brief involvement I'd had with Nate to this point. I could already feel myself getting in over my head and we'd only shared one kiss. One earth-shattering kiss, but still.

"But you deserve an awesome guy and a hot sexy love life, Laney! Every guy I suggest is all wrong—he's too short, he has a weird accent, he wears a fedora, he sweats too much—*whatever!* I can't sit around here and watch you spend another Saturday night watching *The Mentalist* on Hulu and fantasizing about Simon Baker—he's too old for you anyway. You need a real live date with a real live penis—your penis fly trap needs a snack! No offense."

Oh my, it seemed Fiona brought the big guns out tonight. "Wow, don't hold back on my account." I narrowed my eyes at her. "First of all, did you stop by a bar for a shot or seven of vodka on your way here? Second, you seem to have forgotten that one of the guys you tried to set me up with was eighteen years old—his voice hadn't even changed yet! Enough said."

Ready for her rebuttal, I thrust a hand out and intercepted it. "But, as it so happens, dear Fiona, Annette is setting me up on a date with someone this week. He fits all your criteria and he even has a child of his own. I didn't specifically ask if he has a real live penis but I'm assuming that's a given. I'm expecting his call and, barring a disastrous initial conversation, I plan to accept. So there!"

She beamed back at me and I couldn't help but be a little happy that I'd put a smile on her face. "Well, if it can't be hot construction dude, I guess we can give this other guy a chance at snack time. Now, where's the wine?"

* * *

My phone buzzed with a text.

Nate: I got an in at Hops and can skip the line. Just name the night. BTW, when did that place become such a madhouse? It's still just a burger joint, right?

Laney: I know! Ever since it got listed as "Best Burger" on some list you can't get in anymore.

Nate: I noticed that still wasn't a yes on the date?

Laney: I've got Charlotte's phone number for you.

Nate: I don't want to go out with Charlotte. I want to go out with you. Besides, dating married women requires too much effort and I'm not big on subterfuge.

Laney: Smartass. I meant I had her number for the apology you owe her. I haven't forgotten.

Nate: Neither have I. Now, about this date ...

Laney: I've got Rocco so it's not that easy.

Nate: You've also got Gavin and I am his boss after all. I can be lenient if he needs to come in late ...

Laney: Exactly! None of that. I don't think we should get involved.

Nate: You think too much.

That was Tuesday and I chose not to re-engage or I'd get myself in trouble. That same night I got the call I'd been expecting from Annette's guy, Alex. He seemed nice enough on the phone, although we did have the expected awkward moments one gets when trying to organize a date with a complete stranger. We settled fairly quickly on Thursday evening and I have to say I was somewhat relieved to get off the phone. I forgot how stressful dating was—why do people do this to themselves?

* * *

Thursday arrived before I was ready, and it was officially date night. The only problem was that the date wasn't with the guy I actually wanted, no matter what the logical part of my brain said. Nate had continued to text me since Tuesday and I couldn't help but be charmed by him. *Dammit!*

Determined to get me fired up for the date, Fiona showed up early in the evening with a slew of dresses and heels. Since she and I are nowhere in the neighborhood of the same size, my look of confusion must have been evident.

"So I stopped at a couple boutiques. Suck it!"

I would try to argue with her but there was no stopping Fiona and her credit card. So I let her spend the next hour doing my hair and makeup and dressing me up like a Barbie, except one with actual human dimensions. She spent the majority of the time alternating between reveling in her own genius and filling me in on useless gossip that was both totally frivolous and completely entertaining. As only a best friend would do, she'd offered to babysit Rocco during my date. I would have asked Gavin, but I was starting to feel like I was taking advantage of him a bit and I knew he had his, well, drinking or whatever to do in the evenings. Truthfully, I had no idea what he was up to these days.

"This is definitely the one." Fiona stood back and admired her work, finger to her lips.

I looked down at the form-fitting pink dress. It was sleeveless with wide straps—because, come on, there was no way on earth I could forego a bra—and a pencil skirt that ended just above the knee. Running down the center of the dress was a pretty little vertical ruffle of sorts. I tugged lightly at the ruffle. "You don't think this is too much?"

"It adds interest and draws the eye vertically—very slimming," she said.

I was all for slimming, but still. "You don't think I look a bit like … a vagina?"

She gasped just as the doorbell rang. "Shoes!" she shouted.

Oh well, too late. I shoved on the torture devices she threw at me and headed out to the living room. I paused as I noted for the umpteenth time this week that the cockeyed board on the hallway floor lay flat where it had once caused countless stubbed toes as if that had been its sole purpose on this earth. Nate had fixed it on Saturday and dammit if I didn't think of him every time I walked down the hall. *Sigh.* I forced thoughts of Nate aside and entered the living room where Gavin sat on the couch.

"Doorbell," he said oh-so-helpfully. Then he looked me up and down. "That's a lot of pink. No offense, but you kind of look like a—"

"You must be Alex!" Fiona opened the front door with a flourish.

I *knew* it! Crap! Too late now.

Alex stepped inside. Annette hadn't lied—he was super cute. Short-ish blond hair spiked up in artful disarray, and a thin nose held a pair of cool hipster glasses with black frames. He was taller than me in my heels so that was good, and he had great cheekbones, but no scruff, I noticed. Oh well. He wore a gray short-sleeved button down and black pants. Skinny pants. Huh. How did I feel about that?

Fiona swept to the side like the little hostess she is. She motioned to herself. "I'm Fiona, the best friend. That's Gavin, the brother." She spared Gavin the slightest gesture and then motioned to me as if presenting Alex to the queen. "And this … is Laney." Jesus, was she going to curtsey next?

Alex's face broke into a smile. "Wow, Laney, you look beautiful. I love pink."

Cough. Shut up, Gavin!

"Thanks. You look nice too." Didn't they have those pants in your size? I guess I'd figured out my feelings about the pants after all.

God, stop being a bitch, Laney!

He really did have a great smile—nice, even white teeth. But no dimple. Well that's okay, not everyone can have an awesome dimple.

Come on, give him a chance!

Fiona looked at me and seemed to be attempting to communicate the same command. *Let's do this!* "Well, have fun, kids!" she chirped and ushered us out the door.

The drive to the restaurant went as expected for a first date—some overly long silences and some talking over each other in an attempt to ease the awkwardness. Just normal first date stuff.

"I thought we'd try out this new sushi place," Alex said.

"Oh, okay." A bit of a risk for a first date, wasn't it? Not everybody likes sushi. *Shut up! You like sushi just fine.* "Sounds great!"

We arrived at the restaurant and he opened my door for me. Gotta love a guy with manners. He kept his hand on the small of my back all the way to our table which, while not prompting the flight of any butterflies, was nice.

After we were comfortably seated and had a chance to look over the menu, we placed our orders with the waitress. I stuck to the basics with California rolls, tuna and the like, but Alex went full out experimental. I couldn't pronounce most of what he ordered, and I was a bit scared to witness him eating it. Eek.

"So, Annette says you and Rocco just bought your house? That's great. Isn't house hunting fun?" he asked with a smirk. Sarcasm, I like it.

"Yeah, it comes in only a close second to a root canal on my list of favorite activities. But now that it's done I love it." I relaxed and sipped my water.

"I had to get a new place last year too. I thought my daughter, Allison, would have a hard time adjusting. Her mom stayed in our old place, you know, and we share custody."

I nodded understandingly.

"But Allison's been an angel—handling the divorce like a champ. Couldn't ask for a better kid."

That's sweet, I thought. I needed to give this guy a chance. "Wow, that's great for you. I've heard that can be really hard so it sounds like you lucked out." I smiled at him. "There's not even a divorce involved in my move and I think Rocco is going to need therapy to get over it," I joked.

"No luck about it. Allison's just the perfect kid." Deadpan.

Whoa, back it up there, mister. Isn't there some unwritten rule that you can't call your own kid perfect out loud unless you're using deep sarcasm? Before I had to think of a response our waitress came with our food and the hot sake we'd ordered. I think some of Alex's meal was still alive.

He picked up his chopsticks. "So, what do you like to do for fun, Laney?"

"Oh, you know, work and take care of my kid mostly. That's when I'm not flying off in my private jet to Aruba, of course." I popped a California roll in my mouth. Yum.

Alex shook his head and swallowed his bite. "You've got to make time for yourself. You should take up running. It's great cardio."

Was he calling me fat? "Running and I don't really mix." You can only get hit in the face with your own boobs so many times before you have to call it a day. "I like hiking, though, but it's hard to take a five-year-old. Rocco's ready to turn around thirty steps in," I tried to joke again.

"Allison loves hiking. We also do a lot of biking together."

I'm sure she does. And I'm sure your bike shorts are even tighter than your pants. "That sounds like fun for you guys." My appetite was quickly fading. I took a large sip of my sake instead.

"It is. She's really advanced for her age." He took a bite of what looked like a tentacle.

Of course she is. This date was officially over. Why did he need to date me when he had the perfect girl at home? "Well if I can get Rocco to sleep in his own bed by the time he's ten I'll count it as a win on my end," I ground out as I searched in vain for our waitress.

Completely misinterpreting my mood, he continued, "My ex and I employed a nurturing concept called the 'family bed.' Allison sleeps with me to this day."

Aaaand there's that. I was beginning to understand the cause of his divorce—and also the reason Allison was an only child.

"You should embrace Rocco's desire for closeness," he persisted.

I downed the rest of my sake.

Check, please.

* * *

"So it didn't go great?" Fiona asked, looking disappointed.

I don't know what gave it away, my scowl or my complete deflation onto the couch, vagina dress splayed around me. I was surprised to see Gavin in the recliner, leaning back in the same jeans and t-shirt he'd had on when I left. I thought he'd be three sheets to the wind by now at Jake's.

"Obviously," he contributed. "That guy was a douchecanoe."

I couldn't rally myself to protest. "Is it judgy of me to find it creepy that he prefers sleeping in the same bed as his seven-year-old?"

Fiona's expression crumpled with revulsion while Gavin's remained steady. "Dating that twatwaffle could only end in a smartphone full of dick pics. Consider it a bullet dodged and move on."

"Eww," Fiona and I simultaneously pronounced.

Chapter Eleven

WELL, THIS IS AWKWARD

NATE

I hadn't given up. Several days of flirty texting but no date accepted, I still had my ace in the hole with a tentative Saturday plan to resume work on her house.

Nate: *Krispy Kreme again or should I go for Granny's?*

Laney: *Oooh. Tough choice. Surprise me.*

And just like that I had my confirmed invitation to come over tomorrow. It was Friday afternoon and I had to swing by my parents' house to get my dad's signature on a few documents. I hadn't seen him in about a week so I was looking forward to checking out his progress in person. My mom had told me over the phone that he was making her crazy trying to be too active and he was chomping at the bit to start driving again. That sounded about right.

She was also still on her kick to find him a hobby. Bailey had brought over a few jigsaw puzzles earlier in the week, as requested by our mom, and it had not gone over well. Some words were exchanged about nursing homes and bingo, and an alternative—and quite creative—suggestion was made as to where to put the puzzles. Bailey's visit didn't last long.

When I arrived, I let myself in the front door and was surprised to see that Bailey was back as well. Clearly a glutton for punishment.

"I thought you had an appointment this afternoon," I said.

"Canceled," she replied, chugging a coffee from Starbucks like it was her life's blood.

"Does Mom know you brought caffeine in the house?"

"I distracted her when I came in the door so I got away with it."

"How'd you do that?!" I had continued to get the pat down each time I entered the house.

"There he is!" exclaimed my mother, entering the hallway and consuming me in a giant hug. "My Nathan."

Looking over my mom's shoulder at Bailey, I spotted my conniving little sister's shit-eating grin instantly. She just shrugged her shoulders and mouthed, "Sucks to be you." I flipped her off immediately.

I was way too familiar with this look from Bailey. It was the same one she got each time she finagled her way out of trouble by throwing me under the bus. I'd spent many nights as a teenager, grounded in my room, plotting revenge on Bailey for just this kind of shit. It didn't matter that I actually *had* been smoking weed behind the garage or sneaking out my bedroom window to go out late—it was the principle of the thing. I'd been pretty successful with a few of my revenge strategies, the best one being the time I got the whole school to call her "Sabrina" for most of her freshman year. It was short for "Sabrina the Teenage Bitch" and the best part was that it could be used in front of teachers—it pissed Bailey off in the worst way. Ah, good times.

But that was then—this was now. And she would pay—as soon as I found out what the hell she'd done this time.

"Hi Mom," I said a bit warily, returning her hug with a tad less enthusiasm.

She released me and took my face in her hands. "So handsome."

Oh shit. This was worse than I thought.

"Now, tell me all about her. I can't wait to meet her! Bailey said she has a son. That's just wonderful! I miss being around kids."

Jesus H. Macy.

Skewering Bailey with my best "you are fucking dead" glare, I stopped her in her tracks as she attempted to slink away.

"Let's go have a drink in the kitchen and you can tell me all about her and her little boy," my mother cooed.

Trying desperately to get out of this conversation, I asked, "Where's Dad? I really need him to sign some papers."

She waved me off and ushered both Bailey and me toward the table. "He's in the shower. He'll be down in a bit and then you two can take care of that. Sit."

With little other choice, I sat and mentally planned my sister's very painful death. *Do they still have the rack?* No, that was too good for her.

Cups of decaf all around and the inquisition began. "Bailey said you met her at work? Is she Catholic? I'll bet she's Irish, isn't she? Oh, no matter—I'm sure she's wonderful either way." Her eyes passed between me and my sister.

At this point Bailey jumped in and tried to save herself. "That's just what Mark said. I don't really know much about it except for what he told me."

That bastard. Mark was too nosy for his own good and I should have known he couldn't keep his mouth shut. He had seen Laney at the Old Oak Ridge site, though, so there had been no avoiding talking about her. Every guy there had been talking about her for a week, much to Gavin's annoyance. Which only made the guys talk more shit, of course.

"Okay, slow down, Mom. I just met this girl and we haven't even gone out on a date, so hold off on the wedding plans, please."

"But you've been spending time with her, right? That sounds to me like dating. What's she like? I'm sure she's really pretty, isn't she?"

"Her name is Laney. She's beautiful." I couldn't help it—it just came out.

Bailey shot me a surprised glance, totally unused to me saying word one about a woman. Why did I feel like I was shooting myself in the foot?

"I knew it." Our mother smiled. "And how old is her son?"

"He's five, I think. His name is Rocco."

"Awww," came the two female voices simultaneously.

Jesus.

"I know!" My mother straightened up suddenly. "You should invite them over for Sunday dinner! Then we can all meet them. And it would be a great distraction for your father."

Before I could protest that nothing of the sort would be happening, Bailey cut in. "Not this again, Mom. A girlfriend or a potential grandkid is not going to keep Dad from going back to work. You've got to stop with this hobby thing too. You saw how he reacted to the puzzles. What's it going to be next, synchronized swimming?"

Bailey looked to me with a sudden smirk. "We'll have to add that to the list, Nate—can you imagine?" She started to snicker before she realized that she'd just fucked us both. *Have I mentioned what an utter pain in the ass my sister is?*

Our mother's good mood evaporated instantly, and the air turned thick. Her hands gripped her coffee cup so tightly her knuckles turned white. "So, you two think this is all a big joke," she said with a quiet intensity we'd never heard before. "You just wait until you see the person you love more than anything lying on the ground afraid and in pain. Then you see how funny it is to wrack your brain trying to think of any and every thing in your power you can do to keep them with you—to not lose them. Laugh all you want, but if puzzles or grandkids or *goddamned synchronized swimming* will keep your father with me for one more second, you better believe I'll pull out all the stops. Now, if you'll excuse me, I'm going to get your dad's medicines ready for him."

Imagine the shittiest you've ever felt in your life and multiply that by ten. That's how pathetic Bailey and I felt sitting at the kitchen table after the well-deserved beat-down served by our mother.

"God, we're such assholes," Bailey said.

"Yup." She'd hit the nail on the head.

"I'm going after her." Bailey rose from her chair and left the room.

I continued to sit and drown in the guilt. I had even lost my desire to punish Bailey, it was that bad.

Ten minutes later, Bailey poked her head in to tell me she was taking off and that she had apologized and tried to smooth things over with our mom.

Looked like it was my turn. I found her folding my dad's t-shirts in the laundry room.

"Mom, I really owe you and Dad an apology. Making fun of your efforts was cruel," I began. "I think … I think we were joking around and being assholes because we didn't want to acknowledge that maybe the strongest man we knew wasn't the superhero we'd always made him out to be. And even harder to imagine is *him* admitting that fact too. Sure he's human, but just because his heart wants to slow down doesn't mean he's not the same bad-ass ball buster and problem solver. But you're right—he needs to tone it down. And we need to be more cooperative in helping you accomplish what's best for you both."

She looked up at me and said, "I accept your apology, but next time, please try not to use so many curse words." She gave me a side hug and I kissed the top of her head, relieved to be forgiven. "This is hard on all of us—so many changes to consider," my mom said.

"Yeah, the changes are definitely throwing me. You know I'm all in with the company, right?"

"Of course. And you know we appreciate it so much, Nate."

In for a penny, in for a pound. "It's just that, ideally speaking, I would really love it if Dad comes back to take over the administration side of things and I can take over the other side. But I understand if it can't happen. I just want you to know I'm there for you either way, but I'd be lying if I said I didn't miss using my hands on the job."

She set the t-shirt she was holding on the pile. "Nathan, you and your father are different men. That's no secret to any of us. He's spent his career working out how to fit the figurative square peg in the round hole while you've spent yours *literally* fitting the peg to the hole. You don't need to become your father in some effort to rescue everyone. That can only end with you being unhappy and probably resenting us. And that is the last thing I want for any of us." She put her hand to my cheek. "We'll work it out. And I'll bet if you open your eyes and start looking around you'll see there are a lot of people who work with you and your father who'd be willing to step up a bit."

Well shit, why hadn't I thought of that? Why had I automatically assumed the bulk of the responsibility?

"So" she smiled at me and picked the shirt back up. "What time can I expect you all on Sunday?"

Aaand checkmate goes to my mother.

I'd decided on Granny's since I secretly loved jimmies—or "sprinkles" to the uneducated. The front door opened before I even had the chance to climb the first step, and Rocco burst onto the porch. "Is there chocolate?"

Ah, a man after my own heart. "Of course," I told him as if only a complete idiot would arrive without a chocolate doughnut. He snatched the box and ran inside.

"Rocco! Manners!" Laney appeared in the doorway.

"Oh yeah, thanks, Nate!" came the quickly receding voice muffled by what I assumed was a chocolate doughnut.

I paid zero attention to Rocco at that point, however. Laney stood before me in what I can only describe as the outfit that would have caused teenage Nate to sequester himself in his room for two straight weeks. The white tank top was thin, the pink lace bra playing peek-a-boo in several places, and her currently tightened nipples were straining the fabric. The tank was snug at her waist as well, and her hips flared out in a denim skirt which stopped mid-thigh. How I was going to get through this morning without putting my mouth on several parts of her body I had no idea. *Did she wear this fuck-hot outfit for me? She must have, right?* I was going with yes and pushing my luck as soon as the opportunity presented itself. With Rocco around, though, it was going to be a long morning working around the giant boner in my pants. How did this woman make me revert to a seventeen-year-old with one look and a tank top?

I stepped through the doorway and made sure to skim my hand over her waist and kiss her cheek. She smelled like coconut and a hint of flowers. Her sharp inhale did not go unnoticed. This was happening.

I spent the morning mildly flirting with Laney and placing casual touches on her arms and back as often as possible. Rocco resumed his position as my helper but lost interest a bit more quickly this time. When Gavin returned home from the gym and offered to take Rocco for pizza, the kid dashed out the door without a backward glance. Perfect. Alone time with Laney.

However, my normally confident air around women was a bit more elusive today, and I realized the reason with a mix of dread and uncertainty. My insensitivity with my mother yesterday had me consumed with guilt, and I knew I'd have to bite the bullet and embarrass the shit out of myself with Laney. I was going to ask a girl to meet my parents when she hadn't even agreed to go out on a date with me. Was there any way I could come across as more douchey or creepy than that?

Before I could stress any more about it, though, Laney walked into the bedroom with a basket of laundry and dumped it on her bed. "Can you tell me what the point is of folding laundry?" she asked.

"Um, I guess so you can find it later?" I didn't know how to answer. My wardrobe consisted solely of jeans, cargo pants, and crappy t-shirts, none of which required much care.

"I guess so." She sighed and sounded so disappointed I didn't understand how laundry could be such a downer.

"Is laundry really that depressing?" I asked as I finished gluing a floorboard in place.

She seemed to shake herself out of whatever mood had overtaken her and emitted a small laugh. "No, I guess I got stuck in my head for a minute there." She shook her head again and smiled at me. "So, what's it like working as my indentured servant on your days off?" she asked.

"Well, I'll tell you, working inside like this has its advantages. It's air-conditioned for one, and I don't have to hear passersby saying stupid things like, 'Hey, when you're finished there, why don't you come over to my house and fix a few things?!'" I mimicked an idiotic hillbilly tone complete with a fake-ass chuckle.

Her face fell. "I say that all the time … It's friendly."

She looked so disheartened I was without words for several moments. "Hmm, well, this is awkward." That's all I had.

We looked at each other silently for several beats. Then, finally, thank God, she broke out into the fucking cutest fit of giggles I've ever heard in my life. It was impossible not to respond with my own laughter, and pretty soon we were both doubled over. The situation may not have warranted the extent of our hilarity, but it felt so damn good to share this with her. I felt ten feet tall.

* * *

Since there's never an ideal time to humiliate yourself, I chose the moment right before I was leaving Laney's house. I gathered my things and walked into the kitchen where she was at the counter mixing something in a bowl. "Whatcha making?"

Her head turned to me and she had a bit of what looked like flour on her cheek. "Chocolate chip cookies. I figured if the doughnuts didn't put us into a diabetic coma this would finish the job." She smiled and turned back to her task.

I approached from behind and stuck my finger in the bowl. I got the dough to my mouth before she could smack my hand. "Psoo gwood."

"Hey! Taste-testing is only for the baker!"

I swallowed the pilfered bite. "It's just payment for today's work!" I then pressed myself into her back, forcing her closer to the counter. I could hear her breath catch. I leaned down close to her ear and whispered, "You have flour on your face," just to watch her raise her hand to her cheek in that way I found so endearing. I wasn't disappointed.

"Why didn't you say something sooner." She was flustered and started to squirm a bit which did nothing for the situation in my pants, considering my body was anchoring hers to the counter. I had no doubt she could feel my body's reaction to her, so I went in for a soft kiss under her ear. She melted into me a bit and I managed to turn her around so I could gain access to her mouth.

Our kisses were wet, hot, and fervent. Neither of us could get enough, and when my hand found its way to her breast she arched her back and pressed further into me. I rubbed her tight nipple with my thumb and she let out a small moan. My other hand caressed down her back and gripped her ass, pulling her in even tighter to my groin. It felt infinitely better than I'd imagined, and I'd spent a lot of time imagining it.

I was dying to get her out of this skirt and replace my hand with my mouth. Her arms wrapped around me and one of her hands descended to my ass as the other gripped my t-shirt. I was starting to lose control and was ready to prop her up on the counter and splay her out. I knew I had to slow down or I'd scare her away for sure. I pulled back reluctantly with one last squeeze of her ass and we both breathed deeply. She raised her hand again, but this time it was to touch her lips which were swollen from our kisses.

"You still think it's a bad idea to go out with me?" I asked.

She smiled and her cheeks remained pink as we both continued to steady our breaths

"I'll tell you what," I said, my hand caressing up and down her side. "You don't even have to be alone with me for our first date. As strange as it sounds, I'd like to ask you and Rocco to come over for dinner at my parents' house tomorrow." I held my breath and hoped for the best.

A perplexed look crossed her face. "I'm sorry, did you just ask me to meet your parents tomorrow?"

"It's not what it sounds like. My mom's a terrible cook but she wants to have people over to hang out with my dad and I have trouble saying no to her. Don't overthink it—just say yes."

"Um, okay then, I guess we can come." Then she quickly added, "Can I bring Gavin?" It seemed she wanted to make sure this wasn't a date. As long as she was coming, though, I didn't care who she brought with her.

"Sure. The more the merrier. That way we'll have more people to hang out with at the hospital when we all get food poisoning."

Her face fell.

"Kidding. But, seriously, you may want to eat before you come."

I offered to pick her up but she assured me they could get there on their own, so once I gave her the address it was time for me to leave. We walked to the door together and I couldn't help but pull her to me for one more short kiss. She tasted like cookies.

"I'll call you later," I said and walked to my truck, afraid if I didn't leave now I never would.

Once I got to my car I called Bailey and told her the Monroe troop was coming tomorrow and she'd better get her ass on the phone and invite someone too—in order to keep things as casual as possible. I could tell right away she was going to try to bail, so like any good brother would, I employed blackmail to get my point across.

"Oh, did I forget to tell you I gave Vance your number?" Vance was the creepy electrician we contracted with on occasion, and he had a serious thing for Bailey. "I said you would be waiting for his call and were really looking forward to getting to know him better. I think he mentioned dinner at his place—I can't recall all the details, but I'm sure it won't involve any lotion on the skin or anything."

"I hope you choke on your own dick. You didn't actually do that, did you?"

"Not yet, but I do have his number on speed dial."

"Fuck you. What time do we have to be there?"

Chapter Twelve

WE'VE ALL GOT OUR OWN BRAND OF CRAZY

LANEY

"I got an email today that I know was from you, but the sender was 'Mommy Buttlover'? What the fuck?" That was Fiona's greeting when I called her to fret about Nate that afternoon. She was trying not to laugh and doing a piss-poor job at it.

"Christ on a cracker—I know. I'm going to *kill* Gavin. No one will recognize his body. He had Rocco tell Siri to call me 'Mommy Buttlover' from now on instead of 'Laney,' and it changed my outgoing email identifier! I replied to just about everyone in my address book today about a birth announcement. Everyone is going to see that 'Mommy Buttlover' thinks the baby looks just like his daddy. God, how embarrassing!"

"Not to mention confusing." She was cackling by this point and I couldn't help but smile a tiny bit.

"I hate my life," I managed.

"No you don't. Your life is great—awesome kid, cute house, sadistic brother … what more could you ask for? Except maybe … hot construction guy?" I could see I wouldn't have to introduce the real reason for the call. She knew me too well.

"I'm starting to think hot construction guy is going to be a part of my life whether I want him to be or not."

"I knew it, I knew it," she sing-songed loudly in my ear.

"We totally made out again in my kitchen and he asked me to have dinner with his parents tomorrow," I blurted out.

Silence.

"It's weird, isn't it?" I stated more than asked.

"Well, the making out part isn't weird at all—in fact, that part is dreamy—and please tell me you got to touch his butt and it was as perfect as it looks."

"Yes, and *hell yes*."

"I knew it!" The song was back.

"Okay, shut up. The make-out session was so hot I can't even begin to describe it accurately. My breasts physically swelled—I didn't even know that could happen. But the dinner thing is stressing me out!"

"All right, calm down. How exactly did he ask you? Was he like, 'Hey, Laney, since we made out a couple times and we're clearly getting married why don't you come meet Mom and Dad tomorrow and then we can make beautiful babies together?' or was it more like, 'Hey, I'm going over to my parents' to grab a bite. Wanna come?'"

"I guess it was more like the second one. He invited Rocco and Gavin too."

"Then what are you stressing about? I think it's sweet."

"You do? You're sure?"

"Yeah. You worry too much. Go and have fun and then report back to me. Now get back to Nate's ass—I need more details!"

"Why is it we never talk about your love life?"

* * *

After the whole Siri debacle, it wasn't too hard to guilt Gavin into coming to dinner at the Murphy's. It did involve free food, after all, but I neglected to warn him about Mrs. Murphy's supposedly horrific cooking. *Can you blame me?* I fed Rocco a sandwich before we left so he would be all set—Gavin could fend for himself.

I was a little distracted on the drive over. Charlotte and I had met up that morning at a nearby park and I'd been hoping Rocco would play with Aiden, but he mostly just asked me to swing him on the swings while Aiden ran around shooting imaginary villains and mounting attacks from the top of the monkey bars. Charlotte and I had a nice time talking and I was liking her more and more— now if I could only get our kids to be friends.

Feeling a bit down from the park, I'd called my mom to catch up and see if she could offer me some reassurance. She was aware of Rocco's little idiosyncrasies, having lived with him since his birth. I filled her in about the nose thing and his recent behavior.

"I feel like it's getting worse since we moved to the new house." I didn't want to say, "since you moved away" because it was definitely not her cross to bear—she'd gone above and beyond as a grandparent. "And now his teachers are concerned."

"Sweetie, all moms worry about their kids. Rocco's not even

going into real school until next year—a lot can change in a year. And might I remind you of another person in our family who has a little habit of her own—someone who rubs her face when she's stressed?"

Oh yeah, why didn't I think of that? Well, poop, it looked like I'd passed down more of my own issues to the poor kid than I realized.

"And, besides, kids are just small adults—have you ever met an adult who was normal? Of course not. We all have our own brand of crazy. Just love him and that's all you can do," she said.

"I just can't help but feel like *I've* done this to him. *I* deprived him of a father by being irresponsible and *I* moved him away from people he loves. And now it looks like *I* gave him a tic for God's sake!" It felt both good and awful to say it out loud.

"Laney, all parents second-guess themselves and feel 'less than' at times. And we *all* make mistakes. I've never told anyone this, but I dropped your brother on his head when he was about two months old—smack on top of his soft little head!"

"I know."

"How do you know that? Even your dad doesn't know that."

"Well, it's a more believable explanation than the possibility that you experimented with drugs while pregnant with the idiot."

See? I knew my mom could make me feel a bit better.

Now we were on our way to the Murphy's, and I tried to put my worries about Rocco out of my head and instead focus on (i.e. worry about) the evening ahead. At this rate, I'd have an ulcer by next week. Couldn't wait.

"I'm still confused about how I got talked into this," Gavin said from the driver's seat of his beat-up Jeep. I never argued when

Gavin wanted to drive because he is the world's absolute worst backseat driver. I was honestly more likely to run into a tree with Gavin in my car than I would be had I been a blind person.

"Will they have cookies?" Rocco asked from the back seat where he was taking apart a Transformer.

"I don't know, sweetie. Mr. Murphy is on a special diet and I don't think he's allowed to have cookies."

"But I'm not on a special diet," he answered as only a kid can.

"Don't worry, Rock, we'll get you one of your mom's cookies when we get home," Gavin reassured, never one to deny my kid something sweet.

"You know, Gav. You should be happy I talked you into this. It could be a boost for your career," I teased. "It'll give you a chance to suck up to not just the boss but the *big* boss."

"Haha. I don't want to look like a douche."

"What's a douche?" Rocco asked.

I gave Gavin the evil eye. "It's just an adult thing, Rocco. You should never say that word."

"But what is it?"

"It's a special kind of soap for adults," answered Gavin, never understanding that in a kid's hands, too much knowledge is too much power.

"No, Rock, it's a bad word some adults say. Just ignore your uncle."

Gavin came back to the original topic. "I don't want to suck up —I'm just gonna stay quiet while Nate spends the evening checking you out." An overly dramatic shiver coursed through his body. "I can't believe you're dating my boss."

"I'm not dating him! And this is definitely not the time to talk about this." I motioned to the listening ears in the booster seat behind us.

"Whatever. I know what's going on even if you don't. All I have to say is you'd better not mess this up for me, Laney," he warned.

"I'm not messing anything up. We're just having dinner at their house."

"Said the most clueless human on the planet. Oh, and just make sure to keep it wrapped this time around." I had to slap him even if he was driving at the time.

We arrived ten minutes later at a beautiful two-story brick home in an elegant community with big, lush lawns and gorgeous crepe myrtles dotting the tree-lawn all along the street. Rocco and I got out first and headed to the door while Gavin grabbed some things I'd brought along from the back. I carried a bouquet of flowers as well as a tin of heart-friendly muffins I'd baked for Nate's dad, and I let Rocco ring the bell. The door immediately opened and there was Nate in all his perfect scruffy handsomeness. *Sigh*. He wore another pair of faded jeans and a vintage Rolling Stones t-shirt, his hair looking like he'd been running his hand through it. Maybe he was nervous too.

"You made it," he greeted and leaned over to place a hand on my waist and a light kiss on my cheek. "Come in." He moved to the side to allow us entry. "Hey Rocco, how's it going?" Rocco just gave a silent little wave accompanied by a nose twitch and stuck to my side.

Nate seemed to let it roll off his back. "My mom is in the kitchen doing some last-minute stuff or she would have greeted you herself."

"Oh, I totally understand. No problem. Gavin's just grabbing some things from the car—he'll be here in a minute." My nerves were eating at my stomach as Nate led us into a living room and invited us to take a seat. I remained standing and I could hear some banging coming from the kitchen. "Are you sure I can't help your mom with something?"

Nate looked unsure. Then a loud curse rang from the kitchen. "Uh, maybe we should." I followed him, flowers and muffin tin in hand.

"Rocco, go help Uncle Gavin bring the things in from the Jeep, okay? I'll just be right in the kitchen." And that's when I got my first glimpse of Mr. and Mrs. Murphy. He was bent over looking into the open oven and cursing a blue streak while she was slapping at a burning dish towel with a spatula.

"Mom!" Nate exclaimed and grabbed the towel from her hand, throwing it directly into the sink and turning the tap on.

"I just asked if it was overcooking! I didn't tell you to light your damn self on fire!" came the gravelly voice from over by the oven.

"I was trying to pull it out. It's not my fault the towel caught on the heating element! Nate, can you pull the chicken out of the oven for me?" asked Mrs. Murphy, blowing her swath of blond hair from her eyes and peering into the sink at the smoking towel.

"I'm not a cripple, Erin! For Christ's sake, I can lift a damn pan from the oven."

"Not yet, you can't—not until the doctor okays it."

"Nate, hand me that towel. No, the other one. I'm pulling this thing out before your mother burns the house down."

Nate shot me a look that said he regretted inviting me over

more than anything he'd ever done in his entire life. I just sent him the brightest smile I had. Oddly, the chaos in the room served to calm my nerves completely. Turns out my mom was right—everybody does have their own brand of crazy. And the Murphys' brand involved yelling and spazzing out and cussing, and I couldn't have felt more at home.

"Uh, Mom, Dad, this is Laney." Two heads swung simultaneously to me.

"Oh my word. Laney." Mrs. Murphy brought one hand to her hair and the other to her ample hip. "You must think we're insane. I am *so* sorry!"

"Not at all," I laughed. "It actually reminds me of home. It's lovely to meet you, Mrs. Murphy. Oh, and I brought these for you." I extended the flowers and muffins.

She came over, grabbed the offerings and shoved them in Nate's hands and then proceeded to envelop me in a full-body hug the likes of which I'd never experienced before. "Call me Erin." In that moment I think I missed my mom more than I'd realized. "And thank you for the gorgeous flowers and whatever's in that tin—I'm sure it will be delicious," she said, still hugging me.

The sound of the doorbell caused her to finally release me, and she turned toward the foyer.

"That'll be Laney's son and her brother," Nate explained as Erin hurried off to answer the door.

"So, Laney," Mr. Murphy began. He was just as tall as Nate and I could immediately spot the resemblance. They shared the same blue eyes, and although the older man's hair was peppered with gray and he carried some extra weight, the similarities were undeniable. "I hear you've been spending some time with my son. I hope he's treating you right."

"He's a perfect gentleman." *Well, most of the time.* "He's helping me out a lot around my house. Thanks to him my doorbell no longer sounds like a drowning cat and I don't trip over my uneven floor on my way to the kitchen anymore."

"Good, well you just let me know if he steps out of line and I'll straighten him right up." He smiled at me, and wouldn't you know it, there was an identical copy of that damn dimple.

Nate just rolled his eyes at his dad. "You're looking good, old man, but I still think I could take you."

"Yeah, you just try," he responded, the affection between the two obvious.

It was then that Rocco bounded into the kitchen followed by Gavin, who wore an indiscernible expression. He approached Nate and said quietly, "Dude. I don't want to alarm you, but your mom just groped me in the entryway. I think I might be pregnant."

Nate snickered. "Ah, the pat-down. She was just checking for contraband. Don't worry—your virtue is safe."

I didn't even want to know what that was about, so when Erin re-entered the kitchen I quickly made introductions. Rocco was shy, as usual, and I noticed a few nose wiggles, but with three familiar adults in the room and Erin's innate warmness, he was soon emerging from his shell a bit.

The surprise of the evening, though, was how taken Rocco was with Nate's dad, whose name I learned was Riordan. The older man held a seemingly endless store of kid-friendly jokes and he soon had Rocco in fits of giggles. I couldn't help it when my eyes teared up a bit. Nate immediately noticed and laid a hand on the small of my back, not removing it until his sister, Bailey, arrived with a friend and we all sat down for dinner. Nate's arm then moved to the back of my chair and remained there throughout the entire meal.

Erin had set the flowers I brought as the centerpiece to the table and she thanked me profusely for the muffins I'd made using applesauce instead of butter. Who knew how they'd taste, but it was worth the effort.

Conversation over dinner was lively, and I couldn't remember laughing so much in a very long time. The company definitely made up for the almost inedible chicken, and one look around the table showed all parties' creative attempts at hiding their uneaten chicken on their plates. Thankfully Rocco didn't blurt out any embarrassing comments about the food. Instead he just stuffed his face with rolls and exchanged more jokes with Riordan. Within the flow of conversation around us, I noticed Bailey not so subtly checking me out throughout dinner. But with Nate's regular grazes of my shoulder and neck, I maintained my composure and just tried to smile back at her.

I could see some resemblances between Bailey and the rest of her family. She shared Nate and Riordan's blue eyes, but her hair had clearly come from Erin. It was a beautiful shade of blond and she wore it in a ponytail with a big swath of bangs angled across her forehead. She was also fairly tall—I'd guess maybe 5'7"—which was no surprise considering the height of her brother, and she seemed to share my preference for casual clothes.

While Bailey conversed naturally with everyone throughout the meal and entertained us with some stories (as well as some incredibly well-timed insults at Nate's expense), her friend Kia was less than entertaining. She chattered like a sixteen-year-old girl on a caffeine drip and seemed not to realize that none of her stories were hitting the mark. We were all too polite to let it show, of course, responding instead with head nods followed by a change in subject. I caught Nate shooting looks at Bailey every once in a while, which she responded to with wide smiles. It was after a particularly mind-numbing tale of a nail appointment gone wrong that Gavin decided he was done being polite. Why he thought it was a good idea to provoke a confrontation at his boss's dinner table I have no idea, but as I've stated before, Gavin is an idiot.

"Hey, Kia, do you by any chance have an off button, or maybe just a pause button. My head is about to explode."

I was completely mortified. Kia's jaw hit the table in indignant shock. Erin covered her mouth with a napkin that hid what I thought might have been a smile. Riordan stole another roll. Nate and Bailey shared a look across the table and then simultaneously burst out into gales of laughter.

Assholes!! What was going on here?

"You." I pointed at Nate. "Hallway." I stood, and to the rest of the table I simply said, "If you could excuse us for a moment, we'll be right back." I could see Erin smacking Bailey on the arm and Kia standing up in a huff to gather her purse. Gavin sat back with a smirk, too damn cocky to consider he could have just blown his professional reputation. *Ugh*!

Riordan and Rocco went back to business. "Stop me if you've heard this one. A guy with a peg leg walks into a bar—"

"What's a peg leg?"

In the hall, Nate was ready for me and was already defending himself before I could draw in a breath. "Look, you have to understand Bailey. We live to torture each other and when I told her she had to invite someone to dinner to make you feel more comfortable she decided to choose the most annoying person on her contact list. I should have seen it coming but I was so nervous about not freaking you out and about getting this evening to go well, I completely missed the opening I'd given her. It's my fault, but I promise everyone in there, with the exception of Kita or Kia or whoever, thought that whole scene was fucking hilarious."

What was I going to do with him? Having no answer I decided to settle for punching him in the arm. He laughed and pulled me into a hug.

* * *

After many thank-yous and another round of hugs goodbye we all headed to the front door. Riordan opted to stay in the kitchen to wash dishes, but he fist-bumped Rocco goodbye and gave us all a wave.

"What is all of this?" Erin said as we approached the front door and she saw a couple boxes and a tall cylindrical case leaning against the wall.

I bit my lip. "I didn't want to be presumptuous, but I had all this fishing equipment from my parents' house that I was planning on using with Rocco. We haven't had the time and it's just been gathering dust so I thought maybe Riordan might be interested in trying his hand at it. There are some great ponds and reservoirs around here. It's probably stupid, but I used to love to fish with my dad and he always said it was one of life's best pastimes. Like I said, it's a silly idea but if you're interested feel free to use it," I finished, suddenly feeling shy.

Erin wrapped me in another enormous hug and whispered in my ear, "You're an angel, Laney." I guess it wasn't such a silly idea after all.

On the front walkway Bailey stopped me. "Sorry if that whole Kia thing made you uncomfortable. I was so focused on annoying Nate I didn't really think about making it weird for you. Honestly, that girl has had the biggest lady boner for Nate for so long I'm actually relieved I brought her here tonight. Hopefully she'll leave me alone about it now that she sees he's officially taken," she said.

I had no response. Luckily, she seemed to not need one as she waved and jogged to her car.

Nate walked the rest of us to the Jeep. He opened the passenger door for Rocco and me. Before he closed it, he leaned down toward me. "Text me so I know you got home safe."

All signs indicated Laney Monroe had just gotten herself a boyfriend.

Eek!

Chapter Thirteen

IT'S A GRAY AREA

N ATE

Nate: So what night is best for you this week?

Laney: For what?

Nate: For our second date?

Laney: When did I agree to our first date?

Nate: It was implied. You had dinner with my parents and a psychotic person. I really should count that as two dates.

Laney: Ha.

Nate: Just so you know, Gavin is available to babysit on Wed or Thurs.

Laney: You're involving my brother in this? That's extortion—you're his boss.

Nate: It's a gray area. How about Wednesday? I'll cook for you. Don't worry, I didn't learn from my mom.

Nate: I'm getting gray hair over here waiting.

Laney: Wednesday. I can be ready at 6:30.

Nate: I'll pick you up. Later, Laney.

Laney sure knew how to get under my skin. Not to be cocky, but I knew she was into me, so I couldn't figure out the reluctance on her part. I'd never had to work so hard to get a girl to date me, and there had never been a girl I was so eager to date before. She did things to me I couldn't explain. I must have replayed our two kisses in my head a hundred times, many of those times occurring in the shower with my hand in full participation, I am not ashamed to say. I also found myself thinking of her at the oddest times—like when I went to the grocery store and saw some chocolate chip cookies, it reminded me of the ones she'd made (and the kiss involved). Or when I picked up some supplies at Home Depot, I bought a flashlight because I'd noticed Laney didn't seem to have one. This girl was firmly rooted in my head.

Maybe the reluctance on her part was because of Rocco—I suppose that made sense. I'd never dated a single mom before, and it was bound to be more complicated. I confess I don't know the first thing about kids, but I like them well enough. I'd just never had the chance to spend a lot of time with them. Rocco seemed like a cool little guy—maybe a bit shy and kind of unpredictable but that was okay. It was becoming clear that being a single mom was no picnic, but Laney seemed to be doing a stellar job from my inexperienced viewpoint. Rocco was well-behaved and everybody seemed to love him.

Hell, I was beginning to think maybe my mom had the right idea about pairing my dad up with the kid. They'd been having their own little club meeting at the dinner table last night. Truth be told, I was a bit jealous. Huh, that was unexpected. I wanted Rocco to prefer me to my dad—maybe that was a bit juvenile but there it was. I made a mental note to look up some G-rated jokes on the internet.

But I'd gotten a yes from Laney for Wednesday and I was determined to win her over. Crap, now I had to impress her with my cooking, which I may have oversold a touch. Since spaghetti is just about the only thing I can cook, it looked like we'd be having Italian.

* * *

On Tuesday I got a call about another hiccup with a project out on the east side of town, so I spent most of the morning there. Bailey and I had met with Doug yesterday and, just as my mother predicted, he was eager to step up and help us out with some of this troubleshooting, paperwork, and scheduling. Today's debacle sealed the deal in my mind, and I was determined to call Doug in on this new issue and have him take it over. This new resolve had me grinning on my walk to my truck this afternoon. That's when my phone rang. *Laney.* My grin turned into a full-out smile and I believe I may have started to swagger.

"Hey, Beautiful, what's up?"

"Nate, thank God." She sounded harried.

"What's wrong?" I felt my stomach drop.

"Sorry, I didn't mean to panic but I'm in a bit of a bind and I didn't know who else to call."

My breathing returned to normal. "I'm glad you called me. What can I do?"

"I'm completely stuck here at work. We have a deadline that there is no way we can meet if we don't all stay late. Rocco's daycare closes at 6:15, Fiona is out of town, and Gavin's not answering his phone. It's already almost 5:00 and I have nobody to pick him up. Can you please, please, please pick him up for me and stay with him until I can get ahold of Gavin? Or can you somehow find Gavin and have him pick Rocco up? Anything!" She was sounding panicked again.

"Calm down. I got it. I'm done here so there's no reason to involve Gavin. I can swing by and pick up the squirt. Where's the school?"

She released a huge sigh. "Thank you, Nate. Thank you so much. I'll have to call the school and authorize you to pick him up first, but that won't take long. He usually expects me at about 5:15 so do you think you can go soon?"

I told her it was no problem and got the information I needed from her, including the spot where she hides the spare key to her house—on the top of the door jamb, if you can believe that. That particular hiding spot would be changing tonight.

Now that I knew she was feeling better and all was well, I thought a little bit of ribbing was in order. "I have to say I'm a bit surprised you called *me*, Laney. We're not even dating or anything."

"Shut your face, Sparky."

I drove up to Cornerstone Daycare around the same time as every other parent in town, it seemed. I showed my I.D. to the woman in the front office as Laney had instructed, and I found Rocco's classroom right where she said it would be. At least the teacher had told him to expect me instead of his mom or I'd be more apprehensive than I already was. It wasn't like the kid and I were super tight yet.

When I walked in the room there was a guy about my age directing his kid to get his belongings from the lockers across the room. "Tucker, grab your stuff—we've got to go!" The kid was wearing a bright pink shirt with the collar popped and dark blue shorts with—were those fucking flamingos? I looked back to the guy, expecting to find the mortified look any man whose kid was dressed like that should be wearing, but no, nothing. This guy's wife must either have his balls in a vice or be a champion at blowjobs.

I looked around for Rocco, confident that whatever he'd be wearing would be cool because, let's face it, his mom was awesome. I wasn't disappointed. Rocco sat at a table building a giant Lego skyscraper and wearing a t-shirt that said "Support Our Troops" and had a Stormtrooper on it. *Classic.* I also noticed he seemed to be humming to himself and his nose was doing that twitching thing again.

"Yo, Rocco!" I called so he'd know I was here. Before he could acknowledge me, the pink-shirted kid approached him.

The pussy-whipped dad motioned to the Lego table. "Is he yours?"

For some reason I didn't want to think about too much, I replied, "Yup."

The guy crossed his arms and nodded. "It's really great that he's in school with all the other kids … you know."

What. The. Fuck.

"No, I don't know. Please enlighten me." My voice grated and my body turned to stone.

He could not have looked more uncomfortable if a dozen Playboy bunnies had been pointing at his dick and laughing. "Just, you know, he's got some issues, right?"

And just then, out of the corner of my eye I saw the little flamingo bastard swing his hand and knock over Rocco's skyscraper.

We were done here. I used what I like to think of as my Bruce Banner pre-Hulk voice and laid into the prick with the perfect level of quiet power. "The only *issue* he has is that he's at a school with a bunch of stuck up assholes like you and your kid. Tell your kid if he ever messes with Rocco again I'll be giving my kid free reign to punch him in the nuts. And while you're at it, try growing a set of balls yourself and tell your wife to shop where they sell boy's clothes."

I stalked over to where Rocco sat dejectedly staring at his ruined masterpiece. "Hey, kid. Wanna get out of here and get some ice cream?"

His watery eyes came to mine and he twitched his nose. Then he nodded and took my hand.

One stop at SweetFrog (By the way, what ever happened to DQ?) and another at Home Depot and we were headed back to Laney's. Rocco remained pretty quiet, but I'd gotten a few smiles out of him and we'd exchanged a couple jokes. His were clearly made up and made zero sense but I laughed anyway. I'm no idiot.

I retrieved the "hidden" key, and after unlocking the door I placed the key inside the fake rock I'd purchased at Home Depot and set it in an inconspicuous place by the side door. I thought I would see if Rocco wanted to throw a ball around or play something outside, so I went in search of outdoor toys. The coat closet by the door seemed to be the best place to start looking; however, when I opened it an avalanche of purses, coats, shoes, and, oddly, unopened mail spilled around my feet. Hmm. What to do now? Since I didn't spot any sporting equipment, I decided to shove everything back in and pretend I'd never been there. It appeared Laney didn't mind a bit of clutter, to put it nicely. After that I thought it best to enlist Rocco's help, and we located a soccer ball in his bedroom.

I was no soccer player and it was safe to say Rocco was even less of one, but we still had a good time kicking the ball around the yard. We made up our own game, the rules of which he changed every time he started losing. I didn't care one bit. The kid and I were having fun. Rocco ran to the big tree in their backyard, declaring himself the victor, and I finally lay on the ground in submission. I stayed there for a minute looking up into the branches of the tree, and then Rocco came over and lay down right next to me. I put my hands behind my head and noticed him mimic my movements. It may have been the single most adorable thing I'd ever seen, and I felt a tug in my chest. Then a thought occurred to me.

"You know what you need, Rocco?"

"What?"

"A treehouse."

"For real?" His voice was filled with awe.

"For real. Let's build one."

His little fist punched the air. "Yes!"

And that's when I lost the first piece of my heart to that little kid.

✱ ✱ ✱

When 6:30 rolled around we were both starving and nobody else was home yet. We'd gotten dirty playing soccer so Rocco's solution was to shed all his clothes. I opted to keep mine on, despite the aforementioned "pants optional" policy in place at Laney's house. I fixed us some peanut butter sandwiches and threw in a banana to make myself feel like a more responsible guardian.

Laney and Gavin both got home around 7:00. They walked in the door at the same time, and I heard Laney tearing into Gavin about keeping his phone charged. He threw an insult back at her and it reminded me so much of Bailey and me that I had to smile. Rocco and I were on the couch watching some asinine show about a bald kid with some weird-ass name I can't remember and his overly touchy-feely family. I don't even think Rocco liked it, but it was the only cartoon I could find.

"Hey, Nate," Gavin greeted us first. "Sorry about the daycare thing. I didn't realize my phone battery was dead."

"No problem. Hey, things are looking good at the new site. I hear you're picking things up pretty quickly."

Gavin scratched his head a little self-consciously. "Yeah, they're going pretty well. I'm learning a lot." He walked over to the couch and put his fist out for Rocco. "Hey, dude." They exchanged a fist-bump and he turned and headed for the hall. "I'm gonna hit the shower. I've noticed my luck with the ladies hasn't been so great when I head straight from work to the bars."

"It's a learning curve, my friend," I shot back.

"Hey, Rocco," Laney said quietly as she approached next. She was wearing a sheer blouse with some kind of black tank underneath and her ass was perfectly showcased, yet again, in a pair of tight black pants. It took everything I had not to pull her onto my lap and cop a feel. "I am so sorry I couldn't come get you today, buddy, but I promise I'll be there tomorrow." The guilt was plain on her face. Now I felt like a perv and instead wanted to pull her in for a hug. "Did you have fun with Nate?"

Rocco's head swiveled from the TV and his eyes were bright. "Mommy! Nate and I are gonna build a treehouse!"

Laney cocked her head at me, eyebrows to the sky. Perhaps this was the kind of thing you're supposed to discuss with the mom first.

* * *

Even though I may have been in trouble with Laney, my mood was sky high when Rocco gave me a hug on his way to bed. I waited on the couch and switched the TV to ESPN while Laney put him down. She emerged from his room fifteen minutes later and sat down beside me. I turned to give her my full attention.

She cleared her throat. "First of all, I want to thank you for picking up Rocco and taking care of him. I really don't know what I would have done if you hadn't come through for me." She placed her hand on my arm.

Before she could continue I said, "But I shouldn't have made plans to build a treehouse without conferring with you first. It didn't occur to me at the time, but I get it. I'm new at the whole kid thing so you're required to cut me some slack." I went with my most charming grin.

"Goddamned dimple," I heard her murmur.

"What was that?"

"Nothing. Yes, you're right. You should have asked me first but it's mostly just because I don't want you promising him things that don't end up happening for whatever reason. I can't handle him being disappointed any more than he already is."

I was sensing a much bigger issue at hand but I chose to let it go for now and try to tackle it later, once we'd gotten to know each other better. "You don't have to worry. I am 100% on board with the treehouse. In fact, I can't wait. I promise." I crossed my heart.

"I believe you. And thank you, Nate."

Well if that wasn't an invitation to go in for a kiss I don't know what was. But like a complete imbecile, I didn't. Instead, I chose that moment to fill her in on the little incident at daycare.

"Come here," I beckoned and made a space right in the crook of my arm. She didn't hesitate to fill it. Warm, supple woman cradled against me, I could be happy here for a long time.

"I take it things went well with Rocco," she said.

"They were actually awesome," I responded and I'm sure my excitement was reflected in my voice. "But I've got to tell you I was a little pissed about some things at his school."

Her body stiffened against mine. "What things?"

"Laney, I don't know if these people are your friends or if you just happened upon this daycare, but I did not get a friendly vibe, no offense."

"Crap." Her hand covered her eyes.

"It may have been a random one-off kind of thing, but some little prick was messing up Rocco's project and his dad was spouting off some bullshit about Rocco being somehow 'different' than the other kids. The whole thing just pissed me off and I told the guy to go to hell and I may have even threatened his kid ..." My voice trailed off as I realized for the first time how utterly ridiculous this all sounded. Shit.

"You threatened a child?" Her jaw went slack and her eyes shot fire at me.

"Well, maybe not so much the child but I'm pretty sure I insulted the father's manhood and threw a threat or two in there."

Silence.

"In my defense, the kid was wearing women's clothing and still had the nerve to knock over what I personally considered to be an inspired Lego masterpiece that Rocco had worked hard on."

Laney looked down to her lap and then brought her eyes back to mine. "Was the little fucker by any chance named Tucker?"

Feeling somewhat vindicated I responded, "Why yes, yes he was."

"Okay, I can agree that I didn't get a good vibe from a lot of the moms there, his included. But, Nate, you can't go threatening people at daycare. Who knows how these things operate! They could call the cops or something. Or at the very least we could be kicked out for violent threats. You know they have these zero toler-ance rules now?!"

"Well where are those zero tolerance rules when the pink-shirted kid is bullying Rocco and his dad is insulting him along with it? I don't know a lot about kids, but Rocco's skyscraper was at least fourteen stories high and I believe an elevator was being installed. Sounds to me like the simpletons couldn't compete so they resorted to sabotage. Have you never seen a movie like this? Rocco is the brilliant inventor and Tucker is the underachieving mama's boy with something to prove."

She put one hand on my arm again and another behind my neck. "Nate, I need to hear the following words come out of your mouth: 'I understand these children are five and we are not in a Martin Scorsese movie.'"

I started to laugh but her facial expression remained deadly serious so I recited her ridiculous statement. Sheesh. But I added my own addendum. "Laney, I promise you there is nothing to worry about. Flamingo kid's dad was humiliated to the point where he will never utter a word of our conversation to another soul. Still, maybe shopping for a new daycare isn't the worst idea, huh?" Hoping I hadn't gone too far, I waited.

The next thing I knew I was being straddled by the hottest girl on the planet and I finally had her ass in both of my hands. Sweet Jesus, my life was good.

Chapter Fourteen

SCARLETT O'HARA HAD AN EXCELLENT POINT

*L*ANEY

His hands were on my ass and I was throwing caution to the wind. Every inch of my body was straining toward his, and each firm line of his chest, arms, and thighs was colliding with my body. My immediate thought was that we had too many clothes separating us, but we were in my damn living room so I had to stop my thoughts from careening that way.

His hard thighs were a dream and I wanted to strip his jeans off to caress them with my hands and mouth. Muscular thighs were a huge turn-on for me and Nate had them in spades. I don't know if it was just the physical labor from his job or if he did additional working out on the side, but his body was a thing of masculine beauty. I ground down on his pelvis from my straddled position and was not disappointed by the rigid evidence of his desire I encountered through the denim. It was obvious his body was as eager as mine, but I wasn't sure how far I wanted to go tonight. I was still freaked the hell out by him popping up in our lives only to disappear in a few months, so I knew I should be careful. I just had a hard time communicating that message to both my heart and my hoo-hah. He was so freaking hot. And he was so freaking into me. That was a collision of fates that didn't happen in my world. I was too weak to resist.

I ran my tongue around the shell of his ear and sucked his earlobe. Apparently that was the last straw. Nate physically picked me up and headed to my bedroom with his hands on my ass, and I had no choice but to hang on for dear life. This was shocking and a bit embarrassing on many levels, the least of which being the chronically untidy state of my bedroom.

Let me explain.

In all these romance novels, the buff guys are constantly picking the girls up and throwing them on the bed or having vertical make-out sessions—all while not straining a single muscle. I am not that girl. I have tits and I have ass, and I'm not saying that in some cute little "oh, look at her perky booty" kind of way. I have double Ds and a very proportionate ass to match. That very often puts me into the plus-size department and then on to a tailor to fit the smaller parts of me. Everyone loves to talk about boobs and booty like they are thrilled the old bombshell figure is back in style, but I can tell you two things: (1) a rack like this wreaks havoc on your back, and (2) tailors are not inexpensive.

So Nate carrying me to my bedroom, an event which should have been a romantic milestone complete with "Up Where We Belong" playing in the background, was instead an episode that filled me with self-doubt and imagined trips to the emergency room. A hernia, at the very least, was a distinct possibility in this little scenario—how romantic can you get?

Amazingly, though, we made it without injury and he deposited me gently on the bed. He honestly didn't look any worse for wear, and his lustful look implied I'd better kick my insecurities to the curb. Shit was about to get real. *Yowza!*

"You're wearing too many clothes," he growled while gazing at me from his elevated viewpoint at the side of the bed. "Lose the pants and the blouse. I'll take care of the rest."

Holy shit. It seemed someone was putting on his alpha pants.

His gritty voice and confidence were such a freaking turn-on that I couldn't comply fast enough. Clothes went flying and, lying there in my panties and black tank top, I looked up at him from my bed and couldn't quite believe this was happening. I couldn't even remember my last sexual encounter, which I'm sure I should have found depressing but, at the moment, my mind was very much otherwise occupied.

"You're so fucking spectacular." His pupils were large in his intense blue eyes.

Was this real? Nobody had ever looked at me like this before.

Still fully clothed, Nate leaned down and kissed my belly. He pushed the material of my tank up with his nose and began to run his tongue along my stomach, over my belly button and then across the top of my panties. "You smell so good," he murmured and then lifted my tank to reveal my black lace bra. He pulled the shirt over my head and then returned to hover over my breasts. "I can't believe how perfect you are," he said almost reverently. His eyes shifted up to mine and burned through me. "May I?" he asked, and

I felt so stunned and unsure, my hands just rested at my sides while he explored my body. I think they were as shocked as I was.

"Yes," was all I could manage.

His fingers grazed gently over my lace-covered nipples and they pebbled at his light touch. His lips then replaced his fingers and he began to lick and suck me through the lace. I couldn't stand it any longer and had to reach to my shoulders and pull the straps down so he could gain full access to my aching breasts. He groaned at the first sight of my dark rosy nipples before he covered them with his lips and tongue. I cried out when he lightly bit each one.

My hands, finally recovered from the shock of Nate's laser-focused attention, reached for him and I was beyond frustrated when I realized again that he was still dressed. Determined to remedy that, I clutched the hem of his t-shirt, skimming the dusting of hair on his lower belly in the process. I quickly stripped the shirt over his head and within a millisecond my hands were tracing every hill and valley of his shoulders, chest, and abs. Perfection. God, he was firm and smooth and his skin was incredibly sensitive if his occasional shivers were any indication. I could caress him all night and never get bored. Of course, I'd have to invite my lips and tongue to participate as well. I circled one of his nipples with my tongue and he responded with something between a groan and a laugh. God, I loved that.

Soon my playtime was over, it seemed, because his hands firmly gripped my wrists and held them to the bed while his mouth dove down to the waistband of my panties and took the lace between his teeth. He looked up into my face and I swear, at that instant, life as I knew it stood still. I don't know what it was but something profound, something more than sex or teasing or friendship, gripped at my chest and I found it hard to breathe.

What did this mean? I'd never experienced another feeling like it, and I could see in his eyes that Nate sensed it too. I felt heady and strange and his look told me he was similarly afflicted.

"Mommy?" The door creaked open.

No no no no no! Rocco! I can't believe we didn't lock the door!

For some damn reason, kids don't understand that they are not allowed to interrupt epiphanic moments. I threw a sheet over my body and did my best to kick Nate onto the floor. (So sorry, Nate!)

"What's wrong, buddy? Why aren't you asleep?" My heart was beating out of my chest.

"There are two reasons, but I can't 'member the first one." *Ugh.* "I know the second one is that I need to bring a pack of new crayons to school tomorrow," he said as he climbed onto my bed, not noticing the shirtless man on the floor at the other side.

"That's already in your backpack, sweetie," I told him.

"I think the first reason is I need to sleep with you, but I don't 'member for sure."

Nate and I had been on the precipice of something profound—but it was over for tonight. And while one part of me was screaming to get it back right this second, the other decided to be more rational. I was surprised I'd let things go so far in the first place, except for the fact that I was insanely attracted to this man and felt this intense pull toward him.

I maneuvered my way off the bed with the sheet still wrapped around me, and tucked Rocco in with the remaining covers. I then pretended to be a statue until his eyes closed and his breathing slowed. Nate, who had also been impersonating a statue—one that probably sported some bruises from his abrupt tumble to the floor —waited for my signal and then we both snuck out of the room. He pulled his shirt on as I walked him to the door. I wasn't used to having hormones coursing through my body like girls gone wild, so I was kind of twitchy during our goodbye.

He took my face in his hands. "I don't have to tell you that I'm really looking forward to our date tomorrow night. Is 6:30 still okay?"

I almost wanted to tell him to pick me up at 6:30 AM so we could finish what we'd started but I put my libido in check and agreed, "Sounds great."

He kissed me gently on the lips this time, and the contact was way too short. "Can't wait to see you tomorrow."

This was too perfect. I needed to come back down to earth. Any minute now, the wicked stepsisters would storm in and ruin my gown, and some super-hot girl (who did not have any baggage) would capture Nate's attention and steal him away. And then they'd both go riding off into the sunset back to Texas. That's how it works. What was I doing getting all excited?!

Still, I went to sleep with an internal happy dance and a big fat smile on my face.

* * *

Tonight was the night.

"Tonight is the night!" Fiona shouted. "Laney's gonna get laaaiiid, Laney's gonna get laaaiiid!"

"Do you say anything anymore without the 'nanny-nanny-boo-boo' tone? I feel like we're eight years old."

"Well that would be extremely inappropriate given the subject matter."

This time I was at Fiona's where I could make use of her fashion arsenal. She was helping me with my hair and makeup, and then I'd dash home in time for Nate to pick me up. Gavin was getting Rocco from daycare and babysitting tonight so everything was organized. Except my nerves—they were in complete disarray.

"Am I moving too fast? Should I be doing this so soon?"

"Listen, the man defended your kid to a dickhead bully and then offered to build him a treehouse. I'd say you owe him at least a blowjob for that alone."

"Stop being so sentimental—you're gonna make me cry."

"Oh! Did I tell you Terrence is coming to town this weekend?" Fiona waggled her brows and did a booty shake—well, as much as she could with her non-existent booty. Terrence was Fiona's on-again-off-again "friend with benefits" or "fuck buddy" or "boy-toy" or whatever she was calling him these days.

He was a pilot and he was also a very fine specimen—tall, dark, handsome, with lean muscle. And while he didn't have a dimple, he did have this weirdly awesome slightly crooked smile that somehow always made you feel like you made him happy just by standing in front of him. In other words, he was a sweetheart, and besides the cool smile and all the rest, he had the most flawless deep brown skin I'd ever seen. There had been more than one occasion when I'd had a bit too much to drink and had oh-so-casually run my hand down his arm just so I could feel it. Fiona caught me every time but she thought it was hilarious—she would, considering after all the drinking was done, she got to go home to all that was Terrence. So it was a mystery to me why Fiona insisted on keeping things so light between them. I thought he was great for her.

"Fun ahead!" She continued the shake. "And I ordered the sweetest little silk Brazilian briefs from La Perla—they are the lightest pink with these lace panels—Oh! And I saw this ice blue bra and panty set that would look killer on you—please, please let me buy it for you!!" Her face fell at the shake of my head. "You're such a party-pooper."

There were certain things I would let Fiona and her endless money treat Rocco and me to, but La Perla? Not gonna happen.

"Hmm, I can't decide if he and I will go out or just order in and spend the whole weekend thinking up creative indoor activities. I hope the panties come before Terrence," she said.

Sometimes it was just too easy—I bit my lip to keep from laughing. "Well, it is still in the eighties most days so you'd really be saving yourself from the risk of sunstroke. It's the only responsible thing to do."

"I think you have an excellent point. So, what are we doing with this hair?" She led me to her vanity—yes, of course Fiona had a vanity.

"I don't want to look like I'm trying too hard so keep it simple if you can help yourself. And I'm wearing jeans so I don't want any arguments! It's just dinner at his apartment."

"Fine," Fiona pouted and ran a brush through my long hair. "But at least be civilized and borrow some of my jewelry, will you?"

We both regarded my reflection in the mirror as she twisted and pulled my hair, deciding on a style. A rock suddenly settled in my gut. My hands went to my cheeks.

Fiona dropped my hair and her hands held my shoulders. "What is it, Laney?"

"I don't know what I'm doing here. I just feel this, I don't know, *pull* toward Nate but I know he's going to break my heart. Rocco and I are going to get attached to him and then his dad will get better and he'll move away. You know I'm already worried about Rocco enough as it is, and here I am setting him up for another fall. What kind of mother am I?"

Fiona scowled. "You're the best kind of mother, that's the kind you are! You always put that little boy first and, sure, he's going through a little stress right now but you're doing the best you can. Where does it say you can't have a little something for yourself too? If Nate's leaving, what's wrong with a fling? And, anyway, you don't *know* he's leaving—you're making assumptions without all the information. You could just woman up and ask him outright, you know."

At the look on my face, she read that I was clearly not ready to "woman up."

"Just stop stressing. Hell, you could even find out tonight that you two don't really like each other as much as you thought. Then you're just out one treehouse, and you can get Gavin to learn how to form a right angle and put it together. The point is, just have fun tonight and worry about the rest later."

I considered her in the mirror. "Thanks, Fee. You're right. You have any wine?"

She looked offended. "Do I have any wine? Where do you think you are?"

I laughed at her and dropped my hands back to my lap. "All

right, pour some wine, pretty me up, and let's Scarlett O'Hara the shit out of this thing!"

* * *

I had a glass of wine while Fiona did her thing, and by the time the glass was empty my hair looked sleek and sexy and my makeup was a step up from what I'd normally wear but it looked awesome. I headed home to get dressed. Fiona did end up talking me into wearing a flirty skirt and some platform sandals from my own closet, and she made me text her a picture of my final outfit to keep me from cheating. Gavin and Brett were in the backyard tossing a baseball around with Rocco when the doorbell rang. At least I wouldn't have to deal with that awkwardness. I grabbed my purse, took a deep breath, and answered the door.

Nate was wearing a blue button-down shirt that drew attention to his eyes. The sleeves were rolled up to reveal his corded forearms and the first two buttons at his neck were left undone, affording me a glimpse of chest hair. His dark-wash jeans were a perfect fit, and gray Converse completed the picture. Comfortable, casual, and hot as hell. My lower belly warmed and the butterflies took flight. His jaw was freshly shaven for the first time and I wasn't sure which way I preferred it. His eyes were hot and they were focused directly on me.

"You look gorgeous," he said as his eyes roamed my figure.

"You don't look so bad yourself." *Was that my voice?* It was so breathy.

"Are you ready to go?" He crooked his arm out for me to take.

I wordlessly entwined my arm with his and we walked to his

truck where he opened my door and helped me in. Did he cop a bit of a feel in the process? Maybe, but I didn't mind one bit.

"So, what are the boys up to tonight?" Nate asked once he'd seated himself and pulled out onto the street.

"Lord knows. They were playing ball when I left so hopefully they'll stay out of trouble. Although Gavin's best friend is over so it's unlikely."

"You don't like him?"

"Oh, Brett's fine. It's just that when the two of them get together the chances for downright stupid behavior rise exponentially. I'm probably prejudiced, though, because Brett was there when Gavin got in a really bad accident one time and it ended up ruining his baseball career."

"I was wondering about that but I worried it was a sore spot so I didn't want to ask Gavin about it." Nate glanced at me. "After he met Gavin the other night, my dad mentioned that he used to watch him play when Gavin was in high school. He said everyone thought your brother would go pro one day but then never heard another thing after he went off to college."

"You were probably smart not to mention it—it's most definitely still a sore subject." I sighed.

"What happened, if you don't mind me asking?"

"No, it's fine." I smoothed my skirt and tried not to let the memories affect me. "He was playing on a full scholarship and was right on track to make it big. On his twentieth birthday he and Brett and some of their other friends had the bright idea to try out a teammate's motorcycle—having never ridden a motorcycle in his life, mind you." I shook my head at the thought. "Long story short, he broke his pitching arm in three places. Goodbye baseball scholarship. Goodbye big-league dreams. At least he'd had the good sense to wear a helmet. But, *then*, instead of recovering from the surgeries and finishing his degree, he chose to drink and become a bum. And I haven't quite been able to forgive him for it." I gazed out the window and Nate was silent. "Wow, that was probably more than you wanted to know." I forced a smile and looked back at him.

He glanced at me and then his eyes returned to the road. "Sounds very … complicated." That was a safe way of putting it.

I quickly moved us on to lighter subjects and we arrived at his apartment building minutes later. It was pretty dingy as a whole, with cracked sidewalks and weed-infested lawn spaces.

"I know," Nate said as he took my hand and walked me up the stairs to his second-floor apartment. "It's nothing to look at but it's cheap and it's only temporary. It was the only place I could find that would offer a month-to-month lease."

My stomach dropped. His comment removed any doubt I had about his plans. I had the sudden urge to turn around and run home, but the feel of his warm hand in mine somehow kept me anchored there.

He unlocked the door and it opened to reveal a small kitchen, an old sixties style table, and the ugliest couch I'd ever seen.

"Nate?"

"What?"

"Roseanne called. She wants her couch back."

"Who's the smartass now?" He elbowed me. "I borrowed it from my parents' basement. My real furniture is in Austin."

"I'm relieved I won't have to pretend to like your phenome-nally bad taste." I smiled up at him.

He held a few strands of my hair and ran his fingers down until they caressed my collarbone. A shiver ran straight through me. "Let's reserve that thought until you taste my cooking. I hope you like spaghetti."

At that moment I thought I'd like anything he wanted to dish up.

BIG HEAD VS. LITTLE HEAD

𝒩ATE

"Well, that wasn't half bad if I do say so myself." I leaned back in my chair and took a swig of my beer.

"I didn't realize there was any possible doubt. And it *was* good." Laney propped her elbow on the table and sipped from her wine glass.

Conversation over dinner had flowed easily. We talked about our experiences growing up in the same town and realized that we'd probably nearly met each other dozens of times throughout our youth. But with our age difference it wasn't so surprising that we hadn't. Then we moved on to her history with Rocco and his dad, a guy named Dominic who lived in California. The guy sounded like an assclown to me, but Laney was pretty laid back about it, so I obviously didn't have the whole story. It did explain, however, how she was able to afford a mortgage in a decent neighborhood while sending her kid to that stuffy daycare. I was guessing her job didn't pay enough to afford it all on her own. And I knew Gavin had only recently begun contributing.

Her relationship with her brother seemed especially complicated, as I'd noted earlier. There was obviously some tension there, but I liked the guy and by all accounts he was working his ass off and catching on really quickly at work. Regardless, the love between brother and sister was clear, and he was great with Rocco. Thinking of my relationship with Bailey and knowing the intricacies that exist between family members, though, I wasn't going to pry into that one. If Laney wanted to share, I'd let her do it in her own time.

She sat across from me, her hair all glossy and her eyes looking smoky and sexy as hell as her finger ran absentmindedly over the rim of her wine glass. My dick stood at attention—I'd been fighting a hard-on since the moment she answered her door in a short little skirt and sleeveless V-neck blouse that pointed the way to my biggest temptation. Damn, she was the definition of a bombshell and I couldn't wait to get her in my bed and under me.

"So, I'm guessing the home repairs are on hold in favor of treehouse construction?" she asked, taking another sip of her wine. I nodded and stood with my beer, motioning her to follow me to the hideous, but surprisingly comfortable, couch.

"Maybe so. The project has inspired me." I set my beer on the scratched-up coffee table.

That got a grin as she sat down next to me and I put an arm across the back of the couch behind her neck.

"I may have spoken too soon about the couch," she said. "This is actually more comfortable than mine."

"See, I do have good taste after all." I wrapped my arm around her shoulder and pulled her in closer. "About the treehouse, I've already drawn up some potential plans, but I won't know specifics until I take some measurements of the tree. It's going to be pretty amazing, though. Not to brag or anything." I grinned.

She beamed at me, then set her glass next to my beer and snuggled right into my side. If that's all it took to make her happy I'd build a hundred treehouses. I could see right down the front of her shirt and I didn't even pretend not to stare.

"I can tell you Rocco is beyond excited so that is music to my ears. It's really sweet of you to do this for him. It's sweet of you to do *all* the things you're doing for us. I feel like I don't deserve it." She put her hand on my thigh.

"Why would you say that? You deserve all sorts of good things." I turned her in my arms and leaned my head down to kiss her. She tasted of wine and her own unique flavor, which was quickly becoming a favorite of mine. The intensity of our clinch ratcheted up immediately as my tongue explored her mouth wildly, like I'd never get another chance. She moaned and arched her back, and we were soon leaning down into the couch, one of her hands fisting in my hair and the other squeezing my ass. I moved on top of her and ground my erection into the heated apex of her thighs which were still covered by her damn skirt. We were moving at lightning speed and it was hot as fuck.

"Nate," she breathed and began to pull away a bit, but she was trapped under me so I lifted up a few inches to give her some room.

"What's the matter?" We were both breathing heavily and my hand was caressing her thigh, moving closer and closer to the edge of her panties and the heat that waited there.

"I … I … I'm not sure." Her flushed face turned toward the back of the couch.

"Laney, look at me." She turned her face back and her hooded eyes met mine. "We don't have to do anything you don't want to do." My cock called me every name in the book, but judging by the look on her face, this was going no further tonight.

She put her hand to her forehead and I sat up, releasing her. She sat as well and straightened her skirt. "God, I feel like such an idiot. I really want this." She motioned back and forth between us. "I mean, I *really* want this." She attempted a smile.

I had no fucking clue what to do so I just shut up and hoped she'd clue me in.

"But I have more than just me to consider—I have Rocco. I can't just let someone jump into his life, play with him, build him a treehouse, and then just disappear. He won't understand that."

"Who's disappearing?"

"You know what I mean."

"Laney, there is no guarantee in any relationship. I don't know for sure what will happen between us down the road, but I can tell you that I am *more* than into you, if you can't tell that already." I raised a brow at her. "I can also tell you that while I'm seeing you I'm not even remotely interested in seeing anyone else—and I hope you feel the same way."

She nodded but still looked unsure.

I took a breath. "But I understand you're a mom and that has to come first. I just really want us to be able to spend time together and see where this goes." My hand reached out and she took it with hers.

"Can I have some time to think about it?"

My mouth said, "Of course." My dick said, "No fucking way!"

She gave me a small embarrassed smile and stood up, releasing my hand. "Thanks, Nate. I'm so sorry about … this." She waved awkwardly in the general direction of my lap.

"He understands," I said, and that got a laugh out of her. "Let me drive you home."

The ride back to her house was mostly silent and I did not have a good feeling about the way we were leaving things. I felt like I was missing some crucial piece of information, but I couldn't put my finger on it. I hated the uncertain feeling.

"Will you still come over to start the treehouse on Saturday?" she asked. "I know I'm sounding like a complete contradiction right now, but Rocco is so excited."

I shot her a smile. "Of course. I can't wait." We pulled into her driveway and I got out to open her door.

She stepped down. "Hopefully you guys can finish it before it's time for you to leave. Thanks, Nate. I'll call you." And then she kissed my cheek and ran to her front door.

I waited for the door to close behind her before I pulled out of her driveway. That bad feeling I had was turning worse.

* * *

By Friday morning I still hadn't heard one word from Laney and I felt a heavy weight in my gut. My only solace was that I'd at least get to see her tomorrow. I visited a couple sites already today to meet with some contractors, and I was pulling up to the Old Oak Ridge site wishing I could just drive down the street and knock on her door. But I'd promised to give her time and I knew she was at work anyway, so it made little difference.

As soon as I got out of my car I noticed Doug and Gavin walking my way.

"Nate!" Doug called. "I've got Gavin on framing but Mark mentioned he might pull him for some of that siding work. You know anything about that?" Both men approached and I adjusted the bag I was carrying.

I shook my head. "Don't worry about it. Stay on framing, Gavin."

"That's what I thought," Doug said distractedly and hurried away to address one of the contractors who'd just pulled up.

"How's it going, Nate?" Gavin asked, his hands perched stiffly on his hips.

"All right I guess," I responded. Gavin continued to stand that way and then I caught him clenching his jaw like he was mulling over a difficult problem. "Something wrong?"

"I don't know. You tell me." His voice was curt.

"Tell you what?" I was pretty sure I knew which direction we were headed.

"Dammit, I knew this would happen!" His voice rose and we got a few glances.

"What exactly happened, Gavin? I'm at a bit of a loss here."

He looked at me like I was stupid. "Laney. She's been in her room crying the past two nights, and it didn't escape my notice that the timing just so happened to coincide with the early end of your date the other night. So what the hell did you do to my sister?"

I was dumbfounded—it took me a few moments to speak. "Gavin, I didn't do shit. I thought things were going great and she's the one who put a stop to it. I've been the one waiting for her to call and tell me everything is okay."

"Well, shit!" He pulled his hard hat from his head and smacked it to his thigh. "Now I've got to wade into this like some fucking girl and find out what the hell is wrong."

"Don't worry about it—I'll get to the bottom of it. You can keep your man card. She's been hesitant about getting involved with me and it has something to do with Rocco and not wanting to have men going in and out of his life. But I swear I have no intention of ditching them, Gavin."

His hand pulled through his dusty hair and his shoulders dropped. "Damn, I think I get it now. It actually makes sense if you think about it. Rocco getting attached and then, when you leave for Texas, I guess that would suck for the little guy. It probably is for the best to just cut your losses." He dropped his hand to his side and put his hard hat back on with the other one. "Shit, I feel like I'm growing a vagina here. I gotta get back to work. No hard feelings, man."

He waved and left me standing there feeling like the most oblivious fucking moron on earth.

At 6:30 that evening I stood on Laney's front porch pounding on the door. "Laney, I know you're in there. I saw you peeking through the curtains!" I continued to pound on the door knowing that I was being a bit of an asshole but not caring one bit. My girl was in there and I needed to see her.

"Nate, please go away. I'm not ready to talk yet," she hissed through the door. "And stop pounding. I don't want to scare Rocco."

"Open the door and Rocco will be fine. Come on, Laney. Please."

I heard a frustrated huff, but the door opened a crack and I saw her beautiful face. I also saw the dark circles under her eyes and I cursed myself for the tenth time today.

"Laney, baby, please let me in. I need to talk to you—to explain."

Her will seemed to give out and she let the door fall open as she stepped back. I came through the doorway and wrapped her in my arms like I never wanted to let go. And in that moment, it was the God's honest truth.

"Where is Rocco?" I asked, careful not to say too much if he was close by.

"He's in his room watching cartoons on the iPad." Her voice was quiet.

I kissed the top of her head. "I think I get it now, Laney, and I am such an idiot," I declared.

She sniffled and spoke into my shirt. "That's usually a title I reserve for Gavin, but go on if you must." I loved that even when she was sad her sass came through.

"I don't know how I didn't see it before, but like I said, I'm an idiot. You think I'm moving back to Austin, don't you?"

She pulled back from my hold and looked up at me. "Well, yeah, eventually."

"Baby, I'm not going anywhere. I'm here in North Carolina to stay. It was always my plan to come back—my dad's heart attack just sped up the timing."

Her brows drew together. "But … but you kept saying all these things about 'temporary' stuff." I could see the wet in her eyes and I wanted to punch myself.

"I just meant that the apartment was temporary. I don't want to live in that shithole any longer than necessary." I smiled at her. "As soon as I have the time, I'm finding a house or a condo or something."

"Oh." That was all she said, eyes still teary.

"You forgive me for confusing you?" I leaned down and couldn't help but kiss her quickly on her sweet mouth. She just nodded, looking a bit dazed. I wanted to take her to her bedroom and show her how sorry I was, but I knew that couldn't happen for several reasons.

And despite my desire to pull her into my arms and assume that everything would work out perfectly, I knew I had to say one more thing. "But you know as well as I do that there are no guarantees in life. And I understand that you need to consider Rocco in all your decisions. I'm just asking for a chance, Laney."

Evidently over her shock, she finally smiled up at me and ran her fingers down my jaw. "By the way, if I have any say in it, I prefer the scruff." Then she reached up to me for a kiss. We wrapped ourselves around each other for several moments before cooler heads prevailed and we remembered the five-year-old down the hall, not to mention the open door behind me.

"Oh, I almost forgot." I turned around and retrieved my bag from the front porch where I'd left it. "Call Rocco out here. I've got some treehouse plans to go over with him."

Chapter Sixteen

GO ABOUT YOUR BUSINESS

*L*ANEY

I felt like I'd just won a free lifetime supply of doughnuts, along with a magical guarantee that they'd never go to my ass, as I watched Nate and Rocco at my kitchen table poring over treehouse plans. I was also feeling a bit foolish for spending the last two days wallowing in misery when I should have just opened my mouth and asked Nate outright about his plans. Damn that Fiona for always being right. I resolved from here on out to voice my doubts and be clear about any reservations I had.

I also owed Fiona a call to let her know she could halt the cookie dough, wine, and ice cream brigade she was currently preparing. It was her weekend with Terrence, but since she's the best friend a girl could have, she had been checking in with me and was planning to stop by tonight before Terrence arrived.

"We're heading out back to take some measurements if that's okay," Nate said, stacking the papers and rising from his chair.

"Of course. But, Rocco, you're getting ready for bed in half an hour."

"Aw, man, can't I stay up later since Nate's here?" my kid asked, just like any other five-year-old would when presented with the opportunity to do something fun with a friend. No nose twitching, no shyness, no worried look in his big brown eyes. It seemed Nate was *in,* and I didn't care one bit that he was thirty-one instead of five.

* * *

"Just because we're building this treehouse doesn't mean I'm ignoring your house. I think tomorrow I'll go up on your roof to check things out. I'm also taking a look in your attic," Nate said as we were saying our goodbyes later in the evening.

"Are those euphemisms? I love it when you talk dirty," I said, trying to keep a straight face.

"They can be." He flashed a naughty grin. "But actually, I'm just giving you advance warning. I believe your attic access is in your bedroom closet and I wouldn't want to have to turn you over to one of those cable TV shows, if you know what I mean."

Shitballs! My secret wasn't so secret anymore. "Please don't tell me you've seen my closet."

"Okay, I won't tell you."

Double shitballs! My fingers started itching to do a little cheek rubbing. Nate grabbed both my hands before they could reach my face.

"I've decided to find your 'storage system' cute instead of scary."

"Oh God, you're probably one of those people who doesn't even have a junk drawer, aren't you?"

That was met with silence. Who was this guy? Oh, that's right, I forgot—he's Superman's brother. Superheroes don't have junk drawers.

"I have four junk drawers," I confessed.

He nodded slowly. "And, like I said, it's cute. I think. But I had to give you fair warning about the closet since I'll need to fit a ladder in there tomorrow."

He finally released my hands and I used one to smack him on the arm. "Haha. It's not that bad, you big jerk."

Nate's back rested against the wall by my front door. Rocco was safely tucked into bed—for the moment at least—but after the near miss with the little night stalker last time, neither Nate nor I were willing to enter the bedroom tonight. At this rate, we'd never get to do the dirty.

He pulled me in for an embrace. "I'm picking up lumber on the way over tomorrow so I'll be here about ten o'clock. And, Laney, we've got to figure out how to have a real date night one of these days." He growled and gave me a sweet kiss. I wanted to drag him back down the hall and have my naughty way with him, so I was already flipping through my mental rolodex to figure out how to organize some extended alone time for us.

"Definitely. I'll get to work on it." I smiled and kissed him back. My kiss may have been a little less sweet than his.

* * *

Well, it looked like I owed my vagina an apology. Before I could even ask Gavin to babysit I went and pissed him right the hell off, removing any possibility that he'd grant me a favor anytime soon. And the worst part was I thought I was doing something nice.

"Not interested," Gavin said over his shoulder as he tried to walk away.

"What do you mean? You're the perfect person for this, and it's just one night a week and one game on the weekends."

"I don't care, I'm not doing it! And stay the fuck out of my business, Laney!" He hitched his workout bag onto his shoulder and stormed out the door before I could stop him. *That went well.*

It was Saturday mid-morning and Charlotte had dropped by earlier to give me a plant she foolishly assumed I wouldn't kill. *Yeah* … anyway, during the course of our conversation she mentioned that Aiden was signed up for rec league baseball and the coach had just dropped out. She asked if I knew of anyone who could fill in—her husband not being available since he traveled a lot for work. And, in her words, "He's about as athletic as a basset hound in a patch of sunshine." Sometimes I just loved the crap out of her Texas. So, naturally, I told her about Gavin. It was like kismet, or so I'd thought. Apparently, it was more like the worst misfortune to hit Greensboro, so fierce was Gavin's dismissal of the idea. Now he was pissed and I was evidently never having sex for the rest of my life.

Nate showed up at ten o'clock as promised. He and Rocco were out back doing lord knows what, but it seemed like each time I peeked out the window they both had their hands on their hips and were gazing up at the tree in deep thought. This project might take a while.

I still couldn't quite believe this guy was so interested in me—

truthfully, I didn't really feel like I had that much to offer. I knew if Fiona had been here she would have smacked me upside the head for talking trash about myself, but it was hard sometimes to keep a super confident attitude. I'd just have to go with it, though, because I wasn't about to give up a chance to be with somebody who made me feel the way Nate did.

I couldn't help but peek out the window again, and this time I was treated to the view of his cargo pants stretched tightly over his backside as he leaned down to lift a stack of wood. Damn that man could make me swoon.

Back to closet cleaning, Laney! Focus!

A few hours later Nate and Rocco retreated inside to escape the hot afternoon sun. I was fixing us some cool drinks while Rocco washed up in the bathroom when my front door slammed so hard the windows rattled. I thought maybe it was Gavin and he hadn't gotten over his hissy fit, but it was Fiona's petite form that came storming into the kitchen, stopping a few feet from me.

Her purse landed on the counter with a loud thwack, likely reducing its contents to dust. "I'm staying over tonight and I won't take no for an answer! I'm going to eat all your ice cream and watch tragically stupid teenagers on reality TV while you, my friend, are going over to your hot man's apartment and getting your muffin buttered." She pointed a threatening red-tipped finger at me. "I do not want to see your face until at least noon tomorrow and it had better look well-fucked. At least one of us should have an orgasm tonight and it sure as hell won't be me! Now tell Rocco his Aunt Fiona is inviting him to an ice cream party tonight and he can stay up as late as he wants."

When I didn't move she threw both hands out toward me.

"Shoo!" I still didn't move. This was "scary" Fiona—she didn't come out to play very often.

"Uh, Fiona, you remember Nate, don't you?" I motioned hesitantly to the pantry door where my "hot man" had been spraying WD-40 on the hinges but now stood stock still, the can suspended in his frozen hand.

Fiona didn't even flinch. "Hey there, hot stuff. You get all that?"

Nate just nodded slowly while the rest of him remained still.

"Can you please excuse us for a moment, Nate?" I asked as I dragged Fiona down the hall to my bedroom and closed the door.

"First of all, you can't come in here throwing out f-bombs while Rocco's at home and you know it. Second, I can't even believe you just said all of that in front of Nate. Just … oh God." I covered my eyes with my hand.

She huffed in dismissal.

I took a deep breath and shook it off. "And third, what happened? I thought you were doing sexy time with Terrence."

She scoffed. "Don't even talk to me about Terrence." And then she proceeded to talk about him anyway, as pretty much any girl would do. "What about 'friends with benefits' does he not understand? That man wants to, and I quote, 'take things to the next level.' What next level?! There is no next level! So I sent him to his hotel and told him that until he gets his head screwed on straight he needs to lose my number. I can't go back to my place in case he decides to show up to plead his case again." She did a full body shiver. *Dramatic much?*

"Wow," was really all I could say, though. Treading carefully here was essential. Fiona did not do commitment. She didn't do the girlfriend thing. She was kind of like a guy that way, but every other aspect of her was all girly-girl. I knew she had her reasons so I'd given up trying to convince her to give a guy a chance. But this was *Terrence*. They would be so good together. Ugh. I'd have to let it go for now, but hopefully she'd open the door a crack for him if he just gave her a little time. So, it looked like I'd have to give her a little time too. "I'm sorry, Fee." I gave her a hug and she finally let go of her mad a bit and sagged into my arms with a sigh.

"I know. Me too. Can I still eat your ice cream?"

"Every bit," I said, still holding her tight, my chin resting on the top of her head.

"You know, you really do have a great rack. It's like the best goose-down pillows in here." She tried to snuggle in.

I shoved her away. "You perv."

* * *

So it looked like the sex fates did like me a little bit after all. I'd gotten my sitter, although I would have preferred not to have involved Fiona's heart in the process. Nate, I could safely say, was even more thrilled than I was when I told him the news. And it seemed Fiona couldn't get us out the door fast enough. I barely had time to say goodbye to Rocco and elicit a promise from Fiona that more than just ice cream would be served for dinner.

"I need to stop by my place and take a shower, but then do you want to go out to dinner?" We were in Nate's truck and my nerves were jumping already.

"Sure, sounds good, but I'm not dressed for anything fancy." I motioned down to my casual black shorts and blue t-shirt.

"You look perfect to me."

"Aww." I couldn't help the smile I gave him.

The apartment building was just as neglected as I remembered and I didn't blame Nate for wanting to move somewhere nicer. Although maybe he should keep the couch after all, and just re-cover it.

He took my hand once again and led me to the door, not even letting me go to unlock it. Once the door closed behind us, I found myself pinned to the wall beside it and Nate's mouth was on mine. He tasted like the lemonade I'd fixed him earlier, but his mouth was warm and his tongue hot as it pushed past my lips to explore mine. My hands immediately found his thick hair and gripped the back of his neck. I melted into the kiss. Then my hands decided to do a little wandering as his lips left mine and traced a path down my jaw to my neck. On their journey, my hands found their way beneath his t-shirt and began exploring the planes of his abs and back. He smelled faintly of sweat and some kind of spicy shampoo or aftershave, and I was turned the hell on.

"Sorry," he murmured into my neck as his hands rounded my ass. "I'd really intended to take you out and make this romantic but that's gonna have to wait till next time. I need you to get naked right now." Well okay, I guess this was really happening. Holy crap!

Patience was obviously not one of his virtues because he had my shirt pulled over my head in a heartbeat and his hands moved quickly to the button on my shorts. I was feeling both overheated and a bit self-conscious at the same time. Why was it so bright in here? Would he like what he saw once I lost all my clothes? Wait, why was I the only one getting naked? *Again!*

"Quid pro quo." My voice was breathy as I stilled his hands and motioned for him to lose his shirt. I also may have helped a little, letting my hands take their time on the upward journey over his stomach and chest. Lord, was he built. "How do you look like this?" I blurted out.

He laughed. "Look like what?"

"All muscle-ey and bumpy and stuff." *Brilliant, Laney. You should write a book.*

He laughed again. "Well, I run every morning, and construction work isn't exactly sedentary. I also hit the gym a couple times a week." He shrugged. *He shrugged.* If I exerted that much energy I would be dead within a week.

His hands grazed over my taught nipples still encased in my sensible white bra—I really needed to take Fiona up on her offer to sex up my lingerie. "Now, can we get back to the fun stuff?" Nate asked, dropping his hands down to my shorts again.

"Yes, please."

After that we couldn't get undressed fast enough, and although the couch was comfy and all, that was definitely not where the deed would be done if I had anything to say about it. As our clothes were coming off I subtly aimed him toward the bedroom. We fell onto the bed, me in just my panties and him in black boxer briefs, the rest of our clothes littering a trail from the front door. I had to take a moment to lift myself up a bit and admire the view. He was even more breathtaking than I'd imagined—the perfect proportion of leanness and muscle. I took in his wide shoulders, sculpted chest and abs, muscled thighs, and just the right amount of hair covering his chest and leading a trail down to the hardness that waited under his boxer briefs. It seemed while I was conducting my perusal he was doing some investigating of his own and, if the heat in his eyes was anything to go by, he liked what he saw. That gave me just the boost of confidence I needed to go up on my knees and shimmy my panties down from my hips. I didn't get far, though, before he flipped me onto my back and settled himself between my thighs, only the thin material of his briefs separating our heat.

"I'm gonna spend a while here if you don't mind," he said before tracing one of my nipples with his tongue. "Go about your business and I'll let you know when I'm done."

I tried to laugh but it came out as a gasp instead as his teeth nipped at my peak. He let out a little growl and continued to worship first one breast and then the other. My hands roamed his shoulders and hair, and my breath was coming out in pants after a few minutes—I needed him to do something, anything, just *more*. "Nate," I pleaded.

His tongue began a path from my aching breasts to other aching parts farther south. "I know it's only been a few weeks, but I've been dreaming of this for what feels like forever." He groaned as he parted my lower lips and swiped his tongue upward, ending at my clit and sucking it into his mouth.

I may or may not have had a stroke at that moment. I was no longer in control of my faculties as I started making sounds no human should ever make. Nate Murphy was one seriously talented man. Once his fingers joined his tongue, I was arching and keening and holding his head in place as if the fate of the world depended on him continuing to give me head like it was his fucking job. After what seemed like only seconds, I came in a rush of ecstasy and delirium, and I'm pretty sure Fiona could hear my cries from my house and was raising an ice cream spoon in tribute.

Nate lifted his head and looked only slightly less satisfied than I imagine I did.

"Oh my … I mean … oh my … that was … oh my." Yep, I was a poet.

He smiled at my orgasm induced dopey-ness and wiped his mouth on the sheet. "I'll be right back—gotta get a condom." And he walked his fine ass to the attached bathroom.

I did some internal cheering and dancing (in which I was very graceful) and rolled over onto my stomach to wait for his return. I whipped my head around when I felt a sharp pain on my left butt-cheek.

"Ow! Did you just bite my ass?"

He looked way too smug. "Yes I did. And I plan to do it again."

"Oh my God, what is wrong with you?" I laughed and rubbed my sore ass.

"You've obviously never seen your ass."

I rolled my eyes at him. "Speaking of, you'd better lose those shorts or I'm ripping them off *your* ass."

"Oooh, aggressive. I like it," he teased.

And then I lost patience and kind of lunged for his junk. I'm not really clear on how it went exactly, but the important part was he got naked.

Chapter Seventeen

LIFE IS GOOD HERE IN THE BATCAVE

NATE

I think Laney may have actually torn my boxer briefs as she yanked them off me. I had evidently awakened some inner vixen in her. Not that I was complaining. Or thinking. At all. She had my cock in her hand and was stroking me with perfect pressure and rhythm from base to tip, circling the head before moving back down. It was so good, I was worried things would be over before they began.

"Baby, let up a bit. That feels way too good." I stood at the side of the bed while she lay on her stomach, her ass arched up in the air and her hands all over me. I couldn't get enough of the view. Or her taste. I could have gone down on her for hours with her silky thighs cradling my head, but I was way too anxious to get inside her. She was all soft skin and lush curves.

I pulled her hands from me. "Turn over and scoot up the bed." I tore the condom wrapper with my teeth and tossed it over my shoulder. I then rolled the condom on and settled between her thighs, covering her lips with mine. I knew her taste was still on my lips and the idea that she could taste herself made me that much harder. "Is this okay?" I wanted to make sure since the last time we'd been here she had backed off.

"Yes," she whispered, and I began to press slowly into her wetness. "Nate," she murmured, her eyes closing. "You won't hurt me. You don't need to be careful."

That was all I needed to hear before instinct took over and I thrust all the way inside her. She was hot, wet, and fucking tight. I groaned as I pulled almost all the way out and thrust back in. Her returning groan told me she was feeling the same ecstasy I was. She started moaning and meeting my thrusts, and then her legs wrapped around my waist and I was done for. I thrust away like my life depended on it, our skin slapping together and our sweat mingling on our bodies. I brought my mouth back to hers in a frantic kiss.

She cried out her release against my mouth and I followed her a moment later. I couldn't comprehend this experience—it was like no other I'd ever had. I wanted to hold her and fuck her and keep her in my bed for an eternity. In essence, I was screwed.

* * *

"So, is Laney short for something or is that your real name?" I asked her a little while later. We were lounging on my bed, wrapped up in the sheets.

"Oh God," she replied. "I'll tell you but only if you promise not to ever use it."

I crossed my heart.

She flopped onto her back, her head resting on my pillow and her nipples almost revealed by the shifting sheet. "It's short for Elaine. I think my parents were obsessed with Seinfeld. There were even some hints dropped that I may have been conceived during an episode, but my brain refuses to go there. Anyway, it's just always been 'Laney' and I am more than fine with that."

"I think 'Elaine' is pretty."

She rose back up onto an elbow and gave me a skeptical look.

"But you're definitely a 'Laney,'" I reassured, not being a complete rookie.

That seemed to satisfy her. "What about you? I know your full name and I've met your family, but tell me more."

"Well, let's see. You know I've always been into building things—and you know I can't wait to get back to it, of course. Oh, speaking of which, did I tell you my dad started visiting the office for a few hours this week?"

"No. That's great!"

"Yeah, my mom is not too keen on the idea, but she knows he needs to get out a bit or he'll suffocate. Oh, and she wanted me to tell you he's been fiddling around with the fishing gear you brought by. And he may ask to take Rocco fishing sometime soon."

Laney looked like I'd just presented her with a litter of newborn kittens. "Oh my God—that is so sweet. I'll have to run it by him first—he can be shy and a little hard to read, but they seemed to get along great at your parents' house so I bet he'll be excited. We may have to go along, though, just to warn you."

"I wouldn't mind that at all. I'll get you into a swimsuit and we can go off on our own and stir up a little trouble."

That got me a shove.

"You hungry? We never had dinner." I had to feed my woman.

"Starved. Do you have some clothes I can throw on? I'm not sure where mine ended up."

I got out of bed and put my boxer briefs back on—looked like they weren't ripped after all. "I prefer you naked, but I guess I can find something for you." I rummaged in a drawer and pulled out a t-shirt and a pair of athletic shorts.

"You're a prince among men, Nate."

"What are you in the mood for? Chinese? Pizza? Thai?" I asked as I walked toward the kitchen. I got no response. "Laney?"

"Oh, hell no!" was all I heard from the bedroom. I went back to investigate and found her wearing my t-shirt and throwing the shorts on the bed like they'd done something to offend her.

"What?"

"How is it fair that your shorts are too tight on my ass? I could hardly pull them up!"

Having been a guy for thirty-one years, I knew there was no right answer to that question. Silence, however, did not seem to be one of my options. "I love your ass. It's perfect." She still looked unsettled. "If you recall, I actually tried to take a bite out of it I loved it so much."

She still pouted and it was fucking cute. "Whatever … let's order Chinese."

Phew. I might actually be good at this relationship stuff.

We ate delivery Chinese in bed, managing not to make a huge mess, and we talked about everything and nothing. I told her more about my dad and how we were all struggling with the changes that had to be made. We also talked about Austin and my life back there—a life I wasn't missing at all anymore. She told me more about Rocco's dad and about Gavin and some of the struggles her family had been having. After dinner and some more conversation, I finally ended up taking that shower, but it was considerably more fun with Laney. Maneuvering in the tiny stall was a challenge, but we managed. And the next morning I felt quite proud when we walked into Laney's kitchen and, upon examining Laney's face, Fiona gave us a golf clap.

* * *

One Month Later

This last month was perfect. Well, actually, that's a lie. One thing I learned is having a five-year-old underfoot is a recipe for constant blue balls. But outside of that, life was amazing. Laney and I spent every possible moment together, and I didn't know about her, but I'd never felt this way about another girl. I was trying not to think about it too hard and just enjoy. We had to get creative about the locations and times we had sex due to the afore-mentioned little cock-blocker, but let's just say her shower got a lot of action—and, luckily, it was considerably larger than mine. I still hadn't spent the night, though we'd discussed it. She was going to sit Rocco down for a talk this week and feel him out a bit. I knew she trusted me, so I was glad I wouldn't have to jump that hurdle again.

As for work, Doug and my dad had all but taken over the administrative headaches (although my mom constantly looked over Dad's shoulder and tried to keep him on a short leash). I was back to getting my hands dirty. If I'd had to conduct one more bid-development or client meeting, my head would have exploded.

I took over as foreman on the Old Oak Ridge project and helped out at a couple other sites during the downtime. I still couldn't answer the neighbors' concerns about potential tenants, but Laney trusted my good intentions, and her word seemed to be good enough for everyone else.

Halloween was just around the corner and we were sitting on Laney's back patio enjoying a perfect fall afternoon. A cool breeze blew in and the sun was starting its descent, coloring the sky that perfect shade of orange. Rocco squealed out in the yard as Fiona chased him up the ladder of his completely amazing and innovative treehouse—if I do say so myself.

"That thing is ridiculous." Laney shook her head and laughed at me, knowing that I was admiring my own work. I just winked at her. I knew she loved that treehouse almost as much as Rocco did. It had a ladder with safety handles (Laney's idea) and a split-level design with built-in seating and a table. It also had porthole windows and even a pulley system to haul up important kid stuff. If I had a treehouse like that when I'd been his age I would have charged a cover to everybody who came over to play.

As it was, only Rocco and all of us adults had been inside so far, which I knew still bothered Laney. But I thought Rocco seemed like a perfectly happy kid. He was hardly even doing the nose twitching thing anymore, and he was anything but shy with me.

And the best part? Laney pulled him from that "up their own asses" daycare and he was now in a much smaller program run out of a former teacher's house. Charlotte's son went to the same place when she worked at her part-time job, and by happenstance a full-time spot had opened up in the daycare. Laney snatched it up and Rocco was much more at ease with a smaller and less asshole-ish group—my term, not Rocco's.

We had all gone over to Charlotte's house last week and I'd seen the two boys playing together. I'd also seen the gleam in Laney's eyes and could feel her relief. Next step was an invite for Aiden to play in the treehouse, which I liked to refer to as "The Batcave" but Rocco had dubbed "The Fart Fortress." You can't win 'em all. Oh, and in case you're keeping track, I did indeed apologize to Charlotte for being an asshole the first time we met.

"You know what you need?" I asked Laney as I glanced around the yard.

"Uh oh, what now? You've damn near fixed everything in my house and you already have a list a mile long of upgrades you want to make."

I pretended I hadn't heard her. "You need a screened-in porch. I bet you'd spend a lot more time out here in the summer if it weren't for the damn mosquitoes."

She turned to me, flashing some leg in her cut-offs and making me want to haul her to the bedroom. "Nate, I would love a screened-in porch, but you have got to stop doing all these things for me. You have enough to do with work and you haven't even started to look for your own place."

Yeah, about that. It was no mistake I hadn't started looking for my own place. I knew it sounded crazy, but I was in love with this girl and I was jumping ahead in my mind. It seemed ridiculous to buy a place when she clearly loved this house and I was seeing a future with her and Rocco. And besides, The Batcave was here so there was that. But I knew she wasn't ready to go there yet, so I kept quiet except for a small "Meh." It was the most noncommittal noise I could come up with.

"Meh? You're weird."

"And you're pretty." I leaned in for a kiss.

"I think I'm gonna be sick," Gavin's voice came from the back doorway.

I removed my lips from his sister. I could see things from his perspective—if I had to watch some guy pawing Bailey I would probably feel a little ill myself. Gavin wandered out onto the patio and took a seat next to me.

"I'm going to grab a drink. Anyone need a beer?" Laney asked, rising from her chair.

"Sure," Gavin and I responded simultaneously as Laney went into the kitchen.

"Is it strange that I'm jealous of a five-year-old?" Gavin asked, taking in the treehouse and the two faces peering out the window.

"If we're talking about Fiona, I can't answer that, dude. If we're talking about the treehouse, I'm right there with you."

"Definitely the treehouse. I can get laid without pissing my sister off, thank you very much."

I laughed at the mental image of Gavin hitting on Fiona with Laney as a witness. "Smart man."

Gavin sat forward in his chair and put his elbows to his knees. "Hey, I know it's late notice, but do you think there's any chance I can take Thursday off? There's somewhere I've really got to be and I can only do it on Thursday."

"Shit, man," I started, not looking forward to what I had to say next. "You haven't earned any vacation days yet, and if I let you take off it sets a bad precedent. It puts me in an awkward position, especially considering Laney and all, but I have to say no. I'm really sorry." I shook my head. I hated having to do this, especially to Laney's brother, but the rules are the rules and if I let one person break them then it's just a slippery slope. That's not the kind of work environment I can tolerate.

He looked like he'd already known the answer before I told him, but I still felt bad.

"Hey, no problem. Just thought I'd ask."

An awkward silence settled until Laney came back out with the beers and a glass of wine for herself. She hollered out to the tree-house, "Hey, any of you adventurers thirsty?!"

"Only if it starts with 'w' and ends with 'ine'!" Fiona shouted as she and Rocco descended the ladder.

"Who do you think you're talking to?!" Laney answered and headed back into the kitchen.

Fiona and Rocco approached the table, Fiona rubbing at her hands trying to wipe the dirt off. "I swear this red clay dirt is so hard to wash off sometimes."

"You should use douche," suggested Rocco as casually as can be, wiping his own hands on his jeans.

We all froze. Well, all of us but Rocco. His only parent was out of earshot, and the three of us were waiting for each other to come up with the correct response. Nothing.

Just as Laney emerged from the house, Gavin hissed at Fiona and me, "Do. Not. Tell. Laney. I like my balls where they are."

Chapter Eighteen

NOW ACCEPTING APPLICATIONS FOR A CORNER MAN

*L*ANEY

It was official. I was in love. And everything all those damn movies and romance novels said was true. Well, almost. Nate couldn't get it up ten times in a night, and doing it against a wall was ridiculously difficult, not to mention entirely impractical. But all the parts about food tasting better and jokes being funnier and finding yourself with a great big smile during a boring-ass meeting? All true. It was a little like being drunk but still able to operate a moving vehicle and hold down your day job. I was saying hello to complete strangers at the grocery store and complimenting them on their outfits. I was singing in my car and getting caught by other drivers at stoplights and not caring in the least. All I had to do was think about that sexy man and I turned into a fool.

Neither of us had said the words yet, but I had a hunch his heart was right in line with mine. Or at least I hoped it was. Not a day had gone by without Nate sporting the scruff I told him I liked so much, so that had to mean something, right?

And everything else was going well too. Rocco liked his new daycare a lot better, and he was even starting to engage with some of the other kids. The nose twitching was still around sometimes but was not nearly as prevalent as it had been. And he and Nate were getting along phenomenally. Now I just had to tackle asking Rocco how he'd feel about Nate having "sleepovers" at our house. Part of me felt like it was too soon, but my gut was telling me this was *it*. Nate was *the one*.

I'd finally introduced my parents to Nate over Skype last week. Yeah, that wasn't awkward at all. But since we'd spent a few evenings with his parents already, he said it was time to meet mine. Luckily Rocco dominated the online conversation as he usually did, so it all turned out okay in the end.

Fiona was still in a Terrence-free zone but hadn't had a date with anyone else as far as I knew. She and Nate got along well too, which was a big bonus since she and I were a package deal. And Nate being Gavin's boss hadn't turned out to be as troublesome as I'd feared. They hung out like friends when Nate was at our house, and Gavin still appeared to like his job, so all was good.

Until it wasn't.

It was Thursday after work and Nate let himself in the front door as usual. Rocco and I had been home for a little while and I was chopping vegetables, pretending to know what to do with them, while Rocco watched cartoons in the living room. As soon as Nate entered the kitchen I could feel a weird vibe. He didn't come over and kiss me right away like he usually did so that was my confirmation that something was wrong. He dragged his fingers through his sweaty, matted hair and set down his hoodie.

"Hey, mind if I jump in the shower? I'm a mess."

"Sure. You okay?"

"I don't know …" he hedged. "We'll talk later."

That did not sound good. Not at all. My first instinct was to follow him into the bedroom and make him talk. But I forced myself to think like a guy and I left him alone for the time being, as he'd asked.

Dinner was very quiet. Gavin hadn't come home to eat, which wasn't unusual, but it would have been nice to have someone else to relieve the tension at the table. Nate was stewing, and even Rocco's chatter wasn't enough to rouse him. I just spent the time responding to Rocco and asking him about his day.

When dinner was over, Nate grabbed his hoodie and started to open his mouth to speak. I cut him off before he could get one word out. "You don't need to tell me everything if you don't want to, but you don't get to leave here without saying at least something." I leaned against the stove and waited.

He set his sweatshirt back down and then his hand went back to his dark hair. "It's nothing, it's just … well, have you seen Gavin today?"

I looked at him warily. "No. I usually leave before he gets up. Did something happen to him?"

"No, I don't think so."

I pushed off from the stove. "Stop worrying me, Nate. Wasn't Gavin at work today?"

"No. He never showed."

"Are you sure? Maybe he was at a different site today or something."

"Laney, I'm his foreman."

"Well there has to be a good reason, right?" But I was feeling uneasy all the same.

"I'm pretty sure there's a reason all right." He sighed and then threw his hand out to the side. "This sucks."

"What aren't you telling me?" My hand was predictably glued to my cheek by this point.

"Gavin asked me earlier this week if he could take today off. I told him he hadn't earned vacation yet so the answer was no."

"Okay, that makes sense. Why did he need the day off?"

Nate's hand was back in his hair. "He didn't say. He just said he had something he needed to do and it could only be done today. But he seemed okay when I turned him down."

I approached him and laid my hands on his chest. "Nate, I'm sorry he put you in this situation. I hope there's a good explanation and this can all be worked out, but it sucks that you were put in the middle like this."

"No, it goes with the job, regardless of who my girlfriend is." His hands ran up and down my arms. "The problem is now I'll have to dock his pay and put him on probation. I'm worried he's not going to take it well and I don't want him taking it out on you. He can be pissed at me, but he knew the consequences, and I know things can sometimes be tense between you two."

He wasn't wrong. And I was pissed and disappointed that Gavin had put Nate in this position. Things had been going so well, and I thought the big dope had finally grown up a bit. Where in the world could he be and how could it be important enough to risk his job? Not to mention disrespecting Nate like that.

"Listen, I'm sorry I'm being so moody. If it's okay with you I'm just going to go home. I don't really want to run into Gavin tonight and I'll have a more level head in the morning if and when he shows up to work."

I told him I understood and gave him the biggest hug I could muster.

Damn you, Gavin!

It was eleven o'clock when I heard the front door shut—smoothly, thanks to Nate's handy-work. Gavin's footsteps were hardly audible and I'm sure he assumed I was asleep, not waiting on the couch to strike like a freaking rattlesnake—which was exactly how I felt.

"Where in the hell have you been?"

He jumped, his palm hitting his chest. Good, I scared the shit out of him. He quickly regained his composure. "None of your business, *Mom*. Go to bed."

"It is my business when, (a) you have me worried you're dead in a ditch somewhere, and (b) my boyfriend is your boss and you decided to play hooky like you're sixteen again and put him in a really difficult spot." I didn't even try to hide my annoyance.

He stalked into the living room and dropped his bag on the floor. "See, I knew it was a bad idea for you guys to date. I totally saw this coming!"

"You saw yourself acting like an irresponsible dipshit again?"

His mouth went tight. "I wasn't being irresponsible. I weighed my options and decided the consequences of skipping work were worth it."

"Oh, this should be good. What exactly could have been more important? Were you donating a kidney?" My brows shot up and I leaned back into the cushions.

"Don't be such a bitch. I went to see Coach Willis." He inched closer to the couch.

"Why?" I was utterly confused.

"He called me up this weekend and told me he'd be in Charlotte and wanted to see me. But he was only going to be there today. I thought … I thought. *Goddammit!* I thought he was calling because he wanted me back on a team. I don't know what the hell I was thinking, I just got the call and I couldn't *not* go." He slumped onto the couch next to me, his head dropping back.

Well, shit. The guy looked like a kicked puppy, so I calmed myself down a bit. "What did he really want?"

Gavin choked out a humorless laugh. "He's got some camps he's working with and asked if I wanted a temp job coaching some kids. And he said he missed seeing my ugly mug, so he wanted me to come in person."

I didn't know what to say.

"I don't want to coach some snot-nosed kids. I want to *play*. I was supposed to play."

I remained silent and rubbed his arm. My heart broke for him.

But only for a second because then he went and pissed me right the hell off.

"I'm quitting the construction job and going to Virginia."

At his words, my back went so straight I could have taught an etiquette class. "You what?! Are you joking?"

"No. I'm just not cut out for this."

I could almost hear the countdown to my brain's imminent explosion. "Not cut out for what? Being an adult?" The calm I'd regained was a thing of history. I leapt off the couch and pointed right in his face. I couldn't have stopped myself if I'd tried—the urge to rant at him had been bottled up for so long.

"You lived in Mom and Dad's house for two years and never got a job—never paid a dime. You let them buy you a Jeep, for Christ's sake—it may be a shitty one but you still let them pay for it. They were so afraid you were going to fall apart and so disappointed *for* you that they would have done anything—and you let them!

"You acted like a spoiled child whose favorite toy had been taken away and you let them wait on you hand and foot. It only took eight weeks to recover from your injury—an injury that was a direct result of your own goddamned carelessness, by the way— but you milked the hell out of it and acted like a whiny baby. You took advantage of them and refused to grow the fuck up and take responsibility."

My blood was on fire and I couldn't seem to stop. "So life didn't turn out how you wanted it to—join the fucking club. Do you think I lay in my bed as a child dreaming of my future life as a single mom pinching pennies and working a boring-ass job to make ends meet?" I swiped my hair out of my face and kept going. "And don't you even think about throwing the help I got from Mom and Dad in my face. I know I was damn lucky to have them and I appreciated the hell out of it. Never did I take it for granted, and I pulled my weight as best I could. I got dealt a bad hand and took it on the chin, unlike you. I picked myself up and moved on because that's what it is to be an adult."

I was so worked up by this point I felt like I needed a corner man to wipe my face down.

But Gavin, who had been swiping my finger aside repeatedly, was up and facing off with me. He had come to fight too. "You got dealt a bad hand?! Ha! You decided to spread your legs for some douchebag with a guitar and suffered the consequences. I chose to get on that motorcycle and you chose to be a slut, so don't paint me with a different brush, Laney. We both fucked up. The only difference is that my fuck-up killed the only dream I've ever had in my entire life! Yours just changed the timing of what your life had in store for you anyway."

He laughed without a trace of humor. "You got an awesome kid out of your fuck-up, and if I asked you on your worst day if you'd change one thing about how your cards fell you would always say no because a yes would mean you wouldn't have Rocco. You ask me the same thing and I'd answer yes every single time. I would give anything to change that night and get my career back. There is no fallback or plan B. There's nothing." He stepped into me and his voice dropped.

"So you go ahead and be all superior and call me an idiot like I know you love to do, but you will never understand what it's like to be me and lose the one dream you ever had. You've got Rocco, you've got your new house, you've got your perfect boyfriend, and you've even got the fuckwad California kid to fund your life. Wow, I feel so sorry for you!" He sneered and backed away, grabbing his bag again.

Then he turned and headed for the door. "Now, if it's all right with you I think I'll go get drunk with Brett. Because, unlike my sister who's supposed to have my back, he has never failed me. Tell Rocco I'll catch him tomorrow and tell Nate whatever the hell you want to."

I hurried to catch up and stepped right in his way. "You don't get to drop the mic and stomp out of here." I poked him in the chest. "You talk about your dead dreams and, yeah, it sucks ass that you didn't get to play pro ball, but you could do *anything* else in the world! You didn't even bother to finish college. Mom and Dad were standing there, money in hand, offering to help you finish. You could have picked *anything*, but getting drunk with Brett was what you chose—it's what you always choose!"

He tried to push me aside but I wasn't done. "And as for my dreams? I never even had a chance to figure out what they were—I didn't get the time to. I was going to get a four-year degree and a chance to figure out my future on my own time. Instead I'm stuck in a cubicle for the rest of my life doing a job Brett could probably do hungover."

Gavin rounded on me and shoved his finger in my face. "You're so full of shit. You curse me for taking advantage of Mom and Dad and then you tell me I should have taken their money for college? Which is it? And if you hate your job so damn much, why don't you just quit?!" he hissed in my face and pushed me aside to reach the door.

"God, you're such a child! You don't get it at all!" I yelled at him.

He flipped me off, proving my point, and slammed the door behind him, making me feel so agitated that I wanted to scream and throw things. Why couldn't he see that he had the world at his feet if he'd just open his eyes and consider the possibilities waiting out there for him? *Son of a bitch!*

I checked on Rocco to make sure we hadn't woken him up, but thankfully he was fast asleep, upside down on his bed. I felt utterly crappy and there was no way I'd be able to sleep, so I called Fiona, praying that she was still up. I got her voicemail. Well, reality TV it was, then.

* * *

Nate: Did Gavin ever show up last night?

Laney: Yeah, and we got into it. I'm pretty sure we've disowned each other.

Nate: I've done that to Bailey numerous times but she's still somehow hanging around.

Laney: I don't think he's coming to work today. I'll explain everything later, but I'm really sorry he's being such an ass.

Nate: Can't wait to hear this one. Have a good day and I'll call you later.

Laney: XOXO

Nate: You know I can't bring myself to do that crap.

Laney: Oh, come on, just one lousy emoji or acronym and I'll leave you alone ...

Nothing. Damn.

I had just arrived at work and really should have been doing my job, but I had to catch up with Nate—and I still hadn't heard from Fiona. I'd been so pissed off the night before that I'd tossed and turned and waited for Gavin to come home, but he never showed. Not a huge surprise. So, I was basically a zombie this morning, my Diet Coke doing nothing to revive me. I barely made it through the day, and I may have possibly nodded off on the toilet in the early afternoon. If the pins and needles in my butt-cheeks were any indication, I probably did. Is it bad form as an employee to bring a pillow into the bathroom?

I texted Fiona again and finally got a response. "ttyl sorry," was all it said.

By the time I picked up Rocco and got home, I just wanted to pass out. Thank God it was the weekend. I followed Rocco in the door and was pleasantly surprised to find Nate standing in my kitchen making dinner. "Oh my God, I love you."

Yes, that's what I said. *Shit fuck damn!*

Being the wonderful man he is, after a silent beat he just turned around and smiled, flashing me the dimple.

"Can we please just pretend I didn't say that and you come here and give me a kiss instead?" I pleaded.

That got a good laugh and the kiss wasn't so bad either.

"Hey, dude," Nate addressed Rocco after making my belly dip. "I'm making homemade pizza. You want to help?"

"Yeah, yeah, yeah!" he shouted.

"Go wash your hands first," I told my kid, "and keep your clothes on—naked people are not allowed to prepare dinner. It's a health code violation!" He raced to the bathroom, probably ignoring what I said.

"Well," my arms circled Nate's waist and I rested my head on his firm chest. "You seem to be in a much better mood tonight."

"Yeah," he said. "Sorry about last night, but it's all worked out … well, for the most part. We'll talk about it once Rocco's in bed."

This was a revelation to me because I hadn't seen nor heard from my pain-in-the-ass brother since he stormed out of here last night. I was dying of curiosity. But instead of pressing Nate for details, I joined in the pizza-making party and contributed to the total mess my kitchen became. It was pretty awesome.

I put Rocco in the tub after dinner and hoped the flour and sauce that coated his entire body would all wash off. Tonight's song was about pooping in The Fart Fortress so I tried to stay out of the bathroom as much as possible. I have a dirty mind, don't get me wrong, but Rocco's is a totally different variety of dirty I can't quite connect with.

To my shock and great pleasure, Rocco requested that Nate read him his story before bed. This had never happened before, and I could tell Nate was pretty touched, though he macho-manned his way past it like it was no big deal. Afterward, I gave Rocco a kiss and tucked him in, pleading with him to stay in his own bed.

"But I like yours."

"I know, but you need to learn to stay in your own bed all night."

"Why?"

Because I can't sleep very well with your butt in my face.

Because I want to get laid by my boyfriend and you're kind of cramping my style.

Because I love you but mommies need personal space.

But no, I went with, "Because I said so." I had finally done it— I'd turned into my mother. Good God.

Unbelievably, he actually accepted my answer, but I was pretty sure it was just because he was so tired. I would never get that lucky again.

＊ ＊ ＊

"So, tell me how this whole Gavin thing worked itself out. I didn't sleep a wink last night I was so worked up. I'm glad it got sorted."

Nate and I were on the couch, me with my glass of wine and a pillow snuggled in my lap, him leaning back with his legs resting on the coffee table and an IPA in hand.

"Well, I have to say I was pretty pissed last night and I wasn't sure what to expect this morning. He didn't show up—"

"What?!"

"Let me finish. He didn't show up at first. Then around ten o'clock he came and found me. He looked like shit. Then he laid it all out for me like I assume he did to you last night, and we worked out a deal. His pay for yesterday is being docked and he's on probation, but I'm letting him make up the couple hours he missed this morning."

"So he's not quitting," I stated more than asked.

Nate looked uncomfortable.

"Now here's the part you may not like. He's not quitting … for now." I started to react but he put a hand up to stop me. "Listen, Laney, I don't want somebody working for me who doesn't want the job. That's how mistakes get made and people get careless. That can only result in shoddy work and injuries, neither of which I need. If he doesn't want to work construction then he shouldn't."

"But he doesn't want to do *anything*!" My anger from last night was resurfacing.

"You know that's not true. He wants to play baseball."

I almost choked. "But he can't! A gazillion doctors and trainers have told him that. It's over—no big leagues. He needs to get over it and grow up." I set my wine on the coffee table so I wouldn't spill it—or throw it.

Nate put a hand on my leg. "Look, I don't know if he can or can't play, but if he wants to try, that's *his* business, not mine, and frankly, it's not really yours either."

"Excuse me?!" My blood pressure hit the ceiling and I threw the pillow down, knocking Nate's hand aside in the process.

"I know you've been dealing with this situation for a lot longer than I've been in the picture, but I saw the look in his eyes when he was talking about playing. It's his passion—his dream. I know what it's like to be forced to do something other than what you love and it sucks."

I couldn't stay seated any longer. "I can't believe I'm hearing this. Since when am I the only person on earth who is in touch with reality?"

"Cut the sarcasm, Laney. Usually I think it's cute but right now is not the time." Nate sat forward and set his beer down too.

"I'm sorry, I just don't know how else to respond when I'm faced with not one but two delusional people who think you can just wish on a star and all your dreams come true—poof! That's not how life works, and encouraging Gavin will just lead to heartbreak in the end."

"Who's heart? If he wants to risk it, let him."

"Everyone's heart, Nate! Everyone's! That's what happens when people you love make bad decisions and you're left standing as the only responsible person in the room, no matter how much you wish you could say, 'Fuck it! I think I'll skip work and go to Paris tomorrow—that sounds like a shitload of fun!'"

Nate stood and put his hands out in a "let's placate the crazy person so she doesn't shoot" manner. "Okay, I can see I've touched a big nerve and you're getting emotional. Let's take a step back—"

"Emotional? Emotional?! Oh, so now I'm just the hormonal female fucking things up by bringing feelings into it. Oh, and I probably have PMS too so obviously my opinions are invalid!"

"That's not what I said and you know it!" He was starting to get pissed. I should accuse *him* of having PMS.

This was getting way out of hand. "I can't talk to you right now. I think you should leave."

"Come on, Laney. This is crazy!"

Tears pricked my eyes. "Of course it's crazy—the entire world seems to have turned inside out and I'm the only one making any sense!" I physically turned him around and started pushing him to the door. "Please just go. I can't handle any more of this right now."

"I don't want to leave things like this, Laney," he protested but let me lead him, even though he certainly possessed the strength to stay put.

I started to cry. I couldn't help it. "I can't … I just … I need you to leave me alone for now."

I think the tears did him in because he finally caved. "I'll go home but we're going to talk tomorrow and work this out."

I continued to push him out. All I could do was shake my head. My mind was so discombobulated and the tears wouldn't stop. I felt my heart breaking but I wasn't entirely sure of the source.

* * *

"I am so sorry! I had to go to Raleigh for one of the charities—my mother guilted me into it—and everything was so last minute. Gary was pissed so I'm probably fired, but that's actually a good thing. He was starting to flirt with me and you know I don't go there. I've got something else lined up anyway, I think. So I ended up spending the night because my dad got off work and we all went out to dinner. One wine led to another and I stayed at the hotel where the function was. So, what did I miss?" Fiona chattered over the phone.

I laughed but it held no humor at all.

"Oh no! What happened?"

"I have no idea. I mean, I do, but I don't. I think my brother is moving to Virginia and I think Nate and I may have broken up." The tears started again for the tenth time since last night. I'd had to call Charlotte for emergency babysitting this morning because I didn't want Rocco to see me upset—so at least I was by myself while I cried my eyes out. Two nights without sleep and with too many tears—I was shriveling up like a raisin.

"What? No! That can't be true," Fiona protested.

I proceeded to tell her everything I knew, ending with me shoving Nate out the door.

"You really told him you loved him?"

"That's all you took from that whole saga?" I sniffled

"Of course not, but I wanted to focus on the good stuff."

"There is no good stuff. And to top it all off, if I broke up with Nate and Gavin is leaving, I'm essentially stripping my poor kid of his two best friends. Just hand me my 'Mother of the Year' award right now," I sobbed.

"Oh stop. All of this can be fixed. Just listen to your fairy godmother, Fiona, and it will all be okay."

She proceeded to calm me down a bit and try to put things in perspective a little better. My exhausted mind wasn't working very well, but some of what she said started to make a little sense.

"You and Nate did not break up. What you did was have a fight —all couples have fights—and once you patch things up you get to have hot make-up sex. I've known you for years and when you get going there is no stopping you—you're sort of like a *Housewife* in that sense—I hate to be the one to break it to you."

"Hey—that's mean. You're supposed to be making me feel better."

"Oh shut up—you know it's true. Now, listen. I love you and I only want the best for you and Rocco. You've not had the easiest time of it, but I need to lay it out for you, Laney, so please don't be mad at me."

"Oh God—what? Is this the part where you tell me I'm not always 100% right?"

"Yes it is, girl, and you can handle it so here goes." She took a deep breath and dug in. "I think the reason you get so worked up over Gavin and his admittedly sketchy life choices is that you may be projecting a little bit. You're not happy with some of the choices you've made, and after you beat yourself up a bit, you tend to turn it around on him. Maybe you're reluctant to treat him with more patience and compassion because you can't stop being mad at yourself for your mistakes and decisions that didn't work out too well."

I could picture her perfectly on the other end of the phone. She undoubtedly had her bottom lip between her teeth and her eyes were squeezed shut. I couldn't speak as I tried to process what she said and not throw the phone down.

Silence. My wheels turned for another minute.

"Fiona?"

"Yeah?" Her voice was barely audible.

"Did you just fucking Dr. Phil me, you little whore?!"

"Maybe." Her voice went up an octave.

"Aw hell. I'm gonna have to grow some lady balls and dish out some apologies, aren't I?"

"That would be my recommendation, yes." Her normal tone returned. "But I don't think you're wrong about Gavin needing to man up. I think you just need to adjust your sensitivity level a touch. And maybe we should both stop calling him an idiot so much. I think maybe 'bonehead' sounds more supportive. No— I've got it—we can call him a 'boob.' It gets the message across but will give him happy thoughts!"

"Have I told you lately how much I love you? Or how weird you are?" I was actually smiling at this point—a minor miracle given the last couple days.

"No, but it's a given. So, if you're feeling a little better, I have some phone calls to make and a couple errands to run."

"What are you planning, Fiona?" My back prickled with apprehension.

"Never you mind. Like I said, let your fairy godmother take care of it." And then she hung up on me.

Chapter Nineteen

HANGOVERS AND SOFT UNDERBELLIES

NATE

"You should always listen to me, man. Getting serious with a chick? Not worth it." Mark took a deep swallow of his beer before setting it back on the table. When he'd seen what a pathetic mess I was this afternoon, he convinced me that a night out drinking and playing pool at Jake's was just what I needed. I was pretty sure I was wasted because Mark was beginning to make a lot of sense.

"Yeah, you're probably right. I bet I could get a girl here to go home with me and she wouldn't get all emotional and bat-shit crazy." I looked around the bar half-heartedly for a suitable woman. Ah, shit. What did it matter? None of them was the one I wanted.

"Dude, I hope for your sake you didn't tell Laney she was bat-shit crazy."

"No way. I'm not that stupid." I took another swig of my beer. "I may have called her emotional though."

Mark threw his head back with a maniacal laugh. "That's even worse. I can't believe how ignorant you are. That's like rule number one on the list of things never to say to a woman you want to nail."

"You're such a romantic, Mark. I can't believe you don't have a girlfriend."

"Believe it, man. That's the last thing I need. Keep it light, keep it fun, and keep it comin'—that's my motto." He toasted me and I toasted him right back, though my heart wasn't really in it.

"Well, would you look at this." A familiar voice joined in. I turned my head and, after it stopped spinning, I saw Gavin and his friend Brett by our table, beers in hand. "I didn't think I'd see you here tonight. I figured you'd be hanging with Laney and the little man. I'm still a bit scared to go home so I've been hanging at Brett's."

I gave Gavin the fakest smile I could muster. "I want to kill you."

"What did I do?"

"I think Laney broke up with me. I may have defended you and in the process broken some unspoken rule about siding with siblings in an argument. It's all quite … fuzzy."

"Shit. Are you serious?" He cocked his head.

"It's either that or she's insane," I offered.

"Ah, I'd go with insane."

"Unfortunately, it doesn't matter if she's crazy or not because I'm in love with her." My filter-less, alcohol-addled brain prompted my mouth to speak.

"Dude," said Brett.

"Fuck," said Gavin.

"Christ on a bike—seriously?" said Mark.

"Yup," was my response to them all.

Everyone was quiet, contemplating the fucked-up nature of my situation. We all took a swig of our beers.

"All right." Gavin moved first. "Let's fix this." He took hold of my arm and tried to pull me from my barstool. The world tilted a little. Hmm, that was odd. "Shit, you're wasted, aren't you?"

"It seems that way."

"Okay, I'm driving you home and we'll go to Laney's in the morning and iron all this out. You got a couch I can crash on?" He supported me and led me toward the door.

"Yup, and according to your sister, what it lacks in style it makes up for in comfort, if I'm remembering that correctly."

"Don't do that. It's too pathetic. The less you speak from here on out, the better."

* * *

I awoke to shit in my mouth.

Okay, well not literally, but I imagine that's what shit tastes like. I looked around and realized I was lying in my bed but had absolutely no recollection of how I'd gotten there. There was also a small hammer inside my head beating away at my brain to the tune of "You Asshole. Why Did You Drink So Much?" I hadn't heard that one in quite some time. I chanced sitting up and it only got a little worse. I could do this. A glass of water and three ibuprofen rested on the upturned packing box that acted as my bedside table. Thank God, somebody liked me.

Carrying the glass, I shuffled carefully into the living room and found Gavin sitting on my couch fiddling with his phone. Oh yeah, now I was starting to remember.

"Yo," was all I could manage. I swallowed the pills and winced.

"Hey. You're alive. It was touch and go for a while there last night."

"Yeah, sorry about that. I don't usually drink that much."

"No problem." He shook his head. "If I could count the number of times I … well, maybe not the most appropriate story for my boss. But, considering the current situation …" He laughed.

Yeah, I felt like a moron. "Right. So, am I missing any important details from last night?"

"Oh, wow, this is awkward. You mean you don't remember proposing to that stripper last night?"

My stomach dropped right to the floor and I thought I was going to be sick. What the fuck had happened last night?

"Joking, dude. But you should see the look on your face." He was enjoying himself way too much. I would have to remember to punch him in the face when I was feeling better. "Seriously, though, I feel bad that I was the cause of this mess. Laney and I? We just … I don't know. We're kind of like oil and water sometimes and you just got caught up in it. Don't worry, though, I've got a plan."

* * *

One diner breakfast—or more accurately, lunch—of grease topped with grease and a side of grease, and I was feeling much better. I still didn't know if I trusted Gavin to fix my Laney problems, but it couldn't hurt to let him try.

After we ate, Gavin drove us to Laney's house. I was extremely leery—she'd asked me to leave her alone and I really didn't want to get slapped in the face or punched in the nuts. "I don't know about this, Gavin."

He put the car in park and turned off the engine. "Do you trust me?"

"Not even a little."

"Hm. I guess I can see that. Let's put that aside for the moment. Can you answer one question for me?"

I nodded.

"Is it possible for me to work for you part time instead of full time?"

That was not where I thought he was going with this. "Yeah, sure. We've got several part-time guys. It would affect your benefits, but yeah."

"Good. Now let's get in there and get your girl." He paused getting out his door. "And if you tell anyone I said that I'll kick your ass."

"Afraid to show your soft underbelly, Gavin?" I had to rib him. I got out and we started up the front path.

"Fuck you," he grunted.

Before we could get to the porch, the door opened and there was my girl—or at least I hoped she was still my girl. Her hair was pulled up into some kind of messy thing on top of her head and she was dressed in a loose t-shirt and cut-off shorts. Her face was free o makeup and I spotted dark circles under her eyes. She was perfect. Her eyes came straight to me.

"I've been trying to call you. I was worried you never wanted to see me again." Her eyes filled with tears.

"What?" I pulled my phone out of my pocket. Dead. "Shit. My battery's dead. I'm sorry."

"No, I'm sorry—so sorry, Nate, I—"

"All right, let's not give the neighbors a show—get your asses inside," Gavin directed. Laney didn't even spare him a dirty look. Huh. We proceeded indoors and Gavin shut the door behind us.

Laney faced me with her hands to her cheeks. "I was mad at Gavin and I totally took it out on you and I shouldn't have. I said some awful things and I didn't mean any of them. Well, some of them I did but those were more about Gavin, not you."

I stepped closer and pulled her hands down so I could hold them. "I'm sorry too. I shouldn't have stuck my nose into a situation I didn't fully understand. And I probably said some things I shouldn't have either. Can we be done fighting now?"

"Yes, please." She threw her around my neck. I squeezed the living hell out of her in return and kissed her temple.

"Okay, okay, let's stop while we're still at a PG rating. I have a few things I need to say," interrupted Gavin.

Laney and I pulled apart and she turned to face him. I moved behind her and wrapped my arms around her waist.

"I have some things I want to say to you too," confessed Laney.

Gavin tipped his chin. "I'll let you go first if you promise it won't involve yelling. Or punching me in the junk."

She crossed her heart. "I couldn't even if I wanted to—Rocco's just down the hall. Look, I know we fight and that's kind of our thing, but I owe you an apology. I haven't been very sympathetic these last couple years and it probably has more to do with my own issues and insecurities than yours, or so my fairy godmother told me. And—"

"Your fairy what?" I had to interject.

"Never mind—that's not important. Anyway, Gavin, you're important to me and I love you. And I really appreciate all the help you give with Rocco. I'll try to be more supportive and less judgmental from here on out. I promise, and I'm sorry." She released a breath like it had been weighing her down like a ton of bricks.

"Wow." Gavin blinked. "That was … kind of unexpected." He laughed self-consciously and scratched his head. "Um, I was gonna tell you I'm sorry too."

He backed up against the wall and tucked his hands in his pockets. "After our fight on Thursday, I went over to Brett's to get drunk and I started ranting to him about my pain-in-the-ass sister." He shot Laney a sheepish look. "But he kind of hit me in the face with the same truth-stick you did. Nobody besides you has ever gotten on my case about getting my act together, and to hear it coming from him was kind of a kick in the nuts.

"You're my sister and you're supposed to nag me and be full of shit, but he's been my best friend through all this and he said he couldn't keep his mouth shut anymore. So, I've been thinking a lot about it the last couple days and I'm finally coming to terms with the fact I won't play ball for a living. But that doesn't mean I can't play at all—which I know you've been trying to tell me, so just shut up, okay?"

Laney relaxed back into me as Gavin continued, "Anyway, I

made a few calls and then I received a few more. It seems your fairy godmother has some connections, because I have an interview for a job at the Baseball Academy coaching high-level teenage players. It wouldn't be full time, but Nate said I can still work part time with him, so I think I'm gonna go for it. Hell, what is it they say—those who can't do, teach?"

"Something like that," she responded.

Gavin raised a hand to rub over his chin. "And, Laney, I know you worry and you're afraid of making mistakes, but you're not a screw-up—and I shouldn't have called you a slut either."

My ears perked at that one. It was one thing to get into a fight but another entirely to call my girlfriend a slut. Laney must have felt my body tense because she moved one hand to my thigh to keep me in place.

"The same night you and Dominic were getting your drunken deed on, there were hundreds of other couples on campus doing the same thing. The only difference was yours resulted in a pooping, crying, booger-laden, eighteen-year-long commitment while everybody else got to sleep off their hangovers and move on with life."

We all smiled a bit at that one, and Gavin continued, "If you asked anyone what kind of mom you are to that kid, there isn't anybody who wouldn't sing your praises. You didn't screw up his life and you're not going to. You're the love of his life and that is pretty fucking awesome. So, that's it. That's all I've got." He threw his hands to the sides.

"Get your ass over here and give me a hug, you big boob," Laney said in a tight voice, and I let her go to her brother.

"Boob?" he asked.

"Yeah, I'm trying it out." She enveloped him in a bear hug.

Gavin smiled over her shoulder. "I like it."

* * *

Gavin took Rocco to the park to give us some alone time and we made the most of it, combining a much-needed shower for me with some unbelievably hot make-up sex. Laney came at me like a sex-crazed wildcat and I had the marks on my back to prove it. It made the last miserable day almost worth it. We lay in bed afterward, her cheek resting on my chest and her arm thrown over my waist.

"You know, I've been doing all this thinking about Gavin and his ruined dreams. One of the things that's always bugged me was that I didn't *have* a dream that could or couldn't be fulfilled. I guess I felt like you get what life gives you and you move on, but that's not really the best attitude, is it?" My fingers traced lazy circles on her back and I let her talk. "I guess I could learn a thing or two from you and Gavin. If there's something I feel passionate about, I shouldn't let anything stop me without trying my hardest to get it."

"And what do you feel passionate about?" I kissed the top of her head.

She reached down and copped a feel of my ass. "Besides your hot ass, you mean? I don't know—maybe owning an alpaca farm?"

"Seriously?" My fingers stopped their movement.

She laughed. "No, but it sounds interesting, doesn't it? I don't like to shovel shit, though, so that's probably out."

"Probably. What else?"

"I don't know. But I do know I'm only twenty-five and I've got time to figure it out."

"I forgot I was dating jailbait." I pretended to push her away.

"Whatever, old man." She smacked my chest.

"So, there's something I've been thinking about too," I said.

"What's that?" She snuggled back in my crook again.

"You."

"What about me?" I could feel her smile against the skin of my chest.

"Well, there's that awful temper of yours. And then there's your hoarding habit—don't get me started on what I unearthed in your hall closet the other day. And then we have the issue of your cooking—I have to say it's only slightly better than my mother's, and I'm worthless in the kitchen too, so we're kind of screwed. Oh, and of course there's your habit of rubbing your cheeks like you're trying to summon a genie—"

"Is this going somewhere?" she asked, raising her head to look at me with narrowed eyes.

I nodded and smiled. "Yup. What I'm trying to say is I love you."

Her cheeks pinked at my words. "You've got a strange way of expressing yourself, big guy."

I shrugged. "I figured it's easier to list the things that are so very wrong about you than to list the ones that are so very right—I can't really count that high."

"Well, if that wasn't the most romantic thing ever—you big jerk." She smacked my chest again and started coming in for a kiss.

"I guess I forgot to add your violent streak to the list. I'll make a note."

"You do that." And her lips met mine.

EPILOGUE

*L*ANEY

One Month Later

"This was such a great idea, Laney. We should make this a tradition." Erin linked her arm in mine as we stood enjoying the sunny afternoon on the back porch—oh, excuse me, back *deck*.

Nate and I had compromised and I agreed to let him build me a deck instead of the screened-in porch he wanted. I told him he could always finish it off eventually, but for right now I was sticking to my guns. He'd spent so much time and money fixing up my house that I had to draw the line somewhere. Of course, he couldn't make it just any old wood plank deck—he had to add built-in seating and a nook for his kick-ass grill he'd finally brought from Austin.

It was the day after Thanksgiving and I, like any sane person, was avoiding all retail locations. We were hosting an open house of sorts and invited practically everyone we knew to drop by throughout the afternoon to hang out and snack on leftovers—which we supplemented with burgers and brats. Maybe Nate couldn't cook all that well, but the man could *grill*. He explained that grilling was a skill that came along with having a penis—and something else about cavemen cooking meat over a fire, a topic which his dad had been strangely enthusiastic about discussing. Not that Erin would allow Riordan to have any of the grilled meats.

After a token protest, Riordan summoned Rocco to the deck. "Come on, Rocco. I'm going to show you how to clean a fish. Then maybe I'll be allowed to use the grill." With the unseasonably warm weather, they'd gone fishing on Thanksgiving morning and had a bit of luck. So fish had been added to the menu for the day.

I looked over at Erin and said, "Actually, it was Nate's idea, but I agree. It feels like more of a holiday when you can spread it out over a couple days. But I'm kind of shocked I got Fiona to come over. I figured she'd be in retail heaven."

"I heard that." Fiona approached. "I was up at five o'clock this morning, thank you very much, and I may have even bought a few things for you, my friend—of the sexy variety, if you know what I mean." She winked.

"Uh, yeah, I think we all know what you mean. And thank you for talking about this in front of my boyfriend's mother."

"I was young once too, so don't worry about me. And besides," Erin said, squeezing my arm, "Rocco could really use a sibling, don't you think?"

Danger! Danger! Need immediate rescue from the crazy lady!

As if reading my thoughts, Nate walked up and stole me away

from his mother. "Leave her alone, Mom. Go bug Bailey about having babies. I think I saw her flirting with someone inside."

"Really?" Erin's eyes lit up and she couldn't get inside fast enough.

"Thank you." I hugged Nate back. "Who is Bailey flirting with, just out of curiosity?"

"Nobody. She's stuffing her face with pie." He grinned.

I laughed and looked around the yard where our friends and family mingled. My parents were here, having come back to town to celebrate the holiday with us. Rocco was over the moon. They were staying at a hotel, an arrangement that would never be repeated if Erin had anything to say about it. Our families had spent Thanksgiving together and were getting along great. Thankfully both sides had a high tolerance for crazy.

Some of the guys and gals from Nate's work were here too, and I recognized a few of them, specifically Mark with the cock-sure smile and Doug who, for some reason, was wearing a Hawaiian print shirt for the holiday. I also noticed that Mark hadn't taken his eyes off Fiona since she walked outside. *Oh my.*

Nate made his way back to the grill and announced that the food was ready. People wandered over to fix a plate. It didn't escape my notice that Rocco wasn't among them. I spied his little head through the treehouse window, along with that of Aiden and one other little girl from their daycare. If that view wasn't a balm to my soul, I didn't know what would be.

"Hey, Shortcake." A male voice sounded behind me. I turned around to see Mark lean back on the deck railing next to Fiona, doing the oh-so-casual arms crossed to show off my big biceps thing—*hey, it's a thing, trust me*. He was also giving her that super cocky smile and I almost felt sorry for him. He had no understanding that the phrase "big things come in small packages" was coined with Fiona specifically in mind.

"You talking to me, Meat-head?"

Oooh. This was going to be fun.

Gavin came over, draped his arm around my shoulders, and whispered in my ear, "Excellent. Dinner *and* a show." I snorted.

"Hey, I was just trying to say hi. You don't need to be insulting," Mark said to Fiona.

"I was just returning the favor. Run along now." She shooed him away.

Ouch.

Mark's eyebrows rose. "I was also gonna tell you that the kids' table is inside, Tinkerbell."

Not bad.

Fiona's jaw tightened. "What a coincidence because I was just going to tell *you* to go eat a bag of dicks."

Hmm, an odd choice, but it hit its mark anyway.

"Are you always such a bitch to people you just met?" His casual stance was long gone and they were in a face-off.

"Only to complete morons." Fiona's mouth curled in distaste.

"What is your problem? Jesus, I don't need this crap." Mark stalked into the yard and away from my charming little bestie.

Fiona, completely unfazed, stepped up to the grill and grabbed a plate. "Oooh, are those sausages? I love sausage. Give me a big one, Nate."

Gavin and I both started snickering, and Nate shot us a death glare.

* * *

After we'd all eaten and most of the crowd dispersed, I sat on Nate's lap—he insisted and I'd learned not to question him on his opinions about my body. I sighed the sigh of a completely contented Laney.

"I love this day."

He kissed my temple.

"Oh, hey," Nate said suddenly. "I forgot to tell you. We rented the last space in the Old Oak Ridge property." The project was wrapping up and they'd already signed rental agreements with a financial planning firm and some tech business but there was still one space left.

I mentally crossed my fingers and turned my face to his. "Oh yeah, what's it going to be?"

He smiled that smile and I got the dimple. "A doughnut shop."

"Oh my God! I love you!"

~THE END ~

Stay up to date on Sylvie's upcoming books and projects by subscribing to her newsletter! http://bit.ly/NewsSylvie

Use these links to grab special **bonus** content!
http://bit.ly/BonusTheFix & http://bit.ly/TheFixCrossword

USA Today bestselling author Sylvie Stewart is addicted to Romantic Comedy and Contemporary Romance, and she's not looking for a cure. She hails from the great state of North Carolina, so it's no surprise that most of her books are set in the Tar Heel state. She's a wife to a hilarious dude and mommy to ten-year-old twin boys who tend to take after their father in every way. Sylvie often wonders if they're actually hers, but then she remembers being a human incubator for a gazillion months. Ah, good times.

Sylvie began publishing when her kids started elementary school, and she loves sharing her stories with readers and hopefully making them laugh and swoon a bit along the way. If she's not in her comfy green writing chair, she's probably camping or kayaking with her family or having a glass of wine while binge-watching Hulu. Or she's been kidnapped—so what are you doing just sitting there?!!

**Winner of the 2017 National Indie Excellence Award for Romantic Comedy

**Winner of the 2017 Readers' Favorite Silver Medal for Romantic Comedy

Thank you so much for reading *The Fix* – I hope you enjoyed it. If you did, a **review** on your favorite book site is always appreciated!

* * *

Want to stay updated on new releases, promotions and giveaways?
Subscribe to my newsletter! http://bit.ly/NewsSylvie

Want to hang out with me and my other readers?
Join my reader group on Facebook: **Sylvie's Spot - for the Sexy, Sassy, and Smartassy!** www.facebook.com/groups/SylviesSpot

Thanks! XOXO,
Sylvie

Keep up to date and keep in touch!
www.sylviestewartauthor.com
sylvie@sylviestewartauthor.com

facebook.com/SylvieStewartAuthor
twitter.com/sylvie_stewart_
instagram.com/sylvie.stewart.romance

THE SPARK: AN ENEMIES-TO-LOVERS ROMCOM

by Sylvie Stewart

COPYRIGHT

Chapter One

LUCKY

FIONA

"You must be so proud," yet another couple gushed while their eyes tracked me. Not that they were speaking to me, but everyone's eyes were always directed my way at these events. I was a bug under a microscope—a well-dressed and polished bug, but a bug nonetheless. I stood dutifully by as my parents received the compliment and my mother doled out air kisses to the couple decked out in expensive but understated formalwear.

Ugh.

We wouldn't want to go crazy and wear peek-a-boo lace or down-to-there necklines or, well, a color that actually stood a chance at catching someone's eye, now would we?

How inappropriate.

I didn't know how I was going to make it through another one of these yawn fests without at least something sparkly to look at.

Come on, people! It was as if the invitations had read "Attire: Funereal Chic." My gaze swept the room—black, black, black— ooh, charcoal! Wait, *red*! Oh, just the exit sign—my bad.

I was stuck in this receiving line of sorts with nary a glass of champagne to keep me entertained. My only small act of rebellion was wearing the sexiest, skimpiest pair of lilac lace panties I could find, but they were completely hidden under my (modest, of course) black sheath Dior gown. I had forgone the delicious red patent leather Manolos—the poor things were stuck at home in my closet, probably happy they didn't have to endure this evening's event.

"Shut up, Fiona! Positive thoughts, please," my inner voice, Guilt, reprimanded.

Oh, right. *Sorry.*

So right now, you might be curious as to why I was the reluctant center of attention at this function, and you may even sympathize with me for having to stand here sans champagne and bored out of my mind (sexy panties aside). But in a minute, you're going to agree with Guilt and think I'm a bitch.

You see, when all these people approach my parents and say, "You must be so proud," what some of them really mean is, "You're so goddamn lucky and a tiny part of me resents the shit out of you." But it would be unseemly to actually say that so they always go with the former comment.

Regardless of etiquette, behind their eyes I can always see the envy along with the effort it takes to not let it show. They would give anything, and I mean *anything*, to have a daughter like me.

I know, what a bitch, right?

But it's the God's honest truth. Many of these couples would trade their very lives to have what my parents have—a daughter who survived childhood cancer and lived to tell about it.

"I thought that went exceptionally well, didn't you?" my mother asked as she perched on the sofa next to me, her makeup still flawless and her blond up-do as elegant as it had been five hours earlier.

"Definitely," I agreed, removing my shoes to massage my sore feet. I mean, I may not have gotten to wear the Manolos but I wasn't a heathen or anything—I had still worn a pair of stilettos. At five-feet and a quarter (you bet your ass I'm including that extra quarter inch), I always wear heels—the higher the better.

Fact: adults don't take short people seriously. So I do anything I can to even the playing field. If I had a nickel for every time I'd been patted on the head by some patronizing asshole, I'd be—well, I'm already rich, so let's just say I'd be *disgustingly* rich.

To be fair, I, myself, am not actually rich, but my parents are. And they both evidently got straight As in preschool because they are awesome at sharing.

We have this odd relationship where I just exist and they are so tickled that they throw money at me. That, in and of itself, would be pretty pathetic, but along with the money, they also throw unwavering love, affection, and support in my direction and I hope I do a halfway decent job of returning the same to them. Lots of people say they have the best parents in the whole world, but I actually do. And that, in short, is why I can never say no when they ask for my help with The Foundation. That and my ever-present companion Guilt, of course.

"Ah, there are my beautiful girls!" my father said as he entered my parents' massive living room. He'd loosened his bow-tie and removed his tux jacket and was now looking between us and the screen of his smartphone. "Guess how much we netted? Just take a guess!" From his excitement, the answer was clearly a good one.

"$350,000?" my mother guessed.

"Um, $375,000 and Barbara Rogers' hotel keycard—I hear 80 is the new 40," I said, earning a nudge from my mother.

My dad looked at me with the most serious expression he could muster. "Fiona, you know I won't go older than 75—at that point they're more housecat than cougar."

I giggled—what can I say? I'm a daddy's girl. Did I mention how awesome my dad is?

"So, drum-roll please," he said and my mother and I dutifully tapped our respective sofa arms. "$432,350!"

Mom and I enthused appropriately and my dad went to the kitchen to fetch a bottle of champagne—finally, I was going to get some bubbly!

"Totally exhausting, but so worth it," my mother sighed as she let herself relax back into the cushions of the stylish gray sofa, her formal gown somehow remaining completely un-rumpled. I propped my stockinged feet on the designer coffee table and pretended not to see the chastising glance aimed at me. "This is going to make such a difference—I think this may put us over the top to get the new MRI for Children's."

We speak in shorthand around here where medical terminology, facilities, and organizations are so ingrained in our everyday dialogue that I often wonder if we need complete words at all. We're like a depressing version of a teenage text exchange.

Everything is "WBC," "ALL," "SCT," "Children's," and "County" to name just a few. And it's a good thing because if we used all the actual terms, we wouldn't ever have time to finish a conversation. For instance, saying "ALL" is a lot easier than saying "acute lymphocytic leukemia," which just happens to be the disease that has defined and redefined our lives over and over.

All right, so here's the 4-1-1: When I was nine years old I was diagnosed with ALL, and because of a series of unlucky test results and poor response to treatment, it was revealed that my chances were quite shitty. Undaunted, my parents used every resource available to them and refused to let the poor prognosis stick. It took three hospitals, a clinical trial, every alternative form of treatment my mother could find on the internet, and finally a stem-cell transplant to put me in remission. When I tell you that acupuncture was the highlight of my treatment plan, you understand how much the rest of it sucked donkey balls. And anybody who tells you acupuncture is "fabulous" or "so rejuvenating" is a big, fat, lying whore. Just so you know.

Where was I? Oh, right.

Needless to say, we were all elated when we got the good news that my leukemia was in remission and we would finally be able to return to normal life. The only problem? There was no "normal" to go back to.

Suddenly, our whole family was grappling with a host of conflicting emotions. For the two years we'd been fighting the disease, we'd assumed the finish line was remission. Instead, we were almost paralyzed by the simultaneous onslaught of not just the joy, but also fear, guilt, and sadness. What if it comes back? Why did we reach remission when so many others didn't? What comes next? And what happened to the sense of innocence an eleven-year-old is entitled to?

It was at this point in my life that Guilt moved into my consciousness and made herself comfortable. As far as I can tell, she spends her days tsk-ing disapprovingly at the cobwebs in my head and honing her skills as the most spectacularly annoying backseat driver ever. I would not recommend her as a house guest.

After a few weeks, I attempted to return to the life of a typical eleven-year-old, but everything was so different and awkward. My brain didn't seem to want to work the same anymore, and things that had previously come easily to me were suddenly overwhelming. I was having trouble remembering things, and my academic performance, which had always been stellar, began a downward spiral, with tests and homework becoming a huge struggle.

There were also physical implications from the disease and its treatment, the most noticeable of which was my development, or more specifically my lack thereof. While other girls my age were shooting up like beanstalks and wearing training bras, I was still essentially living in the body of a nine-year-old, with stunted growth and hormonal issues, neither of which would ever fully resolve—much to my dismay (see previous short-person rant).

In addition to all these issues, and possibly even because of them, my social life was a mess. My friends, classmates, and teachers treated me either like glass or like I didn't exist, their discomfort achingly obvious—which was all particularly hurtful to a young girl who had spent her childhood as a total people-person, embracing the world with complete exuberance and in the girliest manner possible.

I longed to return to the ease of my pre-cancer life but knew that I should just be happy to be alive. To ease the situation for everyone, I resolved to plaster a smile on my face so no one would think me ungrateful or worry about me. It was a habit I still maintained much of the time.

Meanwhile, out of a combined sense of gratefulness and contrition, my parents dove headlong into establishing a foundation for cancer research and childhood cancer facilities. To this day, it sometimes seems my mother's entire reason for existence is to spare other families the devastation wreaked by cancer. Other times, I'm reminded that about forty percent of her existence is actually reserved for worrying about me and trying to smother me —with love and attention. Although it often feels like plain old-fashioned smothering—you know, like with a pillow.

Obviously, my father is also very involved in what we call "The Foundation." But somebody has to bring in the big bucks, so he also runs the family's tech firm in Raleigh while my mom holds the reigns of The Foundation and I pitch in when called upon.

Then about four years ago, when I had reached my nine-year anniversary of remission, I decided to leave the nest—you know, the one full of pillows—and move to Greensboro to branch out on my own. I was twenty and finding it very difficult to find direction, so I figured becoming more independent might help me out.

My parents naturally fought it at first, but they eventually relented and bought me a gorgeous condo in a downtown high-rise with amazing floor-to-ceiling windows and two balconies. I freaking love it! They wanted to buy me a house, but I am way too much of a girly-girl to be responsible for my own appliances and grass and stuff. No thanks. I did mention the heels, right? Well, there is a whole designer wardrobe to go along with those heels and not a single pair of overalls in it. They also wanted to buy me a Mercedes, but I talked them down to a Prius with a mere mention of environmental effects and carcinogens.

So, I had my own place and my own life in Greensboro, and it was only an hour and a half to Raleigh so my parents could still hover enough to keep them relatively content. The one thing I still didn't have, though, was direction. It apparently didn't come with the new life and new condo like a gift-with-purchase at Nordstrom. I've spent the last four years floating from job to job trying to figure out what I want to do with my life and having very little luck.

The floating around has, however, provided a couple of amazing benefits—some really hilarious and awesome experiences, and some really hilarious and awesome friends. The greatest of these is, of course, my best friend in the whole wide world, Laney.

She and I met when I was doing a brief stint as a receptionist at the same company she was temping for. At the time, Laney had been raising a baby, going to college, and working a part-time job.

Needless to say, Laney rocks, and I am in complete awe of her most of the time. She is a single mom to a five-year-old little heart-breaker named Rocco (Oh, excuse me, he now demands that I say he is five-and-three-quarters) and she almost ties my mom for being the best mom in the world. However, Laney's inability to wear stilettos or any article of clothing made from a material other than cotton will eventually result in Rocco growing up to marry a girl with similarly bad taste—and that's just irresponsible. Therefore, she rates second in the best mom competition.

What my best friend lacks in fashion sense, though, she makes up for in her taste in men. She recently scored herself one seriously hot man in the form of an adorably doting construction god named Nate. I often want to cry tears of joy at his love and dedication to Laney and Rocco—well that and his tight ass.

What? Laney doesn't care that I ogle him. Sometimes we even do it together. It's a bonding thing.

Laney has not had the easiest time since she accidentally got knocked up her freshman year of college and the douchebag dad essentially skipped the scene. So seeing her and Rocco with such a great guy does things to my heart. It almost makes me wonder if that's something I could want for myself. Almost.

But I have my condo and my various jobs and my flitting back and forth to Raleigh, not to mention Guilt to keep me company, so I'm good.

My phone vibrated on the coffee table next to my empty crystal flute, sending me reminders I'd need for the morning. This particular night of flitting to Raleigh was thankfully over and had ended just as I preferred—with a drink and the people I love. Celebratory champagne consumed and the night's events adequately dissected, my parents and I doled out goodnight kisses and decided it was time for bed.

The thought of driving back to Greensboro so late was unappealing at best, and with the bubbly coursing through me, would have been idiotic. I am not the most responsible person on a good day—Guilt can attest—and I have a healthy respect for my own limits, so driving would just be begging for trouble. Instead, I crashed in my old bedroom. This happens often enough that I keep a small wardrobe and stash of beauty supplies at my parents' house for just such times. I consulted my phone on the next day's plans and slipped into my nightgown. As soon as my head hit the pillow, I was out.

Thank God for champagne.

Oh right, and for letting me be alive.

Can I go to sleep now, Guilt?

GO TEAM!

MARK

Maybe if I just opened one eye it wouldn't be so bad.

I slowly lifted my left eyelid but quickly snapped it shut again as the morning light seared through my eyeball on a direct path to my brain.

Ow.

Last night had not been one of my better ideas.

Time to man up. I gradually opened both eyes and then blinked rapidly, finally registering the unfamiliar light fixture above me. The bed shifted slightly and I stilled every muscle. Shit!

I tried to recall last night's events, but things were a bit fuzzy past the numerous shots at the bar. Everything I knew about myself promised that my bedmate was at least of the female variety, but any other details were up for grabs. I was extremely confident in my sexuality, but I was equally confident in the power of Jack Daniels.

Ever so slowly, I looked to my side. Okay, lots of dark hair on the pillow—long dark hair—this was good. I could resume breathing.

Wait, not too fast. I didn't want to wake her up.

I carefully rose onto an elbow to have a look around. My brain throbbed painfully in my skull.

So, not my bedroom. And definitely not my sheets. These had a bunch of colorful girly shit on them. Was that…were those fucking unicorns? It was then I realized I was naked—naked on a shitload of unicorns.

Oh, God, please tell me I did not just spend the night with a teenager! How could this happen? I was at a bar last night, not a high school party! I looked around frantically for some evidence that this was, in fact, an adult's room and not that of an underaged girl. *Sweet Jesus, what had I done?!*

A pink lava lamp on the bedside table—*Shit!*

A stuffed rabbit on a chair in the corner—*Shit! Shit! Shit!*

And the rabbit was holding a baby bunny in its fluffy rabbit paws.

Fuck me—I was going to jail.

I was too pretty to go to jail, and I definitely didn't want to be anyone's bitch. My mom always told me my smile would get me in trouble one day, and here it was. That day had arrived. My perfect smile was going to land me in a twelve-by-twelve cell with a roommate named Attila who would probably want to call me *his* baby bunny.

"Oh goody, you're awake!" a high-pitched voice came from the pillow next to mine. My head swiveled around and I got my first sober look at the girl who would be the cause of my incarceration. Okay, well, Jack had a partial share in the responsibility, but whatever.

She did indeed have long dark hair that was currently in a rat's nest around her head, and she had one of those little pug noses that can sometimes be cute, but when faced with a future in the state penitentiary, I wasn't finding anything cute.

She offered me an extremely wide smile and almost bounced in the bed while remaining horizontal. She was very cheerful. And young.

Cheerful and young…and bouncy…cheerful and young? And bouncy?

Wait one minute—it was coming back to me! I sprang up in bed, ignoring my complete nudity, and searched the floor—and there it was. A goddamn cheerleading uniform.

Nooooooo!

"Baby, what's the matter?" the little jailbait asked.

"You're a cheerleader," was all I could say. Or whimper.

"Duh," she perked up. "Remember? Goooooooo Mark!"

I cringed and then looked back at her. In the midst of her cheer she had lost the top half of the sheet and her plump breasts were on display. I lunged for the sheet to cover her up but she obviously misunderstood my intent.

"Oh, yay, are we playing lion and lion-tamer again?! Rawr!"

"No!" I yelled at her. "No more playing! I need to get out of here. Oh my God." I put my head in my hands and tried to fight off the giant migraine that was forming so I could come up with a plan. A plan that did not involve a three-hundred-pound man feeding me, *ahem*, carrots.

"Oh, okay," she chirped. I chanced a glance at her again to see her shrug and then climb out of bed buck-ass naked.

I was not only going to jail, I was also going to hell.

"I have to go to class anyway. Leave your number if you want —maybe I'll call you sometime. Thanks for the fun night!" She slipped on a robe, blew me a kiss, and opened the bedroom door, grabbing a shower caddy on her way out.

Thank my lucky motherfucking stars—I was in a college dorm.

* * *

"Why does all the awesome stuff always happen to you?!" Brett asked as he slapped the table in frustration and then took a gulp of his beer.

What I was doing at a bar again was beyond me, but I was still freaked out by my near miss from the night before and I didn't feel like hanging out at my place alone. I took a sip of my soda and gave him a look that I hoped communicated exactly how stupid I found him. "Did you not just hear that story?" I looked around the table at the other two guys sitting with us, but they didn't seem to think Brett's comment was anything less than spot-on.

"Dude, you spent the night in a women's college dormitory with a fucking cheerleader. How old are you? Twenty-eight? Twenty-nine? That doesn't happen. And not only did you bang the cheerleading co-ed, she then invited you to come back again and bang her some more. This is like the foundation for every teenage boy's spank bank. Scratch that—every male on earth, not just the teenagers," said Brett.

"I have to say, I'm definitely filing it away," said Gavin, a friend from work. Gavin's sister, Laney, was dating my buddy Nate, who also happened to be my sort-of boss. Yeah, confusing, but we'll get to that later.

"I might be sporting wood right now thinking about it," said Trey, as he raised a handful of peanuts to his mouth.

We all looked at him with a good measure of revulsion.

"Dude, keep it to yourself or just go home," said Gavin.

"You know those nuts have been touched by probably a hundred guys who didn't wash their hands after taking a leak, right?" Brett pointed to the peanuts and Trey dropped them on the table.

"Whatever," I said, sweeping the mess of nuts aside. "You guys don't fully understand the feeling I had when I woke up and thought for just those few moments that I had crossed that uncrossable line. It was…it was…indescribable. I mean, I was scared shitless and I completely loathed myself. It was awful." I suppressed a shudder just thinking about it.

"Okay." Gavin raised a hand like he was asking permission to speak. "Let's assume for a moment that this was really as bad as you say." I nodded and he went on. "What if you, I don't know, stopped drinking to the point where you black out and bang a complete stranger who may or may not have a daddy waiting down the hall with a loaded shotgun?" He shrugged. "Just an idea."

Huh. It was possible he could have a point.

"Nah," said Trey. "I say you go back next weekend. I'll be happy to be your wingman. I used to play football in high school—

I'm feeling the need to hear someone cheering my name again—Trey, Trey, Trey!" He raised his beer in a toast and simulated humping under the table. Why did I hang out with this guy again?

Oh yeah, because I did stupid shit like that too.

God, I was a mess.

* * *

Today was going to be a new day. I was going to clean up my behavior and start acting responsibly—well *more* responsibly at least. It was, after all, completely moronic to drink so much that (a) I couldn't remember who I'd screwed, (b) I couldn't be one hundred percent certain I'd used a condom—*I know. Just don't, okay?*—, and (c) I could have conceivably broken the law as well as about two hundred moral codes. I'd never envisioned myself as such a douchebag.

In general, I'd say I am a pretty dependable guy. I have a good job working for a construction company called Built by Murphy, and I'm well thought of there, as far as I know. My friend Nate's family owns the company and they've been really good to me. I started out working there after high school while I took night classes at community college, and over the years I've worked my way up to foreman and then, more recently, taken on responsibilities on the administrative side. I get paid well, I work hard, and I enjoy the job and the people I work with.

In fact, out of all the guys I know in their late twenties, I'm probably the most responsible among us—in theory, at least. I don't own a home, but I rent a house and I keep it furnished with nice stuff that I take care of. I know what it's like to live in shit and

I don't reckon I'd like to revisit that experience, so I'm generally careful with my things and my work. I have a truck that may not be the latest model, but it does the trick. I've worked hard for my success, which is another reason I was so pissed at myself for losing sight of that and acting like an idiot.

After the night out with the guys, I'd had a hard time sleeping and couldn't seem to shut my mind off. It could have been the caffeine from the soda, but I had a suspicion it was more than likely a guilty conscience. *Yes, even I have a conscience.* Most of my brain wanted to blame my bonehead behavior on the Jack, but there was that one part telling me that maybe I was getting too old to be such a manwhore. Or not. It was too painful to think anymore.

I ended up getting out of bed at five and going for a run before hitting the gym. I gave a chin lift to Blaine, one of the trainers, on my way out of the locker room. The gym was practically empty at this time on a Sunday morning, with only a few of my fellow die-hards present. I threw my towel on one of the benches and began to stack the weights for my first set of reps.

The gym is my zen place. I don't like to brag—okay, that's not true, I totally like to brag—but I'm a super fit guy. I work out religiously and love to challenge myself and push my limits. I do an hour of cardio six days a week and I do weight training five days a week, rotating areas of the body to achieve maximum results. And I definitely achieve the desired results if the looks I get from women are anything to go by. And then there's that smile my mom was always talking about, so you do the math.

I don't have to try too hard to get a girl into my bed when I want one. Which, I'll be honest, is pretty often. I like all kinds of women—curvy, thin, short, tall, blond, brunette. As long as it's not the same girl twice, I'm game.

I don't do repeats. It's too much hassle—feelings get involved and then I have to try to avoid the girl and it's just a headache I don't need. Instead, I'm always upfront and tell every girl I'm with that all I'm looking for is a good time. One night of fun and then we part as friends. Or not precisely friends—in fact, the exact opposite. We part as strangers—just how it was meant to be.

So, the fly in the ointment must have been the alcohol because my fuck-and-run policy was certainly not the problem. It had always worked perfectly for me and I was getting too old to drink like that anyway. I was just going to have to cut down on the booze, just like Gavin had suggested. Awesome plan.

See, I told you the gym was my zen place.

Problem solved.

* * *

"Why are these girls so fucking boring?" I asked Nate for the third time that night as I returned to our table.

"Maybe because you're sober as a judge and you're not blocking out their voices while mentally undressing them?" he returned.

No, that wasn't it. I was definitely mentally undressing them. They were just boring as shit.

Gavin had recruited Nate to help clean up my act—you had to admire his youthful energy and optimism. Somehow they had talked me into going to happy hour after work on Friday to hone my new technique. Ha!

Their plan was for me to attempt to meet an "appropriate" girl without the aid of alcohol and then—*choke*—simply engage her in conversation instead of seducing her and taking her home. What was the fun in that? What were we, high school virgins?

Oh right, now I remembered the reason for this little intervention. I decided to placate them and give it a try, but I didn't really see the point.

"How do you ever expect to meet the right girl if you can't have a conversation with her before you whip it out?" asked Nate as he checked his phone. Probably looking for messages from Laney—he was so pussy whipped I was almost embarrassed for him. He'd turned into a fuckmuppet.

"I meet the 'right girl' all the time," I told him. "I think you and I have different definitions of the 'right girl.' My definition involves the girl who's right for my dick on that particular night." I fist bumped Gavin as Nate's eyes lifted from his phone and he gave me a look you'd give a dog who'd just eaten its own shit.

"What?!" I demanded.

"For the moment, let's set aside the issues of possible incarceration and diseases that make your dick fall off. Do you want to be 'that guy'?" Nate asked.

"You'll have to elaborate—my mind is still numb from the conversation I just had with that girl at the bar. She wouldn't shut up about her pet cockatoo, and I wasn't even allowed to make any awesome jokes about it."

Nate hastily dropped his phone on the table and threw his hand out in exasperation. "The pathetic guy who's in his mid-thirties and still trolling for college chicks while his friends are starting families and not having to spare any thoughts for STDs and psycho one-night-stands!"

"That was only once, and how was I supposed to know she'd just gotten out of rehab?!" I pointed my finger in his face and then grabbed my drink, forgetting for a moment that it contained no alcohol. "Since when did you get so old and boring?!" I demanded and slammed my glass down. "This sucks!" I may have whined a bit.

"Tell that to my cockatoo," Gavin snorted and then ducked as my fist almost connected with the side of his head. I wasn't going to actually hit him but I wouldn't have been too sad if he'd at least fallen off his stool, the asshole. Nothing was going my way tonight.

"Okay," Gavin said once he'd stopped laughing and deemed it safe to resume his position on his stool. "Let's do a little math here." He spared Nate a glance. "I'm not sure I'm with you a hundred percent on this one, Nate." His gaze turned back to me. "How old are you?"

"Twenty-nine."

"So, half plus seven—that gives us twenty-one and a half— let's be safe and go with twenty-two. It's not socially acceptable for you to date or bone anyone under the age of twenty-two… which makes last weekend pretty fucked up." As if I didn't know that already.

"We've established that, thank you, Dr. Drew," said Nate. Why in the hell was *he* so agitated? That was *my* gig tonight—he needed to get in line.

"So, all I'm saying is you don't have to be all domestic like dickless wonder over here—" He gestured to Nate who opened his mouth to object. Gavin's hand shot out to intercept. "Don't even try it—you're dating my sister. It is my God-given right to consider you a eunuch." Gavin then looked back at me. "Maybe you can at least take a girl out to dinner first—wouldn't hurt to try. Hell, I'm a lot younger than you and even I take a girl out—well, most of the time."

Well, shit, now I'd been slut-shamed and kind of felt like a cross between a lecher and Charlie Sheen—wait, was that redundant? Not important. Instead, I made a mental note to go get tested on Monday.

Nate turned to Gavin with a half-awed, half-amused expression. "I kind of want to take a video of your little speech and show Laney—you sound so grown up I think she would cry."

Gavin just responded by flipping him off, making the whole point completely moot.

I felt my phone vibrate in my pocket and pulled it out to see who was calling, hoping for a distraction.

Shit. My mom.

I was not in the right head space to talk to her right now, although she did provide further evidence of why romantic relationships are way more trouble than they're worth. I noted the time —8:15. I'd only be here a bit longer and then I'd call on my way home to check on her.

"So," Nate continued, fidgeting on his stool, "I've gotta get over to Laney's soon, but if you're both done striking out with all the girls in this bar, I need your help with something."

"Anything to get off this topic," I offered.

He paused and folded and unfolded the bar napkin in front of him. He looked weird. Was he gonna puke?

"Dude, do I need to hold your hair back or something? You look like you're gonna puke," said Gavin, echoing my thoughts.

"No, I'm not going to puke!" Nate bellowed as the napkin tore in two.

"Well, you look like it. Oh wait, do you have the shits? Do you need me to walk out behind you? If that's it, you're going to owe me big-time!" Gavin grumbled.

"I don't have the shits—Jesus, Gavin—I'm going to ask your sister to marry me!" He looked dumbstruck that those words had escaped his mouth, and he face-planted on the table.

"Fuck," was all I could say.

"Dude," Gavin said, and then promptly fell off his stool.

Huh, look at that—something finally went my way.

Chapter Three

MY FAVORITE RIVER IN EGYPT

FIONA

"Oh my God. I think I just had a tiny orgasm," Laney whispered under her breath, closing her eyes and licking her lips to retrieve any stray remnants of sauce she may have left behind. "You are more than welcome to work your culinary magic in my kitchen anytime," she said as if she'd forgotten that I cook at her house at least once a week as it is.

"Why, thank you. The pleasure's apparently all yours," I laughed at her. I love cooking for other people—it's depressing cooking for one. And leftovers suck, unless of course it's Chinese takeout.

"Wasn't that awesome, Nate?" Laney asked her hot-ass boyfriend who was silently staring at her mouth with his fork stock-still in midair. His dark hair was in need of a cut, but it did nothing to detract from his general hotness.

I snapped my fingers in front of his perfect scruffy face and he suddenly came to. "Oh no, lover boy—no dirty thoughts allowed at the dinner table. I have to eat here too and I don't need mental images of you two going to pound town on this table."

"Tell her to stop moaning and maybe I can accommodate you," Nate addressed me but his eyes were still glued to my best friend.

Okay, this was just getting gross. It was time to either stage an intervention or get laid myself *very* soon.

Laney blushed on her side of the table and put a finger to her mouth to shush us as her other hand gestured to the living room where her son Rocco was playing. He'd started the dinner with us, but it would seem my pork tenderloin masterpiece had missed the mark for him if the number of rolls he'd consumed was any indication. He'd been let off the hook early.

As if he'd been summoned, the little guy yelled from the other room, "I have dirty thoughts all the time, Aunt Fiona!"

We all stilled and Laney glared at us in a manner that would give Anna Wintour a run for her money.

"POOOOOOP!"

"Rocco!" Laney scolded.

"What?" he asked. "I think about poop a lot. What's dirtier than that?"

She shook her head and Anna Wintoured us again.

"What?" Nate and I asked simultaneously.

"Soooo, this is a new development," I said to Laney as she and I sat on her couch having a glass of wine after dinner. Nate had taken Rocco to get ready for bed without any assistance required from Laney. "I knew Rocco liked it when Nate read to him, but the whole routine? I'm impressed."

"I know," she said with that annoying dreamy look on her face. Okay, it wasn't annoying—it was frickin' adorable. "Aside from his freakishly organized living habits and maybe his obsession with Notre Dame, I can't find a thing wrong with him."

"Go Tar Heels!" We erupted simultaneously. Enough said.

"Is he finally going to move in?" I asked. He'd been having "sleepovers" at Laney's since the holidays and it was March now, so I didn't see what the hold-up was.

Laney's brow creased and the dreamy look disappeared. Uh oh. "I thought he was. I mean, we've talked about it and it just seems like the next natural step." She gestured toward the hallway. "Rocco absolutely worships him and I know Nate loves us. But he's been acting a bit…*off* these last couple weeks." Her hand rose to her cheek and she rubbed it—this being her habit whenever she gets stressed or uncomfortable.

"It's probably just work." I waved her off, hoping I was right. "And besides, I was moments away from excusing myself at the dinner table so you two could go ahead and play hide-the-pork-tenderloin in private—I wouldn't be too concerned."

She smacked my arm and I almost spilled my wine.

"Hey! Watch it," I scolded her. "I just bought this blouse and I don't want to soak it in red wine if you don't mind. It's not like I could borrow anything from *your* closet to wear home—how embarrassing," I teased and then shielded myself from further assault.

I love giving her a hard time about her uber-casual wardrobe— I mean the girl wears athletic shoes to work, for Christ's sake (oh, and I'm not referring to Jesus with that expression—"Christ" is just my pet name for Christian Dior). But as long as she lets me dress her up like my own personal Barbie now and then, I'm usually content.

Laney is one of those women who should have lived in the fifties, although she would never have survived as a stereotypical housewife type considering her closets are those of a hoarder and her idea of a home-cooked meal is frozen pizza. However, she has boobs and booty for *days* and I love dressing her up and showing off her, ahem, *assets*. She is also a good five inches taller than me (sigh) and has thick, glossy hair that hangs in a dark sheath halfway down her back. I try to buy her clothes all the time but she has very strict boundaries, which I can respect even if I don't totally understand. A sweater from a local boutique is okay, but a nightie from La Perla is sent right back—it's not like I could wear it. Please, my whole body could fit in her bra cup, sadly.

"Whatever." She blew me off, as usual. "So, on to *your* love life…any hot dates lined up?"

"Unfortunately, no. My muffin will remain unbuttered this weekend. No pork tenderloin in sight." I stuck my lower lip out in a pout. I was in a dry spell, as in the Sahara, and I was in desperate need with no prospects on the horizon—only mirages where my vibrator then had to play stand-in-stud.

"Why don't you call Terrence?" Laney asked so quietly I almost didn't hear her. She was hiding her face behind her dark hair.

"Um, excuse me?"

She faced me fully again. "I know—you don't want a relationship, but we love Terrence," she pleaded.

"*You* love Terrence. *I* love Terrence's man parts."

"God, you're such a guy," she said in disgust.

"Love and commitment are perfect and dreamy for you and Nate, and that's awesome—for you. I'm just not wired that way, and you know I don't feel that way about Terrence. We had a perfect arrangement and then he screwed it up by asking for more. I'm sure his 'more' girl is out there, but she is not me."

It was Laney's turn to pull out the pouty lower lip.

"As much as I love you, Laney, I'm not getting into a relationship just so we can double date and have a Brady Brides wedding. Although, if that were to somehow happen in an alternate universe, you know I'd be Marcia, right? I mean, just admit it. She was always the better dresser."

"Fine," she conceded, to which part I wasn't sure, but I was relieved to have the subject closed.

* * *

On my drive home, I was distracted by thoughts of our conversation and of Terrence. Thinking about him always made me alternately mad and nostalgic. Thinking about my love life in general usually conjured conflicting emotions.

Terrence and I had met a little over a year ago when I had been traveling to one of The Foundation's events to stand in for my mother. I was flying to DC and found myself killing time in the Ambassador's lounge, waiting for my delayed flight, when an extremely handsome pilot strode into the room. He was tall with short cropped hair and dark brown skin, his face bright with a smile.

I remember wondering who elicited such a response and feeling a flash of jealousy—or maybe just longing—to be a person who could provoke that kind of joy. I kept watch out of the corner of my eye as he flirted with a flight attendant, and I was all but captivated by his laugh. I don't know how to describe it, but it just made me feel happy and weirdly carefree.

After the flight attendant left, the man who later introduced himself as Terrence Dunbar seated himself across from me. I surreptitiously assessed him from my seat—and was evidently not as subtle as I'd intended to be because it was only moments before he struck up a conversation with me. His slightly crooked but utterly charming smile was almost as captivating as his laugh, and he had an uncanny talent for making me feel like I was the most important thing in the world to him at that moment.

We ended up talking and laughing for an hour before I had to rush to my gate. I only found out later that he'd intended to stop in the lounge for a mere five minutes but had stayed just to talk to me. I'd given him my number and he'd promised to call the next time he was in town.

Thus began our friends-with-bennies arrangement. It was perfect—neither of us wanted the entanglements of a relationship, and we both happened to find each other attractive and fun to be around.

And the sex was hot.

H-O-T.

But, just as I'd known they would, things came to an end. Terrence came to Greensboro one weekend for one of our sex-a-thons and declared that he wanted to move things to the "next level." I'm ashamed to admit I became a bit enraged and I'm sure I completely overreacted, but I was pissed that he had taken what I found to be a perfect arrangement and ruined it. I told him what he could do with his "next level" and hadn't spoken with him since.

Harsh, I know.

But it's for his own good. I promise. There is something broken in me. Or more accurately, there are a lot of things broken in me.

Terrence deserves better. He deserves a woman who will adore him and who he can adore in return—one who will give him babies with his gorgeous skin and crooked smile, and that woman will wake up every morning confident that she is the center of his world.

I know Laney was disappointed that Terrence and I were unable to, in the immortal words of Tim Gunn, "make it work," but I knew deep down that I'd done the right thing by breaking it off. He had certainly lit up many parts of me, and the things he could do with his—well, I digress. Suffice it to say, as much as he lit up my lady bits he never lit up my heart, and once it had become clear that he wanted to involve that organ, as opposed to just the one below his belt, I knew it was time to move on.

So, if I had to pretend to be glib about it to avoid talking about my "issues," so be it. Denial is not just a river in Egypt, as you well know.

Chapter Four

ET TU, PA?

FIONA

"Dr. Brandon is ready to see you, Fiona," said Darcy, one of my favorite PAs in the oncology department. Tearing my attention from my phone, I smiled and followed her, chatting about her kids and what had been happening in both our lives in the year since we'd seen each other.

I was there for my annual "make sure the bitch isn't back" appointment—my thirteenth such visit, so I was very familiar with the routine. For those of you lucky enough to be unschooled in the world of cancer, an annual visit to one's *pediatric* oncologist after thirteen years of remission is not exactly normal. However, in the world of my overprotective mother, it's required—unless I want to look into her tear-filled eyes and try to explain why I don't need to go. Yeah, not gonna happen. And despite the lack of any suspicious symptoms to suggest a possible illness, I still get chills running up my spine every time I approach Dr. Brandon's door.

"Fiona," Dr. Brandon said as he came out from behind his desk and wrapped me in a bear hug. "How are you, sweetheart?" He is a tall barrel-chested man in his sixties and has a neatly trimmed beard that has grayed over the years. His reading glasses are an ever-present decoration around his neck, and his tie is permanently askew. It was nice to see that nothing had changed in the last year.

"I'm good," I told him, hugging him back. I love this guy. He'd been my knight in shining armor when I'd been a petrified nine-year-old and he'd held my hand and told me we'd slay the mean old leukemia dragon together. And to this day I hold on to some of that old hero worship. I can't help it—he's like Santa Claus and Pa from *Little House* combined into one awesome guy.

"Where are you working these days?" he asked, knowing my penchant for drifting from job to job. I released him, and he walked back to the chair behind his giant oak desk, a smirk on his face. Did I say Santa Claus? Maybe not.

"Haha," I responded, but really had no good comeback. I had only been at my current job for two months after quitting my last one where I'd been working as a gofer for a promotions company and getting a skeevy vibe from my boss. Can you blame me for quitting? Well, technically I was fired, but who's keeping track? My new job wasn't anything glamorous, but at least my boss was cool and he didn't hit on me. "I'm working for a landscaping company answering phones and filing and stuff," I answered, knowing just how unexciting it sounded.

"Do you like it?" he asked, genuinely interested, I knew.

Ugh. I felt like I was disappointing him. "Yeah!" I said cheer-fully, hoping to move on to the next topic. My job was only slightly more interesting than watching golf on TV, but I didn't mind. It was stress-free and it didn't hurt my brain.

"Hmph." He let out a small sound, communicating just how unconvincing I'd been. "All right. I'll let you off the hook and get down to business." He raised his glasses to his eyes and opened the file sitting on his desk.

My heart rate suddenly skyrocketed and I had the distinct sensation that I might actually faint. What was wrong with me? My breathing picked up. Surely he wouldn't have been so nice and casual if there was bad news to deliver. Pa Ingalls would never do that!

Breathe, Fiona. It's been thirteen years.

"Your blood tests look great."

Mini heart attack averted. Whoa, Nelly.

See what I did there? Nelly from Little House?

No? Okay, whatever. I was nervous—you can't expect perfection.

My hand went to my chest where my heart was still working overtime. "Wow, I didn't expect to feel this anxious after all this time. I mean, I know you only see me because my mother hounds you," I noted with the best grin I could muster.

"You know I look forward to our visits, sweetheart. And your smiling face always brightens my day." I knew what he meant without him having to explain. We share an unshakable affection for one another, but he is a pediatric oncologist and doesn't get to deliver tons of good news on a daily basis.

"As do I," I told him. "Kind of." I smiled.

He gave a low chuckle. "Okay, lab work aside, I also got the results back from your cardiologist and things look good on that front as well. Have you noticed any changes either physically or mentally that I should be aware of?" he asked.

Ugh. "Not really. My memory is still a bit screwy, as usual, and my cycle is practically nonexistent. I'm still waiting for that growth spurt I know is coming any day for sure, though," I joked, trying to keep things light. I even threw in a cheesy smile and a thumbs-up.

"Are you able to keep a handle on it?" he asked, ignoring my lame attempts at humor.

"Pretty much." I held up my phone. "That's why I have a phone that's smart—so I don't have to be," I tried to joke again but he was having none of it. I took in his chastising expression and thought about trying again—*I'll tell you, doc, the damn thing vibrates so much it almost eliminates the need for a date!*

Maybe not.

Quick! Change of topic!

"So how are your kids?" I blurted out.

Dr. Brandon has three grown children and is amassing a collection of grandkids that seems to grow like a rabbit colony every year. It's as if the women in his family are in competition with the Duggars to see whose uterus will fall out of her body first. Perhaps that was a bit hostile—I expected my wine to taste a tad sour this evening.

"Wonderful, as usual—Jenny and Isaac just opened a spa in High Point—did I tell you that?" he asked, already knowing he hadn't, but proud of his daughter and needing to brag on her a bit. "And three new grandkids since I saw you last." He pointed to a corkboard on his wall that was crammed with photo after photo of cute little kids (and some not so cute, but I oohed and aahed anyway). "What about you?" he asked.

I was momentarily shocked as I wondered what would possess him to ask such an insensitive question—until I noticed his pose. He was leaned into his desk with his hands folded perfectly in front of him and his head lowered just enough that he could look over his glasses.

Oh no. Lecture pose.

Retreat!

"What about me?" I laughed lightly, fooling no one.

"When are you going to find a nice guy and settle down?"

I waved him off. "Doc, I'm only twenty-four. What's the hurry?"

"Uh-huh, I know, but that's been your excuse the last four times I've asked and I know for a fact you haven't had a single boyfriend."

I inhaled sharply. "How do you know that?!"

"How do you think I know that?" His left eyebrow quirked.

Damn meddling mother! Damn HIPPA—I sign away my privacy way too quickly.

Crap!

Dr. Brandon is a close friend of my parents, as they've worked together on many projects with The Foundation since he became my oncologist years ago. He has offices in Raleigh and Greensboro, and I swear his presence in this city was one of the reasons my mother relented when I wanted to move here. Additionally, I unfailingly sign my stupid HIPPA paperwork every year, allowing the good doctor to discuss my medical information with my mother and father at will. Unfortunately, my mother doesn't seem to find it inappropriate to reciprocate by sharing my dating history with him! *Dammit!*

"I'm disowning her," I declared.

He laughed. "She's just worried about you."

"Well, she'll be a lot more worried when I disappear to Fiji and stop speaking to her."

"Fiona." He looked at me over his glasses again.

I couldn't help it. I hung my head and folded my hands in my lap. "What?"

"What you're feeling is not at all abnormal. Lots of survivors have a hard time forging personal and intimate relationships. I just don't want you to miss out on the good stuff in life because of fear. You may not believe it but you're one of the toughest people I know and I—*we*—want you to be happy and fulfilled. Moving from job to job and guy to guy without establishing any roots? Is this making you happy?"

I started to tear up because he wasn't telling me anything I didn't already know. But I'm usually great at putting on a happy face and shoving the truth down deep where I don't have to acknowledge it.

"I know it's not as simple as I'm making it sound and I don't want to upset you, but I wouldn't feel as if I were doing a good job as both your doctor and your friend if I didn't at least bring it up. Please, Fiona, give it some more thought and, for God's sake, pick up the phone and call me if you want to talk. I'm always here." He stood. His glasses went back around his neck, settling over his crooked tie, and he opened his arms for another hug.

Damn Pa! I went to him like Laura after someone pulled on her braids.

Chapter Five

I'LL TAKE HELL IF PURGATORY IS ANYTHING LIKE THIS

MARK

"This is ridiculous!" I thought to myself. The woman sitting two seats over got up and switched to a seat across the room from me. So maybe I hadn't said it to myself after all.

I dropped my head down, elbows on my knees, as I waited for my mother to reappear from behind the closed double doors of the emergency room. My hand scrubbed at my short hair in a futile attempt to release some of my frustration.

Why did they have to make these waiting room seats so uncomfortable? And what was with this reading material? The least they could do was give me *Men's Health* or even *Car and Driver*, but all they had were chick magazines. And I already knew how to bring a girl to orgasm in less than five minutes, thank you very much. That thought brought the first smile to cross my face all day.

It was the Friday after Nate's momentous announcement, and

the mental replay of Gavin falling off his barstool had kept me entertained all week.

What? I'm easily amused.

We'd been of absolutely no help in coming up with a good proposal plan, but Nate should have known better. He needed to talk to his sister, Bailey, if he wanted advice that didn't include a reenactment of Justin Timberlake and Andy Samberg's famous "Dick in a Box" skit. Pretty sure the answer would be a right hook if he took guidance from us. Although come to think of it, Bailey would probably give even worse advice so he was pretty much screwed.

I'd been behaving myself all week, not drinking and not even going out to the bars to scope out the talent. And what was my reward? A phone call from my mom at four this morning begging for a ride to the ER. Let me tell you, that is not a call any son wants to get, early morning or any damn time.

Luckily, she was not the one who'd been injured.

No, as if the Fates were punishing me for my bad behavior with the co-ed, it had been my dad who'd landed himself in the ER —my piece-of-shit dad whom I hadn't seen in eight years and whom I'd hoped to never see again. Thus the reason I was going out of my mind in the waiting room while my mom was somewhere back in the ER with the dirty son-of-a-bitch.

Why? I had no damn clue.

When I'd picked up the phone this morning, I hadn't been able to understand a word my mother was saying, but I did finally catch something about a hospital. Once I'd calmed her down a bit, she'd been able to explain.

"It's your father," she'd said, sniffling.

"What the hell do you mean?" I'd asked, still half asleep but relieved to hear she wasn't hurt.

"The hospital just called and said that your father was brought in late last night by ambulance and he was unconscious and b-b-beaten." She started to cry again.

What. The. Fuck?

"Mom, calm down. Everything's gonna be okay."

This was bullshit. That asshole had ditched her thirteen years ago and now he was calling her from the hospital in the middle of the night?

"Sweetie, I need you to drive me to the hospital. I'm too upset to drive. I'll get in an accident."

"I don't mean to be insensitive or anything, Mom, but why did he call you?"

"He didn't," she said. "The hospital did. He's unconscious and I guess I'm still his emergency contact."

Note to self: When he wakes up, knock him out again.

So here I was at the hospital on a Friday morning—instead of working like I should be—wishing I were anywhere else for any other reason. Getting a prostate exam? Sure—lube up that glove and bring it on. Nothing could be worse than this. I couldn't for the life of me figure out why my mom gave the tiniest shit about what happened to my dad.

Had I been the emergency contact, the conversation with the nurse would have been a short one: "What's that? My dad's been beaten and he's unconscious? Good. Tell him I hope it hurts." Click.

How could she still care about him? Let him make her cry? He'd caused enough tears when he'd been around, I would have thought she'd want nothing to do with him after all this time. I guess I was wrong.

Growing up in my family had not been a picnic. While we didn't live in a trailer park or starve, we didn't have a whole lot. My dad had a hard time holding onto a job, mostly due to the fact that he was the laziest human being to ever walk the earth. His exceptional talent for shifting responsibility off himself and onto absolutely anyone else didn't hurt either. He'd once blamed the family dog for losing a job because he claimed the dog "distracted" him and made him forget he was on shift.

He would constantly do idiotic things like using his unsteady paychecks to buy dozens of scratch-off tickets instead of milk or peanut butter. Or he'd get fired from a job and then get the brilliant idea to come home with fifty dollars' worth of takeout for dinner. My older brother, Jake, and I were luckily pretty good at making friends, so we spent a lot of time at other families' dinner tables.

Most nights, our father would come home after a day of work or hanging out with other deadbeats and proceed to tell my mom everything that was wrong with her. Or me. Or Jake. He had a brilliant knack for undermining and belittling and for finding just the right vulnerability to poke at.

For Jake, it was his natural charisma and his less-than-stellar performance at school. For me, as paradoxical as it sounds, it was my better-than-average success at school—and also my scrawnyness. I was only slightly less awkward than a drunk newborn giraffe. And for our mom, it was just about anything she did or sometimes simply the fact that she existed.

I'd spent many sleepless nights conjuring up confrontations the adult Mark would someday have with my dad, meticulously outlining all his faults and putting him in his place, never comprehending that a man like him would never be swayed in his stubborn perception of his own superiority.

Despite his general surliness and his miserable treatment of our family, he never got physical with any of us—apart from the occasional smack to the back of the head.

"I don't understand how any man could lay a hand on a woman," had been a phrase I'd heard him utter many times.

We were, after all, a God-fearing family, and hitting your wife would have been a grave sin. However, he didn't find verbally and emotionally abusing his family or failing to provide for them to be frowned upon by God, so he went whole-hog and developed quite the talent for those pursuits.

When we were little, my mom worked the night shift as a cashier at a convenience store so there would always be an adult around to care for us in the event my father found himself employed. On nights when my dad was too drunk or too busy being a deadbeat to feed us, the older lady on the other side of our duplex would usher Jake and me to her kitchen.

Her name was Mrs. Finley and she was a widow whose husband had died in the Korean War. We knew this because every time we came over she told us the same story about how kind he'd been to her dying mother right before he'd left for the war and she only hoped someone had been as kind to him before he died. Being the young kid I was, the sadness of that didn't register until much later.

Mrs. Finley was a petite woman with short silver hair, and she wore a variety of housecoats that zipped up the front. Her house smelled like roses, despite there never being any fresh flowers in sight, and she made gingersnap cookies that were so spicy they burned our taste buds. For some reason, this made them even more appealing to Jake and me, so she baked them constantly.

The other thing I knew about Mrs. Finley, besides the fact that her husband was dead and she baked strange cookies, was that she *did not* like my father. Not one bit.

With my mom working nights, there was always some money coming in, just never quite enough. Looking back, I'll never understand how my mother managed to take care of us during the day and still get enough sleep to make it through her night shift, but she somehow did it. Mrs. Finley pitched in when she could, but it was mostly just my mom.

As time passed, though, it became apparent that the home environment my dad created was taking its toll on our mother. There would be many times when I'd hear her crying through her bedroom door or days when we'd come home from school and find that she'd just been sitting on the couch and staring at the TV all day instead of eating and getting some much-needed sleep to make it through her night shifts.

Although Jake and I had inklings that this wasn't quite normal, it was all we knew so we didn't think to question it much. Once we were a bit older I think we finally recognized our mom's tendency toward depressive behavior, and as the years progressed she became more and more "delicate." Not sure if that was the right word to capture the nature of it, but it seemed to fit.

Then two things happened.

First, Jake graduated from high school and signed up for the Marines the same day. I was fourteen and was suddenly alone with a depressed mother and a deadbeat father. By that point, my mom had moved to a better-paying job as a waitress, but there were a lot of times when she couldn't get out of bed and I worried she'd get fired. I got a part-time job as a busser at a local pizza place—the owner knew I wasn't sixteen when I lied about my age, but he hired me anyway and paid me under the table until I was legally allowed to work. We ate a lot of pizza at the Beckett household in those days.

Needless to say, I was more than a little resentful toward my brother for ditching us.

The second thing that happened was better than the first, although I may have been the only one to see it that way. About a week before my sixteenth birthday I awoke to the sound of my mother crying, which wasn't unusual, I'm sad to say. I found her at the wobbly kitchen table holding a piece of paper. Tears streaked her cheeks and her eyes were puffy and red. I took the paper from her and read the words written in my dad's messy scrawl.

I can't let you drag me down anymore—I deserve better.

That was how my dad chose to leave our family. If his departure hadn't wounded my mom so sharply I would have thrown a fucking party in celebration. I was certain Mrs. Finley would have pitched in with decorations and ginger snaps, but sadly she'd died the previous summer.

It had happened peacefully in her sleep, and I remember thinking at the time that I hoped I'd been especially kind to her the last time I'd seen her. Although she wasn't there to celebrate with me, I was sure Mrs. Finley was whooping it up in heaven that the bastard had finally flown the coop.

That was thirteen years ago, and apart from a visit from him in my early twenties—where he asked me for money—I hadn't laid eyes on the old man since.

As far back as I can remember, I've thought of it as my job to worry about my mom and to this day I constantly wish to be a better son. I should have taken better care of her. Maybe if I had, she wouldn't be in an ER crying over a guy who never deserved her tears.

I rubbed my hands over my face as I mentally cursed him one more time. How much longer was this thing going to take? My ass was falling asleep and I needed a caffeine fix. I approached the main desk and asked the nurse if there was anywhere close by to get a coffee. She informed me that the hospital actually had its own Starbucks.

Of course it did.

I stumbled in the direction she pointed and sniffed the air for the scent of a caffeine trail. After a couple wrong turns, I finally approached the ubiquitous green and white sign and got in line.

I was completely zoned out so it took me a moment to realize that someone was staring at me from a few feet over.

Sitting at a small table in the corner was a tiny shift of a girl I'd encountered once before.

The encounter had not gone well.

I'd tried to hit on her and she'd not only rebuffed me, but she'd insulted me repeatedly and without reason. It was just my luck to run into Fiona Pierce on what happened to be one of the shittiest mornings I'd had in a long while (the cheerleading incident notwithstanding).

Unable to cease being a member of the male species, I looked her over and, despite her diminutive size and overall insulting tone,

I still found her to be physically appealing. What can I say? I own a penis.

She has delicate features but huge green eyes and light blond hair that falls around her shoulders and sweeps over her forehead. It's almost as if a breeze accompanies her wherever she goes, causing her hair to float around her face in constant motion. There was just…something about her, some hint of fire I'd noticed the very first time I'd spotted her across Laney's backyard. It was the very thing that had propelled me toward the deck where she'd been standing, where I'd then proceeded to bomb in a most spectacular fashion. That had been the day after Thanksgiving and I hadn't seen her in the months since.

Until today of all days.

She wore a light jacket and a knee-length skirt and sat with her legs crossed, one leg bouncing and showcasing some strappy heels. For a brief moment, my mind wandered and I imagined those heels biting into my back as her legs wrapped around my waist—and then I remembered what a harpy she was and forced my mind back to coffee.

I'm sure I looked like shit, and that had to be the cause of the small smirk on her face. I didn't think I was up to the challenge of sparring with the little spitfire, but the fact that she kept her eyes on me told me I wasn't going to have much choice in the matter.

It was all a little baffling to me. She was Laney's best friend and—according to Nate—was really sweet, smiled a lot, and was funny as hell. He had mentioned that she had a bit of a temper, but that was no news flash to me. I simply couldn't reconcile the two versions of this girl in my mind.

It was my turn at the counter so I looked away from her to place my order. A moment later a voice came from my side.

"Care to join me?"

I turned to see Fiona standing next to me, coffee cup in hand, wide innocent-looking eyes peering up at me. Hmm.

The top of her head barely reached my chin even with the heels. How short was this girl? I bent down in an overly exaggerated manner.

"I'm sorry, can you say that again? I couldn't quite hear you from way down there." I was determined to fire the first shot over her bow. And it seemed my aim was impeccable.

Her cheeks pinked immediately and her mouth got tight. "I was *trying* to be nice, but I'm obviously wasting my time," she hissed and spun around to stalk back to her table, her hair swinging gloriously around her.

Okay, so maybe I'd completely misread this situation.

But she'd totally blindsided me with her bitchiness at our last encounter and I must have still been harboring a bit of resentment. After all, if memory served, she'd called me a "meat-head," a "moron," and had suggested I "go eat a bag of dicks," all within the span of sixty seconds. If it hadn't been aimed at me I might have found it impressive. And all I'd done was say hello—and I might have called her "Tinkerbell" and directed her to the kids' table—that part was a little fuzzy.

Since I couldn't afford any more bad karma, I decided to go apologize once I got my coffee. I took my first sip to steel myself for what promised to be a delightful exchange.

"Hello, Fiona." I approached and she pretended not to hear me as her thumbs typed away on her phone—probably texting Laney about what an utter dick I was.

I sagged into the seat across from her. "I'm sorry for what I said. It's been a shitty morning and, based on our last meeting, I wasn't prepared for civility."

She set her phone on the table and eyed me speculatively for what seemed like an eternity. Finally, she spoke. "I suppose I can understand that." She tossed her hair and sipped her coffee. "I accept your apology."

We were both silent.

Her leg bounced.

I spun my coffee cup around in circles.

We both pretended to find the décor of this particular Starbucks to be fascinating.

It was awkward as shit.

I almost wished I were back in the waiting room.

Or at the proctologist's office—yes, it was almost that bad.

Chapter Six

MYSTERY SOLVED: TONY SOPRANO IS ALIVE AND LIVING IN NORTH CAROLINA

FIONA

Shit, this was awkward. Why wasn't he saying anything? I was the last one to speak, and according to the common rules of conversation, it was his turn, dammit!

Fine.

"So…" I said. *I know—brilliant.*

"So…" Mark replied.

Seriously?

We were a match made in heaven—the dumb blonde and the dumber jock.

Had his neck gotten thicker since the last time I'd seen him? I just didn't understand the point to all these muscles—it was all a bit excessive.

Don't get me wrong. I love the solidity of a guy who works out and takes care of himself, and I wouldn't turn my nose up at a nice set of abs and biceps—or a nice ass, of course—but this guy was like a walking ad for steroids. Okay, well, maybe that was a bit harsh, but he was just so…so…bulky. I mean, his boobs were ten times bigger than mine and there was something exceedingly wrong about that.

Aside from his overly-muscled physique, though, I had to admit he's kind of a babe. He has a great smile, not that I'd seen it yet today, but I remembered it from our last encounter. And I usually don't care for the whole buzz-cut thing, but it so works on him. His eyes are also a rich deep brown and—holy eyelashes—how was that fair? All the mighty forces of Sephora couldn't produce lashes that nice! Oh well, it wasn't as if a nice smile and some eyelashes could make up for the fact that he is completely insufferable.

He finally spoke. "What brings you here at—" he checked his watch, "ten-twenty-four on a Friday morning?"

"Just a check-up," I answered. I certainly wasn't going to elaborate on my visit with Dr. Brandon. "How about you? You mentioned a shitty morning." I sipped my coffee and hoped I had successfully transferred the focus to him.

He must not have been lying about his crap-tastic day because he looked like he hadn't slept at all last night. His brow held what looked like a permanent crease big enough that I could potentially store my eyeliner pencil in there, and the area under his eyes had a greenish-gray cast that even those lashes couldn't disguise.

"Yeah, you could say that. Just some family stuff—had to come in early this morning to the ER." He scrubbed a hand over his light brown hair.

Before I had time to think about it, I covered his other hand with my own. "Oh God, is everything okay? Who got hurt?" My heart pounded and I suddenly regretted any of my negative thoughts toward him. *Muscles are great! And who needs a silly old neck anyway?*

He waved me off. "Nobody." He stared at my hand on his and I couldn't read his expression. I removed my hand as nonchalantly as possible and used it to grab my coffee—super casual-like. *Ugh.*

Mark leaned back in his chair and sighed. "Well, somebody, but he's nobody important. My mom wanted to come in to see him so I drove her—that's all."

I let out a breath I hadn't realized I'd been holding, although I was a bit confused by his comment. "Oh, well that's a relief I suppose."

"Yeah, I guess," he said distractedly.

Clearly there was something going on that I was not privy to—and why should I be? I didn't even know this guy. Apart from sharing a few insults and a cup of coffee we were virtual strangers. Our only connection was some mutual friends and that didn't necessarily amount to anything much in the grand scheme of things.

"Listen, I'd better get back to the waiting room. I don't want my mom coming out and wondering where I am." He stood from the chair. "I guess I'll see you around, what with Nate and Laney and Gavin…" he trailed off.

He stood still for a moment, looking oddly pathetic in an old threadbare t-shirt and track pants. I don't know what possessed me, but out it came. "Would you like some company while you wait?"

His head snapped up, almost as if he'd forgotten I was there. Then he blinked a few times and I saw the crease in his brow release a bit. "Actually, that would be nice."

* * *

I had never realized before how uncomfortable the chairs were in the ER waiting room. Back in the day, I'd spent many a night waiting in similar rooms, but I had usually been too nauseous or in too much pain to care about the hard chairs. I made a mental note to ask my mom to add new chairs to the ever-growing list of fundraising efforts. Not that is was that important, but sometimes it's the little things that can make a difference.

I was flipping through my texts and trying not to laugh out loud at something Laney had texted about Rocco—totally inappropriate to laugh in an ER waiting room, I know, but that kid cracks me up! I don't have to deal with him on a daily basis, however, so I'm allowed to find his antics funny.

Rocco is an exhibitionist of sorts, always preferring to hang out in his underwear and absolutely nothing else.

Am I the only one who finds tiny boxer briefs to be completely adorable?

Anyway, according to Laney's frantic text, Rocco had accidentally seen Nate naked and kept asking when his wiener would be big like Nate's. She then caught Rocco walking around the house wearing Nate's boxer briefs with a belt cinched around his tummy to hold them up. If I hadn't been sitting next to a very seriously brooding Mark, I definitely would have laughed my ass off.

Laney: *I'm worried this has scarred him for life!*

Fiona: *Shut up. This is hilarious. These are the moments you store in your memory only to be brought up at his rehearsal dinner when he gets married. Please tell me you took pictures of the belted underwear!*

Laney: No way! Now Nate is never going to move in! He's worried CPS is going to come and arrest him for letting Rocco see him naked!

Fiona: Calm down. He didn't "let" him. It was an accident. Plenty of little kids see their parents naked. How many times has Rocco walked in on you naked?

Laney: But Nate is NOT his parent.

Fiona: Seriously?

Laney: What??!!

Fiona: Don't be ridiculous. You know you're going to get married and have more beautiful babies and Nate will be a father to all of them.

Fiona: Your silence speaks volumes. Stop worrying.

Laney: I love you.

Fiona: I love you too.

Laney: Oh my God—I am a horrible friend! I totally forgot! How was your appointment?

Fiona: All GOOD!

Laney: Yay! I'm so happy!

Fiona: Me too.

Too bad my heart didn't quite agree with my text. Damn Pa and his thought-provoking nuggets of wisdom.

What was wrong with me? I'd just gotten good news and I was sitting next to a guy who, while claiming this ER visit was no big deal, was obviously grappling with something monumental.

Guilt shook her finger at me. Yes, Guilt is a woman because women are better at head weaving and finger shaking so it's more effective. If Guilt were a guy he'd just shrug his shoulders and say, "Eh, just rub some dirt on it."

I pushed the negative thoughts aside and peeked over at Mark. We'd been sitting in a somewhat companionable silence for the last half hour, but it was clear he was getting restless. We had both finished our coffees and he sat with his hands clenched over his knees while I had been occupying myself with my phone. I quickly glanced at my calendar one more time before putting the phone back in my purse and turning my body toward Mark.

"How are you holding up?" I asked.

"What do you mean? I'm just waiting for my mom," he scoffed.

"You are quite possibly the worst liar I've ever met in my life," I informed him with a smile.

"Not possible. I'm awesome at poker." He turned to me and—damn those eyelashes!

"Then I have never met the terrible liars you play poker with," I returned.

That earned me a hint of a smile.

"Come on, give me your worst joke," I said.

He looked at me like I'd just escaped the psych ward.

"Oh, don't give me that look. Your worst joke. Go."

He shook his head. "Fiona, I don't…" he trailed off.

"Okay, fine. I'll go first." I sat up straight and smoothed my hair as if preparing for a presentation. "Why don't crocodiles eat clowns?"

He peeked at me from the corners of his eyes and I swore I saw his lips twitch. "Fine. I don't know. Why?"

I gave him a "duh" look and answered, "They taste funny." I followed that up with jazz hands.

He face-palmed.

"Pretty bad, huh? Your turn."

Mark sat up and looked at me. "What exactly is the point of this again?"

I started to answer before I thought better of it. "My dad and I used to do this all the time when we were waiting—" I stopped myself just in time. "You know, for appointments and stuff. It passes the time."

It was actually one of my sweetest memories of that dark time in my life—my dad smiling at me and telling the worst jokes ever in an effort to distract me from fear or pain, even if it was just for a moment.

Mark let out a short mirthless laugh that startled me.

What was that about? I needed to chill him out.

"Just go with it. Your turn," I prodded.

He looked sideways at me again before giving in. "Fine, let me think for a minute." His eyes went to the ceiling for a moment before he continued. "Okay, prepare yourself. This is horrible."

I wiggled in my seat in anticipation. What can I say? I love a bad joke.

"Did you hear about the fire at the circus?"

I shook my head.

Mark cringed and said, "It was in tents."

I couldn't help it. I giggled.

"You're not supposed to laugh—it was awful!"

"That's why I'm laughing. That might be the worst joke I've ever heard." I still couldn't stop giggling.

Mark just shook his head and I finally got a full-on smile, the same one I remembered from Laney's deck. The same one he's used when he'd acted like a total sleazebag. I'd almost forgotten.

But before I could give it another thought, the double doors to the inner sanctum of the ER opened and a slim woman with dark brown hair, puffy eyes, and a harried expression emerged. "Mark, sweetie," she said, looking bewildered and a bit shell-shocked.

Joke time was most definitely over.

Mark rose abruptly from his chair and went to her, enveloping her in a hug. If the situation hadn't been so sad, the image would have been almost comical—such a slight figure secured in an unbelievably expansive embrace. It almost looked as if he could have wrapped his arms around her twice. Perhaps it would have helped, she seemed so devastated.

I wished I knew what was going on, but I reminded myself that I was a virtual stranger who had no business butting in—even if all I wanted to do was help.

After several moments, Mark released her from his embrace but held onto her upper arms and peered into her face. "Tell me," he said, his jaw tight.

The woman, who I could only assume was his mother, swiped at some fresh tears. "It's bad. He's awake, but he owes some money to some really bad people and they tried to beat him to d-d-death." She started to sob quietly.

I frantically searched for a packet of tissues in my purse.

"Shit," said Mark.

"I don't understand," his mother said. "This kind of thing doesn't happen to people in real life. We need to help him. We need the police but he said no."

Mark cursed again as I finally unearthed the packet and approached cautiously. I handed the tissues to Mark. He spared me a momentary glance and then offered them to his mother.

She turned her eyes to me, a bit surprised to see a stranger with her son. "Thank you," she managed and then wiped her eyes and nose.

Mark led her to a seat across the room and bent down to talk quietly with her. I couldn't make out anything he said, and I just stood awkwardly, not quite sure what I should do. He rose a moment later and approached me. The deep furrows had returned.

"I think I can take it from here."

Oh, okay, that was a bit abrupt. "Sure. Of course," I said and reached out to touch his hand in reassurance. "Take care, Mark."

"Thanks. You too," he said distractedly, but he was already on his way back to his mom.

* * *

"Okay, so you know I'm a terrible gossip, but this is *not* gossip. This is just something you need to know but I'm afraid it's going to come out as gossip," I announced as I burst through Laney's front door that evening.

"Um, hi," she said, but she was smiling—she knew me too well to expect any other kind of entry into her house from me.

"Something is wrong with Mark," I said as I stalked into the kitchen and put a bottle of Kim Crawford on her counter—her new *granite* counter, thanks to sweet Nate. He'd been slowly updating the kitchen, and the counters were the latest addition. Before that had come the cooktop, much to my delight. "We've got to figure this out and help him." I brought my mind back to the situation at hand.

I turned around and realized she wasn't there. "Laney?!"

She rounded the corner. "Excuse me, but did you just tell me something about Mark? Mark from Nate's work?"

"Yes! Keep up, woman!"

"I thought you hated Mark." She tilted her head to the side and crossed her arms over her giant rack. I sometimes marveled at her ability to stand up straight with all of *that* going on up front.

"Meh."

"What does that even mean?" she demanded.

"Not important. Get your hot piece of ass in here—we need to talk business."

"My 'hot piece of ass' is still at work so you'll have to settle for me," she said, blowing her hair out of her face. Now that I took a good look at her I noticed that she was dressed in a ratty t-shirt and an old pair of denim overalls, her messy hair partially pulled back. There was dirt smudged on her face—and she was sweaty.

I circled my finger in front of her. "What's all this? Are you a farmer now? I have to say I'm not a big fan of this look."

"Thank you, Joan Rivers," she said, evoking a little sigh of pride from me that she made a fashion reference—one that actually made sense (although technically Joan is no longer with us, but whatever. RIP). "And no. I'm cleaning out Gavin's room." She gestured to the stack of packing boxes in the attached living room.

"Holy shit! Is he finally moving out? Let me guess—one too many awkward midnight encounters in the hallway with the guy who just finished banging his sister?"

Laney choked on the air, I assumed.

"Now all you have to do is get a white noise machine for Rocco and you and Nate can play 'feed the kitty' as loudly as you want. Bow-chicka-wow-wow." I threw in a hip swivel to reinforce my point. Hey, if you can't be real with your best friend then what's the point?

She gave me a look she mostly reserves for Rocco when he sings about genitalia while at the grocery store.

"Hey, speaking of Rocco, where is my little man?" I had an urge to hand out some tickles. I started down the hall to find him and to check out Gavin's empty room.

Laney recovered her voice and called out after me, "I had to send him down the street to play with Aiden. He was unpacking the boxes as fast as I was packing them. I don't think he wants Gavin to go."

I stopped outside Gavin's door. Huh, this was a little sad now that I saw the empty room. All that was left was a stripped-down bed and an old dresser. It was all a bit pathetic. Poor Rocco. Who was he going to learn bad habits from now that Gavin would be gone? Without his uncle around he was never going to learn how to belch the entire alphabet. Nate was a more civilized guy—the most he could probably teach him would be to blame a fart on the dog.

I was actually very fond of Gavin, and not having any siblings of my own, I sort of saw him as my little brother too. When Laney bought her house last year, Gavin had moved in with her to help with Rocco and with renovations on the house. With the arrival of "Tall, Dark, and Holy Hotness," though, Gavin had gotten out of the work on the house. But he was an important part of this little family and, while it was definitely time for him to strike out on his own, it was bittersweet.

Laney joined me and leaned against the doorjamb. "I'm gonna miss his stupid face," she sighed. "But he's promised Rocco lots of sleepover parties, and I have to say it has been getting a little cramped around here. I'm proud of him, though."

"Me too," I said and squeezed her arm. Gavin had basically gone from industrial-strength barnacle to semi-independent adult in the span of the last six months. A derailed baseball career had turned him into a freeloading cloud of grumpiness, and it wasn't until recently that a series of events kicked his butt into growing up and moving on.

He was now working part-time for Nate's family's construction company in addition to coaching advanced level players at the Baseball Academy in town. I may or may not have had a tiny bit to do with the latter, but I'll never tell. *Yeah, right.* I totally abused my parents' contacts to get Gavin an interview for the job, but in my defense, he was completely qualified. He was finally coming to terms with never going to the Big Show and was actually enjoying helping other guys work toward that dream.

"Where is he moving?" I asked.

"He and Brett are renting a townhouse just north of High Point."

"I fear for their neighbors." Gavin and Brett have been best friends since high school and let's just say that they are pretty adept at bringing out the idiot in each other.

"That is no joke," she agreed, swiping her face with the back of her hand and leaving another dirt streak.

I hated to imagine the things Laney had found while cleaning up that room. Perhaps the entire Kim Crawford should go to her.

Or not.

"So tell me this mysterious news you have about Mark Beckett?" Laney nudged my arm.

"Is that his last name? Right. So, I ran into him at the hospital this morning and he was almost as insulting as he was the last time I saw him—well, at first anyway."

"Did he make more short jokes?"

"Yes! What is up with that? Was he traumatized by a politically incorrect circus clown or something?"

Laney snickered. "I have no idea, but that's a solid theory. Now go on."

It's true—I'm easily distracted, but Laney is good at getting me back on track without making me feel like a complete spaz.

"I thought at first that he was hungover because he looked all zoned out and tired, but he had actually been waiting since early morning for his mom. He drove her to the ER to see somebody who'd been hurt. He wouldn't tell me anything about who it was, but he was totally distracted and stressed out. When his mom came out she was super upset and Mark seemed really pissed off. I overheard his mom say that the guy—whoever he is—had been beaten unconscious by somebody he owes money to and that they tried to kill him! It was all very *Sopranos*, but without any of the funny stuff."

"Are you being serious right now?" Laney asked, looking skeptical.

"Dead." Oops. "I mean yes! This actually happened."

Her hands went to her hips. "Holy shit. I'm calling Nate."

"That's what I was saying—we need his help!"

"No—we're gonna need more wine!"

Chapter Seven

TAG – YOU'RE IT

MARK

"What the hell, man?!" Nate's voice thundered over the phone so loudly I had to pull it away from my ear. I knew Shortcake wouldn't be able to keep her mouth shut.

"Take it down a notch—I'm not hearing impaired."

"You called in for a personal day and now I'm hearing there is some guy your mom's involved with and he's being stalked by loan sharks. I repeat, what the hell, man?!"

"Oh, it gets worse."

"How is that possible?"

"It's my dad."

Silence. Then, "You've got to be shitting me."

"I shit you not. I couldn't come up with this level of FUBAR if I tried."

"Where is he now? Where are you and your mom?"

"He's still in the hospital and I'm at my mom's with her."

As if the morning hadn't been a treat in itself, this day just kept piling on the shit. After Fiona left us at the hospital I'd been able to talk to a nurse and get some information on the extent of the sperm donor's injuries. He had a broken collarbone, broken ribs, a broken leg (likely from a baseball bat to the knee), and head trauma. Terrific. He would need surgery for the leg and knee and would be in the hospital for several days. I didn't know the status of his medical insurance, and I didn't want to.

Thankfully, I had been able to talk my mom into going home since the nurse informed me that the bastard needed rest and was on serious pain meds. I doubted he even remembered talking to my mom, and I was hoping to keep it that way. Keeping *her* away may prove to be a bit more difficult.

She'd spent the afternoon intermittently pacing and quietly crying, despite my efforts to distract her. She called in to work and got the evening off, although I personally thought it might have been a good way to get her mind off the whole situation. But I got her to eat something in the late afternoon and then finally convinced her to lie down in her bedroom.

I had no idea what to do. And since I couldn't say what I wanted to, which was, "Just leave him there and forget about him," I was at a total loss. So, I'd been sitting on the couch stewing while my mom rested.

On the other end of the phone, I heard Nate sigh. He knew all about our history with my dad. "I can't believe he had the nerve to call her."

"That was my first thought, too, but he was out cold. If you can believe it, he still had her listed as his emergency contact—after thirteen fucking years!"

"What an asshole. And your mom actually wanted to go to him?"

"I will never understand women," I replied.

"I've been told it's an impossibility so don't even try. What are you going to do?"

I swiped my hand over my head for the umpteenth time that day. "I have no fucking clue."

"Did the cops come?"

"Yeah, I guess it's routine in this kind of situation. The old man was out of it a lot, but apparently he told the cops he'd just had an accident so there is nothing they can do if he doesn't want to pursue it or press charges. My guess is he's scared shitless, as well he should be."

"Will your mom listen to you if you ask her to stay away from him? The last thing she needs is some loan shark coming after her once they find out he's got a wife—estranged or not."

"Shit! I didn't even think of that." I stood abruptly from the couch. "This is getting worse by the minute."

"You want us to come over tomorrow and try to help you talk to her?"

"Nah, man. I'll figure it out, but thanks."

"Well, if you change your mind, just give me a call. We're here if you need it."

"Thanks, man. Later."

I hung up and stared at my phone. I did need help figuring this out, but I wasn't about to drag Nate and Laney into this mess. It wasn't their problem—it was a family problem. And I knew just who deserved a call.

I scrolled through my contact list and hit the call button.

"Yo, dickhead! What's up?"

"Jake, you cocksucker, it's time to get your ass home. Dad's back."

* * *

It was Sunday night and I sat in my truck outside Piedmont Triad International Airport waiting on my brother. The Zac Brown Band rang from the speakers but did little to distract me. I drummed my fingers on the steering wheel wondering what the hell was taking so long. Jake's flight had landed twenty minutes ago.

Then I caught a glimpse of him in my rearview mirror and the reason became clear. Duffle bag slung over one shoulder, my big brother swaggered out the automatic doors with a tall, stacked blonde by his side. She was laughing at something he said and ducking her head coyly.

Jesus Christ.

Leave it to my brother to use a family crisis to schedule some horizontal refreshment.

I rolled my window down and shouted, "Yo, Jake! Your wife just called and said she's going into labor. If we hurry, maybe you'll make it in time to cut the cord!"

Jake looked at me like he might go all Vito Corleone on my ass, and the blonde practically sprinted in the other direction, shouting some pretty choice expletives behind her. He stomped over to the truck and threw his duffle in the back. "I forgot what a dick you can be," he said as he folded his tall frame into the passenger seat.

He looked the same as always—three days past needing a shave and built like a Mack truck. His hair was buzzed like mine but that's where the resemblance stopped. Jake's looks are more dark, favoring our mother, while mine are more fair, favoring the sack of shit. Jake also has a good four inches on me, a fact he never lets me forget.

"Always here to help." I settled my hands on the steering wheel and pulled away from the curb.

"If cock-blocking is your idea of help, you need me more than I realized."

"Oh please, the only reason a girl would fuck you is if she ran out of batteries."

He turned to me and narrowed his eyes. "I think it's time you shut up, little brother, and give that hole in your face a chance to heal."

I smiled at him. "Good to see you too."

The corner of his mouth lifted a fraction of an inch. "Whatever. Just drive—I can't wait to get this shit show over with."

Jake sighed.

I pulled onto the highway. "You and me both."

"Jake?" Our mom sat on the couch, looking as if she'd just awakened from a dream and wasn't sure if Jake was real or not. She blinked furiously as my brother made his way to her, a giant grin on his face.

"Mom!" Jake exclaimed as he bent to encompass her in a hug and draw her to her feet. She wasn't short, but she was thin and looked frail in his big arms.

She returned his embrace and then pulled back so she could gaze up at him. "What are you doing here?"

"Can't a guy come home now and then?" he teased her.

"Of course you can. It's just such a surprise!" A smile lit her face for the first time since Friday. Thank God.

"Well, I missed you and I happened to have some time off so I thought, what the hell!"

Yeah, not exactly how it had gone down, but good enough.

The fact that she didn't seem the least bit suspicious of the expedient timing of his visit indicated just how addled she was.

Earlier this morning I'd had to drive her to the hospital to check on my dad since she'd threatened to drive herself if I didn't take her. Luckily, he'd been sleeping so she didn't get a chance to talk to him.

Ever since Nate's comment about the thugs possibly coming after my mom, I'd been nervous as hell and I was reluctant to let her out of my sight. But nothing seemed amiss at the hospital—not that I would have known what to look for anyway. It's not as if these guys would be swinging around baseball bats and wearing t-shirts saying "1-800-Loan Shark. Text rates apply." But just to be safe, I accompanied her to the hospital room and got my first look at my old man in eight years.

Time—and the baseball bat—had not been kind to him. His hair was long and scraggly and mostly gray, no longer the neatly combed sandy head of hair from my childhood. The muscular frame I'd never been allowed to forget was also diminished. His face was swollen and colored in various shades of purple, green, and yellow from the beating he'd taken. Had I seen him out of context, there wouldn't have been a single trace of recognition.

There were various tubes and wires attached to his arm and hand while his leg hung suspended above the bed, wrapped in plaster and bandages. I wondered vaguely if the hospital had contacted the correct family. Maybe this was all a big mistake. But then I glimpsed the familiar faded tattoo peeking from the sleeve of his hospital gown and I was swiftly returned to the shitstorm that this week had brought to our lives.

Once the nurse confirmed that his pain meds were keeping him asleep most of the time, I was able to coax my mom to leave.

I took her to lunch at the Village Tavern, hoping to cheer her up, but she just picked at her salad and remained distant. Maybe she sensed the fury brewing just beneath my skin and that was the reason for her continued silence on the topic, but I was desperate for her to open up. Thankfully, I'd known reinforcements were on the way.

"I just can't believe you're here." Our mother stared at Jake, dumbfounded. "When you didn't make it home for Christmas I was worried about you." She didn't mean to scold, but I secretly felt a bit smug that her comment piled a little guilt on Jake. He certainly deserved it, in my humble opinion.

He looked appropriately chastened. "I know—I'm sorry. I really couldn't get out of the project we were working on. But there's no need to worry about me, Mom."

I wasn't entirely clear on what my brother did for a living. After his stint in the Marines, he'd seemed to wander the country aimlessly for a while, coming home from time to time. He worked odd jobs and then somehow got involved in landscape design, which took him to Florida. This was unsurprising, as I could perfectly picture Jake sweet-talking rich retirees into installing ridiculously expensive outdoor fountains surrounded by hedge mazes or some such shit. All he'd have to do is turn on the smile, flex his biceps, and throw a little "Aw, shucks" in there and the rich ladies would swoon. My smile hadn't been the only one our mom had worried about.

"I should go get your room ready." Mom brought her hand to her dark hair. "Are you hungry? I should make you some dinner. Where are your bags?" She looked around.

"Don't worry," Jake said calmly and grabbed her hand. "I just have the one bag, and I've already eaten. I'm also perfectly capable of making a bed. Just relax and catch me up on what's been going on lately."

We'd agreed it best that Jake play dumb and pretend he didn't know Dad was back. Hopefully, once he got our mom talking she would finally share some of what she was thinking and we could get a bead on her mindset.

"I have to make a phone call," I said and excused myself from the room. I went into the kitchen where I could still hear their conversation. Part of me felt guilty for putting on a ruse, but the situation was so messed up I could easily let it go.

"Didn't Mark tell you…oh my goodness, Jake. Normally I wouldn't have much to share, but I have some news and I'm not sure how you're going to take it."

"What's that?" Jake asked quietly.

She proceeded to tell him the facts as we knew them, with the addition of a new piece of unwelcome information—it seemed the old man was into these guys for thirty grand.

"Wow," said Jake, the fucking genius.

"I know," our mother replied, but then she went on. "Jake, I just don't know what to do. I've been thinking about it nonstop and I feel like we need to help him."

Shit. Shit. Shit.

I clutched my phone so hard I was surprised it didn't crack.

"Hmm, well, I guess I can see how you'd feel that way." At least Jake was doing a good job of keeping his cool. "There are a lot of things to consider, though, Mom." He sounded like a fucking talk show therapist.

"I know. I don't have that kind of money to give those awful people. But we can figure something out. He's your father."

At this point, I was incredibly fortunate to be standing a room away. There would be no way I could school my expression at that last comment.

Unbelievably, Jake continued with a calm tone, "True, but let's think this out a bit. Do you know if he has insurance? Do you know where he was living when he got mixed up with these guys?"

"Um, well, the hospital said he doesn't have insurance." She seemed to pause.

"Mom, did they have you sign anything at the hospital?"

"No, nothing. Why?"

I could hear Jake's sigh of relief that echoed my own.

"Okay, well that's good at least. Make sure you don't sign anything or you might become liable for his medical bills. You're still technically married."

"Oh my God—I hadn't even thought of that!"

"It's okay. We'll figure this out. Now, was he in North Carolina when he got involved with these guys?"

"I don't know. I just know this is where they found him and attacked him. I really think he was trying to come home to us."

Fuck. Fuck. Fuck.

Again, Jake kept his cool. I was going to have to buy him a beer and stop calling him derogatory names. "Well, that aside, we have to be careful, Mom. It might be best to stay away from the hospital in case these people are watching and they figure out your connection to him. I'm worried they might try to harm you in some way."

"What? Why would they do that? I didn't do anything to them." She sounded breathless at the thought.

"These kinds of people don't think that way. They want their money and will do just about anything to get it. Look what they did to D...dad." He stumbled over the word and I couldn't blame him one bit. "That's probably why he lied to the cops too."

"Oh."

Things were silent for a few moments so I figured it was safe to return. They were both sitting on the couch and Jake's arm rested along the back, behind our mom's head. Unsurprisingly, she looked a bit dazed.

"Anybody need anything to drink?" I asked, trying for distraction so my mom had time to digest the reality of the situation. I was hoping against hope that it sunk in and stuck. We'd have to worry later about her misguided belief that anything but money had brought dear old Dad back to Greensboro.

"Sure," said Jake. "Why don't you bring Mom a glass of wine and I'll take a beer."

"Coming right up," I said, happy to retreat to the kitchen once again.

Jake and I had our fair share of differences and I certainly still held on to some resentment that had built since his abrupt departure years back. But right now?

It was damn good to have my brother home.

Chapter Eight

A GOOD BEST FRIEND IS HARD TO FIND

FIONA

"I know you told me you and Nate would take care of it but, for reasons I can't examine right now, I can't get the whole thing out of my head. I know he's a big boy—lord knows if he were any bigger he'd need his own small country to fit in. What is up with that, by the way? Isn't there a point where a person looks in the mirror and realizes that there are wimpy people in this world who need the muscle more than he does? Did his mother never tell him about the muscle-impaired children of the Third World?" I rambled, as usual, as I hefted the grocery bags to Laney's kitchen.

A new recipe idea had been niggling at my brain and I'd decided to make use of my guinea pigs again tonight. "Anyway, I hope you like beef tips because I woke up this morning with a hankering for some juicy tips. Yum!"

I heard a sharp intake of breath, a poorly muffled giggle, a deep chuckle, and what sounded like a growl all coming simultaneously from the living room off Laney's kitchen.

Fuckity, fuck, fuck my life!

I really had to stop running my mouth without checking for witnesses first. I turned slowly from the counter and walked to the half wall separating the two rooms.

I thought for one brief moment that I might actually die of humiliation.

I'm sorry, Mr. and Mrs. Pierce, there was nothing we could do. It was acute systemic embarrassment (which the medical community will henceforth refer to as ASE or perhaps "Fiona's Curse"). She unfortunately brought it on herself—you are aware your daughter was a complete and total wackadoo, aren't you? Again, I'm very sorry.

On the recliner in the corner of the room sat Laney on Nate's lap, both of them wearing shit-eating grins on their fat stupid faces. Assholes! Rocco played with some monster trucks on the coffee table, and if only I'd been able to stop there, I wouldn't have been forced to see the faces of the two men sitting on the couch, one stern and familiar, the other jocular and completely foreign to me.

Oh yay, I was expanding my audience to include random strangers now. Why did these things always happen to me?

"What's a beef tip?" asked Rocco, lifting his sweet brown eyes to me.

I ignored my flaming face and looked at the child who I decided was going to be my only friend from here on out. "It's a cut of meat that comes from the bottom loin under—"

"Okay!" Laney interrupted, barely stifling another giggle— what was up with her?! "It's steak, Rocco."

"Gross."

Oh well, more for me.

Then, instead of creating a diversion and allowing me to slink back out the front door like a true best friend would, Laney gestured to the couch and forced me to act like a grown-up. "Fiona, you remember Mark, of course. And this is his brother, Jake. Jake, Fiona. Fiona, Jake."

Sending Laney my best "I'll cut a bitch" glare, I tried to regain my composure and step down the two steps to the living room. Of course, my heel caught on the threshold and I bobbled a bit before grasping the wall to regain my balance.

There would be no regaining my pride, however.

I proceeded to the couch and looked up, and up, at Jake, who was now standing politely with his hand out. What did their mother feed these boys? I took his hand as I also took in his slightly naughty smile. Don't ask how I knew it was naughty. It just was.

"It is so nice to meet you, Fiona," he said, appearing quite amused. Oh yeah, this guy was trouble.

"You too," I managed to say. "I'm here all week if you'd like to catch another show."

Jake chuckled and I looked around him—which was not an easy thing to do as it seemed the brothers were both greedy where muscles were concerned—to find Mark, who was scowling for some reason. Okay, so maybe he was mad I ranted about his physique, or maybe it was my inability to stay out of everyone's business.

Whatever.

"Hi, Mark," I mumbled.

"Shortcake," was all he said.

Oh no he didn't!

"So!" exclaimed Nate. "How about those beef tips? Sounds awesome!"

* * *

As tempted as I was to claim there was not enough food to go around and then suddenly invent an important meeting that required my presence (because you know, Monday evenings are usually fully booked with work for landscaping receptionists), I sucked it up and cooked dinner for everyone. Who was I kidding? Laney knew I always made too much food, so there would have been no fooling her anyway.

I have to say I was quite pleased with the results of my efforts, and from the little moans and the lack of conversation at the dinner table I'd say my bourbon and honey steak tips were a hit with everyone else as well—Rocco excepted. He did, however, enjoy my roasted garlic mashed potatoes with his hot dog. Future foodie in the making.

At least I assumed it was the food that kept everyone quiet, not the weird tension between Mark and me. Was I the only one who felt it, though? He had me discombobulated. I'd been thinking about him and about the scene at the hospital all weekend, unable to get him out of my head. And while I'd been cooking I'd caught him staring at me several times—it had rattled me to the point where I'd nearly burned the glaze.

Gah! Out of my head, you brute!

"Fiona," Jake finally said, wiping his mouth with a napkin. "Will you marry me?"

Ha! I knew it! How could you not like a good beef tip?! I smiled at him.

"That depends, Jake. What can you bring to the proverbial table?" I took my last bite and sipped my wine, determined to focus on brother number two. He was a little yummy himself, but he lacked the eyelashes and general surliness of Mark. Wait. What?

"I can build you a backyard oasis and probably get you a seat at the hottest Bunco night in Florida," Jake said after a moment of thought.

"Tempting," I said, pretending to consider his offer. "But I live in a condo. And I prefer Mahjong. I hope you understand—it's not you, it's me."

"So you're saying I have a chance."

Laney and I laughed and then Nate chimed in, "Seriously, Fiona, that was so good. I'm going to have to up my workouts if you keep feeding me like that."

I smiled at Nate and then I snuck a quick glance at Mark, sure he was going to volunteer to train Nate or something, but he was just sitting back in his chair eyeing me and sipping his beer. Hmm.

"Can I be excused?" Rocco asked, his little lisp making the question quite possibly the most adorable thing I've ever heard.

"Sure, baby," answered Laney, and the little guy ran off to his room.

I got up and started to grab the dishes but Laney and Nate stopped me simultaneously, as was their custom on Fiona nights. I don't know why I still tried.

And then, because I couldn't seem to keep my giant yap shut, I proceeded to butt into everyone's business. "So, how is your mom?" I asked Mark and Jake.

Jake glanced at Mark and they did some silent brother communication thing before Mark finally answered, "She's okay."

To any normal person, this succinct reply would have signaled that it was time to switch topics. But me? I pressed on, for some ridiculous reason. "And her friend who was hurt?"

Mark threw a glance to Nate at the counter, maybe having assumed that Nate had filled me in on some details—which he had *not*, much to my annoyance. I hadn't even been able to crack Laney.

This idea of Rocco as my new best friend was proving to have more and more merit by the second. Sure, he was just a kid, but if I fed him enough ice cream I'm sure he'd go shopping with me. Plus, I'm pretty good at talking about gross stuff and that totally impresses boys.

Jake was the one to finally speak up. "It was actually our father, and he's pretty racked up but he'll pull through." Mark shot him a warning look while my chin hit the table.

Oh my God! It hadn't occurred to me that it could be Mark's dad. That would certainly explain why he and his mom were so worked up at the hospital. "I'm so sorry! I had no idea," I said. "That must be really upsetting. I'm glad he's going to be okay." I continued to ramble.

"That would make you the only person," Mark muttered, effectively shutting me up.

"Mark, everyone here knows what's going on so why not see if anybody else has ideas on how to clean this up quick?" Jake turned to his brother.

I raised my hand like a kindergartner. "Um, I don't think I really understand what's going on."

"And we don't want to bother you with our problems, Short-cake. Right, Jake?" His look was so pointed it was almost comical.

This was all so shocking I forgot to be mad about the "Short-cake" moniker.

Jake looked back and forth between Mark and me as if suddenly realizing something interesting. Huh? Then he smirked like the goddamn troublemaker I'd known he was, and I could practically hear the *bling* bounce off the naughty twinkle in his eye.

Oh, hell no! Back this truck up before anyone gets any ideas.

Jake went on, "I'm sure Fiona would be happy to help. So, long story short, Fiona, our dad is a douchebag who our mom is somehow still hung up on—even though he walked out on her years ago—and he has loan sharks after him because he stupidly borrowed a shitload of cash from them. Now he's back in town, we can only assume, to suck us into his shitstorm and all our mom can think about is how to help him and/or win him back."

"Holy hell," was what came out of my mouth.

"You can say that again," Laney said from the sink.

After that, we all migrated back to the living room with our drinks and proceeded to brainstorm a bit. From what I could under-stand, the goal was to keep their mom as far away as possible from not only their dad, but the hospital's billing department and these guys who had beaten up the douchebag dad.

"Not to be insensitive to the serious topic at hand," I began, "but does anyone else's mind immediately picture Chevy Chase in a shark costume whenever the words 'loan shark' are mentioned?"

"Thank God I wasn't the first one to say it, but I've been dying to!" said Nate, who was then firmly swatted on the arm by Laney.

"Shut up, you two. Am I the only grown up around here?" she scolded. "And besides, that was *land* shark, not *loan* shark," she added quietly. "If you're going to be assholes, at least get it right."

Nate and I just grinned at each other and shrugged before we schooled our expressions. Nate cleared his throat and I looked down at my lap.

"The whole thing is so oddly surreal, though, isn't it?" Mark commented.

Phew—my big mouth hadn't pissed him off again.

"Why can't we call the cops?" asked Laney.

"Because the old man has at least some sense of self-preservation. If he goes to the cops he'll most likely end up with cement shoes, and as long as he's alive there is a better chance they'll keep after him and not go looking for relatives," explained Jake, who then turned his attention to me and said, "I've always wanted to have a legitimate conversation where I could fit in the phrase 'cement shoes.'"

I couldn't help it—I giggled a little. Until I saw the look on Mark's face. If I were Jake, I'd find another ride home lest I be the one to end up in those shoes.

What was up with that? He needed to pull his panties out right quick before his scowl caused premature wrinkles. Did he understand nothing about skincare?

"So what's the end game here?" asked Nate. "Not to be harsh, but do you want to leave him to the mercy of these guys? Or do you want to spirit him off to Mexico or something? Do you want to come up with the money and then threaten him to never come back?"

"I say let them have at him again," said Mark.

Ouch.

"It's not that simple and you know it, little brother," said Jake.

Aww.

"I know, but a guy can dream, right?"

"Okay, so option one is out," Nate stated. "How about option two?"

"What's to keep the guys from going after Mom if the asshole suddenly disappears?" asked Jake.

"We don't even know if she's on their radar," replied Mark.

"Best to keep her far away then," concluded Laney.

"Yeah, that's the problem. She wants to be involved," Mark returned.

"Well then, we'll have to figure out a way to remove her from the picture without being obvious while you guys deal with the rest," I said with a little smile, my mind already spinning with plans.

I looked at Laney. "You in?"

"Hell yes."

Nate put his head in his hands and muttered, "Here we go."

I do love a good project.

Chapter Nine

SO MAYBE IT'S A THING

MARK

"I can't believe I let you guys talk me into this," I muttered to Jake on the way home from Laney's house that night.

The food had been incredible—Shortcake could cook like a fucking champ. I'd spent more than a few minutes watching while she'd chopped, stirred, and sautéed, and I liked witnessing the relaxed pleasure these actions brought to her small features. It had felt oddly intimate, though, so I had tried to force my attention away, to little success.

I'd be lying if I said she hadn't been on my mind since the ER waiting room. How she'd gotten me to smile on a day like that was a complete mystery, one of many where this woman was concerned. The problem was I didn't have time or energy for more complications in my life and she had "complication" written all over her. It's not like I could bang her and then never see her again. Not an option.

After hearing her little tirade about my body earlier tonight, though, I hadn't been able to help myself from calling her "Shortcake." If memory served, that had been part of my opening line the first time we'd met. She hadn't liked it then and she sure as shit didn't like it now. I just couldn't help having a little fun with her.

And I'll admit, after the initial discomfort of discussing what I considered private family business, it was somewhat of a relief to share some of the load, even if it did involve sharing it with Fiona. As always, Nate was great at breaking things down into manageable pieces, and by the end of the evening I felt as if we had some semblance of a game plan.

At one point, Fiona and Laney had excused themselves, ostensibly to put Rocco to bed but it was clear they were scheming.

This made me nervous.

I knew logically that my mom could weather a lot of shit, but in my opinion she was always to be handled with care.

When they returned to the room, the girls attempted subtlety while asking questions about my mom—where she worked, what kind of hours she had off, what her interests were. They eventually abandoned all pretense and just asked for her number. Jake answered most of their questions, although how he knew these things living several states away I had no clue. Maybe he paid more attention than I gave him credit for.

Completely sick of the serious tone the evening had developed, I made a concerted effort to switch topics and soon we were arguing about college basketball—I do so love to torture Nate about his devotion to Notre Dame.

At one point, after a particularly well-placed insult, I dropped the mic and excused myself to the restroom. When I was finished and emerged into the hallway, my attention was grabbed by a low melodic sound coming from one of the rooms. I turned left to investigate instead of taking a right and rejoining the group. Maybe Rocco was listening to music instead of sleeping. I'd been over here a few evenings and I knew the kid liked to stall his bedtime as much as possible.

When I got to his door and peeked in, however, I saw Fiona perched on the side of his bed, singing softly to him. The scene was simultaneously endearing and bizarre. Here was this smart-ass, ball-busting woman—barely bigger than her pajama-clad charge—singing an old Beatles song to the sleepy little boy. She was dressed to the nines in high heels and what I could only assume was a ridiculously expensive designer outfit but strangely looked right at home sitting on a rumpled pile of fire-truck bedsheets.

My skin warmed. I began to feel like an interloper, a voyeur, and tried to back away. In my haste, I inadvertently hit my boot on the doorjamb and immediately drew Fiona's attention.

She stood up suddenly, forgetting her task before quickly checking to make sure Rocco was indeed asleep. That damn hair fluttered around her face and she tried tucking one side behind her ear as she looked at the floor and quietly made her way into the hall. Her cheeks were pink.

"You have a beautiful voice," I whispered, unable to help myself.

"Oh, thanks." Apparently, that hadn't been what she'd expected me to say. "I was just trying to help him get back to sleep. Nightmare," she explained quietly, still clearly uncomfortable at being caught in the act.

"I used to sing to my dog," I blurted out.

What?! Shut up, you asshole!

I don't know what possessed me to say that except I didn't want her to feel self-conscious about what I had seen as a genuinely sweet moment—that and, well, it was true. Daisy had loved it when I sang to her—that dog was a huge fan of Notorious B.I.G.

Fiona smiled and looked up at me. Then she started to giggle and I shushed her while closing Rocco's door.

"I'm sorry. That was really rude. It's sweet. Really." She tried to get ahold of herself.

"I have no idea why I said that," I muttered. "If you're done laughing at me, let's go back and torture Nate some more." I tried to scowl at her but it didn't work.

She bit her lip.

Damn, that was hot.

"Deal," she finally said and sashayed her way back to the living room.

Watching her cute little ass as she walked ahead of me, I suspected I was in a bit of trouble.

When Jake and I got up to leave later in the evening, Laney gave us both hugs while Fiona stood to the side somewhat awkwardly. She seemed to finally make up her mind and settled on a smile and wave for Jake and a punch to my arm, after which she let her gaze linger a moment too long on the bicep she'd just assaulted. Was it possible little Miss "Go eat a bag of dicks" didn't find me that distasteful after all?

Interesting.

Jake interrupted my reverie. "What? These people obviously care about you—what's the harm in letting them help?" he asked from the passenger seat of my truck.

"Fiona doesn't give two shits about me. She's just a bored little —emphasis on *little*—rich girl looking for a project." I knew I was laying the denial on a bit too thick.

"Whatever you say, man."

"What is that supposed to mean?" I took my eyes off the road to glare at him.

"It's so obvious. You guys are doing the whole 'I hate you so much I want to fuck you to death' thing."

"That's *not a thing*! And, no, we are not. She thinks I'm a steroid-obsessed idiot and I don't even find her attractive. I've seen small children with bigger tits than hers." Okay, that was a bit overboard. And creepy. So her tits aren't big, but they are definitely there. And I may or may not have noted that they're perky. Kind of like her.

Shit.

"For what it's worth, I think she's hot, if not a bit…what's the word I'm looking for?" Jake closed his eyes in concentration and I hoped he'd just drop it. "Hyper?" he tried and then shook his head. "Dramatic?" He turned to me.

"I think the word you're looking for is 'blond.'"

"That's it!" He pointed his finger at me and I rolled my eyes. "I suppose I could do a whole lot worse than a hot little blonde, though," he mused with a quick glance at me.

I tamped down the rising in my chest. He was so pitifully obvious in his baiting technique I almost felt sorry for him. "Oh gee, Jake," I deadpanned. "Please don't bang her, man." I turned to him and resumed my normal voice, "Is this the part where I'm supposed to growl possessively?"

"Okay, dickhead. Touché. But I know you think she's hot," he said and then smirked and whispered, "Shortcake."

I flipped him off. "It doesn't matter what I think—she hates me and the last thing I need right now is more drama anyway. Speaking of which, what the hell are those two witches going to do to our mother?"

"Who the hell knows, but they seem to have something up their sleeves so I'm all for letting them run with it while we worry about the rest."

And then, apropos of nothing, he said, "Hey, did you know Mom still has middle school trophies on the shelf in our old room?"

I cringed. Part of me was happy that we were dropping the subject of the tiny terror, but the other part wasn't ready to talk about Mom's behavior. "I'm aware." It was no secret that part of her lived in the past—a past that she somehow managed to senti-mentalize.

"Who keeps debate team trophies? I mean, sports trophies, maybe..." he goaded me. "I saw those things last night and laughed my ass off. I'll bet Mom has an entire album of pictures stashed somewhere of a pimply little Mark in a crooked tie lecturing like a 90-pound politician at some podium." He snickered.

I wasn't about to tell him he was right. "Laugh it up, asshole."

He seemed to have lost his mind because he proceeded to do just that and practically bust a gut in my passenger seat.

"If you're going to piss yourself, I swear I will pull over and punch you in the throat." He held his index finger up, indicating he needed a minute. "Seriously, out of three hundred million sperm, you're the one who made it? It boggles the mind." And that just sent him off again.

Mom was working an evening shift at her waitressing job, but I decided to come in the house instead of just dropping Jake off, hoping to check in with her. We were relieved that she'd made it to work without comment and especially without trying to stop by the hospital again. I was hoping the information Jake had dropped on her last night was making an impact, but it would be nice to see for myself.

Walking into our childhood home rarely made me think of my father anymore, but that had changed in the last few days. All I could see when I walked into the little duplex now was the stained and time-worn carpet in front of the recliner where my dad used to settle his clay-encrusted work boots and then complain about dirty floors later. And the mirror above the entry table with the crack in the corner from when it had fallen during one of his tirades, only to be picked up and repaired by my mother that night. Then the wobbly oak table in the kitchen where Jake and I had bitten our tongues so hard we'd nearly drawn blood in our attempts to refrain from back-talk as the old man had hurled thinly veiled insults and criticisms.

I could see him plain as day in the farthest chair, his hair combed back, a full plate in front of him and a can of Old Style in his hand. "Joey Walker, now there's a great kid. I'll bet you money his father is damn proud of that one. Did you see that pass he threw last night? And I noticed he doesn't do too poorly with the ladies either, huh? Did you see that cheerleader he was cozying up to after the game? Hooey!"

"Do you know him?" he'd asked me. "What am I saying?" He'd then chuckled. "Of course you wouldn't know a guy like that." His focus had switched to my brother. "Jake, you know him. Maybe if you put in a little more effort at practice you'd get more playing time like Joey, huh? That is some kid. Pass the potatoes, Mary." Mary, of course, being his nickname for me.

My trip down memory lane was interrupted by Jake as he stepped in front of me. My eyes snapped from the table to focus on Jake and the IPA in his outstretched hand.

"Nah, man, I gotta drive home in a bit."

"Suit yourself," he replied and dropped onto the sofa. At least that wasn't the same couch from our childhood. I'd finally gotten our mom to agree to a new one last year when the springs on the old one were literally pushing their way through the threadbare cushions. This new one wasn't fancy, but she'd let me buy it for her and at least I didn't have to risk my nuts being cut off when I sat on it.

She was always touchy when I tried to fix things up at her house, insisting that it was fine as it was and she didn't want me spending my money on her. Since I work in construction, though, I'd been able to make some improvements to the place using spare pieces from other projects. That was how she'd gotten a new foyer floor and kitchen countertops. The kitchen floor I'd had to pay for out-of-pocket, but I didn't tell her that. I just wanted her to have something nice for once in her life.

"Damn, it's weird being back," Jake said as he took a swig and looked around.

"How long has it been anyway?" I let my sudden moodiness spur my comment, knowing full well how long it had been and just wanting to hear him say it. I began to pace the small room.

Oblivious to my mood, Jake replied, "I think it's been over a year—Christmas before last maybe?"

I just grunted in response.

"What crawled up your ass all of a sudden?" my brother asked, trying and failing to pull off a casually amused expression.

"Oh, I don't know—maybe just a bit tired," I said through clenched teeth. The room was starting to feel claustrophobic. I wanted to pick that old recliner up and throw it out on the curb. Fuck, what was wrong with me?

"Oh, just spit it out—I knew this was coming anyway so go ahead." Jake tossed an arm out in invitation.

"Don't try to make it sound like I'm having some kind of teenage hissy fit—if we're going to talk about who the grown-up is in this room, I think we both know it sure as shit isn't you!"

He scratched at the side of his dark scruff. "I'm sorry, okay! I was eighteen. All I could think about was getting the hell out of that man's house before I killed him. Don't you remember what it was like to be eighteen? We're all selfish idiots at that age."

I stopped my pacing and stared at him with incredulity. WTF?!

"Yes, Jake. I *do* remember what eighteen was like—clearly our experiences were worlds apart. You ran off to 'find yourself' and I was stuck here!" He opened his mouth to interrupt but I was on a roll. "*My* eighteen meant taking care of mom and making sure she took her meds every day—making sure she made it to work so she could keep a roof over her head and not lose her insurance. It meant sticking around town working full time and taking classes at community college because God only knew what would happen if somebody didn't stay here to keep an eye on things. That's what it was like to be eighteen, Jake," I spat.

Jesus, it felt good to get that out, but I simultaneously felt like kind of a douchebag—this was practically ancient history and I was indeed starting to resemble a teenager throwing a hissy fit.

Shit.

I slumped next to him on the couch, the fight having left me entirely.

"Exactly how long have you been waiting to say that to me?" He shoved my arm.

"Oh, only about fifteen years. Not long." I sighed.

"I'm sorry, little brother. I know it's no excuse, but I was a young, selfish asshole who couldn't see past the immediate future. If it's any comfort, I regretted signing up for the Marines about thirty minutes into boot camp."

"Maybe a little. Wait, I thought you liked the Marines?" I turned to him.

"I don't think anybody 'likes' the Marines. I did end up learning a lot and it helped me grow the fuck up, that's for sure. I should have come home after. I should have helped you watch after Mom. I just didn't know how to make it up to you and then I kept putting it off, telling myself you were always better at this shit anyway. I know it was stupid."

"Fuck," I swiped his beer. "You're here now. And you seem to be able to get through to Mom a hell of a lot better than I can."

He grabbed the other beer I'd refused minutes earlier. "That's because I've spent the last several years honing my skills at charming older women."

"Don't. That just sounds disturbing as shit."

"Asshole." He shoved me again.

"Dickhead." I shoved him back harder and managed to push him off the couch.

I *knew* I was stronger than him.

"You're gonna have to get to the gym here in town if you want to keep up with me, big brother."

Just then, the front door opened and our mom walked in, spying me on the couch and Jake sprawled on the floor. She smiled. "Isn't this a nice surprise—my two boys hanging out together. It feels like old times." She seemed to be in a good mood.

"Hey, Mom," we both said simultaneously, making me feel like we were indeed kids again.

"How was work?" Jake asked, picking himself up off the floor, trying not to spill his beer in the process.

"The usual—it was fine." She set her purse down on the entry table and turned back to us. "Oh, and I got the strangest phone call. It was from the girl who was with you at the hospital the other day—Fiona?"

Oh shit.

"What did she say?" I was afraid to ask but did anyway. It was like pulling off a bandage—better to get it over with quickly.

"It was the oddest thing. She invited me out to lunch." She had a small smile on her face, obviously recalling the details of the conversation. She let out a little laugh.

Interesting.

"Anyway, we're going out on Wednesday." She walked toward the kitchen, calling out behind her, "You boys need a snack?"

"Always," replied Jake.

I stayed silent, too preoccupied with what Fiona could possibly have said to not only draw such an unexpected reaction from my mom, but to get her to agree to lunch with a complete stranger.

I *knew* Shortcake was a witch.

Chapter Ten

THE A-TEAM AIN'T GOT NOTHIN' ON ME

FIONA

I was like frickin' Hannibal from the A-Team. This plan was coming together like a mo-fo! I wasn't lying when I said I liked a good project—it's one area where my list-making abilities come in super handy.

Even before the Beckett boys had left Laney's house, she and I had schemed out a solid strategy. The plan was to call their mom, whose name we learned was Kelly, and invite her to a welcome-home dinner for Jake that we were planning to host. Who doesn't love an excuse to eat yummy food and drink wine while making new friends in the process? Naturally, the true purpose of the call was to lure Kelly into spending some of her free time with us, therefore keeping her mind off her husband and her ass out of his hospital room.

I called her cell phone and happened to catch her on her way out of work. While the introduction was a bit awkward since I had to mention the hospital, I quickly glossed over it with my typical flightiness and moved right on.

I may have inadvertently implied that her sons and I had known each other for longer than we actually had. Okay, I outright lied, but it was for a good cause! And I did know them through Nate, whom I knew through Laney—and something involving Kevin Bacon makes it okay. Speaking of Kevin Bacon, that dude has gotten scary skinny—eat a sandwich, man.

Anyway, I asked Kelly about Jake's favorite foods when he was growing up and then suggested that a few embarrassing photos would be a good addition, all while drawing her into friendly conversation.

I wasn't too surprised to find that she was a lovely woman with a good sense of humor. And I knew just how to make a mom of two grown men warm up to me. It involved a careful balance of both praising and insulting the shit out of her offspring. Every mom loves to hear good things about her sons while also under-standing that a girl who is blind to their faults or is a pushover is never going to make the grade. Especially with those two beasts she'd raised.

By the end of the call, I had secured a lunch date for Kelly, Laney, and me on Kelly's next day off. She said a cheery goodbye after promising to bring photos with her. I was secretly hoping there would be a few embarrassing shots of Mark as well, but I didn't ask.

"And that's how it's done," I proclaimed to Laney as I pushed the end-call button and set my phone on the counter.

"I have to say I'm pretty damn impressed. You were charming as shit!"

"What a lovely compliment." I glared at her playfully.

"You know what I mean." She scrunched her eyebrows. "You can talk to anyone, and you're never shy or anything—it's really an extraordinary skill."

"Aww, that's sweet. But you know it's just because I'm so used to making a fool of myself that it doesn't really faze me anymore. I just open my mouth and shit comes out." I paused for a moment. "Wait, that didn't come out right, did it? See? It's true!"

She laughed at me as Nate rounded the corner into the kitchen. I took a moment to admire him, as I often do, and oddly found myself comparing him to Mark. Had Nate's arms gotten a little scrawny since the last time I saw him? No. Not possible—that was only a couple days ago.

My mind wandered back to the moment in the foyer when I'd stupidly decided that an arm punch was a proper farewell to Mark. His arm was like steel and apparently I was starting to develop a steel fetish. I'd practically mentally undressed him right there in the foyer—how pathetic. And from the look he'd given me, I don't think it went unnoticed. Damn. It must have been that story about his dog that got to me. Double damn.

"What's so funny?" Nate asked, pulling my attention.

"Fiona," Laney responded, still smiling at me.

"Naturally," was his comeback so I punched him in the arm. What was it with me tonight? At least Nate had the good grace to pretend it hurt.

"So, I don't really get it," Laney said.

"What? He insulted me so I punched him." Did I sound a bit defensive?

"Not that," she said. "If somebody owed me a bunch of money, why would I try to kill them? Then I'd never get my money back."

Nate leaned against the counter and crossed his arms. "Not that I have any personal experience with this, obviously, but I've seen enough movies that some may consider me an expert." Laney and I both rolled our eyes at him but he continued undiscouraged. "My theory is either they never intended to kill him—just hurt him badly enough to scare the shit out of him—or he'd been screwing them around to the point where they figured they'd just off him and take all his possessions. Then they'd at least have something— and they could go after people in his life for the rest. Obviously, that's what has Mark and Jake the most concerned."

That all made sense, I guess. It also pissed me right the hell off —what had Kelly done to deserve even the threat of something like that? It made me even more determined to help them all out and to befriend her in the process. Us girls have to stick together, after all. Vaginas unite!

There has got to be a potential superhero story with that awesome tagline! It's a shame I'm not into comics.

* * *

I managed to make it to Wednesday, the day of our lunch with Kelly, without thinking too much about Mark—or his arms. And by that, I mean I only thought about him a couple times in the shower and maybe a few times at work when I was supposed to be filing. Not bad at all. But even I, the queen of meaningless sex, could admit that this had the potential to become a problem. I mean, casually screwing someone who was part of your friendship network was a terrible idea. Even if that person happened to be hot and used to sing to his dog. I'd just have to try to remember how good he was at annoying me and then I wouldn't want him at all. Yes—good plan.

Technically I only had an hour for lunch but I was good at finagling more time here and there—it was one of life's great mysteries why I got fired so often. Since Laney tended to actually follow her company's policies, we decided to meet up closer to her office for our girls' lunch.

Venturing inside the little Italian bistro in my best skinny jeans and some killer Tory Burch wedge sandals, I spotted Kelly immediately and was suddenly struck by her resemblance to Jake—dark hair, olive complexion, and striking cheekbones. Kelly was also fairly tall, which obviously wasn't saying much coming from me, and was quite beautiful now that her face wasn't streaked with tears as it had been the last time I'd seen her.

It was also clear to me that she was one of those women who didn't know how to play up her beauty and spent very little time on herself. She wore old jeans, a cardigan that was two sizes too big, and not a speck of makeup. I sensed another project looming, and my Inner Fashion Maven cackled gleefully. Unlike Guilt, she was a wonderful house guest.

Kelly hadn't noticed me yet as she stood near the hostess stand gripping her purse while shifting on her feet.

"Kelly!" I approached her with a welcoming smile. Her eyes turned to me and a gorgeous smile lit her face. What in the hell was this woman doing pining over a loser like her dickhead husband? I gripped her hand in both of mine. "It's so good to properly meet you."

"You too, Fiona—thanks for inviting me," she said a bit shyly.

"Of course," I responded and then looked around. "I don't see Laney yet, but let's go ahead and get a table."

She nodded, and by the time we'd been seated at a window table and handed our menus, Laney had arrived.

"You must be Kelly," Laney greeted, shaking Kelly's hand.

"Yes," she smiled, "I've heard a lot about you, Laney. From all accounts, Nate is a very lucky guy."

Laney blushed a bit as she sat in her chair.

"Yes," I agreed. "Nate gets lucky a lot." I opened my menu.

Laney sucked in a breath, but Kelly let out a laugh.

"You'll have to excuse her, Kelly. I would try to explain, but there is really nothing adequate to say." Laney skewered me with her eyes. Anna Wintour was back.

"Please, don't worry about me," Kelly replied with a small smile. "Until I talked to Fiona on Monday I hadn't realized how much I needed a good laugh."

Laney reached out and touched her hand. "I'll bet you do—I know you and your boys have been under a lot of stress this past week."

"Yes, well…" Kelly looked down at her lap, and Laney and I exchanged worried glances. We were supposed to be distracting her, not stressing her out. Shit. "All the more reason to focus on better things—like this dinner you're hosting for Jake. It's very sweet of you," Kelly said, raising her eyes to us again. She fiddled with her water glass, almost knocking it over.

Taking her cue to move on, I said, "Oh—did you remember to bring the pictures? I can't wait to see!"

Her expression immediately brightened and the tension in my

gut eased. Kelly pulled an envelope out of her bag and handed it over to me. I leaned toward Laney so we could both have a look.

Sweet mother of Judas Priest! We'd hit the jackpot.

There were, of course, the adorable diaper shots and then the traditional toddler-holding-baby-brother ones. But then we hit the motherlode of blackmail material. Shot after shot of the brothers together, Jake usually in some pose with his chest puffed out or showing off his adolescent biceps. And then there was Mark—Mark wearing round, wire-rimmed glasses, hair a floppy mess, and weighing about as much as a Chihuahua, and probably with about the same size muscles too.

By the time we got to the last photo—one where Jake had Mark in a headlock with Mark's skinny little ass facing the camera —Laney and I were both in tears.

Kelly reached over and picked up a picture. "They were adorable, weren't they?" This just sent Laney and me off again in another fit of giggles.

"They were…something," Laney managed, swiping a finger under her eye.

"I just never would have guessed that Mark," I extended my arms in the classic giant-fish-story pose, "was ever so scrawny. I mean, he could have given me a run for my money." I laughed. Inwardly, though, I was "mwahaha"-ing as any good villain would do.

"Oh God, I know. He was most definitely a late bloomer. But such a sweet boy—still is." She gazed at the photo with a mother's love.

"We are definitely blowing some of these up—I'm thinking life-sized!" Laney proclaimed, sifting through them again.

I was still stuck on the "sweet boy" comment and the look in Kelly's eyes. No! Mark wasn't supposed to be sweet—he was supposed to be rude and unbearable so I could ignore my attraction to him. Shit.

Thankfully the waitress came to take our order so I could think about something else. Like what kind of dessert I was going to have after lunch.

Conversation flowed easily over lunch and although Kelly certainly wasn't gregarious or particularly outgoing, she did contribute and seemed to feel more comfortable with us by the end of the meal. It was clear though, however much she tried to be engaged and put on a cheerful face, there was a cloak of sadness about her that made me understand Mark's protectiveness when it came to his mother.

The fragility of a parent was an entirely foreign concept to me. I'd spent most of my own life as the fragile one with my elders consistently lending me their strength. What had life been like for a young Mark to assume this opposing role? It was obvious his mother's disposition wasn't merely a result of recent events but one honed over years of struggle.

This thought tempered my good mood, but I maintained my smile as we all parted ways in the parking lot and I headed back to work—all the way thinking about scrawny little Mark being sweet to his mom and then handsome grown-up Mark doing the same. Damn the man. He and his stupid eyelashes and not-so-off-putting muscles were getting under my skin—I could feel it!

✱ ✱ ✱

I heard my phone signal a new text message on Friday morning as I sat at my desk trying to remember what my boss Jax had asked me to do on his way out the door. My hands had been busy so I hadn't written it down, and I was having no luck recalling it. Oh well. I picked up my phone and saw a number I didn't recognize along with a very strange message.

Unknown Number: *I need your help!*

I suddenly imagined myself in one of those movie scenarios where the kidnapping victim discovers a forgotten phone and dials a random number in the hopes that a good Samaritan on the other end of the line will save the day. I could totally do that!

Fiona: *I'm here! What is ur name? Do u need me to call the police?*

Unknown Number: *Huh?*

It was worse than I thought. This person had obviously been put in a confined space and was running out of air. What else could explain the confusion?!

Fiona: *How much air do u have left? Do u know where u are? I need to give the police something to go on!*

I just hoped I wasn't too late. Guilt would never let me forget it if I let this poor person die!

Unknown Number: *Are you high right now, Shortcake?*

Shortcake?

Shortcake!

This was no desperate kidnapping victim. It was Mark Fucking Beckett.

Fiona: *Mark?*

Unknown Number: *Who the hell did you think it was?*

Fiona: *How did u get my number?*

I quickly put his name into my contacts so he couldn't catch me unawares again.

Mark: It didn't take Sherlock Holmes.

Gah!

Mark: What the hell was all that stuff about the police and air?

Never being one to actively pursue humiliation—it preferred to find me on its own—I decided to skip that topic.

Fiona: What do you want?

Mark: My mom is planning on going to the hospital tomorrow and we can't talk her out of it.

Crap! This was about Kelly so I couldn't be mean and tell him to suck it.

Fiona: When?

Mark: Morning sometime. She works in the afternoon.

Fiona: On it. Later.

Mark: Thanks, Shortcake. I owe you.

Fiona: Stop calling me that.

Mark: It's an endearment.

Fiona: Endear this!

I followed that up with a lovely middle finger emoji. Thank you, Steve Jobs, for giving me the tools to adequately express my feelings.

Chapter Eleven

RULES OF THE PLAYGROUND

MARK

I had to laugh as I set my phone down on the desk. I loved torturing the little spitfire, and now that I didn't have to worry about my mom tomorrow I was feeling much more relaxed.

"What are you laughing at?" asked Bailey as she walked into the office. "And get out of my chair."

Bailey Murphy is Nate's younger sister and the one I never had —or particularly wanted. Like Nate, she works for the family construction company and spends her days dealing mostly with interior design and space planning. The rest of her time is spent insulting Nate and me, as far as I can tell. Well, that and painting. Bailey is actually an artist at heart, but she feels an obligation to the family, and having a real job also keeps her from living in a cardboard box—or her parents' basement. I'm unsure which she would consider to be worse.

"I was here first," I said, pointing out the obvious.

"What are you, eight?" she responded and then reached toward my phone. I snatched it up before she could grab it.

Bailey stands only a few inches shorter than me and, thankfully, she isn't into heels like somebody else I know so she never tops me. Lord knows she'd love it, though, so I make sure to never suggest she dress like an actual girl. Objectively, I suppose she's attractive—long blond hair, bright blue eyes, decent rack—but it's impossible to see her as anything other than just *Bailey*.

"You may as well just tell me. I'll find out eventually anyway."

She wasn't above pick-pocketing or blackmail, so I gave in.

"I was just texting Fiona. I get an inordinate amount of pleasure from torturing her."

"Aw, that's so adorable. I can't imagine why you're single," she deadpanned and then proceeded to try and pull me out of her chair. Silly woman.

I just ignored her as she strained herself for another minute.

"You're not pretty enough to be this much of a bitch, Beckett." She stopped pulling at me and flipped me off instead.

What was it with girls giving me the finger today?

"Oh, I'm sorry," I feigned innocence and rose from the chair. "Did you want to sit here?"

"Asshole," she said and flopped into the chair like the graceful angel she is.

"Who peed in your Cheerios this morning?" I asked her.

"Eww. And nobody peed in my…anything. Just yuck." She gave me a disgusted look—one you might give to, well, somebody who peed in your cereal.

"Come on," I coaxed. "Tell Uncle Mark all about it." I took the seat opposite her and folded my arms on the desk.

Her disgusted look morphed into more of a disturbed frown.

"Are you always this creepy or am I just noticing it now?"

"Shut up and tell me what's wrong."

She waved her hand like she was swatting away an annoying bug. "It's nothing—I'm just frustrated—I'll get over it."

"Frustrated about what? Work stuff or…personal stuff? I would say 'guy stuff' but with the way you dress I'm never sure which way you swing." I gestured to her outfit of khaki pants and a company polo.

She gave me a huge fake smile. "I hope the steroids make them shrink up and a mouse eats them while you sleep."

My hand immediately covered my zipper in an attempt to protect my balls from her insults. "Hey—you know I don't take that shit!"

"Whatever you say, Buffy. Anyway, it's nothing you need to worry about—I'll get over it and be fine by Monday."

"Are you sure you don't want to talk about it? I can try my best to be nice and listen. Scouts' honor." I gave her the salute, or possibly signaled a Vulcan code, I'm not really sure—I was never in the Scouts. But I genuinely cared about her and didn't like to see her upset. If this was girl shit, though, I was going to regret it for sure.

"I'm positive. Now before we deal with the boring-ass bid paperwork, I want to hear about Fiona." She waggled her eyebrows.

"So *you* don't have to share but *I* do?"

"Yup."

"Well, there's nothing to say about Fiona anyway. She's just helping me with the situation with my parents and giving me the added bonus of being easy to pick on. You know how much I love that."

"I'm aware," she responded, leaning forward in her seat and searching for some papers on her desk.

"I'm wondering," I mused, "why is it that you and Fiona both have blond hair but she's the only one who's *blond*?"

Bailey eyed me, started to speak, thought better of it, and then finally said, "You know how I said you were acting like you're eight? I'm thinking that's the same thing you're doing with her."

"Huh?"

"You know, pulling her pigtails on the playground, calling her ugly, spitting in her applesauce at lunch…"

"Spitting in her…what the hell kind of school did you go to?!"

She waved me off again. "Andy Pulaski, first grade—the kid was in love with me but didn't know how to show it."

"Are you sure he didn't actually despise you? It sounds like he hated your guts."

"Eh, I guess we'll never know for sure. The point is, you teasing Fiona is so transparent—you should just ask her out and be done with it."

"I don't want to go out with her!" I insisted. "And besides, I tease you all the time and that doesn't mean I want to bone you."

"Yeah, but I'm the exception to the rule. We've known each other too long. And besides, I find you about as desirable as William Shatner's left nut."

"Ouch."

"The truth hurts, Beckett. Just ask her out. What's the worst that could happen?"

Obviously, she didn't know Fiona very well or she'd never ask that question. I'm relatively certain Shortcake could singlehandedly bring on the zombie apocalypse and then just shrug her shoulders and suggest a trip to the mall.

* * *

"She's going where?" I asked Jake.

I was driving home from work that evening when Jake called to tell me that Mom had changed her plans for tomorrow morning. Thank God.

"I told you—some spa or something."

I had heard him the first time but I just hadn't believed it. Our mother had never been to a spa in her entire life. She isn't a spa kind of person.

But I knew a diminutive mastermind who most definitely was.

"Fiona," I said.

"Fiona," Jake echoed. "I don't know how the hell she did it, but that woman is a genius."

Maybe not the word I would choose, but I was grateful nonetheless.

"Anyway," Jake went on, "I called the hospital today and they're planning on transferring the old man to a county rehab facility tomorrow."

"Does Mom know?"

"I don't think so. She hasn't been there since we warned her off on Sunday, but I can't be sure she hasn't been calling on his status.

Anyway, I think this might be a good opportunity for us to stake out the place and see if we can spot anybody while he's being transferred—you know, see if anyone is paying close attention or even tailing him."

"I can't believe I'm saying this, but you have a good point. That would be a great time for someone to try to approach him—when he's sort of out in the open with no security to worry about."

"That's what I was thinking too."

"Okay, any idea what time they're transferring him?"

"Sometime in the morning, but they weren't more specific than that," he told me.

"Okay, I'll bring the coffee and doughnuts and pick you up at 7:30."

"Sounds like a plan, little brother."

I couldn't believe we were staking out a hospital for bad guys. My life had suddenly turned into an eighties buddy flick.

I hit the gym earlier than usual the next morning, determined to get in a workout before potentially sitting on my ass all day. Contrary to some people's experience, a workout actually energizes me so I knew I'd be all set for the day. After showering and dressing in old jeans and a long-sleeved thermal, I headed over to my mom's, stopping for refreshments on the way.

"Rise and shine, people!" I shouted as I unlocked my mom's front door and let myself in.

"Hey, sweetie," came her voice from the kitchen. I followed it and found her in an old pink robe at the table with a cup of coffee and a pile of mail. "What are you doing here so early on a Saturday?"

"Jake and I are running some errands," I semi-lied to her as I handed over a fresh latte from the drink tray I was carrying.

"Wow—thanks!" she said, not needing to check what kind of drink I'd gotten her. I knew her vices.

Just then Jake sauntered into the kitchen dressed very similarly to me, only the color of our shirts differentiating us. He went directly for the drink tray and lifted the lid on the only untouched coffee there—we both took our coffee black. After taking a long sip, he finally spoke. "Ready?" he asked me.

"Ready," I replied. "See you later, Mom," I said.

"Not sure when I'll be back but you'll probably be at work so I'll see you tonight, okay?" Jake addressed our mother.

"Sure," she said, distracted by a letter in her stack of mail. "I'll see you later."

We drove toward the hospital mostly in silence as we sipped our coffees and Jake devoured two of the doughnuts from the bag between our seats. I turned up the radio to give us something to distract ourselves, although it didn't do much except eliminate the need for conversation.

When we finally pulled up to the hospital, I parked in the visitor lot and switched off the ignition. "Well, I guess this is it. I feel like we should have brought something with us—like some brass knuckles or a pocket knife. I feel unprepared."

"The goal is not to get arrested, dumbass. We're just waiting and watching—no big deal. Let's go," he said, opening the passenger door and stepping out.

We ventured in the main doors of the hospital and up to the

floor where our old man's room was. The nurses' station was bustling and there was a constant stream of people up and down the hallway. How in the hell were we going to spot these guys, assuming they would even show up?

As if sensing my irritation, Jake whispered, "Calm the fuck down. Just pull out your phone and act like a normal person, dickhead."

We leaned against the wall several doors down from the asshole's room for the next hour or so, taking turns strolling around the floor in a (hopefully) casual manner. The only pleasant distraction was a surgically enhanced red-haired nurse who did her own "casual" strolls by our spot in the hall. Her eyes raked over us each time she passed and we returned the favor, but after the first time I just wasn't feeling it. Jake, on the other hand, most definitely was.

"What's your name, darlin'?" he asked on her third lap.

"Lexie," she answered and tilted her head to the side. "What's yours?"

"I'm Jake. This is Mark. Think you can help me out with something, Lexie?"

"Sure." She smiled up at him.

"That patient in room 320 who you guys are moving today—has anybody been around asking questions about him?"

She suddenly looked unsure. "Oh, I can't give out any patient information. Sorry." She attempted another smile, seemingly disappointed she couldn't give him what he wanted.

"No, I don't need any patient info—just wondering if any visitors have been hanging around or asking about him."

She was ready to retreat so I took over. "Listen, Lexie, that guy in there is our dad and we're worried some people who aren't so friendly are looking for him. We're just trying to protect him."

"Oh." She seemed to consider that. "Um, now that you mention it, I did notice a couple guys hanging around yesterday who seemed a bit out of place. They kept walking by the room and then the nurses' station and were clearly eavesdropping. We ended up calling security but they split before security got here. I didn't think much of it until now. We get odd people around pretty often —usually bored from waiting around."

Mark and I exchanged a glance. Shit. "Do you remember what they looked like?" Jake asked her.

She bit her bottom lip in concentration. "They were kind of unremarkable, you know, just everyday guys. They both had on baseball caps—I think one of them had a red logo. The other guy had a leather jacket and they were both in jeans. That's about all I can remember, sorry. Do you need me to call security?"

"No, that's okay," I said. "Do you happen to remember if either of them had facial hair or a noticeable tattoo or something?" Yeah, I've watched some TV. I know some things.

"Oh, yeah, the one guy had a goatee—I do remember that. No tattoos I can remember but they were both wearing long sleeves so ..." she trailed off.

"Thanks, Lexie," Jake said and then winked at her. "Just one more thing—do you think you can find out what time our dad is being transferred without making a big deal out of it—we kind of don't want him to know we're here."

She gave us a curious look and put her hands to her hips. "Show me your ID and I'll see what I can do." Smart girl.

Jake smiled at her and pulled out his wallet, extracting his driver's license and handing it over. Lexie took it to the nurses' station and started typing into the computer. Seemingly satisfied with what she'd found, she returned a few minutes later with the license in her outstretched hand.

"Okay, Jake Beckett. I can tell you the rehab transport is supposed to arrive at 11:00 and he'll be discharged by then."

Jake took the ID and gave her a grin. "Thanks, Lexie. You've been very helpful. Now, maybe you can help me with just one more thing?"

"That's what you said five minutes ago. I do have a job, you know," she scolded but did it smiling. "What else could you possibly need?"

"Your number would be a good start."

* * *

"You know, it may be time for you to branch out and try dating a girl with tits she didn't pay for. It opens up a whole new demographic," I suggested to Jake as we walked out to the parking lot. All I got was a pointed look with a raised eyebrow in return.

We were back in the truck, which I'd moved for a better vantage point. That way we could watch, hopefully unnoticed, when our father came out, keeping our eyes peeled for anything suspicious.

After another half hour of waiting with just the radio and our own thoughts, Jake said, "You know, I wanted to be in the FBI when I was younger." He tapped the buttons on the radio looking for actual music instead of commercials or cackling deejays.

"Seriously?"

"Yeah. I thought it would be cool and it sounded interesting too —I could be a real-life bad-ass, you know. Although, now that I'm an actual adult I realize the job doesn't really involve much of that."

"So why didn't you go to college and try going for the FBI instead of enlisting out of high school?"

"Why do you think?" He sat back in his seat, having found a good country station.

Oh, right. "Dad somehow found out," I stated more than asked.

"You know it—laughed his ass off and told me the government would never hire a dumbass like me unless it was to shine their shoes."

God, our dad was an asshole.

"Still, you shouldn't have let him stand in your way," I said, knowing it was unhelpful at best.

He just grunted in return and then pointed to a car backing out of a prime spot. I quickly put the truck in reverse and maneuvered to the new parking space.

"Anyway, you seem to have a good thing going with the land-scape design, right?" For some reason, I was set on pulling him from any dark thoughts—ironic given our current circumstances.

"Sure," he replied. "Hey—didn't Fiona say she works for a landscaping company?" He attempted nonchalance. Unsuc-cessfully.

"Uh, yeah, why?" I asked cautiously, not sure I wanted to know where this was going.

"No reason." Jake shrugged.

Yeah, like I believed that. It was like a dog asking where the shoes were stored and then passing it off as a mere bit of curiosity.

I scoffed. "What—" I began but Jake cut me off, suddenly pointing out the driver's side window.

"Check it out," he said quietly, but with an intensity that made me shut the hell up.

I turned my head to look out the window and saw two guys standing next to a black sedan, smoking. One wore a black cap with a Red Sox logo and the other had on a black leather jacket and sported a dark goatee.

Shit. Fuck. Damn.

I really wished at that moment that Jake had, in fact, followed his childhood dreams and could call in a crapload of reinforcements. But as it had always been and probably always would be, we were on our own to deal with the oncoming shitstorm.

Chapter Twelve

THE POWER OF THE PEDI

FIONA

"I don't know about this," Kelly fidgeted in the front seat of my Prius as I parked outside the Youtopia Day Spa in High Point.

"What do you mean? Free mani-pedi! Life rarely gets better than that," I encouraged. I hadn't anticipated her level of discomfort. I mean, I'd figured she rarely had the chance to treat herself, but she looked downright scared. I glanced to the back seat hoping Laney could step in and somehow fix the situation.

Reading my mind as usual, she leaned forward, eying the spa's sign through the windshield. "It's been *forever* since I had a pedicure. You ever had one, Kelly?"

"Not yet." Kelly shook her head and tucked a strand of stray hair behind her ear.

"I was kind of weirded out the first time too, but as soon as the woman started massaging the knots out of my calves I was a goner." Laney sighed.

"They do that?" Kelly asked, incredulous.

"Sheer heaven," I confirmed.

"Girls, you are young twenty-somethings with what I am sure are beautiful young twenty-something feet. Mine look more like something out of a horror movie. I'll be too embarrassed. Maybe I'll just do the manicure."

"No!" we both cried at once.

"The pedicure is the best part—and they always have massage chairs…" Laney cast out the lure and prepared to reel Kelly in.

"And I'm sure they have seen much, much worse than whatever you think you have going on in those shoes. I promise—they won't bat an eyelash."

"Crap. Maybe. I don't know…I guess. Okay. Fine, I'll do it."

"Yay!" Laney and I both did a happy car dance.

"You girls are nuts," Kelly commented, but she was smiling as she opened her door and got out.

I had been due for a mani-pedi anyway, so as soon as my middle finger text to Mark had been sent, I was on the phone with Dr. Brandon asking him for more info on his daughter's new spa. He was happy to put me in touch with Jenny and I escaped the call with only a few short questions about my wellbeing. Overall, a successful chat, I thought.

I went ahead and called Jenny, hoping she'd have three available spots—which was pushing it considering it was Friday afternoon and I was looking for Saturday morning appointments. As luck would have it—for me, not so much for Jenny—the new spa was slow-going and she indeed had more than enough open spots for us. In fact, she offered us all free services in exchange for honest online reviews, hoping to drive in more traffic. I tried to protest but she was having nothing of it, so I just planned on tipping the crap out of our technicians.

Appointments made and Laney on board, I called Kelly and told her about our family friend who'd just opened a spa and needed people to come in and try out the services for free. Based on her hesitancy, I now realized I may have bullied her into it a little—with overenthusiasm and friendliness, I hoped.

But it was the perfect opportunity to kill two birds with one stone. I would keep Kelly away from the hospital and the creepy bad guys (her husband included) and I could begin Inner Fashion Maven's grand plans for a Kelly makeover—insert non-evil cackle. I didn't know anybody who deserved it more than she did, and if she was open to it I was going to be on her like white on rice, or Laney on Nate, or whatever.

We walked through the front door and were immediately surrounded by a lovely spicy-minty scent and relaxing background music that sounded like tiny bells. The entire reception area of the spa was painted an earthy green combined with cream and rust accents, and a beautiful stone fountain sat in the corner bubbling quietly. Comfy chairs lined one wall and tempting products were on display throughout the space. It was, in fact, what I imagined heaven's waiting room to be like. All that was missing were some cherubs and a giant gold gate.

"Fiona!" I heard my name being called and turned to see Jenny emerging from behind the sleek cream reception counter. We exchanged hugs and I congratulated her on the new spa. She and I kind of knew each other from the years our families had been attending the same fundraisers and functions. She was in her thirties and had three kids, though you'd never be able to tell—she was slim and pretty and she rocked an awesome head full of burgundy curls.

"It's so beautiful!" I told her. "You'll be beating customers back in no time."

"Your lips to God's ear," she responded with a smile before introducing herself to Laney and Kelly. "Come on back, gals, I've got you all set up—you just need to pick your colors and then relax." She led us to the back, which was more of the same nirvana but this time with massage chairs.

We all chose our colors—I went with a citrus theme while Laney chose a palette of blues and Kelly chose clear.

Clear.

I did not think so. I grabbed the bottle and put it right back. "You can't pick clear! At least if you're going to do the clear look you need a French manicure."

"What's that?" she asked and I refrained from crossing myself —just barely. I looked up and down the colors and pulled out a pretty pale pink and a slightly darker one. "How about these? The lighter one is for your hands and the other is for your feet. You're probably the only one who's going to see your toes, so why not have a little fun?"

She agreed and we all sat down in our cushy chairs at the manicure tables. Jenny declared she was doing mine, and she introduced us to Laney's technician, Evelyn, and Kelly's technician, Nari.

"This is Kelly's first mani-pedi so go easy on her, Nari," Laney teased.

"You're kidding," replied Nari. "You just relax and I'll take care of you. We won't be able to keep you out of the spa by the time we're done with you today." She smiled at Kelly and got another in return.

Phew.

Thirty minutes later, we were sitting side by side in our massage chairs while Jenny and the gals worked on our feet.

Kelly let out a giant sigh. "I can't believe I've never done this. What was I thinking?" She had her eyes closed and her head leaned back.

Nari laughed as she applied the scrubby stuff to Kelly's legs. "I told you."

"And I don't know what you were talking about with your feet being old people feet or something," I said.

"They are," she insisted. "I've been working on my feet for thirty-five years. It does things to a woman's feet."

"Nari, be honest, how bad are her feet?"

Without hesitation, Nari replied, "Not even top 100 in nasty feet. You wouldn't believe the things I've seen."

"Amen!" said Jenny and Evelyn at once.

We all laughed, even Kelly.

I decided here was my opening. "Jenny, do you do other services too? Besides nails and massages?" I asked.

"We're starting out with just this for now, but we have more space and we'll have hair styling, facials, and waxing if we can get things going soon. I'm actually a stylist, but I'm a certified nail technician too so right now this is what I'm doing."

Excellent.

"Don't you think Kelly would look great with a cute layered bob?"

"Oooooh," said Laney. "I like it."

Jenny considered Kelly with her professional eye. "That could totally work with some caramel highlights. That would rock."

"Stop right there, girls," said Kelly who was leaning back with her eyes closed again. "I'm still getting used to the idea of having painted nails so don't rush me. And, besides, stuff like that needs upkeep and I'd rather eat than have pretty hair."

I knew not to push too hard, so I let it go. Sort of. "We'll skip the highlights then," I said quietly and Kelly gave my arm a shove.

An actual shove! This was awesome. I looked over at her and her eyes were still closed but she had a grin on her face.

* * *

I had promised to have Kelly home in time for her to run a few errands and get ready for work—and I kept my promise, pulling up to her house with time to spare. She'd gone quiet again on the drive home, but I was hoping it was just because she was super relaxed. Turned out, not so much.

She turned in her seat so she could see both Laney and me. "Can you girls come in for a minute? I have something I need an opinion on." She looked nervous as all get-out again.

Shit.

We didn't even answer. We just opened our doors and followed her into the house. It was one side of an older duplex and it was a bit dated, which I had sort of anticipated, to be honest. I could see where little updates had been made here and there, but nothing disguised the age and wear of the place. The tile in the entryway appeared almost new, but the carpet had definitely seen better days. A nice couch sat along one wall of the living room, but the rest of the furniture looked old and beaten up. The kitchen counters and floor were not original to the house and I could see Mark's hand in all of it. Despite the mix of old and new, the entire place was tidy and free of clutter. Kelly definitely liked her living space neat.

She led us to the table in the small kitchen and invited us to take a seat. Once we were all sitting, she withdrew an envelope from the stack of mail sitting on the table in front of us. She handed it to Laney.

"Does this mean what I think it means?" Kelly asked.

Laney opened the envelope, took out the letter, and read it over. "Crap," she swore and handed it to me.

It was a plain sheet of white paper with just a few words printed on it.

You have one week. $32,000 cash.

"Shit," I said and put down the paper.

We all just stared at each other.

"I kept telling myself it must be a bad joke or something, but it's not, is it?"

"We have to call Mark," I said.

"No!" Kelly exclaimed. "I don't want to worry him or Jake. I'll figure something out."

"But you can't!" insisted Laney. "You need their help! And we should call the cops too—this is a threat!" She pointed to the paper. "It's one thing if your husband doesn't want to call the cops but now they've threatened you, so you can call!"

Kelly just shook her head. "But it's not an actual threat. There's nothing the police could do about it," she said.

Laney and I both read the paper again. She was right. It was deliberately vague.

"I'm going to the hospital to see Jim tomorrow and find out where the money is. Then I'm going to get it to these people." She pointed to the paper.

"What makes you think he still has any of it? Wouldn't he have handed it over the first time instead of being beaten half to death?" I asked, wondering if Kelly was thinking straight.

Kelly shook her head again. "I don't know—you'd have to know Jim. He's so…stubborn and always sure he's in the right. He *could* still have at least some of it. Anyway, I'm going to find out tomorrow. If he doesn't have it, I'll figure something else out from there. These guys obviously know about me but they don't know about the boys—and I intend to keep it that way."

"I understand you wanting to protect them, Kelly, but they'd want to do the same for you. They're worried about you."

"I know, but they don't need to be. As soon as we get this money thing worked out, things can go back to normal."

Laney and I exchanged a glance.

"Normal like 'last-week-normal' or normal like 'with Jim'?" I asked, afraid of the answer.

"What do you mean?" She seemed genuinely puzzled.

"Well, from what Mark and Jake said, not that it's any of my business you know, but from what they said it sounded kind of like you maybe, you know, still kind of had—"

"Oh for God's sake," Laney cut me off. "What she's trying to ask is if you still have feelings for your husband and want him back."

Kelly's head jerked back. "What would make you think that?"

I mumbled, "Mark and Jake may have mentioned something or other…"

"Oh," she said and looked down at the table. She remained silent for a few moments before speaking again. "The whole middle-of-the-night hospital thing was just so crazy—I'm not even sure what I said to them. It was all so shocking, you know?" She lifted her head. "Seeing Jim again and especially in those circumstances—it took me a few days to get my head on straight."

"So…you don't want him back?" Laney asked.

Kelly gave a slight laugh that held zero humor. She tilted her head back and blinked like one does when trying to stave off tears.

We waited silently, hoping she'd elaborate. After getting a handle on her emotions and bringing her eyes back to us, she did.

"My boys, they remember all the bad stuff, you know?"

Laney and I both nodded, waiting for her to continue but afraid of what we'd hear.

"But I remember the beginning. I was so in love, and I have to believe Jim was too. There is nothing as magical as young love, and God we were young. I was seventeen. He was nineteen and was going to be my knight in shining armor, taking me away to a life that would be so, so beautiful. It felt like no one else in the world could possibly have a love as pure and strong as ours—it would last forever. We were kids." She shrugged.

"The thing is, change happens gradually, not overnight. Things…happen. Real life happens. Lord knows I should have been a better mother and stepped in when Jim got out of line. But it's so easy to see that in hindsight. Looking back, I just remember being tired and I remember making excuses—at least he didn't hit us, at least he didn't do drugs. I understand it's no real excuse and never will be. He was just so clever in the way he put us down and made us feel like we should be grateful he even put up with us."

She gave another humorless laugh. "I'm not stupid. I don't actually want him back." She ran a hand through her long hair and looked up at the ceiling again. "I guess part of me just wants to feel worthy of *someone* wanting to come back for me, even if it is my loser husband. I know that sounds ridiculous. It *is* ridiculous."

My heart broke into a billion pieces and my throat was so tight with tears that I didn't dare try to speak. One glance at Laney showed her similarly affected, her cheeks streaked with tears she hadn't been able to hold back.

I reached out my hand and gripped Kelly's. Laney did the same on the other side. We held on for dear life.

There were two things I was certain of at that moment. One, this was something even an entire day at the spa couldn't make a dent in. And two, I was going to kick the ever-loving shit out of Jim Beckett. They might be tiny, but these fists were gonna fly.

Chapter Thirteen

LOU AND TERRY AND THE SUCKER PUNCH

$\mathcal{M}$**ARK**

Fiona: *Where r u?!*

There was no way I was about to tell Fiona I was sitting in my truck outside the hospital looking at two thugs who may be planning on kidnapping or killing my father as soon as he emerged.

I ignored her text.

It was 12:30 and we still hadn't seen any signs of our old man or the transfer vehicle. Jake had just returned from a little recon mission where he'd gone through the back of the hospital and confirmed that our father was still there. As is typical in healthcare, things weren't running on time.

The goons—I was trying out different terms to refer to them and I may have found a winner—were back in the black sedan and Jake and I were doing our damn best not to be noticed.

My phone chimed again.

Fiona: *Where the hell r u?!*

"You gonna answer that?" Jake asked me, leaning forward in his seat and looking as restless as I was.

"No."

Before I could move a muscle, he'd snatched my phone and put a hand over my face to push me away from him.

"Fiona," he said with a smirk as I grabbed my phone back and punched him in the arm.

"Next time it will be your pretty little face," I warned him.

My phone chimed yet again and Jake smothered a laugh.

Fiona: *Mark, if you don't tell me where you are I will publish this picture on Instagram, Twitter, and my Facebook page.*

What followed this was something I had difficulty wrapping my brain around. It was a photo from when I was about 12 and Jake was maybe 16. He was standing shirtless, flexing his bicep on one arm while choking the crap out of me with his other arm. I was maybe 80 pounds soaking wet and was wearing my damn glasses and a bow tie. How in the hell did she get this picture?

And then I remembered who I was dealing with.

Mark: *Let's not do anything rash, Shortcake. I'm at the hospital.*

Fiona: *Perfect. On my way.*

Fuck!

Mark: *DO NOT COME HERE!*

Fiona: *Don't you shouty caps me! I can go where I want!*

If the goons didn't get to me first, this girl was going to be the death of me.

Mark: *Seriously, Fiona. The bad dudes are here. Stay away and keep my mom away!*

Fiona: *Shit. Okay.*

I could breathe again.

Fiona: R u okay?

Mark: We're fine. Just watching right now. Nothing has happened.

Fiona: Should I call the police?

Mark: No! What is it with you and the police? Is this a fetish thing?

Fiona: What? Please speak English.

Mark: No cops. Dad is being transferred to rehab. Do NOT tell my mom.

Fiona: She's at work anyway. Had a lovely time at the spa.

Jesus H. Christ.

Mark: We're gonna follow the rehab transfer to make sure he gets there safe. Will text you later.

Fiona: Stay safe. Later.

I read her last text and then noticed that Jake was staring at me with a shit-eating grin. "Do you realize your face went through about thirty emotions in the last five minutes and at one point you actually growled?"

"No I didn't."

He nodded with that stupid-ass grin still glued to his face. "You've got it bad, little brother."

"Whatever. She just drives me crazy," I lied.

He put on a mock frustrated face and balled his fists. "Oooh, that little minx, she just drives me so crazy I'm gonna fuck the hell out of her."

What an asshole. "You know, Jake, all I can think of right now is how jealous I am of all the people who've never met you."

He laughed, completely unoffended. Douchebag.

"Oh shit," he said, his expression sobering. "Here comes the transfer." He pointed out the windshield to a vehicle that resembled a combination of an ambulance and a van. On its side were the words "Guilford County." This vehicle was either taking someone to rehab or to prison. Either would be fitting.

I looked to the sedan and saw that the driver had opened his door.

Jake and I both opened ours, but we hadn't yet determined exactly what we were going to do.

"I'm thinking you may have been right about those brass knuckles, little brother," he said quietly.

My heart was beating a mile a minute as the vehicle came to a stop and the transfer driver got out. He was not a big guy—by any means.

Just then, the double automatic doors of the hospital parted and there was our old man on a stretcher, looking not a whole lot better than the last time I'd seen him. A lone woman in scrubs was pushing the stretcher. Shit. We needed more people around, preferably ones with muscles and weapons.

"Is that him?" asked Jake, his voice surprised. I forgot he hadn't seen our father in fifteen years.

"Yup."

"He looks so…" Jake started.

"Old, I know," I said.

"I was gonna say small, but yeah. Holy shit."

"Speaking of holy shit, here we go," I said as I gestured to the sedan where both men had now emerged and were heading slowly toward the transfer vehicle.

We let them get a head start and then fell in behind them, careful to keep a good distance.

They were about twenty feet from the vehicle when the one with the goatee shouted, "Yo, Jim! Fancy seeing you here. Haven't seen you since Vegas."

We picked up our pace and closed the distance a bit. I could see my father turn his head to them and then mouth the word "Fuck."

The orderly and the driver seemed to hesitate, not quite sure if this was a friendly meeting or not.

That would be a firm "not."

"Lou, Terry, hey," said the old man, feigning cheerfulness. "Uh, you can see I'm not really up for visitors right now."

"Yeah, what happened, man?" said Lou or Terry, whichever one had the Sox hat on. At this point, they were about five feet from the stretcher. The driver and orderly, seemingly having decided this was an exchange of friendly pleasantries, went about their business and began loading our father into the back of the vehicle.

"Oh, you know…" said the old man, nervous as shit.

"Oh yeah," said the thug with the goatee. "I think I heard something about that. You should be more careful who you hang out with, Jim. Maybe you should spend more time at home—with your pretty wife."

"Oh shit," said Jake at my side.

"Yeah, maybe," was all the old douchebag said. Son of a bitch!

"We'll stop by your house next week and check on her for you —see how she's doing while you're healing up. Sound good?"

"Uh…" said my piece-of-shit father.

"It's all set then, next Saturday. Later, Jim."

And they walked away, right past us and back to the sedan. Jake and I pretended to be in conversation as they passed and the doors of the transfer vehicle slammed shut with a bang.

It was official. Our old man was the shittiest husband and father in the world and we were all up shit's creek without a paddle.

* * *

It turned out I didn't get a chance to text Fiona to update her—she wasn't patient enough to wait. By the middle of the afternoon, she'd found Jake's number and we both had three new texts along with a renewed threat to post more incriminating photos if I didn't "call her ass immediately."

I also had an apology text from Laney.

And another from Nate.

Exactly when had Shortcake become an integral player in this debacle? How had she wormed her way into this so deeply that she now required regular "briefing"?

Still, not wanting to subject myself to widespread ridicule over social media, I dialed the little harpy's number while my brother made himself at home in my kitchen and grabbed a soda from the fridge.

"The bad guys know about your mom," she said as soon as she picked up the call. "She didn't want me to tell you and I've been going back and forth about this for hours, but I'm so worried for her, I just had to tell you. And now I'm probably going to hell, or at least Karma is going to have it out for me. I'll probably break my leg or lose my job—of course, that's probably going to happen anyway, but whatever. Anyway, I'm prepared to suffer the consequences if it means we can protect your mom. I was thinking I could hire a bodyguard for her or, you know, buy an attack dog. Although what we'd do with the dog when this is over, I don't really know. My building doesn't allow dogs over thirty pounds and I doubt we could find a good attack dog that small. And now that I think about it, I'm not sure I'd want an aggressive dog as a pet anyway. You think we should go with the bodyguard instead? Maybe I could find a hot guy close to her age and it could be like that movie, *The Bodyguard*, except he and your mom would stay together in the end. Oh, and nobody would die," she finished on a breathless gasp.

"Shortcake!" I finally shouted when she stopped for a beat.

"Yeah?"

"Shut it!" I said, trying to get a moment to take it all in. She was like a forest fire—once she got going it was fucking hell to stop her.

"Rude!" she responded but did, in fact, shut it.

"I know they know about my mom. The question is, how do you know?" I mentally braced for an answer I knew I wouldn't like.

"They sent her a threatening letter. Can we please call the cops now?"

Shit.

"Hold tight. Where are you?"

"My place."

"Where's that?"

She gave me the address and I told her I was heading right over.

"Just call up and I'll buzz you in when you get here. In the meantime, I'll call my parents' driver and ask him if he knows any hot older bodyguards. Drivers usually know these things, don't they?"

I couldn't take it—I hung up on her.

I put my phone on mute in case she called back and then relayed all the details to Jake.

Let me rephrase—I relayed all the *pertinent* details to Jake. I left the crazy where it was—in a high-rise building downtown.

"I'm heading over to Fiona's to find out as much as I can. I'll drop you off at Mom's and you see if you can find this letter."

"Shit. Okay," he said and we both headed back out. "You know, Florida is much less dramatic than North Carolina."

"I'm thinking after this shit blows over I might need a vacation —you'd best prepare for a houseguest."

I parked on the street a block down from the high-rise. Damn, this girl was money incarnate. I work in the business and I know how much condos go for in a building like this.

Way out of my league, just like her.

Wait, no. I didn't want to be "in her league" anyway. That's the kind of thing relationship people think. I don't date—I fuck and run. So who cares how much money a chick has? It's never been an issue when she's under me. Not that Fiona was going to be under me, or over me, or against the wall, or on the kitchen table— hey, with all those fuck-me heels she wears, who can blame my male brain for wandering there from time to time? Or all the time. Dammit.

I buzzed her.

No response.

I buzzed her again.

Still no response.

I called her on my phone.

After five rings, she finally picked up.

"Yes?"

"Buzz me up, Shortcake. I'm getting strange looks out here."

Indeed, there was a guy who watched me buzzing repeatedly and felt it necessary to comment, "Damn, man, you must have pissed her right the fuck off."

"Oh, I'm sorry. Did you want to talk to me? Because it sure didn't seem like it when you *hung up on me!*" she shouted.

"It was just a bad connection," I blatantly lied.

She muttered something unintelligible and then I heard the buzzer go off. I was no moron—I grabbed that door as fast as humanly possible since I was certain there would be no second chances, regardless of loan sharks and goons and my little spitfire's need to be a do-gooder.

The entire lobby area was decorated and designed in a very clean, modern style. A bit minimalist for my taste, but then again, it seemed that rich people often paid more for less. I found the elevator and, I must admit, I was a tiny bit disappointed to see she did not live in the penthouse, but on the floor below. If she'd had an entire penthouse to herself, it would have made it that much easier to dismiss her completely as a spoiled little rich girl who was just dabbling in my family's drama for entertainment. Not that a condo on the fourteenth floor of this building would be anything to sneeze at.

I imagined Fiona in my mother's dilapidated house and felt a twinge of both humiliation and anger that I couldn't quite reconcile. Fiona was simultaneously too good for the abysmal place and not good enough for it—or my mother, or me, or Jake for that matter. It made no sense, but the familiar feeling of never being good enough produced an amazing amount of resentment that built over time like an unnoticed thorny weed and often stung innocent passersby. It was yet to be determined if Fiona fell into that category or not. She'd never struck me as innocent at any rate.

The elevator took me up to her floor and I found her door, which was propped open a few inches. I took this as an invitation and entered her condo, ready for her verbal attack and the possibility of physical assault as well.

I took in the place. Yup, money.

The apartment and its furnishings weren't particularly stuffy or ostentatious, it was just that everything in there was expensive. Expensive in the way where it doesn't scream it cost a mint but it would probably automatically repel dusty cargo pants or beer in a can. The owner of said items would find himself mysteriously thrust into the hallway with no clear understanding of how he'd gotten there while the couch pillows inside would wipe their imaginary hands and say, "Well, now that that's done let's get back to being splendidly rich."

I was so distracted in my perusal of the condo that I didn't see Fiona at first. Then I wondered how I couldn't have spotted her right off. She was, for once, not wearing heels. In fact, she was barefoot. She was also dressed in form-fitting jeans and a simple wide-neck white t-shirt—which, let's face it, probably cost as much as the couch I'd bought my mom. Her hair floated about her face as usual and I realized she wasn't wearing any make-up.

My Shortcake stood in the threshold of the kitchen with a wounded look on her face and red puffy eyes. She'd been crying. The mere thought that either I or my situation was the cause of the tears had me wanting to take back every negative, sarcastic, insulting thing I'd ever thought about her or said to her. My gut roiled at the same time it was hit with the biggest sucker punch I'd ever felt or imagined. Because despite all my big talk, my history, and common sense in general, she was *my* Shortcake.

She was mine.

What on God's green earth was I going to do with this revelation? It turns out that standing there like a big fucking jackass was the only move I had.

Brilliant.

Chapter Fourteen

WE DO LIVE IN A DEMOCRACY, AFTER ALL

FIONA

In my defense, I didn't really think he'd show up after he hung up on me like an asshole. But by the time I realized he was indeed downstairs and wasn't going away, I refused to primp or even apply so much as a swipe of lip balm, and I just buzzed him up. So what if I looked like a twelve-year-old homeless person? Oh, wait, that thought was too depressing—I'd totally want to embrace a twelve-year-old homeless girl and adopt her. So what if I looked like a very short crack whore? That was better. Mark would just have to take me as I was. No, I didn't mean *take me*, I meant *put up with me*. That's what I meant. Wait, did I just compare myself to a crack whore? *Get it together, Fiona!*

When the door swung open and Mark stepped inside, my breath hitched a bit. He was dressed in a *very* form-fitting olive green long-sleeved thermal, an old pair of jeans that were worn in *all* the right places, and work boots. He had that creased brow and a day or two of scruff on his face, and my lady bits decided they liked this look very much. A fire started down below from just the kindling of his scruff and the spark from his sheer hotness. How had I thought all of...*that*...was excessive? He was fucking sexy as hell!

He looked like he'd just walked off a runway and I looked like I'd just walked out of a crack den. This was completely counter to the familiar order of things in my little world. *I* was runway! *He* was gym rat material—rude and conceited. Right?

Oh, of course not. I'd known for at least a week that he was more than that. Much more.

His eyes finally found me and Uterus spoke up. *"Fallopian Tubes, Vagina, and I have all voted and the results are in —JUMP HIM!"*

Well, crap. I could usually reason with Fallopian Tubes and Uterus, but Vagina? There was no swaying her. In fact, she and Inner Fashion Maven were often in cahoots as they shared a mutual hatred of Guilt and a mutual affection for hot sex. Thank God Clit hadn't weighed in or I'd already be across the room and climbing Mark like the human mountain he was. Everest be damned! It was Beckett I would conquer!

Shut. The Fuck. Up.

I had to gather my wits. This was not about crack whores, female anatomy, or mountains that needed scaling. This was about a very real threat to good people and I needed to clear my freaking head.

"Shortcake," was all he said as his shoulders dropped and he lost any sense of defensiveness he'd entered my condo with. "What's all this?"

I was confused. "Um, my condo?" I asked more than said.

"No, that's not what I mean. The tears, Shortcake?" He approached slowly, his thigh muscles straining his jeans.

Panty Dropper, party of one!

"Don't call me that," I said with only half the indignation I'd meant to use.

He was standing directly in front of me by that point. I looked down, suddenly self-conscious at my appearance when I had been steadfastly resolute just minutes before.

I felt his finger on my chin, lifting my face so he could look directly at me without having to bend down. I realized this was the first time he had ever touched me and I felt goosebumps rise on my arms. It really was quite ridiculous how big he was in comparison to me. I wondered for a moment what those muscles were called that rose above a person's collarbone to create that slope Mark had. Then I dismissed that thought altogether as I caught his scent and nearly swooned. What was that? Whatever it was, it had the effect of a hot fudge sundae on all my various lady parts because they all swooned simultaneously, leaving me responsible for keeping our entire body upright. Bitches!

"I like calling you that," he responded quietly. "Please don't spoil it for me."

I was evidently under some kind of spell he'd cast because I inexplicably said, "Okay."

Okay?! What? I hated when people pointed out my height—it was so patronizing. Like I wasn't aware of my size already and just needed a freakishly large person to point out something my tiny scale-appropriate brain couldn't possibly configure on its own! *Wow, thank you for pointing that out—I was wondering why I had so much more oxygen down here. Feel free to go on with your busi-ness, you freakishly tall human being, you.* Gah!

But apparently, Mark was now using some sort of wizardry on me because I capitulated like a puppy with a peanut-butter-filled Kong.

"What the hell, Fiona?" cried a new part of my subconscious. I wasn't familiar with this one. *"Pride,"* she introduced herself.

Oooooh. Wow, it's great to meet you—I think we need you right about now.

"Yeah, no shit," she said. But before she could say more, Mark cut in.

"I don't like seeing you cry. Are these tears about my mom? Please say you just watched something sad on TV or missed a giant sale instead," he said as his thumb swept over my right cheek.

My knees wobbled and I could only hear Pride as a very faint echo in the back of my brain yelling, *"Hold on!"*

"I just...don't want any of you getting hurt," was what I managed without breaking down again.

This afternoon, I had waited until I'd dropped Laney off and was safely ensconced in my own space before I'd broken down. I cried my eyes out at the unfairness of it all. Why were some people so cruel? Why did Kelly have a shit husband who, even after disap-pearing for years, could still rain hurt down on her and her kids? Why did my family have money when *she* was the one who needed it to protect her family? And why did people like me, who had those financial resources, have to fight a different battle—one that money couldn't win? It was all so misaligned.

Of course, I knew without asking that if I were to offer the money it would ruin any kind of friendship I may ever hold with any member of their family. I would forever be the little rich girl who offered her "spare change," oblivious to the true struggle it was to live a normal life. If it were only that, I probably would have risked it regardless, but I knew they would never accept my money in a million years. I wasn't the only client Pride had, of that I was certain.

So, I did what any normal girl would do—I sat in my apartment, broke down in tears, and downed a pint of Ben and Jerry's. All right, I may have also had a couple glasses of wine, only remembering after the first sip that wine and ice cream don't really go together very well. Somebody needs to invent alcohol-infused ice cream. Oh yeah, I guess that's kind of what frozen margaritas are. Oh well. Moving on.

Anyway, it was at that point the phone had rung and it had been Mark, *finally* calling me back, so I'd gotten my act together and told him about his mom and the note, even though Guilt gave me hell about it. Oh, what did she know anyway?!

I did make the decision, though, to keep some of Kelly's business private—certainly the emotional and very personal struggle she'd shared with us, but also the fact that she was going to see Jim tomorrow. I was hoping the bad guys would stick with their plan and leave her alone until next weekend, but it was still a bit risky. And I knew if I told Mark, he and Jake would try to stop her—to protect her, as usual.

Their care and concern for her was indeed very sweet and endeared them to me, but I knew only too well what it felt like to constantly be on the receiving end of such care. It was always well-intended and came from a place of love, but to be reminded how fragile, how breakable, you are on a constant basis can have the unintended effect of making you feel even more broken. It can make you forget that you *can* be strong if given the chance. So, I wanted to give Kelly that chance, and hopefully it wouldn't turn out to be a mistake. That's why I was planning a little stake-out of my own in the morning. I've watched *Enter the Dragon*—I've picked up some things. Nobody was touching a hair on Kelly's head.

"Shortcake," Mark said again and then wrapped me up in the same hug I'd witnessed him giving his mother last week—the one where it seemed his arms could wrap around me twice.

And I needed it.

I reveled in it.

I let out a huge involuntary sigh and burrowed right into his chest where I was again consumed by his scent—something woodsy and earthy—and the goosebumps turned into a whole-body shiver.

"Are you cold?" he asked.

"Yes," I lied.

At which point he bent down, picked me up as if I were a child, and carried me over to the sofa where he plopped down with me sprawled sideways across his lap—kind of like he was Santa and I was a big baby, only in a sexy way. Okay, drop the whole Santa thing—that analogy is totally inappropriate. Just focus on the big hot guy.

He grabbed the cashmere throw I keep over the arm of the sofa and bundled it around me, tucking it almost up to my chin. It made me smile stupidly at him.

"Better?" He smiled back and looked at me with his amazing brown eyes bordered all around by those obscene eyelashes.

"*What's taking so long?*" asked Uterus.

"*Yeah, enough with all the boo-hooing—just sit on his face already!*" Vagina chimed in.

"*Shut up, you filthy little whores!*" scolded Pride.

I had to work very hard to block these bitches out or I was definitely going to throw common sense out the window and start feeling Mark up.

"So," Mark interrupted the turbulent musings in my mind, "tell me more about this letter and everything that happened."

Oh, right, back to regularly scheduled programming—except that I was sitting on his lap and his thumb was stroking my arm.

"Um, well, we went to the spa and it was really fun—your mom is great, by the way—and we got mani-pedis. See?" I lifted my feet from under the throw to show him my toes.

He grinned. "Very nice, Shortcake."

"And I had to talk your mom into getting her nails painted an actual color instead of clear—can you believe that's what she picked out?" I looked up into his face again and I could practically see his internal struggle to maintain patience.

Oh, right, back on track, then.

"Anyway, when we were done and were dropping your mom off she asked us to come in to have a look at something. It was the letter from those loan sharks."

"What exactly did it say?" he asked, tension lining his mouth. His thumb had stopped moving.

I concentrated and tried to remember the note. "It said something like, 'You have a week. $32,000.' I'm pretty sure that's what it said because Laney and I insisted it was a threat and your mom should call the cops, but Kelly pointed out that the way they'd written it wouldn't necessarily be seen that way."

"Shit. The price went up by two grand. I guess I shouldn't be surprised," Mark said, shaking his head. "And it goes along with the timeline we overheard at the hospital."

"So what exactly happened over there? You had me worried."

He looked at me intently and then, I kid you not, bent and kissed the top of my head!

What was going on here? Had I blacked out for a week and we were now people who hugged and kissed? Or, in the midst of a coma I don't remember being in, had his mother decided to adopt me, making me his little sister who he affectionately kissed on the head? Help! I don't know what's going on!

"Calm down and pay attention," Guilt said. *"This is a lot for him to take in so give him some leeway without freaking out like a thirteen-year-old with her first crush."*

Right.

His thumb started making circles on the back of my hand this time. Oooh, that looked really good with my new manicure.

Mark's voice pulled me from my consideration of our hands. "Not much, really. The thugs approached my old man and issued a very thinly veiled threat to my mom if they don't get their money by next Saturday. The asshole just laid there like the useless pile of bones he is."

I brought my hand to my throat. "Oh my God—poor Kelly. This is so unfair! What are we going to do?"

"Well, first, *Jake and I,*" he said while giving me a pointed look, "are going to convince our mom we've got it covered. Then we're going to use a contact at the hospital to get the old man's address. From what those guys said, he's probably not living here in North Carolina—just came back to try and hide and be the parasite he is. We're going to go snooping and see if we can find anything to sell or—if he's dumb enough, a safe assumption at this point—see if he has any hidden cash. That is, if the thugs haven't already tossed the place."

I nodded my head. That sounded like a pretty decent plan to start with.

"What did my mom say about the note?"

Hmm, here's where things got tricky. I'm relatively certain it's wrong to lie to someone while they're cuddling you and just kissed you on the head.

"She was upset, obviously. I don't know. We just did some girl talk?"

"Is that a question?"

"Um, no?" Dammit all.

"Again, is that a question, Shortcake? What aren't you telling me?"

I huffed. "Some things are just private, Mark—between girls."

"There's not anything important you're not telling me, though?"

I tried to evade. "Well, if you consider stories about your childhood important…" I trailed off, hoping I'd distracted him enough.

"Yeah, about that—I can't believe my mother gave you those pictures!"

"Aww," I teased. "Are you embarrassed that you used to be as tiny as me?"

He just narrowed his eyes and squeezed me.

"Careful, He-Man, you may just crush me with your big bod if you don't watch out. I will say, though, that seeing those pictures gives me a little insight into why you and your gym have such a bromance going on."

He scoffed. "Whatever. I just like being in shape, Shortcake."

"Uh-huh," I said, eying him up and down quite leisurely.

And at that moment I became acutely aware of some very specific movement under my bum. Let's say a *rising* of sorts.

Oh my.

Oh my!

I abruptly sat up and practically jumped off his lap—this was so confusing! I threw myself across to the other end of the sofa and tossed the cashmere blanket on top of his lap to cover any evidence. My sharp movements caused some groaning and grunting from Mark. Perhaps I hadn't been very graceful in my panic to escape the confusion-inducing penis salute. Ugh. Kill me now.

What was wrong with me? I was completely attracted to him, and I now had hard evidence (*oh, come on, I couldn't resist*) he was attracted to me too. *He* only did casual sex—*I* only did casual sex. On paper, we should be boning right now. Well not actually *on* paper because that might involve paper cuts in some extremely inconvenient—*oh, you know what I mean!*

Only it wasn't that simple and we both knew it.

Time for distraction!

I snuck a peek at Mark. He seemed to still be recovering from my unintentional assault to his man parts.

"So, there's one thing I think you haven't considered in this grand plan of yours to ransack your dad's place."

"Oh yeah?" he muttered with his eyes closed, head resting on the back of the sofa like he'd just run a marathon. Seriously? How badly could it really have hurt?

"Yeah. Assuming he lives far away, if you and Jake both go then there won't be anybody here to protect your mom in case the thugs decide to come calling early."

His eyes opened and shifted to me. "Crap. You're right." He sat up, seemingly back to normal. "Maybe I can ask Nate…no, I don't want to put him in harm's way, especially with a family to worry about."

Damn straight. "That's why I'm going to go with you, and Jake will stay with your mom."

What? Did I just say that?

"What? No," said Mark.

Phew.

Then he tilted his head, looked me over slowly from head to toe (turnabout being fair play and all, I suppose), and announced with complete certainty, "Actually, that's a great idea. Can you get off work if need be?"

Shit. I'd really done it now.

"Yay!" cried all the lady bits, even Guilt and Pride because being helpful is a good quality in a human being.

"Sure," was all I could say. It seemed I was out-voted.

I believe I'm the only person I know who lives in a democracy consisting of a slew of imaginary crazy people and only one actual human.

Oh well…road trip!! I just hoped it didn't interfere with my stake-out. I was one busy bad-ass woman.

Chapter Fifteen

THE CHRISTOPHER COLUMBUS OF LIKE

MARK

I had absolutely no fucking idea what I was doing. This was akin to braving a new world—I'd never had *feelings* for a girl before. And I'd certainly never wanted to hold one on my lap, unless of course she was straddling me.

After Fiona had kicked my hard-on and practically crushed my nuts in her attempt to scramble off my lap, I'd thought all was lost and she was repulsed. Then I remembered how she had thoroughly checked me out—the very perusal that had caused said hard-on— and I recognized the deer-in-headlights look on her face.

She was just as perplexed as I was, and more importantly, as turned on as I was. I already knew she was mine, as foreign as that thought was, but I was guessing she didn't yet realize I was hers. All of which would be remedied by the concentrated alone time we'd have while traveling to, and subsequently searching, my dad's place, wherever that may be.

So, back to the plan. A call to Jake was in order so I pulled my phone out of my back pocket and hit connect on his contact, keeping Shortcake in my sights all the while. She fidgeted like mad in the corner of the sofa. It was fucking cute. And now that my dick had recovered, it was clamoring its approval. However, as soon as my brother picked up the phone, it did the appropriate thing and calmed the hell down.

"Yo," Jake greeted.

"Hey, you find anything?"

"Not a thing. She must have taken it with her. You at Fiona's?"

"Yeah. Don't worry about finding the note. Bottom line is we already know the deadline is Saturday, but the amount has been upped—thirty-two grand."

"Shit."

"Yeah. So, the plan to search his place is still on, but Fiona brought up a good point. If we're both gone, who's going to watch out for Mom in case the goons get restless?"

"Right—crap."

"So I think you should still get the address from Lexie, but then Fiona and I will go to his place." I kept my eyes on her and she smiled nervously. Then she stood and headed for the kitchen, mimicking a drinking motion on the way. I'd let her go for now.

"What the hell, man?!"

I maintained a calm demeanor. "We've got it covered."

"I hope you know what you're doing," he said.

"Not a fucking clue," I responded once Fiona was out of earshot.

To which Jake laughed his fucking ass off.

✳ ✳ ✳

"Okay, it's all set," I told Fiona when she finally came back to the couch carrying a glass of red wine in one hand and a beer in the other. "Jake is going to get the address tomorrow and then, depending on where we're headed, we can either leave tomorrow afternoon or Monday morning. How does that work with your schedule?"

I noticed she sat about as far away from me as possible as she set her glass on the end table and picked up her phone from its spot on the coffee table. She tapped at it for a moment and then put the phone to her ear.

"Hey, Ollie, it's Fiona," she greeted the person on the other end of the line, then paused and laughed before saying, "Oh, you know me too well." And then she giggled.

I decided I hated this Ollie person.

"Yeah, I was hoping to switch things around and get Monday and probably Tuesday off…uh-huh…uh-huh…oh, really? Uh-huh. Okay, thanks hun. Later." And she hung up the phone.

Hun?

"So?" I asked with my teeth clenched, hoping she didn't notice how hard I was gripping my beer bottle. That was new. Apparently, I was the possessive, jealous type.

"Ollie is going to smooth it over with Jax so I can get both Monday and Tuesday off in case it takes that long."

"Ollie, huh?" I asked, failing colossally in my attempt at nonchalance.

Fiona turned to me and cocked her head to one side. Then a

little smirk hit her face and I wanted to drag her back to my lap and kiss it right off her.

"Yes. Ollie. He's great," she said oh-so-causally as she picked her wine glass up and took a sip.

I growled. Huh—seemed like Jake was right for once—I did in fact growl around Fiona.

Okay, so this was how we were going to play this game? She was going to run away like a frightened rabbit and then turn around and try to make me jealous? This rabbit obviously didn't know who she was dealing with.

I rose from the sofa, taking one last pull on my mostly full beer. "Well, Shortcake, I should probably get going—got some shit to take care of."

Her head snapped up and she almost spilled her wine. "Already?"

Ha! Don't mess with the bull if you don't want the horns, little rabbit. I play to win and I hate losing, especially now that I knew what I wanted.

"Yup. I'll call you tomorrow with the details once Jake gets the info." I fake stretched and knew my shirt lifted to reveal a portion of my abdomen and happy trail. I heard a little whimper from her side of the couch but pretended not to notice. "Thanks for the beer," I said as I headed for the door.

I heard her scramble off the couch and her glass nearly crash into the table in her haste to set it down. "Oh, okay. I'll walk you out." I felt her come up behind me at the same time I grabbed the door handle.

I turned momentarily and saw her tongue poke out to swipe over her bottom lip. Damn, this was not as easy as I'd hoped, but I stood my ground. "Later, Shortcake." I stepped into the hall, pulling the door closed behind me just before I collapsed against it as quietly as possible. I looked down at my tented jeans and silently promised my dick that I would make it up to him.

* * *

"Atlantic City? Seriously?" I asked Jake.

"I shit you not."

This just kept getting better and better.

It was Sunday mid-afternoon and I was in the trailer at my current work site when Jake's call came in. I'd decided to come in on a Sunday to get things organized in anticipation of my unexpected time off. The guys had assured me they would cover for me, but I didn't want to be a bigger pain in their asses than necessary. Getting as much organized as possible should ease the way and make things go smoothly in my absence. But I forgot all about the blueprints and work orders littered in front of me when I heard the words "Atlantic City."

There was nothing intrinsically wrong with Atlantic City other than our father living there being the biggest cliché ever. But it was not lost on Jake or me that this was the place our old man had always talked about as being some kind of mecca we'd all visit one day when we had money and could make a big deal of it. I think he'd figured he could spend the vacation gambling while our mom took us to kid-friendly activities and venues. He would spend as little time with us as possible and call it the best family vacation ever.

So, I suppose we shouldn't have been too surprised when

Jake's flirting with Lexie had brought this information to light. Jake had looked it up on the map and it was only an eight-hour drive—no problem for an overnight trip, but not really feasible for a round trip in one day.

Fiona and I would have to get a hotel.

"All right, man," I said. "Text me the address and I'll let Fiona know we're leaving in the morning."

"No problem. I sure as shit hope you guys find something. All my money is tied up and I can't get it fast enough. In the meantime, I'll keep wracking my brain and see if I can figure out a way to borrow a shitload of cash on short notice."

"Hopefully it won't come to that, but if it does, I've got some saved and available. Not enough, but some."

"Well, I guess we'll see," Jake said. "By the way, I'm at Mom's and she's not around—hasn't been all afternoon. Think we should be worried?"

"Nah, probably just got called in to cover for someone at work."

"Okay. I'll text the address. Later, little brother."

I hung up and was about to hit connect to call Fiona but decided to text her instead. I still didn't want to expose my hand too much.

Mark: Destination New Jersey—tomorrow morning.

Fiona: OK, what time?

Mark: 7:00 and pack a bag—I'll pick you up.

Fiona: OK—I'll bring the music.

Mark: No way, Shortcake. My ride, my tunes.

Fiona: Whatever.

She followed that up with a devil-face emoji. Hey, it was better than a middle finger. I set my phone down and got back to work, but I did it with a grin this time.

Chapter Sixteen

YOU CAN'T TEACH AN OLD DOUCHEBAG NEW TRICKS

FIONA

I set my phone back down and looked across the table at Kelly, thankful that Mark had texted me instead of calling. I didn't know if I'd be able to maintain a casual vibe if I had to actually speak with him, given what I'd just found out from his mom. It was all I could do to remember to throw a little sass in the text exchange so he wouldn't be suspicious.

So, it turns out I'm not as sneaky as I thought. When I'd ventured out in the morning for my super-secret stake-out, I'd been all kinds of confident. But apparently, parking your bright blue Prius right by the building's entrance goes against the very first rule of a super-secret stake-out. I also suspect turning the radio up and jamming out to Twenty One Pilots may conflict with rule number two.

I was just getting to the good part of "Stressed Out" when I heard someone yell my name and knock on the passenger side window.

Kelly.

Oops.

I turned the music down and put on my best sheepish smile as I lowered the window.

She folded both her arms on the door frame and peered at me. "I'm not even going to ask," she said, shaking her head.

I thought about making up a story about why I was there, but even I'm not talented enough for that level of bullshit. Instead, I pointed at her and said, "I've got your six. You go do your thing and I'll keep my eye out for bad dudes!" Turns out reading military-themed romance novels had taught me important lingo for this kind of operation.

She just shook her head again, in resignation I assumed, and said, "In that case, you may want to move your car and keep the music down if you don't want to attract attention." It seemed somebody had watched better movies than I had.

"Roger that!" I gave her a thumbs-up and put the car in reverse. She watched me park, and I waved before she turned and entered the building. I checked my phone for reminders, then for texts, and then I played a game of solitaire. This stake-out stuff was boring as shit. I couldn't believe I'd forgotten coffee!

After what seemed like forever, but was probably only about twenty minutes, I spotted Kelly practically sprinting out the front door of the building. She made a bee-line for my car and I quickly lowered the window again.

Her cheeks were pink and her eyes were a bit wild as she looked in at me. "Holy crap!" was all she said before standing back up and looking around the parking lot. "Let's get out of here. Just pick a place and I'll follow you," she said before racing off to her car.

She didn't have to tell me twice. I put the car in gear and headed straight for Starbucks, making it in record time. It was all I could do not to explode from anticipation while we got our drinks and finally sat down at a secluded corner table.

"Spill it, woman!" I demanded, and Kelly finally got down to business.

As it turned out, Jim being moved to rehab was no big secret and all she'd had to do was ask at the hospital to get the info. Then she'd headed on over to confront him and had immediately spotted me in my super-secret stake-out position by the fucking front door. Sheesh. I hurried her past that part and on to the dirt.

"So, once I'd signed in and finally found his room I was so nervous," she said.

"Of course." I nodded in understanding and sipped my iced coffee.

"But I gave myself a pep talk and then I just barged right in. He has a roommate and I think I may have scared him with the look on my face," Kelly said with a little smile. "Anyway, I walked right up to the bed and just said, 'Jim' in a really snarky tone of voice." Her face scrunched up in a perfectly appropriate snooty countenance. Awesome.

"What did he do? What did he say?" It seemed all my patience had been used up in the parking lot.

"I have no idea what I ever saw in that man—you wouldn't believe it. He smiled at me. *Smiled* at me! And then he went on with 'Kell, honey, you look great—I'm so glad you came—blah, blah, blah.'"

"He did not?!" My jaw dropped. What a douchebag. "I have got to call Laney and get her on speakerphone for this—do you mind?"

Kelly just waved me on, confident as can be, and I dialed Laney. She picked up immediately and we filled her in before Kelly continued. Laney must have been just as anxious as I was to hear the story because she didn't even give me shit for not including her in the super-secret stake-out.

"So I told him to cut the crap," Kelly said with a little smile. "Luckily, he didn't remember a thing about seeing me in the hospital, he'd been so drugged up, so I was able to fudge a bit about the details. I told him I already knew why he was back in town and there was no way on earth I would help him out of the mess he'd made. I might have threatened more bodily harm as well." She covered her mouth, obviously a bit surprised at her own boldness.

"Good for you," Laney chimed in.

"Oh, it gets better," Kelly continued and sat up straight in her chair. I loved seeing her on fire like this—it was such a change from the meek woman I'd met last week. "He totally tried to back-track once he knew I wasn't going to fall for his 'oh honey, just help a guy out' crap. He's such an idiot. He told me he has a line on a 'sure thing' and that's why he needed the cash he'd borrowed. The problem is the money for this sure thing needs to be in the investor's hands by next week and he's still a little short." She grinned and raised her eyebrows.

I gasped and brought my hand to my mouth. "You didn't?!"

I may have created a monster.

"I sure did!" Kelly said, leaning back in her chair.

"Did what?" Laney screeched over the phone's speaker. "What?!"

Kelly spun her coffee cup on the table. "I told him I may have a little cash squirreled away and I might be interested in making an investment myself. But I made it clear I wasn't going to just hand it over to him. I wanted to be fully involved and make sure he didn't just run away with my cash. He tried to act all offended, but then I pointed out that he was the one who'd come to *my* town in the first place so I knew he didn't have any other way to get more cash."

"So wait, he still has the cash from the loan sharks?" Laney asked.

"Yup," said Kelly.

"Oh my God," Laney and I both said.

"Now to the best part," Kelly continued, totally on a roll. "Being not just a giant idiot but also the world's biggest jerk, he's managed to alienate just about everybody he's ever known. And now that he's laid up and can't get himself back home—which happens to be Atlantic City—to get the bulk of the cash, who do you think he's sending?"

At that point, I couldn't hold in my hilarity any longer. Laney and I proceeded to laugh our asses off.

"What a moron!" I heard Laney cry over the phone.

"Oh, that's not all." Kelly's expression suddenly turned dark. "Since he's safely tucked away in rehab for a while, his plan is to wait it out until he gets the payout from the sure thing. Then he'll pay the loan shark back with more interest and be done with it. He said by then we'll both be rich."

She took a breath and continued, "It was very important to him, though, that I go get his money right away and have it in his hands before Saturday." She looked at me meaningfully. "He has no idea I got a direct threat from these guys and I know that Saturday is the deadline."

I sobered up completely then. "So he was just going to let your ass swing out there while he sat in a secure facility with the cash?"

"Yup," Kelly replied quietly.

"I am going to kill that asshole!" Laney shouted from the phone.

"You'll have to get in line after Mark and Jake find out about this," I said.

"No!" Kelly cried. "Like I said, I don't want them involved. I'm going to talk to my boss and hopefully get a few days off so I can drive up there and get the money. Jim told me where he stashed it so it won't take long. And if I can't get the time off, I'll just have to deal with it and find another job—it won't be the first time I've been unemployed. Better unemployed than dead, though, right?" She said.

It had been at this point in the conversation that Mark's text had come in saying we were leaving for New Jersey in the morning. After our quick text exchange, I looked at Kelly.

"Um, I have something to tell you."

She looked suspiciously at me as I continued.

"Mark and I are already planning a trip to Atlantic City in the morning." I closed one eye and turned my head a bit, steeling myself for her reaction.

"What?!" she and Laney said in unison.

"Well," I tried to defend myself, "Jake and Mark were planning on going up there and searching Jim's place and I pointed out that it may be a good idea if one of them stayed in case the thugs came after you in the meantime. So, I volunteered to go with Mark."

"Wait, wait, wait," Kelly interrupted. "How do they know the thugs are after me? And how do they know where Jim lives?"

At this point, I had to decide whether to rat myself out or to rat Mark and Jake out for keeping their exploits from their mom. Guilt hung her head at the mess I'd made, and I decided full disclosure was probably best. So, I told Kelly the whole thing about me confessing to Mark about the note—but not about her visit to Jim in rehab—and how he already knew she was in danger because he and Jake had overheard the guys at the hospital.

"Look, Kelly, we all just care about you and don't want you to get hurt. Don't be mad at us." I put on my best innocent face.

She sighed. "I know, sweetie. I should have suspected something like this when you showed up at the rehab place earlier. And had I not just pulled off a little con of my own, I might be more upset." She reached over and squeezed my hand. "Besides, I know Mark is impossible to stop once he gets an idea in his head. As long as everyone is careful and we can pull this off without anyone getting hurt, I guess I can deal with it."

"Fiona…" I heard Laney say.

"Yeah?"

"Are you sure you know what you're doing?"

"Don't worry about me. We'll lay low, pick up the money and come right back. I promise." Then I turned back to Kelly. "One more thing—can you avoid Mark until we're gone and not go all 'mama bear' on him? I'll have to fess up about everything before we get to Atlantic City anyway, and that way he'll have a day or so to calm himself and won't come down on you so hard for going to see Jim on your own. Win-win." I explained.

She seemed to consider that. "Actually, that sounds like a pretty good plan now that you mention it." She gave me a little smile.

"Let's do this thing!" I said and toasted her with my coffee.

* * *

The next morning, I was up bright and early, determined to make the most of the time with Mark before I had to go piss him right the hell off with my news. Hopefully he'd get over it quickly, though. In the long run, it did basically solve the problem so he had to be happy with that, right?

I checked my purse one more time before stepping into the elevator to go down and meet Mark. Despite his rejection of my mad deejay skills yesterday, I had three new playlists on my phone and I was determined to win him over with my superb taste in music. Also on my phone was the detailed description of the hiding place of the money, so I had to make sure I didn't forget to bring it. Not that I could survive even an hour without my phone, much less an entire road trip.

I stepped out into the spring sunshine and drew my Prada sunglasses down over my eyes. I was dressed comfortably for the long car ride, but that didn't mean I had to forego designer apparel. Instead of stilettos, I had opted for platform espadrilles and a three-quarter-sleeve silk romper with a gorgeous paisley print. I also carried a light sweater since I knew we were headed to colder weather. My overnight bag—okay, my suitcase—was stocked with a mix of spring and winter wear since I wasn't sure what to expect.

As soon as I stepped on the sidewalk I spotted Mark exiting his truck. I sucked in a breath. He was in comfortable attire as well, not that it made me comfortable at all—in fact, it made my heart rate pick up and my palms sweat. He hadn't seen me yet so I took my time looking him over. He wore gray cargo pants, those same work boots, and a tight as hell t-shirt with a weathered denim button-down over it. The denim shirt was completely unbuttoned and the sleeves were rolled up to expose his corded forearms. I remembered those arms around me on Saturday and I tried to swallow but my throat was suddenly dry.

Just as my eyes reached his face he noticed me standing there. I thought he would look me over too, but his eyes just did a cursory sweep of me before homing in on my suitcase.

What? Where was flirty, affectionate Mark from Saturday? I wanted my head kiss at the very least. Thank God I was so used to being confused or this turn of events would have had me in a tailspin.

"Seriously?" he asked, hands on his hips.

"What?" My hands perched defensively on mine in response.

He tossed a hand out, gesturing to my suitcase. I considered for a moment that maybe he was as impressed as I was that Diane von Furstenberg had a designer luggage line, but then I remembered who I was dealing with.

"We're going for *one night*, Shortcake."

I huffed and lifted my chin. "Well, it'll be cold up there and I wanted to be prepared." So maybe I wouldn't necessarily need *two* pairs of boots, but one pair had a sturdier heel on the off chance that we'd have to do some running from mobsters. It was New Jersey, after all.

And maybe, just maybe, I had packed some additional articles to make sure I looked extra cute. My head was still telling me that hooking up was a bad idea but I didn't have much confidence in my grip on my control. Did I mention it had been a long time since I'd gotten laid? Based on the recent tirade from my lady parts I assumed people in Australia knew the status of my sex life. We were all getting desperate for some attention of the non-battery-operated variety.

"And besides," I said to Mark, "you have this giant truck. What do you care?"

He finally gave me the up and down appraisal I had been waiting for and seemed to make the mental connection that a full suitcase ensured a variety of visual distractions for his man brain. At that point, I got a shrug and a small smirk. "Suit yourself."

Aha! I had him now.

He approached and got right up into my space. I refused to back up, assuming this was a test of some kind. Based on his casual departure from my condo yesterday, he was obviously up to something. He just raised an eyebrow, along with one side of his mouth, and then reached down for my suitcase, never breaking eye contact. He lifted the case as if it weighed no more than a handbag and placed it in the bed of his truck. I started to object, worried what would happen if we ran into rain, but then I stopped myself. I'd have several battles to fight on this journey and this one was definitely not worth it.

I took his hand when it was offered to help me into the cab of the truck. I'm pretty sure my head only came up to the door handle, but there was the running board thingy for me to step on so he didn't have to completely lift me up into the seat. I settled in while he rounded the front and I pulled out my phone before securing my seatbelt. Mark hopped effortlessly into the driver's seat and started the engine.

"So," I said, "I've got three playlists all lined up. Are you by any chance a Justin Bieber fan?"

His hand froze on the key and I could practically hear his jaw crack.

Oh goodie—this was going to be fun.

Chapter Seventeen

SHAKEN AND STIRRED

MARK

This was going to be a nightmare.

Fiona sat in her cute-as-fuck little outfit and fiddled with her phone, no doubt trying to figure out how to connect wirelessly to my truck's sound system. That should take her awhile, considering my truck had nothing but a good old-fashioned radio and a CD player. In the meantime, I pulled from the curb and started toward the interstate.

She was apparently ready to move on to a new topic. "Can we stop for coffee?"

I was beginning to comprehend just how long this trip was going to take. "Sure, once we get out of town we can get coffee from a drive-thru, but if it's going to make you have to take a leak every ten minutes, then you have to get the smallest one they have."

"Whatever you say, big man."

I was surprised she didn't fight back.

"Speaking of big," she said and I choked on my own saliva.

"Are you okay?" she asked, smacking me on the back.

I did my best to recover. "I'm fine. What were you saying?"

"Well, ever since I saw those cute pictures of you as a kid I've been meaning to ask you about the whole working-out thing. What exactly do you do to get all of *that*?" She gestured vaguely up and down in my direction.

"Why?" What was she up to?

"Just making conversation. Geez, you don't have to be so sensitive." She went back to her phone, huffing a bit in frustration.

"I go to the gym," I responded.

"Well, duh," she said and I could just hear the eye-roll in her voice. "What I mean is, what do you do at the gym?"

"Lots of stuff—cardio, some machines, and mostly free weights. You planning on starting a training regimen, Shortcake?"

"Um, no. I don't exercise," she said as though I'd suggested she join a BDSM club or buy the generic brand of…anything.

"How can you not exercise? That's so unhealthy!"

"I don't like it." She brushed some invisible lint from her thighs. "I find the whole thing sort of ridiculous."

"Excuse me?" I was taken aback and a little offended, to be honest.

She proceeded to enlighten me. "Take weight lifting, for instance—it's just a lot of picking stuff up only to set it right back down. What's the point?"

I literally had no response to that. Talk about ridiculous—I was beginning to wonder if this girl was actually of this Earth or was, in fact, some strange alien sent to test my patience and sanity.

She continued, "And besides, it makes me all sweaty and stuff." She did a full-body shiver.

"That's how you know you're doing it right."

"No thanks. I'm generally a pretty healthy eater so I think I'm all set."

"Suit yourself," I said as I checked my blind spot and pulled onto I-40, "but don't come crying to me when you hit thirty and your metabolism shuts down. You're cute now, but you short chicks need to watch out when the pounds start piling on." I couldn't help myself—I loved getting a rise out of her. And she kind of deserved it after completely dismissing what I considered to be an essential part of my lifestyle.

She gasped in indignation as I'd known she would. "I cannot believe you just said that!" She slapped my arm.

"Hey! No assaulting the driver." I turned the radio up just to annoy her some more. An old Rascal Flatts tune filled the cab.

She reached over and snapped the power button off. "Did you just call me short *and* fat?"

"No, Shortcake. You need to listen better. I said you're *going* to be fat." I tried and failed to keep the smirk off my face. This was fun.

"I cannot believe you *ever* get laid with the way you speak to women."

"There's not much speaking involved, sweetheart." I raised an eyebrow and tilted my head toward her. She looked at me as if I'd just asked her to smell my finger. God, I was doing an awesome job at being an asshole.

Why was I doing this again?

Oh right, we had a long trip ahead of us and I couldn't afford to

have her being all sweet and adorable like she'd been in her apartment this weekend or I'd do something stupid like tell her about
my *feelings*. She already thought she had the upper hand on me
anyway and that couldn't stand.

Although, she's incredibly hot when she's mad so it was
entirely possible we wouldn't make it to Jersey without me having
to pull over and feel her up in my truck anyway.

Don't act surprised—you should understand me by now.

"Did you have to train hard to become such an asshole or is it
in your genetic code?" she asked and then gave a little gasp as she
realized what she'd just said.

I guess fun time was over. I couldn't blame her—I had done a
good job of riling her up. That didn't mean it felt great being
compared to my dad, maliciously or not.

"Mark, I'm sorry," Fiona said quietly. "I didn't mean it like
that. I…"

"It's okay, Shortcake. I deserved it. I was acting like an ass—
it's just so easy to piss you off I couldn't help it."

"No—" she began but I cut her off.

"Really, it's fine. And I mean that in the way a guy says it's
fine, not a girl." I gave her a grin so she'd know everything
was okay.

"Fine," she said and crossed her arms, sinking down in her
seat. I didn't miss the little smile she tried to keep to herself.

* * *

We stopped to get gas about halfway into the trip and Fiona practically sprinted to the restroom. I knew she'd been bluffing when

she promised the large coffee she'd ordered wouldn't slow us down.

After I filled up, I decided to go inside and pick up a drink and a snack. I found Fiona perusing the snack selections as well, with a bag of Cheetos in one hand and a bright red slushy in the other.

I came up behind her and whispered in her ear, "I see you're making those super healthy choices you were telling me about."

She jumped in surprise and nearly dumped her slushy. "Don't scare me like that!"

I just chuckled and grabbed a bag of peanuts for myself.

"I don't know what it is about road trips, but my body somehow sends a signal to my brain telling it to do very bad things," she said as she reached for a Snickers bar.

I almost choked. "Do tell," I managed to say.

"Huh?" She just shook her head and sashayed her way to the check-out counter. I took my time selecting a drink before following her.

This trip was going to be even longer than I thought.

When we stepped back out into the sunshine, she pulled her sunglasses on and said, "You know, I was only teasing about Justin Bieber. I actually have excellent taste in music. I even have some country on my playlists just so you know." She gave me a smug smile.

"Well, it doesn't matter what you have because unless you're planning on listening to it on headphones there isn't any way to play it in my truck."

"What do you mean? You just plug it in or you do the whole Bluetooth thing."

"Shortcake, what year do you think my truck was made?"

She looked from me to the truck and back again. "Oh," was all she said before sauntering over to the passenger door.

I followed to help her in, kicking myself for forgetting that we come from totally different worlds. She was all upper crust and I was all "Eat your crust cuz there ain't no more food in this house." What in the hell had made me think any kind of relationship—my first relationship—would work between us?

I helped her up into the cab and stalked back to the driver's side, my mood suddenly cloudy. It wasn't until a few minutes down the road that I noticed Fiona had unearthed a bunch of shit from her bag and was setting it up on the bench seat between us.

"What are you doing over there?" I asked.

"I'm exercising one of my many skills—resourcefulness."

And then, from a tiny black box on the seat, came the crystal-clear sounds of Parachute's "Kiss Me Slowly."

I looked at the box and then at Fiona. She gave me a killer smile that made me want to pull over, and then she just closed her eyes and leaned her head back in her seat with a sigh.

Well, color me impressed. My little Shortcake was full of surprises.

This was what I got for letting Fiona handle the directions. And, for once, I was not being a dick about gender roles. She and her GPS had gotten us perfectly to our destination—or rather, *her* destination.

"Yes we are," she said for the third time as she wrapped her sweater around herself and grabbed the door handle. The temperature here was a definite drop from North Carolina.

I held her arm to stop her.

"We are not staying at a fucking five-star hotel, Fiona! The valet parking charge is probably more than a night at the Days Inn, which is where I *told* you to direct us!"

"First of all, this is a *four*-star hotel, and second of all, I'm using points so it won't cost anything anyway. Just cancel your reservation."

"You knew I was going to be pissed off so you purposely didn't tell me," I hissed at her.

"Precisely." She gave me a breezy smile and hopped out of the truck. "I'll go check us in while you take care of parking. Oh, and don't forget to tip the valet." She winked and sauntered off to the entrance, her cute little ass swaying.

Shit.

Well, there was no way I was letting the valet park my truck. Once we checked in, we'd have to pull it right back out of parking again so we could go to my old man's place. That meant two tips—not gonna happen. I reluctantly let the bellhop take Fiona's suitcase and tipped him a couple bucks. I then waved off the valet and went in search of street parking. This would never have been an issue at the Days Inn.

A half-hour later I made my way through the entrance of the ridiculously over-the-top hotel and pulled out my phone. Turns out the valet parking is a racket—there is exactly zero street parking within a mile of this place. Good thing I was in shape—another thing I could add to the list of reasons Fiona should work out.

Or not.

Honestly, I'd hate to see her any other way than she already is.

I thought about going up to the desk and asking about my room, but I figured a call to Fiona was needed since it was surely in her name. She picked up and spoke before I could say a word.

"Where in the hell have you been? Never mind, don't answer that—just come up. We're in room 1244." She hung up before I could utter a syllable.

One room? This just got more interesting.

Unfortunately, this hotel was huge and it was like navigating through some rich person's idea of a corn maze. It was almost as if they didn't want you to find the elevators so you would just spend all your time on the main level blowing your money. Oh wait, I'm sure that was exactly the point. By the time I finally found the elevators and made my way to the twelfth floor, my patience was waning.

I knocked on the door to room 1244 and it was immediately opened by Fiona who had, in the time it had taken me to park the car and find the room, transformed into an exact replica of a ski bunny from a James Bond movie. She was wearing fur-lined boots, skin-tight pants, and a fluffy cream sweater with a big drapey neckline. The lights in the room were dimmed and a fire roared in the fireplace behind her—yes, this room had a fireplace. I felt as if I'd been transported to an alternate universe. I half expected a butler to appear out of thin air and ask me how I liked my martini.

"Exactly how long have you been here without me?" I asked, still in shock.

She stepped back to let me in and then closed the door behind her. "Yeah, about that, what the hell took you so long? Did you get into a wrestling match with the valet over your truck keys?"

I continued to look around and noticed that, in addition to the sitting room with the previously noted fireplace, there was a full kitchen, a dining area, and several doors leading to other rooms. I answered absently, "No, I didn't let him park my truck."

"What?" She had her hands on her hips and her hair was floating around her face as always. God, she was stunning. I felt that punch to the gut again.

I shook my head to recover my wits. "We're leaving in like five minutes to go to the old man's place. Why would I pay to have my car parked for five minutes?"

She took a deep breath and then bit her bottom lip and closed one eye.

Shit. This could not mean good things.

"Mark, there's something I need to tell you."

Yeah, those are perhaps the most dreaded words in the English language for a guy—and for good reason. They are usually followed by phrases such as "I'm pregnant" or maybe "I have crabs" or "Sorry, man, I didn't know she was your mom." I was suddenly having flashbacks to the hospital when I'd welcomed the idea of a prostate exam to escape my reality. What the fuck was wrong with my life that all these horrible alternatives were beating out my actual circumstances? I braced myself and forced my eyes to meet hers.

She took another deep breath and then said quickly, "I know where the money is."

Chapter Eighteen

THE PROS AND CONS OF WHITE KNIGHTS AND BAKED POTATOES

FIONA

I still had one eye closed, hoping it might shield me from some of the blowback I knew was coming.

Part of me—okay, it was mostly Inner Fashion Maven and Vagina—had thought that if I dressed cute and set the right mood he'd take the news a little better. I'd been fooling myself that it would have any effect. Nevertheless, I'd had the bellhop light a fire and I'd changed into my best sexy/cozy New England outfit, even if it was just New Jersey. I'd also booked us a lovely little two-bedroom suite on an upper floor with a balcony and some great views, even though it was freaking freezing out. Hey, they were my points—I may as well use them.

"Excuse me?" His jaw was tight and his eyes narrowed. Yup, no appreciation for ambiance.

"I know where the loan shark's money is." At this point, I switched things up and decided confidence was the right tone to strike, so I raised my chin and looked him right in the eye with both of mine this time.

"Are you shitting me right now?" He advanced on me.

"No. I am not shitting you. Your dad never spent it. He hid it to use on a bigger deal and we need to go get it—that is, if the bad dudes haven't figured out where it is already. But, honestly, if they had I doubt they'd still be after your parents."

He looked around as if searching for an explanation somewhere in the room before bringing his eyes and tense-as-hell face back to me. "Do you mind telling me what the hell is going on here?" He tried to keep his tone measured, but it was like attempting to contain a raccoon in a paper bag—or his chest in one of his ridiculously form-fitting t-shirts. Didn't these shirts come in a bigger size? I swear it seemed as if most of his shirts would be snug on a baby for God's sake. Did he do this on purpose to distract me?

Oh right, back to the topic at hand. I gave him the short version of his mom's exploits and tried my best to put a positive spin on the whole thing by reassuring him that I'd had her six with my stake-out—I thought the macho phrasing might make me sound more credible. Yeah, that didn't work so well. I knew he was upset about his mom possibly being in danger, but then he turned the whole thing on me.

I did not think so!

"Since when are you heading this operation?" he snapped at me.

"I'm not! If anyone is, it's your mom. She finally grabbed her lady balls and took charge!" I threw right back at him.

"Her what? Don't talk about my mom like that. This was all

your idea, wasn't it? Before you came along my mom never would have done a thing like this."

I huffed and stomped my cute booted foot. "And why is that, Mark? Is she too weak and vulnerable to take care of business like a man would?" I let the sarcasm drip from my tongue.

"You don't know anything about her—or my family!" He turned around and stomped toward the kitchen. Then, realizing he had nowhere to go from there, he turned around and stomped toward the door.

Like I was letting him walk out!

I lowered my voice and tried to let the anger and tension ease. "I know more about it than you think I do, and I know your mom doesn't need to be coddled nearly as much as you assume she does. You need to open your eyes and see that even though she's had struggles, she is *not* weak. She's a strong person who hasn't had the chance to show it. You're too busy taking care of her to notice that she needs to find her own way on her own terms, Mark." I was suddenly pleading with him and I was so afraid he'd walk out.

"So you know everything about everything, is that it?" he asked, but I noticed that, like mine, his tone had calmed a little and he wasn't reaching for the doorknob anymore. However, his back was to me so I couldn't be sure of his emotions without seeing his eyes.

"No, Mark. I don't know much at all in the grand scheme of things. But I know you are a wonderful and caring son. I know you love her more than anything, but you can't protect her from every-thing. Nor should you."

He finally turned around and faced me again. "And it's just that easy? Just let go?"

"No, of course not. It's not all or nothing. But let's just take things one step at a time. We've got a great lead here and there's something we can finally do to fix this mess." I took a hesitant step toward him.

He ran a hand over his head in clear frustration and then flung it out toward me in a last-ditch effort to prolong his waning tirade. "Fiona, you can't just go sticking your nose into everybody's business and think you know what's best for everyone."

Gah! I was so sick of being accused when all I was doing was trying to help! "Mark, I'll stick whatever I want wherever I want. You can't tell me where to stick my…my…stuff! I'll stick it where I want!"

Take that!

He smirked and gave his head a little shake. "You'll stick it where you want, huh?"

Huh? How was this suddenly funny?

"Yeah!" I responded with deadly seriousness as I crossed my arms over my chest.

He took me in from top to toe and then inexplicably threw his head back and roared with laughter.

"What?!"

He just kept laughing and eventually bent at the waist with the power of it.

"Have you lost your ever-loving mind?"

Maybe he was in shock. Is maniacal laughter a symptom? No, pretty sure it's not.

"Well," I said, "I guess this is what you get from hanging out with Gavin and Brett so much. Do you need me to call a doctor?"

He started toward me again, having laughed so hard there were actual tears gathered on his ridiculous eyelashes. Uncertain of his motives, I backed up a step—I mean, who knew what he intended in his current mental state? Undaunted, he advanced further and abruptly bent down, gathered me by my thighs and lifted me up off the ground.

"Aarrgh!" I shrieked, unable to extricate myself and completely confused as to what was happening here.

He gave one last chuckle and just said, "Shortcake," as he lowered me to slide down his body until we were nose to nose.

Ooh, tingly.

His eyes hit mine before they traveled down to my mouth and I realized what was happening. Mark Beckett was going to kiss me!

I watched as his head tilted slightly to one side and I considered for one millisecond that maybe I should stop him, but before I knew it his lips covered mine and I told all my inner voices to take a hike. Mama was gettin' some.

The kiss was slow and exploratory—no intense assault or plundering as I might have anticipated from this giant man—just a beautiful, sensual teasing of his soft lips against mine. After a moment, he pulled his head back a fraction, presumably to assess my reaction to the surprising turn of events, but I was having nothing of it. My hand slipped up to the back of his head and pressed him back into me as my mouth sought his again. He emitted a low growl and the next thing I knew, one of his hands pulled my thigh up alongside his hip and I could feel his hardness press against my pelvis. I may have moaned a bit at that point, and I nipped his bottom lip so he would get the message that I needed to taste more of him.

Our tongues explored each other and my head was filled with

that wonderful scent I now just associated with Mark's pure male-ness. All my senses were buzzing as the kiss progressed into a frenzied clashing of lips, teeth, and tongues—our hands wandering in the need to feel as much of each other as possible. My hands decided to prioritize and tried to find his ass, but the damn things couldn't reach with him holding me above the ground like this. So, I decided to improvise and went for his arms and shoulders.

Holy. Shit.

This was undoubtedly the nicest body I'd ever come in contact with, and my fingers were ecstatic to have free reign to explore all the various dips and curves available to them. Mark was just so hard—everywhere—but surprisingly warm as well. I could only imagine how much more fun this would be without his shirt.

I was so caught up in my own voyage of discovery, I hadn't noticed that one of his hands had made its way to my ass, because of course *his* arms could reach—totally unfair. I swear his palm encompassed the entirety of one of my ass cheeks, but I couldn't dwell on any feelings of booty-inadequacy because it was clear that whatever he was feeling he was liking a whole lot, if you know what I mean.

His lips left mine and trailed a path down to my neck, and I couldn't help but tilt my head back to give him better access as he kissed and nipped his way down to my collar bone, brushing aside the neck of my sweater as he descended.

Oh wow. This was good. Really good.

And then came three swift knocks on the door.

Shit! No!

"Ignore it," Mark mumbled into the crook of my neck where his tongue had started doing wonderful things.

"Yes," I responded on a moan, not quite sure what I was saying yes to.

The knocks came again.

Mark growled for real this time.

Then I remembered. "Shit. I ordered room service. I totally forgot," I groaned.

"We don't need food." He still hadn't moved his head. "Just sex. Lots of sex."

Aaaand then I realized what we'd just been about to do and remembered why it was not such a great idea. Not to mention, we should be focusing on the money and getting the scary-as-shit situation ironed out—not sex! Damn hormones!

"Mark, you're going to have to release me so I can get the door. I may be feisty, but even I can acknowledge that me trying to best you physically would be an exercise in humiliation."

He finally raised his head and scowled at me, but the effect was lost because his eyes were all sexed up and soft. Damn, I could get used to that look.

But now was not the time. He reluctantly set me down, and I was surprised to find that my knees didn't hold me up quite as well as they usually did. I steadied myself with a hand to Mark's chest and then walked as nonchalantly as possible toward the suite door, thankful I'd donned my sturdier boots—see, packing for every eventuality was a smart move after all.

It also turned out my instinct to save myself with room service worked out, just not in the way I had intended. I'd originally placed the order for a steak dinner when I'd been anticipating needing something to distract Mark when I confessed. In the end, the dinner had saved me from unintentional sex instead, though I wasn't entirely sure how to feel about that. Sometimes a girl doesn't want to be saved, even if it comes with a side of loaded baked potato.

I let the server in and stood awkwardly to the side as he set our dinner out on the dining table. I wanted to look at Mark to gauge his mood, but couldn't bring myself to do it, so I finally went after my purse to retrieve a tip. The server asked if I'd like him to open the wine but I declined and walked him to the door.

"So," I finally said as I forced a smile and met Mark's eyes, "I hope you like filet."

Chapter Nineteen

DEAD HOOKERS CAN'T DO THE RUNNING MAN (TOO FAR? MY BAD.)

MARK

I scrubbed my face with my hands and let the cool water hit my back as I lathered up. At my age, I should be used to the occasional cold shower, but Fiona was a whole different story. She had damn near lit me on fire and my cock was still screaming at me to just go out into the main room and take her against the wall.

After the best kiss of my life and the mood-crushing interruption from room service, I hadn't been up for steak, even if it was filet mignon and probably cost as much as my grocery budget for a month. There had also been Fiona's swift change in mood, which didn't sit well.

Did she regret our kiss? Well, I suppose calling it just a kiss was a bit of an understatement, but still. I hoped like hell she didn't regret it because it was happening again when the time was right. We may be playing this little game right now but I hadn't forgotten the end goal was to win her over, as strange as that still sounded in my head.

So, I'd asked her where the bathroom was and took my bag in for the obligatory cold shower. I'd promised to return for dinner in a few minutes and told her to start without me. Good thing, too, because this was not working. Cooler temperatures alone were not going to calm my raging hard-on so I had to take the situation in hand.

Ten minutes later, I had changed into fresh clothes and felt a bit more relaxed thanks to the shower activities. I ventured out into the main living space again and spotted Fiona leaning against the kitchen counter biting her lip and staring out the window. When I passed through her line of sight she seemed startled and her cheeks immediately pinked. Oh yeah, she wasn't unaffected by our kiss in the least.

I was hoping we could pick up where we'd left off after we ate and grabbed the money, even though I still thought her story was too good to be true. But I was willing to go check out the location if there was even a remote possibility we could be over and done with this crazy-ass situation. Half of me could believe my old man had acted so selfishly and idiotically, but the other half knew it couldn't be that easy. I guess we'd see.

"Hey," Fiona said with an awkward little wave. "I thought I'd wait for you." She gestured toward the table where the plates still had those silver dome covers.

"You didn't have to," I replied, but she didn't meet my eyes. I sighed. "Look, I can tell you feel uncomfortable about what happened between us, but you don't need to. We can just set that aside for now and focus on food and then the money if that will make you feel better."

I hated to see her discomfort and I reminded myself not to act like a Neanderthal and attack her over the table. I could be patient.

No, really.

She sighed in return and the tension seemed to drain right out of her. "Thanks." She graced me with one of her beautiful smiles. "I think the craziness of this whole situation is finally catching up with me."

"You know, Shortcake, I realize I haven't thanked you for your help and I really should be showing you better appreciation instead of constantly yelling at you like I seem to do. So, thank you, Fiona," I said, chagrinned.

She kept smiling as she sat down gracefully in her seat at the table and gestured for me to join her. "You're welcome."

* * *

"Are you sure this is right?" I asked for the tenth time since we'd gotten in my truck.

"I'm absolutely sure—stop being such a wimp," Fiona responded.

I couldn't even let her comment get me riled up, I was so confused. "I just can't picture my father ever walking into a place like this."

"What's that supposed to mean? 'A place like this.'"

"Well, you know."

"No, please enlighten me. Exactly what is wrong with this place?"

"There's nothing *wrong* with it, I mean if you like that kind of thing, but you don't know my father—he'd never be caught dead here."

She swung the passenger door open and said, "Maybe that's the whole point. Ever think of that?"

And then she jumped out of the truck and strode toward the entrance of the most garish nightclub I'd ever laid eyes on. The outside looked like a neon flamingo factory had vomited all over it and I was relatively certain the inside wouldn't be any subtler.

I reluctantly opened my door, knowing I had to stay with Fiona, even if it may be more for my sake than hers.

"You'd better hurry and catch up to me, Champ, or they're gonna be all over you," she said as she strutted in her hard-on inducing boots and laughed.

That was all I needed to hear to get my ass in gear and race to catch up. She could call me a wimp and laugh all she wanted as long as she didn't ditch me in the middle of a gay nightclub in New Jersey on Go-Go-Boy night.

When Fiona had said she knew where the money was, I'd assumed it was hidden somewhere in the old man's apartment, but I should have known it wouldn't be that simple.

After our dinner, I had gone to get the truck and told Fiona I'd meet her at the hotel entrance in twenty minutes. There was no way I was going to do the valet thing and go retrieve her from the room like a gentleman. I was all for wooing her in the long run, but I had my principles and the gentleman stuff could wait. That valet wasn't getting a dime from me.

Sure enough, when I pulled up the expansive drive, there she was. Gone was the ski bunny ensemble. Instead she now wore a low-cut slinky green top with skin-tight jeans, spike-heeled black fuck-me boots that went clear up to her thigh, and a shit-hot leather jacket.

Holy. Fuck.

She was a wet dream come to life.

She sauntered over to the truck before I could get my wits about me and open the door. I felt like a douchebag when the valet helped her up into the truck and she gave him a huge smile and a tip. Dammit.

"Um, you look, you look…amazing," I mumbled like a complete moron.

She smiled, pulling on her seatbelt and settling a black leather satchel on the seat between us. "Thanks."

I just sat there until she actually had to prompt me to move.

"Um, Mark, there are people behind us waiting to pull up."

"Oh shit. Right. Sorry." Still behaving like a fucking moron, I hit the gas a little too hard and the tires squealed. Could this get any more embarrassing?

Fiona tried and failed to cover a laugh in the passenger seat.

"So, where to?" I asked, attempting to gain some control over my behavior. My plan to play it cool was going all to hell.

She pulled out her phone and tapped a few times. "Looks like his apartment is about fifteen minutes from here. Take a left at the next light." She proceeded to direct me to what turned out to be a run-down converted motel in a shitty part of town. This did not surprise me in the least. There were several late model cars in the parking lot and a few lights were on in various windows. We parked in front of unit 122 and got out.

My eyes swept the parking lot, and the hairs on the back of my neck stood up. I didn't see anything out of place, though, so I chalked it up to adrenaline. When I turned back to the unit, Fiona was turning a key in the lock and opening the door. Shit!

"Wait!" I said and jumped toward her, startling the crap out of her.

"What?!" she screeched and jumped back.

"Nothing. I just didn't want you to go in first in case there was anybody in there or, I don't know, anything I wouldn't want you to see."

"What, like a dead hooker or something? This situation may be strange, but I highly doubt we're going to find a dead body in there." She shook her head at me. "You watch too much TV."

"All the same," I said as I pushed in front of her and entered the apartment, switching a light on as I did.

The place was a complete disaster. It was obvious that Lou and Terry had already tossed it, and my hopes of finding the money were immediately dashed.

Fiona, on the other hand, walked right in completely unfazed.

"Shortcake, I think we're too late."

She just continued to walk through the filthy place, stepping effortlessly around overturned chairs and dresser drawers until she got to the sink outside the bathroom. There, she crouched down and pulled a small flashlight out of her satchel.

WTF?

She reached behind an exposed pipe and tried to move her head as far under the unit as she could in an effort to get a better look.

"Aha!" she declared and popped out from under the sink, holding up a small key. "Victory!"

And then she proceeded to do a very adorable version of the

running man while singing some made-up rap about not messing with the A-Team. It was a little unreal and a lot crazy.

I finally had to put a stop to it. "I hate to interrupt your little touchdown celebration, but do you mind telling me what the hell is going on?"

She stopped dancing. "Oh, right. Well, this little old key goes to a padlock where the money is."

"Seriously? And where is that?"

"At some club. Your dad knows the owner and the lady lets him keep a locker in the staff room. I didn't get the whole story, but I have the address. Let's roll, Chief!"

I shook my head. "You are something else, Ms. Pierce."

"I know." She winked at me and I felt that sucker punch again.

Ten minutes later, as I followed her into my first gay club, I was feeling a whole other kind of sucker punch. *Oh, don't judge— you weren't there. And, by the way, is it really that surprising that a guy whose dad called him Mary might be a little sensitive in this area? I'll wait for your apology.*

Um, still waiting.

Chapter Twenty

PICK A PENIS! ANY PENIS!

FIONA

I felt kind of bad that I'd been evasive about the club. I'd known what we were in for the moment Kelly had given me the name of the place—there aren't too many ways to misinterpret "The Manaconda Club." I'd figured Mark would do better if given less time to contemplate potential upcoming scenarios.

I was not surprised to have him right on my heels as I opened the door to the club and found my eyes and ears assaulted by what I could best describe in two words—flash and fierce.

It. Was. Awesome.

If not a bit loud for the night's purposes.

Club music pounded from the speakers while colored lights skittered across the crowd that packed the central dance floor. Bodies jumped, shimmied, and swayed to the pounding beat. Every few yards was a circular platform standing high above the main floor and each had a very fit half-naked—okay, more like four-fifths-naked—young guy dancing on a pole. In addition to the scorching entertainment was a long black bar against the side wall where several bartenders stood under more neon lights, serving up cocktails and joining in the vibrant mood set by the crowd.

This was Monday night in Atlantic City? I was suddenly pissed we'd missed the weekend goings-on.

With my eyes darting around so quickly to take everything in, I didn't immediately notice the very large mustachioed man standing to my right. He wore black pants and a tight black t-shirt that could have given one of Mark's a run for its money.

"ID and fifteen-dollar cover," he said to me. Then he looked Mark over quite thoroughly and said, "No charge for you."

I had to stifle a laugh as I reached into my bag for my money and license, but when I went to hand it to the bouncer I saw that Mark had already paid my cover and was trying to pay for himself as well. The bouncer wouldn't take the extra money so Mark scowled and put it back in his pocket.

"Hey, is it always this busy on Mondays?" I asked loudly as he checked over my ID

The large man bent down to be heard over the noise of the club. "Nah, just once a month on Manaconda Monday." He gestured toward the platforms. "Go-Go Boys."

"Gotcha," I responded when he handed back my license. Then I remembered we'd better get down to business. "Is Angie around tonight?" I asked.

That got me a sharp look. "Whaddya want with Angie?"

I gave him my best smile, the one that got me out of trouble at work all the time. "I'm a friend of a friend—just need to ask her about something."

He looked at me with suspicion. Apparently, gay mustachioed men from New Jersey were immune to my charms. Huh. Well that sucked.

"Angie doesn't have friends, and we don't need any trouble here."

Shit, this was going to be harder than I thought. And now this guy was going to be watching us like a hawk.

Out of nowhere Mark grabbed my hand and said, "No worries, Toots! Let's get our fine asses on the dance floor." And then he dragged my stunned-as-hell ass into the crowd.

"Holy shit! Did you really just say that?" I laughed and shouted up at him once we were safely away from the bouncer.

"I had to do *something*—you were painting giant bullseyes on our backs!"

"Oh my God, wait until I tell Nate and Laney—oh, and Jake too—I have his number now. Could you maybe say it again so I can take a video? It would just be easier if I could send out a mass text," I pleaded with him but just got a snarl in return.

"Look, we're gonna have to figure out a way to get into the staff room without being caught. Any ideas? I would say we could go with distraction but this whole fucking place is one big distraction." He scowled as he looked around.

Okay, this was clearly not his scene. Fair enough.

"Well, there's always at least one straight bartender at gay clubs so I could try to find one and flirt my way into the staff room with him," I suggested.

"No fucking way."

So, that was a firm no. I guess he had a strong opinion on that idea. "Well, why don't we just look around? Maybe we'll get lucky."

It turned out my choice of words could not have been more perfect. As we made our way around the club, I couldn't count the number of times Mark got hit on and/or had his arms groped. His face was beet red by the time we got to the back of the club where the bathrooms were, but it was unclear if the color was from embarrassment or fury. I didn't ask.

We ventured into a darker hallway that had four closed doors. Two were restrooms, although it was impossible to tell if they were designated for any specific gender since they were both just marked with abstract paintings of penises.

Hmm, the painting style was actually quite nice—I wondered if the artist took on any other subjects besides dicks. I'd have to file that thought away for later.

The other two doors in the hallway were unmarked. One of them had to be the staff room.

I casually wandered by the first door and tried the knob. Locked. Mark saw what I was up to and blocked me from view as I tried the second. Unlocked. I slipped in and closed the door behind me before Mark could object or utter a syllable.

"Staff only, sweetheart," came a voice from behind me. "You don't like dicks in the bathroom with you then this ain't the club for you."

I turned around and saw one of the bartenders from earlier leaning against a locker and eying me. I flipped my hair, hoping I had managed to single out a straight one, but it had no effect.

"No offense, sweetcheeks, you're all kinds of adorable and those boots are hot as shit, but you need to turn around and scoot."

Damn.

"Oh, sorry," I giggled and worked the hell out of all the dumb blonde I had in me. "I thought this was the girls' room."

It got me nowhere. He stayed put. "Like I said, across the hall —just pick a penis."

Had I not been desperate to get to the very lockers he was leaning against I would have found this situation hilarious. Unfortunately, this wasn't the right time.

"Right," I said, giving up the ruse. "Later." I turned the knob and walked out, slamming right into a very firm chest belonging to a very annoyed Mark.

"Stop doing that!" he demanded.

"Okay, fine. But that was definitely the staff room. There's a bartender in there and he does not mess around."

Mark scowled at me again. Somebody sure was grumpy.

"Give me the key and make yourself scarce. I'll take care of it."

I put my hands up in the air in surrender. "Fine, if you think you can do a better job then be my guest." I handed him the key. "The lockers are along the far wall and from what I could see there were only a few with locks."

"Got it. Now go hide in one of the bathrooms in case the guy comes out."

"Wait, don't you need a bag or something? That's why I brought this." I held up the satchel.

"Shit," he grumbled. I could totally understand him not wanting to carry a woman's bag, but it wasn't very girly—in fact, it was pretty utilitarian. And given where we were…

Mark snatched the bag from my grip and I snuck into one of the penis rooms, entirely unsure what to expect.

Huh. Well, it turns out it was just like any other bathroom. I was sort of disappointed—I kind of felt the door treatments promised something a bit more exciting. Oh well, may as well pee while I was there.

I did my business, washed my hands, ran my fingers through my hair to smooth it and did as much primping as possible without my bag, all while chatting with the guys and girls who came in and out. But there was still no sign of Mark. At this point it had been ten minutes, so I chanced a peek into the hallway. No Mark—just a group of drunken guys making their way to the back exit for a smoke.

Where in the hell was he?! I closed the door again and leaned against the sink, tapping my fingers on the surface.

Just then, the door burst open and in came Mark, looking flushed. He grasped my hand and pulled me so hard I almost lost my balance. He practically sprinted out of the bathroom and made a beeline for the back exit, with me stumbling along behind him. Crossing the threshold, I begged for him to slow down and only then did he seem to realize I wasn't capable of moving like a cheetah, heels or no heels.

"Sorry," he said as he slowed his pace a touch and rounded the side of the building toward the front parking lot and his truck.

"Well?" I was dying to know what happened.

"I got it," was all he said.

"Seriously?!" I jumped up and down and squealed. "Oh my God. This is so awesome! I can't believe you did it. How did you get past that guy?"

"I don't want to talk about it," he said as he opened the passenger door and lifted me up into the seat, not waiting for me to assist at all. He slammed the door and stalked over to the driver's side.

Uh oh.

As soon as he got in, he cranked the ignition and we sped out of the parking lot. I don't think either one of us had any idea where we were going, but I was just as happy to escape as he was. I had to sit on my hands and bite my tongue really hard to keep from quizzing him, but I was *dying* to know what had happened.

Five minutes later, he pulled into the empty parking lot of a grocery store and cut the engine. "Now don't get too excited until we count it—I don't know how much is there." He handed me my satchel and I opened it, peering inside.

In addition to my own things, there was a plastic grocery bag filled with stacks of cash. Now, I may come from money, but to me that meant credit cards and vacations and awesome clothes. I had never actually laid eyes on this much cash in my life. It was so strange. I pulled out the grocery bag and handed several stacks to Mark. We both began counting.

Forty-seven thousand dollars. *Forty-seven thousand dollars!*

We looked at each other once it had been tallied and I finally got a grin out of him. I returned it and then his morphed into a full-on killer smile. "We did it, Shortcake."

I couldn't help it. I jumped across the bench seat and kissed the shit out of him.

After he got over his initial surprise, Mark joined right in with gusto. Even though the position was awkward with the bag and money between us, we managed to engage all the right parts. His tongue swept across mine and had me moaning as I grasped the back of his head, wishing for the first time that he had longer hair so I had something to hold onto.

One of his hands traveled down to my waist and he effortlessly lifted me over the contents of the seat and onto his lap. I squeaked a little in surprise but he quickly silenced me with his mouth over mine again. I breathed him in and let out an inner sigh as my hands started to wander. They didn't make it very far, however, because just as things were getting good there was a tap on the driver's side window.

My first thought was that we'd been caught by cops making out like teenagers in a steamed-up truck. But then it occurred to me that cops probably wouldn't knock on a car window with the muzzle of a gun.

Shitballs.

Chapter Twenty-One

TRIP TO JERSEY: $200, ROAD SNACKS: $30, CONNING AN ASSHOLE: PRICELESS

MARK

"Sorry to interrupt your little make-out session, but we need a word," came the voice of the man holding the gun. A man whose name I knew to be either Lou or Terry.

Dammit.

I'd been so thrown by the events at the club I hadn't given thought to anything other than getting the hell away with the money. I had to try to smooth this over and protect Fiona. I suppose the good news was we had the cash so I hoped like hell that would be enough.

Fiona's mouth was agape and she was staring at the gun, speechless. I lifted her gently off my lap and placed her as far from the weapon as possible.

"Shortcake, look at me," I coaxed.

She finally tore her eyes from the window and held mine. Her gorgeous green eyes were wide with terror.

"It's gonna be okay. I'm just going to give them the money. You stay in the truck, do you hear me?"

She must have been in a bit of shock because for the first time in her life she didn't utter a word. She just sat there and gave one jerky nod.

I opened the door and looked back at her one more time before stepping out to face Lou and Terry. "Stay here."

I closed the door behind me, bag of cash in hand, and stepped as far away from the truck as I could without alarming them.

They were both dressed in leather jackets and jeans, just like any other guy. Just like me, in fact. The only glaring difference was that the goateed guy held a gun.

"You amateurs can't spot a tail for shit," he said, and then thankfully tucked the gun in the back of his waistband.

Somehow I didn't feel so bad that I lacked that particular skill. I was hopeful that this was the one and only occasion in my life where I might give someone cause to tail me.

I put my hands up in a defensive pose. "We don't want any trouble. We have the money."

"Yeah, no shit. Why do you think we were tailing you? Now put your hands down before somebody sees us and thinks this is a car-jacking."

I did so immediately. While this might have been my first time working a "deal," it was obviously something Lou and Terry were way more practiced at. I deemed it prudent to go with the voice of experience here.

"We figured your old man would spill the beans to someone sooner or later. It was just a waiting game. Now, you mind handing it over so we can get outta here?"

"No problem," I said and reached into the bag.

"At least step behind the truck, kid. Jesus, it's like you're begging for the cops to show up," the second guy said. "Fucking amateurs, Lou," he mumbled.

Again, I did not feel the least bit inadequate for not knowing the appropriate etiquette for this situation.

And, bonus—now I knew which one was Lou and which one was Terry.

I moved behind the truck and they followed. I mentally counted the stacks as I walked so I would pull the correct number out on the off chance they'd let us keep the rest.

I unexpectedly heard Lou say, "Sorry about scaring your girl with the gun. Just had to make sure you weren't going to try to skip town with the money and disappear."

I turned to him. "Do we look that stupid?"

"Well, no, but given who your old man is, the odds weren't in your favor if you get my meaning."

"Point taken," I responded since that did indeed make sense. "So, if we hand over the thirty-two grand you'll just let us go?" I was afraid there was too much hope in my voice.

Terry scoffed as if offended and Lou said, "Yeah, kid. Despite how it might seem, we're really not all that bad. We run a business just like anyone else."

I wasn't about to argue the point. I just wanted to get the hell out of here. I started to hand over the bundle I'd gathered when Terry cut in.

"The price actually went up to thirty-three. Gas money, you know." He scratched his chin.

"Of course," I said as if I were an idiot for not thinking of it myself. I reached into the bag for another thousand and handed it over.

Terry counted all the money and nodded to Lou before putting it in a Health Foods grocery sack, of all things. Apparently bad guys liked to eat organic.

Lou held out his hand and I had no choice but to shake it. "Nice doing business with you, kid. If you ever need a loan…"

"Yeah, thanks. I'll keep you in mind." I began backing up toward the driver's side, unwilling to turn my back to them until they were gone.

"But you best tell your old man if we ever see his face again he won't be as lucky as he was this time."

"If I ever have the displeasure of speaking to him again I'll be sure to pass that right along," I responded.

Lou grinned and they turned and walked to their car. I waited until they'd pulled out before getting in the truck and closing the door.

"Did that just happen?" came Fiona's incredulous voice from the other side of the truck. I looked over and noticed she had her window open—she'd heard the whole damn thing. Her green eyes were wide and wild.

"Yup, pretty sure it did." I held up the bag with the remaining cash. "And we just became fourteen thousand dollars richer." I couldn't help the smile that spread across my face.

She lost the shocked expression and returned my smile. "Well, big man, I'd say you damn well earned it!"

* * *

The first thing we did once we were safely back in the hotel suite was call everybody and tell them that the situation had been taken care of and we could all breathe easy. It felt fucking great to share that news. We did not share the bit about the gun and the extra money, however, since we didn't want anyone to worry about the first and we had no idea what to think about the second.

The next thing we did was order a bottle of champagne from room service. I didn't even particularly like the stuff but it seemed obligatory given how much we had to celebrate.

After the server popped the cork and was appropriately tipped and ushered out, Fiona turned to me for a toast.

"To conning a con-artist," she said, and I had to laugh as I clinked my glass with hers and we each took a sip.

"Now," she continued with a grin, "are you going to tell me what happened in that club?"

I cringed. I so did not want to talk about this, but since she was the most tenacious person I'd ever met, I knew she'd get it out of me sooner or later. I had an inkling she was even worse than Bailey.

"Fine," I gave in.

"Wait, wait, wait!" Fiona said. "I need to get comfortable for story time." She proceeded to set down her champagne flute and practically undress. First to go was the leather jacket and then came the boots. She had absolutely no clue what a turn-on this whole scene was—with the descent of each boot's zipper my dick responded in the opposite direction.

This girl was going to kill me.

By the time she finally settled on the sofa in just her slinky top and skin-tight jeans, I was a fucking mess. I sidled my way to the other end of the sofa where I plopped myself down and immediately snatched up a throw pillow to hide the bulge behind my zipper. I was wishing I'd at least thought to keep my jacket or button-down on. My t-shirt and pants didn't hide much.

"Okay, I'm ready," she said, taking a sip from her drink.

"Right." Thinking back to the club helped my awkward situation resolve itself. "It really wasn't a big deal—I was just way out of my comfort zone, that's all."

She glowered at me. "That's not how you tell a story. A story involves details and must contain any dialogue that was exchanged." She gestured as if addressing a small child. "Adjectives and adverbs are also much appreciated. Try again." She nodded encouragingly.

What was this? The story-time version of "Mr. Mark Visits the Go-Go-Boys"?

I scowled back at her and continued, "Okay, okay. So, I went in the staff room and that bartender was still in there. He wasn't rude or anything, but he was obviously going to kick me out. Before he could, I asked him if Tony was around tonight."

"Who's Tony?"

"No idea. I just figured we were in New Jersey so it was a safe bet that somebody named Tony worked there."

"You're smarter than you look," Fiona cupped her chin and said with a teasing smile.

"Gee, thanks. Anyway, turns out my hunch was right and he said Tony would be in later. Now this is where the awkward part comes. I don't think this guy and Tony like each other too much because the bartender guy suddenly became much more friendly." I was hoping to leave it at that.

No such luck.

"Oh? Do tell," she said. She didn't even have the decency to try and cover her excitement at my night's torment.

"God, you're nosy! And you're getting way too much enjoyment out of this."

"Oh, I definitely am. Now go on." She was a puppy waiting impatiently for a walk.

I huffed out a sigh of frustration but continued. The sooner this was over, the better. "Fine. He introduced himself and then started to hit on me and ask me all sorts of personal questions."

Fiona covered her mouth in a failed attempt to stifle her laughter.

"I'm glad I can amuse you, Shortcake."

"I'm sorry, I'm just getting the most spectacular visual." She then proceeded to snort and it all just descended from there as she lost her mind.

I scrubbed at my hair. "Let me know when you're done and I'll finish the story." I took a large gulp of my champagne and got up to fill my glass again.

"Is it safe to continue, or did you pee your pants?" I asked once I was resettled on the couch and her hilarity had subsided somewhat.

She just nodded, apparently afraid to speak yet.

I rolled my eyes at her and prepared for further humiliation. "I was so close to the money, I just had to play the part. So, I told him Tony was driving me crazy and I was trying to shake him loose but he had some of my shit stored in one of the lockers. Since I had the key, it must not have seemed too suspicious to him. I took a look and all the locks were combination locks except one, so I opened it and got the money. You want some more champagne?" I asked, standing up again.

"Oh no you don't." She pointed at me. "There's something you're not telling me. Spill it!" she demanded.

I knew I'd been too quick with my ending. Dammit.

"God, you're good at nagging. Did you earn a Girl Scout badge for that?"

She rolled her eyes.

"If you must know, while I was blocking the locker from his view, he may have grabbed my ass and said some really inappropriate things in my ear. There. That's everything. You happy?" God that was embarrassing.

She beamed. "Oh, more than you know. I'm adding this to the part of the story where you called me Toots. Ha! Now where is my phone?" She began searching around for it.

"Not a chance in hell." I snatched her phone from its place on the coffee table and put it in my back pocket before sitting back down, essentially blocking her access.

"Oh, come on. Let me have my fun. What was his name?"

"Whose name?"

"Duh, the bartender! You said he introduced himself. Did you give him your number?"

"Are you insane?"

"I won't stop until you give me my phone."

"No way in hell."

"He was awfully good looking now that I think about it. You two would make a cute couple," she continued to tease. "Now hand it over!" She put her hand out and stomped her bare foot on the floor.

"No." I crossed my arms.

"Isn't it so great that gay marriage is finally legal?" she goaded.

"Actually, I do think it's great. And I'm sure what's-his-face will find true love in due time."

At that, she growled and then let out some kind of maniacal battle cry while launching her entire body at me. I didn't move a muscle as she exhausted herself trying to pry my body forward with a variety of moves. After a few minutes, she admitted defeat and slumped over my shoulder with her head resting on the back of the sofa. This put her ass at a particularly delightful level, and I uncrossed my arms so I could give it a few encouraging pats. "There, there," I said and circled her thighs with my arms.

She lifted her head and leaned back so I could see her face. She was flushed from exertion and her blond hair was a wild mess. "Did you just pat my butt like a baby and say 'there, there'?"

"Well, I wouldn't say you were like a *baby*."

She blew some wayward strands of hair from her face. It was all kinds of cute.

"It's okay, Shortcake. Maybe you'll do better next time," I told her and then flipped her down so her back was flat on the couch and I was hovering over her.

"You're going to kiss me again, aren't you?" she asked, a bit breathlessly.

"I was giving it serious consideration." I lowered my face so our noses almost touched.

"I don't know if this is a good idea," she said.

"Kissing? I think it's a great idea." I smiled at her.

"You know what I mean—getting involved."

"It's just a kiss. And, besides, we're celebrating."

"Very funny. We have mutual friends. What happens when one of us is done with the other?"

This was where I had to tread lightly. I couldn't see a time when I'd be done with her, as foreign as that idea was to me, and as talented as she was at annoying me. But she was skittish as hell and I suspected she was more like me—or like the old me—than I'd realized. She didn't do relationships. At least not yet.

"Let's just play it by ear." I was hoping that response would work.

"But I kinda like hanging out with you. You're not nearly as irritating as I thought you were." She smiled.

"Again, gee, thanks."

"What I mean is, if we have sex a few times and then move on, won't it be awkward? I don't think I've ever been friends with someone after sleeping with them."

I hadn't either, but I wasn't going to share that bit of info.

"You worry too much. And besides, you never know what will happen."

"Yes I do," she responded, all lightness gone. Shit. This was the look of a girl who had baggage. Normally that would have sent me running for the hills, but I found myself getting worked up on her behalf.

Had she been hurt? Had some guy treated her like shit and thrown her away? I had to save those thoughts for later and focus on the moment.

"Shortcake, let's take it one step at a time. You know I'm attracted to you. Are you attracted to me?"

"You know I am. That's not the problem."

"As far as I can tell right now the only problem is that we're not kissing," I tried to joke but it did nothing to break through her solemn mood. So, I felt compelled to say, "I promise I won't hurt you. You can trust me." I kissed her nose. First I was kissing her head and now her nose? This was uncharted territory for me.

For some reason, the small kiss brought tears to her eyes. "That's not what I'm worried about either."

"Tell me what I can do to make this better." I kissed her forehead. "Do you want me to let you go? If that's what you want, I will. Just say the word."

She bit her lower lip and blinked the tears away, then looked me dead in the eyes for what felt like minutes but was probably just seconds. With that, she seemed to come to a decision.

"No, don't let me go. Just kiss me."

So, I did just that.

Chapter Twenty-Two

OH DEAR GOD THAT IS HOT

IONA

What was I doing? I mean, I knew what I was doing—I was kissing this incredibly hot man. This man whom I'd discovered was so much more than some simple-minded, conceited meat-head. He was funny and caring and generous, and he took care of his own. He was also very interested in what I thought and did—even when I let my mouth wander from the topic at hand, he seemed to find me somehow entertaining. And he wanted good things for me. It was all so unexpected, but here I was in a hotel room in Atlantic City making out with a guy who felt so utterly right I didn't know what to think about it all.

But it didn't matter if it felt right. I wasn't the one for *anybody*. Not that Mark had exactly declared his undying love or anything, but I could feel it in my bones that he wanted to pursue something —as counter as that was to all my initial impressions of him. But any relationship that went beyond sex was asking for trouble.

Sex was easy—it was physical connection with a few laughs thrown in. A relationship meant transparency. It meant vulnerability. It meant he would find out who I really am and all the things about me that are broken. It meant he would have the power to break me and I would most certainly break him eventually. It would end in him being disappointed at best—heartbroken at worst —and me cuddling up with Guilt for an ice-cream marathon and listening to her say, "*I told you so.*"

And now that I knew him and what he was all about, I could just picture his reaction when I finally confessed about the cancer and its side effects and about the distinct possibility it could come back. Anytime. He would want to take care of me—I'd seen it with his devotion to his mother—and I would suddenly be fragile, just like I am with my parents. I was so sick to death of being weak— to see that reflected in Mark's eyes might just kill me.

"*How many times do I have to tell you to stop your boo-hooing?*" said Vagina. "*If you miss out on this chance to get some, I will cut you!*"

Take it down a notch, bitch, and give me a minute. Geez Louise!

But, dammit, she was right—what was I doing wasting my time with all these negative what-ifs? I was smack dab in the middle of Sexy Muscle Magic Land and I was having a pity party instead of enjoying the rides! And besides, I didn't know for sure that he wanted anything other than casual sex so this could work out great. Yes, let's go with that.

"*Now you're talking!*" said Uterus and all the other girls, except Guilt and Pride, but they're a bit prudish anyway.

I yanked my brain back to the moment just as Mark's mouth

left mine to trail down my neck and give me a whole-body shiver —how did he do that? While he focused on my neck, I maneuvered myself to finally cop a feel of that ass.

Wow. Consider me a convert—exercise is awesome! Let's hear it for all those reps!

My hands caressed and stroked wherever they could go—his hips, his back, his shoulders. I had no idea the human body could have that many ridges and contours. It was time to get his shirt off and get a better look.

I pulled his head up from my neck and couldn't resist another kiss before I said, "Mark, if you don't take your shirt off I'm going to tear it in two." His eyes were a little glazed over, as I'm sure were mine, but he grinned and then rose to his knees.

Holy shit—that was a sight!

He then reached behind his head with one hand and pulled his shirt off in a single fluid motion, revealing a chest, abs, shoulders and…everything a man like him had going on. In other words, I think I stopped breathing and was technically dead for a moment.

Laney and I have often discussed this ultra-sexy and impressive male talent of removing a shirt in this manner. We both firmly believe they know exactly how it affects a woman—not that we're complaining. We decided to try it ourselves one time but had very little success. Laney's enormous rack got in the way during her attempt and I had to help her extract her arms from the straight jacket she'd created. My attempt wasn't much better—I was able to get the shirt off but it completely messed up my hair and stretched out the neckline of my Stella and Jamie shirt. Also, Laney declared that it really wasn't as sexy when a girl did it.

Oh right, back to Mark and his incredible bod—*you should*

know by now I'm scatterbrained, so just deal with it! His shirt was quickly discarded and I got to take in the full view.

Unfortunately, my little viewing party was cut short because Mark was on top of me again seconds later. But I had been right in guessing that my sensory journey of his body would be so much better without a shirt. His skin was smooth and hot, with the contrasting hardness of his muscles beneath—and there was that heady scent that filled my brain with all sorts of naughty thoughts. I was going to have to find out what cologne he wore and keep a bottle with me when our little affair was over.

Gah—stay in the moment, Fiona!

By this point, Mark's hand had slipped under my blouse and was pushing it up above my bra. I helped by lifting my arms and head so he could pull it off. Now it was his turn to check me out, but in truth, there wasn't a whole lot there. I hoped he wouldn't be disappointed. If his growl was anything to go by, I guess I had nothing to worry about. His head dipped down and his lips blazed a trail from my waist up to the center of my mostly non-existent cleavage. He lifted his eyes to mine and I noticed his pupils had almost overtaken his brown irises. And I swear his damn eyelashes batted themselves at me!

"Your skin is amazing," he said, and then leaned back down and took a little bite of my neck—just hard enough to make me groan. I was so turned on at this point I couldn't unhook the front closure of my lacey bra fast enough. I needed his mouth on my breasts ASAP. Luckily, Mark could read my mind and immediately covered one firm peak with his lips while his calloused hand caressed the other. A wave of relief coursed through my body at his touch. It felt like my whole being had been waiting for this—for his touch and possibly for this particular man. It was such a startling and unfamiliar feeling.

I didn't have time to dwell on the thought, though, because everything moved at lightning speed after that. We couldn't get our clothes off quickly enough and before I knew it, my legs were wrapped around his waist and he was lifting me up and striding toward the master bedroom. Yes, please!

"*Yippy!*" I heard the girl parts shout.

He put a knee to the bed and lowered us both down, his mouth crashing down on mine in a frantic kiss. I kept my legs locked around him and caressed his arms, reveling in their warmth and strength. It was like running my hands over a relief map, but in a super sexy way.

"Oh my God," I panted into his mouth as my center clenched. "More."

He didn't need to be told twice. His hand smoothed over my booty and thigh until it found its way between our bodies and his thumb found my clit, stroking and circling until I thought I'd go mad. And then I believe I did go mad as my orgasm suddenly crashed over me and I continued to pant and moan into Mark's mouth, feeling like I was losing my grip on reality.

He bit my lower lip gently. "You are so fucking sexy when you come," he groaned.

Just as my heartbeat was beginning to slow, he suddenly got up off the bed and I started to panic. That is, until I realized I was finally getting my first full-body view of naked Mark and– holy mother of male perfection! This guy was like a living breathing statue, the title of which would be "Oh Dear God, That Is Hot!"

The moonlight coming through the window cast a gazillion

shadows across his sculpted body, and the breath left my lungs again. I had never seen such a thing in real life. His hip "v" was so cut it was a capital "V" with an exclamation point!

"Where are you going?" I managed to croak through my breathless state.

"Condom," he responded and then turned around presumably to find his pants in the other room. Oh, this view was just as delicious as the first. Exactly how many muscles comprise the human ass? I pondered that for an extra couple seconds before stopping him.

"Here," I said, rolling over to open the nightstand drawer. "I'll bet the Days Inn doesn't supply condoms." I looked over my shoulder at him and noticed his eyes planted firmly on my bare ass. Huh, he seemed to think my booty was nice the way it was too. This guy was great for my ego.

I held up the condom and he quickly climbed back onto the bed to lie next to me.

"I may have been hasty in my judgment of this hotel." He took the condom and ripped the packet open with his teeth, while I moved my hands down to encircle his rigid cock and begin to stroke him. He groaned and allowed me to explore him for a few moments before he nudged my hands aside and rolled the condom on. Somebody was impatient.

Having been deprived of the pleasure of stroking his cock, my hands moved to his chest and flattened against his pecs. I could both hear and feel his chest rumble at my touch, and my heart sped up again.

This was really happening. God, I hoped I wasn't making a

mistake, but at this point everything felt so good and so right there was no way Guilt or Pride or any army of inner girl voices could stop me.

As Mark finally pressed into me, he actually sighed my name. I moaned in response like a wanton hussy, a role I was just fine with. We began to set a perfect rhythm and his mouth sought mine out again.

"You feel so fucking good," he groaned between wet kisses.

In response, I wrapped my legs around him and held on for dear life as our tongues and lips explored one another and our bodies joined over and over. I flicked his ear with my tongue and felt him shiver over me as he continued to thrust and I met his every movement.

I may have lost consciousness at one point when he lifted my leg up to rest on his shoulder and his thrusts became almost frantic. In this new position, I had a clear view of his gorgeous face and chest and he kept hitting the exact right spot. It was so good I was essentially just a lazy ball of goo, not really contributing anything and just letting his muscles do what they do best.

It. Was. Fucking. Hot.

Mark began to grunt with effort and intensity and I could tell he was as close as I was. I grabbed onto his hips and bit my lower lip hard—that was all it took to send us both over the edge. It was quite possibly the best orgasm of my life, and if Mark's gasping breaths were anything to go by I was thinking his had been damn good as well.

He collapsed next to me, thank God, as I was guessing the full weight of him would smash me like a bug. "Shortcake," he said on an exhale, "I'm pretty sure you're going to be the death of me." His labored breathing continued and I could do nothing but laugh and plant a kiss on his chest. He lowered his chin to look at me. "Not that I'm complaining, you understand." And then we both pretty much passed out.

It had been quite a long day, after all.

Chapter Twenty-Three

IN FOR A PENNY...IN FOR AN UPHILL CLIMB

MARK

I watched Fiona sleep, feeling only slightly like a creeper. It was going on two in the morning and I knew I should get some shut-eye for the drive home, but I couldn't seem to make myself settle in. Fiona had passed right the hell out after our earlier activities. I'd taken care of the condom and come back to the bed, where I pulled back the covers and shifted her so her head rested on a pillow. Then I couldn't help myself so I rearranged her as she had been earlier, with her head resting on my chest and her arm across my stomach. That was better.

If I hadn't been sure about how right she was for me before tonight, I was damn certain now. Somehow this tiny, feisty, beautiful spitfire had been made just for me, and I thought back to all the times I'd given guys like Nate shit for being pussy whipped. I actually got it now, and it didn't even make me feel like a girl as

I'd assumed it would. That right there is what I call personal growth.

Now the hard part would be keeping things low-key until Fiona came around to the same conclusion. But I could do it—I would do it. There was no other choice. She was mine and I wasn't letting her go. With that thought, I finally felt the weight of my eyelids and I drifted off, looking forward to another day with my girl.

* * *

"Sour cream and onion or salt and vinegar?" she asked. Apparently, now that we'd had sex she was willing to share her snacks with me.

I had awoken this morning to Fiona trailing kisses down my sternum and I'd be lying if I said I couldn't see myself waking up to that every morning. We'd rolled around in a tangle of limbs and lips and tongues for a while before taking the action to the shower where we managed to spend a good half hour going down on each other. Then I had no choice but to demand she brace her hands against the shower wall so I could take her from behind. I had to say I was gaining a whole new appreciation for this fancy hotel and its endless supply of both hot water and condoms.

When we were both sated and clean, we realized how late it was and quickly packed up our things so we could get on the road. This time I didn't object when Fiona ordered the large coffee. I knew we'd be stopping for snacks every couple hours anyway so what difference did it make? Fiona was not only a chatty traveler but a hungry one as well, not that she hadn't earned that appetite after the last twelve or so hours.

We were just pulling out of rest stop number two when she asked my chip preference. "Neither. I'll just stick with my peanuts, thanks," I told her.

"You just love your nuts, don't you?" she asked.

I was preparing a nice little comeback along the lines of, *"You seem to like them too,"* when I looked over and noticed she was just smiling and humming to herself, oblivious to the blatant double entendre she'd just dropped. I couldn't bring myself to respond so I kept my laugh to myself but couldn't contain my smile.

That caused her to lean over in the seat and kiss my cheek. Damn, this girl was going to be a handful and I didn't think I'd want it any other way.

How had I gotten here? A few weeks ago, I was swearing off relationships or even just simple repeats. Suddenly I was putty in this girl's hands. Damned if I could do anything about it now, though. I'd just have to steel myself for the verbal beat-down I'd get from all the guys.

Oh well, in for a penny…

"How about one of your playlists, Shortcake?"

We arrived back at her condo after dark and we were both exhausted. I didn't know how to play the sleeping-over card, so I took her lead when she yawned and said she was going to take a quick shower and crash. I pulled her suitcase from the bed of my truck and offered to carry it up for her, but she insisted she'd get it on her own since it had "those wheelie things."

I could take a hint so I didn't press the point. Shortcake was getting skittish again. I did, however, make sure to give her a searing kiss before sending her through the doors of her building. Let her stew on that for a while.

I knew Jake and my mom would be waiting for me to stop by so they could grill me about the trip. I'd been thinking about that extra money, too, and had concluded that my mom should just take it. If anybody had earned it, she had, and the old man could just assume the loan sharks had taken it in return for their trouble.

As predicted, the lights were on inside the little house as I pulled into the drive and parked. I barely had a chance to get up the front steps before the door flew open and I was tackled in a giant bear hug by Jake.

"I can't believe you fucking did it!" He smacked me on the back hard enough to dislodge something vital before pulling back and patting me on the shoulder. "You did good, little brother." He was all smiles.

I fake scowled at him. "Maybe you could show your appreciation by getting me a beer instead of manhandling me."

He laughed. "Coming right up." He moved back to the doorway and was replaced by our mom who hugged me as well, only hers was the normal type, not the kind that caused internal bleeding.

"I can't tell you how relieved I am to see you in one piece. I was worried sick." She took my face in her hands and inspected me for any damage.

"It all went fine, Mom, but I do have a bone to pick with you," I started to scold.

"I know, I know, you're mad I went to see your father without telling you. And you did some scheming of your own without telling me. What's done is done. Let's focus on the good stuff." She held my eyes firmly.

"I can do that," I finally said.

After we'd settled in and Jake had gotten me my well-deserved beer, I told them about the extra money and my thoughts on it.

"I can't just take it! It's not mine. And who even knows where he got it," my mother objected.

"Mom, you can definitely take it, and you should." Jake backed me up. "He probably got it gambling or playing poker anyway. Just think of it as back child-support."

I pointed to my brother. "Exactly."

"I don't know," she said and bit her lip. "And what about my taxes—won't it look strange if I suddenly have fourteen thousand dollars?!"

I waved her off. "There are ways around that—we'll figure it out."

"At least give me a little time to think about it, okay."

"Sure," I said and Jake nodded his agreement even though we both knew, in the end, she would get the money whether she agreed or not. She always resisted when I tried to pitch in financially, but this time I was standing firm, especially since the money was coming from the sperm donor's pocket.

"Hey, I'm meeting up with Nate and Gavin for a game of pool. You should come," Jake said.

I was torn. The drive had wiped me out, but I was afraid if I went home to my empty bed I'd just think about Fiona. "Maybe just for a bit," I said.

We kissed our mom good night and then took separate vehicles, Jake borrowing our mom's tiny car. The visual of him cramming his six-foot-four-inch frame into the compact vehicle had me chuckling as I pulled out of the drive and headed for the bar, ironically named "Jake's." What could I say? It was our favorite place even if it did have the same name as my dickhead brother.

It turned out the whole crew had decided to hit Jake's tonight. Brett, Gavin, Trey, and Court—another guy from work—were shooting pool, and I spotted Nate at the bar picking up another round.

"Hey! It's the man of the hour!" he called out when he caught sight of me.

I just grinned and stole one of the beers the bartender had just set in front of him. I took a sip of the draft—a nice hoppy IPA. Nate always had great taste in beer.

Jake walked up to the bar and I noticed he was rubbing the base of his spine. "Goddamn car—that thing is designed for the vertically challenged."

Which of course made me think of Fiona, again. I groaned.

"What's up with you?" asked Nate, giving me a sideways glance.

"Nothing. Let's play some pool."

Gavin and Brett cleaned up the floor with all of us, although Trey and Court were still insistent that they could turn things around. Seeing the writing on the wall, Nate, Jake, and I bowed out and took a seat at a nearby table. We all switched to water, knowing we'd be driving soon.

Once we were settled, I gave the recap on the Atlantic City adventure, this time including the parts about the gun and the extra money. I pointed at Nate. "You cannot tell Laney about the gun or she will flip the fuck out about Fiona."

He put his hands up. "I hear you. If she found out she'd have your balls and I don't think I could live with the guilt."

I knew he was right. Laney was protective of Fiona and would definitely, and rightly, blame me if any harm had come to her best friend. Thankfully it hadn't. In fact, Fiona had been amazing.

"Why in the hell are you smiling at the thought of having your balls cut off?" my brother asked.

"I wasn't smiling."

"Yes, you were," they both said at the same time.

"If I was, it wasn't about my nuts, I can promise you. I was just thinking about Fiona. You should have seen her up there." I shook my head. "That girl isn't afraid of anything."

"There it is again," said Jake, gesturing to my face.

"What?" I asked.

"Holy. Shit," said Nate, sitting up straighter.

"What?!" I demanded this time.

Jake looked at Nate and then back at me, seemingly as confused as I was. Until his lips slowly turned up and he threw his head back with a barking laugh.

I was starting to get pissed. I took a quick drink of my water and then slammed it back on the table.

Nate looked dumbfounded but Jake slapped his palm on the table. "I knew it! You totally boned her!"

Oh shit.

It wasn't as if I was going to keep this a secret forever, but I was at least hoping to secure things up with Shortcake a little more tightly before the entire world weighed in.

"You did, didn't you?" Nate asked, finally having recovered his ability to speak.

"Something might have happened. That's all I'm going to say. And that does not go beyond this table!"

"Man, have you met Laney? There is no way she will let me live if she finds out I knew this before she did," said Nate.

"Maybe Fiona already told her?" I offered up. "As far as I can tell, she has absolutely no filter so it's apt to come up soon. Just work with me."

"Yeah, okay."

Meanwhile, Jake was still having a good time at my expense. "Hate-fucking is supposedly really hot, not that I've ever experienced it personally, but I can see the potential. All that energy refocused on fucking each other's brains out." He hooted.

"Hate-fucking?" Nate looked at me. "Seriously?"

"Yeah," Jake responded before I could. "Those two are always bickering and driving each other crazy. It's classic—annoyance channeled into a good screwing."

I put my head in my hands. Shit.

Nate was pissed. "I actually care about that girl and you'd better not use her or treat her like shit. I mean, I know she doesn't do relationships either, but that doesn't mean you're allowed to be an asshole."

Double shit. I now had confirmation of my suspicions that Fiona wasn't into relationships. This was going to be a difficult road ahead.

"It was *not* hate-fucking and I was not an asshole." I lifted my head again and shot daggers at Jake. "It's complicated. Besides, is it really anyone's business besides mine and Fiona's?"

Nate took in my expression and seemed to come to a satisfactory conclusion. "Okay, okay. I get it." He put his hands up. "I've just got to look out for Fiona—she's kind of the crazy, foul-mouthed little sister I never had. Oh, wait, I *do* already have one of those." He smiled.

"It's cool, man," I told him and then turned to my asshole of a brother. "It's almost as if you're *asking* to be punched in the throat. Why is that?"

"Damn, little brother, I'd forgotten how fun it is to get under your skin." He grinned at me.

I vowed at that moment to never torture a child of my own by providing him with a sibling. Then I sat with my water, contemplating my next move.

There were two things at the top of the list—say goodbye to dear old dad, and get Fiona to fall for me.

Piece of cake.

Fuck.

Chapter Twenty-Four

LIAR, LIAR, PANTIES ON FIRE

FIONA

It was the following afternoon and I yawned as I sat at my desk and checked my phone for the tenth time in the last five minutes. Nothing.

Which was fine since I didn't want to pursue anything with Mark anyway, right? It was an adventure and we had some hot sex. Best to leave it at that.

Oooor, maybe doing the friends-with-bennies thing would be the better choice. We could make it work even if we had mutual friends to deal with. It wasn't like either one of us was going to want to take it up a notch and have an actual relationship or anything.

Ugh. This was hurting my brain.

The phone rang and I jumped in my seat, only to realize it was the office phone. Oh right, my job. Oops.

"Good afternoon. Precision Lawns and Landscaping. This is Fiona. How can I help you today?"

"Hey, Fiona! Just the girl I wanted to talk to," said the voice on the other end. It was familiar but I couldn't place it.

"I get that a lot, but I'm afraid you have me at a disadvantage. Exactly who is this?" I asked with a light-hearted tone.

"You wound me, Fiona. It's your future husband—that is, if I can convince you to develop an interest in Bunco."

I smiled. "Hi, Jake. Why are you calling on this line? Don't you have my cell?"

He laughed. "Mark deleted your contact. He said I only manage to screw things up when I open my mouth so I'm not allowed to talk to you out of his presence."

I couldn't help but giggle. Hmm. Interesting.

"What can I do for you today? I'm assuming you're not calling about lawn service since you don't live here."

He didn't respond right away. "Actually, that kind of *is* why I'm calling."

"What do you mean?" I was genuinely confused at this point.

"I did some checking around and your boss Jax has a really impressive reputation around town."

For some ridiculous reason, his comment gave me a little kick of pride—which was so misguided since I'd only worked here a couple months and the only thing I contributed to the business was answering phones and forgetting to fill the coffee maker.

"Well, that's nice to know," I responded, still not understanding where this was going.

"All right, I'm just gonna lay it out for you. I'm considering moving back to the area and I want to work with the best. That happens to be your boss. Any chance I could get an introduction? If I'm overstepping or that makes you uncomfortable I totally understand, but I thought it wouldn't hurt to ask."

I was totally shocked. "You're moving back? When did this happen? Does Mark know? Does Kelly know? Oh my God, she will be so thrilled. This is so exciting! Now our welcome home party can be for real. Oh wait, you're not supposed to know about that—forget I said anything. Oh my God, this is so exciting! Oh, and of course I'll introduce you to Jax, although it might actually work against you. I'm not exactly the best reference, but we'll figure it out. Wow. Just, wow!"

"Take a breath, Fiona. I said I'm considering it. It's by no means a sure thing. I have lots of things to think about."

I scowled into the phone. "Party pooper. So, in other words, keep my mouth shut? You so picked the wrong person, Jake, you know that, right?"

He laughed. "Just do your best."

"You mind me asking what caused this sudden turn-around? From what Mark has told me, you have a pretty sweet gig down in Florida." I leaned back in my chair and twirled a pen in my hand. I immediately dropped it. Why do people always make that look so easy?

"Yeah, well, things aren't always exactly how they appear," he said. And boy did I know a thing or two about that. "And besides, this whole debacle with my mom and dad has got me rethinking some things."

"That's understandable. Well, I'll do my best to keep my mouth shut but I can't make any promises. I can, however, promise to introduce you to Jax."

I grabbed another pen and jotted down some notes about the meeting arrangements before we said our goodbyes.

* * *

"I still don't understand what we're doing here," Laney said as I prowled the fragrance counters at Macy's. She trailed behind me with her Caribou hot chocolate in hand. I would never understand how she couldn't recognize coffee as humankind's greatest invention—well, that and Diane von Furstenberg's wrap dress. It really does look good on everyone, you know. And now that I think of it, penicillin wasn't such a shabby invention either…oh well, I digress…

It was Thursday and I still hadn't heard a peep from Mark. *It had been two days, people—two days!* So, I had concluded that our hot night of sex was a one-and-done kind of thing. This was not entirely surprising, even though I found it remarkably disappointing for reasons I did not want to contemplate. Sometimes you don't realize what you want until you don't get it. There has to be a song in there somewhere.

Anyway, I thought I'd get confirmation that our one-nighter was in line with Mark's general MO and he hadn't, say, fallen off a cliff in the last two days. That info was definitely worth a trip to Caribou Coffee where I could casually quiz Laney. Then I could put the whole thing to rest and move on with normal life—life without *Sopranos* dudes and guns and Manaconda Mondays and road trips and sexy muscled arms and searing kisses and toe-curling orgasms and sweet hugs and—oh for Christ's sake!

I hadn't seen Laney since the weekend so we'd agreed to meet up for a coffee/hot chocolate date after work. I had been so busy obsessing about Mark I hadn't even spilled the beans about Jake's potential move back to Greensboro. Yay me!

She and I still had the dinner to plan and I was dying to know if anyone had been to see Mark's dad to share the news that his money was gone—boo hoo. But I could not bring myself to text or call Mark. A silent brushoff was enough—I didn't need verbal or text confirmation from the source himself.

I waited for Laney at a table by the window, having already ordered both our drinks, and I was trying to come up with the best way to casually ask about Mark's sex life. Ugh, this was going to be hard. I'd finally resolved to just wing it in my normal spazzy way when Laney walked through the door.

"I know, I know, Skechers are not appropriate work attire. Ward off the fashion demons and move on," she said as she approached the table and dropped into the seat opposite me.

I took in her outfit which did, in fact, include Skechers, but I had to give her points for her cute asymmetrical top. However, since I knew it amused her, I crossed myself and whispered a request for forgiveness on Laney's behalf to Inner Fashion Maven and Christian Louboutin while I was at it. "Done," I said.

She rolled her eyes at me, took a sip of her drink and sighed. "Nate picked Rocco up and they're going out for guys' dinner so I've got the whole evening free."

"Yay—that's awesome. Maybe we can grab dinner after this or something. You know we still have to plan a party for Jake," I began.

"I was just thinking about that today. I know it started as an excuse to hang out with Kelly, but I'm still excited to do it," she said. "But first, I haven't even seen you since you got back from Atlantic City. I need the full recap!"

I leaned forward in my seat, eager to finally share the good stuff. "I already told you just about everything, but I did leave out one juicy bit. You have to swear not to tell Nate, though, or Mark will lose his shit." I proceeded to tell her all about the club and the guys who had a thing for Mark's hot bod.

We were both laughing like idiots by the time I finished. Laney snorted and then said, "Too bad for all those guys Mark doesn't swing the other way. I get the impression he's a total manwhore— he could have lined up a record number of dates." She continued to giggle, but my mood fell flat on its face.

Shit. This was the information I'd come here for, so why did I feel like someone had just sucked all the air out of the room.

Unfortunately, I wasn't able to mask my emotions quickly enough to avoid Laney's notice. She smiled and crinkled her eyebrows at me in silent question. I attempted a grin that I'm sure came off as more of a grimace and then tried to hide behind my coffee. Her smile died right there on her face and her left hand came up to rub her cheek. Shit! That was her tell.

"Oh, Fiona," she said.

"What?" I responded, setting my coffee back down and shooing her with my hand. "It was no big deal. I've had one-night stands before. So what?"

She rested her elbow on the table, still cradling her face. "I guess so. But you don't really seem okay. What happened? I mean, I don't need the details of the deed itself, but did you guys talk about it? Did you know what you were getting into?"

"No…I don't know. We didn't talk about it—before or after—

but we'd been kind of dancing around each other so I suppose it was bound to happen." I picked at the seam of my coffee sleeve.

She grabbed my hand. "About what I said before, I don't know for a fact that he just does hook-ups. It was just a guess. I mean, maybe you guys can do the casual thing like you usually do. Unless that is, you want…do you want…do you want a relationship?" There was way too much hope in her voice.

I huffed. "Oh, God no. You've known me for how long and you ask such a question? I'm a little worried about the state of our friendship." I attempted to joke but even I knew it rang false.

"Oh." She pulled her hand back and picked up her hot chocolate again.

"What?"

"It's just that I guess part of me was hoping you'd finally be open to a relationship. That's all."

Yeah, no shit. She was about as opaque as cling wrap.

But she looked so darn sad I was kind of mad at myself for disappointing her.

"Look," I said. "I may not be 'relationship girl' but I can admit that maybe I was hoping for a friends-with-benefits deal."

"You said 'was.' Why can't you still do that? And then maybe see where it goes…"

Gah!

"Because he hasn't called or texted since he dropped me off on Tuesday, and I can't stop thinking about him and I am going out of my mind mentally reliving the best sex of my entire life!" I blurted —maybe a touch too loudly judging by the pinch-faced glares I was receiving from the two older women across the way.

Oops.

Well, clearly neither one of them had ever screwed a man who was built like a fucking mountain and was sweet to his mother. Dammit.

"Oh my God," Laney said.

I knew that look—and that tone of voice.

Retreat!

"You like him."

I rolled my eyes at her. "Well, of course I like him. Do you think I have sex with people I hate? Who does that?"

"No, I mean you *like* him."

I scoffed at her, "Yeah, right. You know what I like?" I slammed down my almost empty coffee cup. "I like how he smells. It drives me out of my ever-loving mind and makes me think things I never think. And it lights my panties on fire!" I looked over to the disapproving, awesome-sex-deprived women. "That's right, ladies. Panties. On. Fire. And I'm not even a liar!" I pointed at them and taunted like some mentally unstable version of a coffee-house poet.

At this point, Laney took over since I had evidently lost my mind. "Let's go," she said as she stood and gathered my purse along with all her things. I stood up and beelined for the door ahead of her. I was done with this. I wasn't going to let some man turn me into a nut-job!

Laney attempted an apology to the women who had tragically never been to Sexy Muscle Magic Land and then raced to catch up to me as I stomped down the sidewalks of Friendly Center in my four-inch heels.

"Where in the hell are we going?" Laney asked. When I didn't answer, I heard her mutter, "Well at least I wore comfortable shoes."

So now we were at Macy's, trolling the men's fragrance department on the hunt for whatever that damn intoxicating cologne was that Mark used to lure me in and catch me unawares.

I turned to Laney to explain my strategy again. "I'm going to buy a big-ass bottle of whatever it is he wears so I can do some good old-fashioned immersion therapy and rid myself of my damn Pavlovian response to that scent!" I was white knuckling the theory that it was his scent, not the man himself, that had tricked me into possibly having—*gag*—feelings.

"I guess," said Laney, in a pathetic attempt at encouragement.

"There are too damn many of these." I looked around helplessly, which was a little sad because I don't think I've ever in my entire life felt anything less than blissful at a department store.

"Maybe I can help. Describe the scent," Laney pitched in with much-needed enthusiasm. This is why I love this girl.

I thought about Mark's scent and my lady parts immediately sighed. *Shut it, bitches! Mama has demons to exorcise!* I blocked them out and tried to concentrate. "I don't know—a little spicy and kind of herby and woodsy, but in a way that's like a favorite blanket you bring out from an old cedar chest." I was staring off into space and almost missed her stifled snort. "What?!"

"I hate to break it to you, but you've got it bad."

Did I just say I loved her? Well, forget that. She was dead to me.

I groused, "Oh shut up and help me find this shit."

Laney snickered and then dutifully approached the first counter.

Chapter Twenty-Five

LADY GAGA WOULD MAKE A TERRIBLE NINJA

FIONA

"I've got some news," Laney sing-songed over the phone later that night.

"You found the cologne?" I asked excitedly. Maybe Nate had known what it was all along! Or not, because that would be weird.

We had completely struck out at Macy's, and by the time we'd smelled the fortieth scent our olfactory senses were numb and everything had started smelling like old feet dipped in sporty deodorant. We'd finally given up and decided to grab dinner, where we vowed not to discuss Mark and/or the events that led up to me shtupping him.

Instead, Laney told me about Nate's increasingly peculiar behavior, but this time she wasn't finding it worrying. Instead, she was getting a kick out of it. This was a surprising, but welcome, turn of events.

Apparently, Nate was up to something because twice in the

past week Laney had come up behind him, unintentionally startling him, and each time he had jumped sky high and then stuttered and stammered like Woody Allen. The man was undoubtedly guilty of something.

"He wouldn't…" I began. I could never see Nate cheating on Laney, but I had to make sure her mind wasn't going there.

"No, no—definitely not," she reassured. "Both times I surprised him he had been typing into his phone and tried to hide it from me really quickly."

"Umm…" I uttered and then stopped because wasn't this exactly the type of behavior a cheater would exhibit? *Sorry, Nate, I have total faith in you, but whatever you're up to you need to be a bit subtler, dude.*

"No, you don't understand. He doesn't have a password on his phone and he's always asking me to answer it for him or check his texts when his hands are busy. That means he's been planning something online." She raised her eyebrows and smiled.

The lightbulb finally turned on. "Your birthday! Of course! Oh, I wonder what he's planning. Do you think it's a trip? You totally deserve it, and if your parents can't take Rocco you know I will." I was so happy for her that she had such an awesome guy.

"I don't know yet, but I'm excited anyway. And I haven't told you the best part—he gave his landlord his notice so, as of next month, Nate will officially be living with us!" she announced.

I squeed. "Oh my God! I'm so happy for you guys." I reached across the table and hugged her. "I feel like we should order a bottle of champagne or something, but then we can't drive." My smile turned into a pout.

She waved me off. "Another time."

I looked at my best friend and she was glowing with contentment. "Laney, I can't think of anybody who deserves happiness more than you."

She'd smiled at me and then grabbed my hand across the table. "I can."

Aaand with that I'd switched the subject to planning Jake's party while we'd finished our meals.

It was now past dark and I'd been getting ready for bed when Laney's call had come through.

"No, I didn't find the cologne. This is better!" she taunted.

"Sweet Jesus, Nate's taking you to Paris! I love that man!"

Laney laughed. "No, it's about Mark."

Visions of springtime in Paris were replaced with those of me enjoying late night reality TV with my buddies Ben and Jerry. Kim would probably be invited too, but unless she figured out how to pair deliciously with ice cream she'd have to wait her turn.

"Hello?" I heard.

"I'm ignoring you." I tucked the phone between my ear and shoulder and opened the toothpaste.

"It's good news—I promise," she pleaded.

"Fine. Go on, if you must."

"So when I got home, Nate and I were talking and I very casually asked him about Mark's dating habits and—"

"YOU WHAT?!" The toothbrush fell into the sink and I braced my hands on the counter. *Deep breaths, Fiona.*

"Shut up and pay attention! I was a total ninja—he had no idea why I was asking."

I huffed at that.

She ignored me. "Anyway, he said Mark always makes it clear

to anybody he's with that he only does casual one-nighters—"

I stood up straight. "*This* is your good news? What do you have planned for tomorrow? Are you going to buy me a pony and then say 'just kidding'?"

"If you don't shut up and let me finish I may do just that!" She was using the tone she reserves for Rocco when he's done something super inappropriate, like the time he asked Nate's mom if she liked having a big butt to sit on.

In other words, my choices were to listen while she finished or hang up and incur her wrath. I chose to listen.

"Fine." I didn't say I would be nice about it.

"As I was *saying*," she stressed the word pointedly, "according to Nate, Mark always—*always*—makes sure he and his 'partner' are on the same page *before* the deed is done. And—listen carefully—he never sleeps with girls he hangs out with." She sounded like she'd just delivered some kind of awesome news and was waiting for accolades. Um, thanks for the news that the guy I boffed is a totally indiscriminate manwhore?

"I don't understand," was all I could say. At this point, I dropped to the bathroom floor on my butt with my back pressed against the wall. I felt weird.

"Fiona, it means he went totally off-script with you. He never gets to know a girl first. He never hangs out with her casually or as friends. He never dates. Until you!"

"What do you mean? We're not dating. He hasn't even called me in two days!"

She sighed. "Answer me this: what was the last thing he said to you before you parted ways the other night?"

I thought back to the scene on the sidewalk where I'd been

feeling all kinds of confused. I'd been tempted and scared at the same time, and when he'd tried to find a way up to my condo I had brushed him off with excuses of being tired.

And then that kiss! Gah!

"Um, I believe he didn't actually use words—more like just his tongue," I muttered into the phone.

"Ha! I knew it. He's totally into you!"

"Then why hasn't he called, dammit?!" I hollered before I could think better of it. "I mean, wait. No. I don't want to date him. I just want hot sex with him, Laney," I may have whined.

"Keep telling yourself that, girlie, but you're the only one buying it. And he hasn't called because he's obviously giving you a little space. I guarantee he will call you within the next twenty-four hours. And, besides, Nate said he's been working late trying to catch up. And then there's the whole thing with his dad—they're all arguing over who is going to tell him about the money. Cut your new boyfriend some slack." She snickered.

Bitch!

"He is not my boyfriend!"

"We'll see. Anyway, I just wanted to tell you the good news. And, like I said, don't worry, I was a total ninja so Mark will never know I was snooping."

I had too much else to think about to remind Laney that she was about as subtle as Lady Gaga. I hung up the phone and sat there for a few more minutes before picking my ass up and finally brushing my teeth.

Boyfriend?

No.

Absolutely not.

Chapter Twenty-Six

LOOK AT ME BEING ALL SENSITIVE AND SHIT

ARK

Nate: Heads up, man.

Mark: About what?

Nate: Laney was quizzing me about you. Fiona's flipping the fuck out.

Mark: Shit.

Nate: What are you going to do?

Mark: I'll figure something out. I've been so swamped I've hardly come up for air.

Nate: I know—that's why I'm sending the heads up. You'd best get your ass in gear if you want a chance with her. "If" being the question.

Mark: Okay, thanks, man. Prepare all your jokes and insults now. I'm going all in.

Nate: You just made my day, you pussy-whipped little douchebag! Wow, that felt good. Later.

I deserved it so I figured I'd better be prepared for all the payback coming my way. Who was the fuckmuppet now?

It was ten at night on Thursday and I was exhausted. I'd taken work home with me the last couple nights and was playing catch up. It wouldn't have been so bad except while I had been in Atlantic City we'd had an order fall through on one of my jobs, and the client on another one was threatening to fire the architect, which would push our start date way out and screw up our whole schedule.

And, as if that wasn't enough, Jake, Mom, and I were in a stalemate over who was going to go see the old man and break the news to him that his money was all gone and his disregard for everyone's safety had earned him exactly what he deserved—a huge hospital bill and no prospects.

Thankfully, it now seemed our fears of our mom wanting to get back together with the asshole could be put to rest. She was as fired up as we were, if not more so. I know Jake and I both relished the thought of finally sticking it to him in person, but our mom was insistent that she be the one and only person he spoke to. I think she was afraid he'd hurt our feelings or something, but she just kept saying that he didn't deserve to see how well we'd turned out and she didn't like the thought of us in the same room as the asshole. Well, she'd said "loser" but I'm sure she'd meant "asshole." We had to decide soon, though, because he'd been expecting her to show up by now, money in hand.

Given all of that, coupled with the frightened rabbit impression Fiona had pulled again on Tuesday, I was letting that whole situation stew for a few days. But it looked like my time was up. I didn't want her flipping out and dismissing me—I'd only meant to give her time to miss me a bit and get comfortable with the notion of having me around. Apparently, my plan had flaws. Now I had to figure out a new one. Fast.

Mark: Hey Shortcake. You awake?

Fiona: I am now, thanks to this annoying guy who just texted me.

Mark: Aw, I love it when you get all sweet and charming.

Fiona: Haha. Is there a point to this?

Mark: You bet. Been swamped since we got back but I wanted to know if you were free for dinner tomorrow night. Sorry for the short notice.

I was proud of myself for being all sensitive and shit and not allowing her to bait me.

Mark: Fiona? You still awake?

Perhaps my idea of sensitive and hers were slightly different.

Fiona: Sorry—just checking my schedule and it turns out I need to wash my hair tomorrow night.

What a little smartass.

Mark: Look, I'm sorry it took me so long to contact you. If it helps, I've been thinking about that thing you did in the shower…

Honestly, I just wanted to tell her I hadn't stopped thinking about her at all—and not just the sex, although that was part of it. I *am* a guy. But if I told her I missed her or got overly attentive, I would definitely scare her away.

Fiona: Well I should hope so—that was some of my best work.

Mark: Yes, ma'am. So dinner?

Fiona: You seriously want to go out on a date?

Mark: Yeah.

Nothing.

Mark: Shortcake, I've already seen you naked and shared several meals with you. I think you can handle it.

Fiona: Fine. What time and how should I dress?

I was tempted to suggest getting take-out, but that wouldn't go well with my new strategy. It would just turn into naked dinner and the plan was to woo her instead of just jumping her.

I know. I'm just as surprised as you.

Mark: 7:15 and wear whatever you want—we're going to The Marshall Free House.

Fiona: Okay. I'm going back to sleep now.

I wanted to tell her I wished I were there.

Mark: Sweet dreams, Shortcake.

That would have to do for now.

* * *

"I was gonna park and come up to get you!" I shouted out my window as I rolled up in front of Fiona's building. She looked up, startled, as if she hadn't been expecting me. There she was on the sidewalk, phone in hand, with her brow furrowed—though it loosened when she saw me. Huh, that felt pretty damn good. Then she smirked at me and the sass was back.

"Hey there, He-Man. Thought I'd just meet you down here," she said as she started toward the truck, tucking her phone back in her purse.

She looked like a magazine ad—her hair was pulled back into some messy knot which I'm sure was intended to look casual but in fact required tons of time and precision. And she was wearing these pants that hung daringly low on her hips. The only words I possess in my vocabulary to describe them are M.C. Hammer pants —but totally kick-ass in a girlie kind of way.

Okay, I'm just going to stop now because it's beyond obvious I don't know the first thing about fashion. And I am totally comfortable with that.

Suffice it to say, my future girlfriend was all kinds of hot. She officially had permission to stick her nose into my business anytime she liked.

I did wonder, though, if she had "people" or something to prepare her whenever she exited her condo and went out into the world. I've heard of that before, but I'm pretty sure that's only for rich people who live in New York and L.A., not the great metropolis that is Greensboro, North Carolina. I was sensing I had a lot to learn.

I stopped staring at her like an idiot long enough to shift into park and hop out to help her with her door. The Hammer pants looked just as good from behind. I shut her door and soon we were pulling away from the curb for the short drive to the restaurant.

She opened her mouth to speak but I beat her to the punch, wanting to set the tone for the evening. "You look beautiful."

Her jaw snapped shut, stifling whatever she'd been about to say. Her cheeks turned a little pink and she finally said, "Thanks. You don't look so bad yourself."

I regarded my cargo pants and plain cotton button-down. If she said so. "Thanks," I replied.

Just then her phone rang from inside her purse and I swear she growled at it.

"You need to get that?" I asked.

"Absolutely not."

"Okay, then." There really was no other possible reply.

The ringing stopped as the call presumably went to voicemail and then a few seconds later it started again.

This time, Fiona threw her purse on the floor of the passenger side only to change her mind and pick it up a couple seconds later, rifling through it for the offending device. She stabbed at the phone and put it to her ear.

"I'm only answering to tell you that I'm turning my phone off so you may as well stop calling. I will not be answering for the rest of the night and I felt it only fair to tell you that because I don't want you to jump to some insane conclusion that the reason your calls are going unanswered is because I'm languishing on the side of the road somewhere grasping in vain for my phone in one final attempt to speak with my beloved mother before I die under the heap of mangled steel that was once a car. I don't need you and Dad trolling the sides of I-40 all night looking for my body. I'm not dying, I'm not answering my phone, and I'm not talking about this. Goodnight and I love you." She started to pull the phone away from her face but brought it back up one more time. "Tell Dad I love him too."

She stabbed the end button, threw the phone back in her purse and let out a giant sigh. Then she turned to me. "Do you think Kelly would adopt me?"

"Shortcake, given that we're currently on a date and I've seen every inch of your naked body, I'd say that question is a tad inappropriate."

Her mouth twisted to the side. "Hmm. Yeah, I guess you're right."

"I would ask if everything is okay but I think even the people in the next town over know it's not."

"Ugh. It's my mother." She shook her head.

"I gathered that."

She rolled her eyes at me. "I told her I had a date."

"And?" I didn't see what the problem was. I switched my turn signal on and made my way toward Battleground Avenue.

"I don't exactly date much," she confessed.

"Me neither." I glanced over and grinned—in a way I hoped came off as conspiratorial as opposed to, say, lascivious.

"Yes, I know," she muttered under her breath. Crap, somebody had been hearing stories about me. I knew it would happen but I had to nip this in the bud.

"Until you," I said, flat out. I looked over again to gauge her response.

She squirmed in her seat. "This is a bad idea," was all she said.

"Why would you say that?"

"It just is," she sighed. Well, that wasn't going to cut it.

"Give me one valid reason," I challenged.

She looked out the passenger window and I thought for a moment that she wasn't going to answer me. Then she said, "It's complicated."

It was my turn to roll my eyes. "Quit dancing around it and give me something solid, Shortcake."

She twisted her body toward me. "Fine. I don't want our friends to have to choose sides when this is over. That right there is a damn good reason!"

Yeah, she was still under the impression that this was going to be some kind of temporary friends-with-benefits thing. Granted, if we dated like I wanted to and then for some unforeseen reason did indeed break up down the road, her point would be valid. But who wants to dwell on that kind of depressing thought? So, I went with the best response I could come up with.

"Fine. If things between us end, you can have them. Except Jake—that one would be a bit awkward at holidays and family reunions," I attempted to joke.

She scoffed. "Not 'if,' '*when*' things end."

"Are you psychic or something? You carry around a crystal ball I don't know about in one of your giant handbags?"

"You know, Mark, normally I'm a huge fan of sarcasm but I'm being totally serious and you're just making light of it."

I pulled into the parking lot of the restaurant and put the truck in park. Turning to her I said, "If I can promise you one thing, Fiona, it's that I'm not taking any of this lightly." And with that, I released my seatbelt and got out to retrieve my girl. Because she was—she just didn't know it yet.

Chapter Twenty-Seven

THE WORST KIND OF TROUBLE

FIONA

What the hell was that supposed to mean?! What-ever it meant, I was definitely in trouble—double-dog-doo trouble, otherwise known as *fucking* trouble. It seemed perhaps Laney had been right—Mark wanted to *date* date.

I didn't know how to do that!

I didn't want to do that!

I wasn't capable of doing that!

Pride cut in at this point. *"For the love of God, please don't hyperventilate and pass out in the parking lot of The Marshall Free House. We are getting those Scotch eggs if it's the last thing we do! Get your shit together!"*

I was beginning to really dislike her, but she did have a point—the one about the Scotch eggs, not the panicking and hyperventilat-ing. That was completely justified.

Mark opened my door and put a hand out. I had no choice but

to take it, noticing as always how warm and strong it was, but mine was shaking—although my breathing had miraculously calmed a bit.

The motherfucker just smiled at me as if he knew just how panicked I was and couldn't be happier about it.

Those Scotch eggs better be worth the heartache that awaited.

As we walked into the restaurant and the hostess led us to our table, I forced my mind away from the scary topic of dating. Unfortunately, that meant my brain decided to wander back to the phone conversation I'd had with my mother earlier in the evening.

I'd been having a perfectly lovely day and was looking forward to seeing Mark, even if it did make me all sorts of anxious. I hadn't messed up anything at work, an occurrence that had Jax and Ollie a bit flummoxed. They were already so used to me screwing stuff up that it was a wonder I hadn't been fired yet.

Ollie always assured me that Jax had seen my resume before he'd hired me, so he was aware of my job-hopping and knew there had to be a reason for it. Luckily Jax had been in such a bind when I'd sent my resume in, he'd had little choice but to at least interview me. That's where I shine, I've been told. Ollie said Jax was under my spell and offering me the job before he even knew what had happened. I guess I am pretty charming.

At any rate, I'd had a great day, and then my mom had called right after work.

She began talking before I even had a chance to greet her. "Sweetheart, I know it's really last minute, but is there any way you could pop over tonight and make an appearance at Barbara's dinner party? She adores you and she said her grandson wants to know more about the LLS Regatta. He's very involved in his sailing club and this could mean a big boost for the event. He'll be at the dinner tonight—it's at 8:00 so you have plenty of time. Is there any possible way you can make it? I'm sure he'd be much more interested in talking to you than all of us old folks."

"Hello, Mom," I said.

"Oh, I'm so sorry, sweetheart. I don't know where my head is. How are you?" I could perfectly picture her standing in the kitchen poring over paperwork and trying to organize a hundred things at once.

"I'm good," I said, dropping my purse and flopping down on the couch. "Work is going great and I got to do girls' night out with Laney last night."

"Oh, how is she? I still can't believe I haven't met the famous Nate yet! Although from the pictures she's posted I'd say she caught herself a live one." She chuckled.

"Nah, she keeps him in line," I joked. "And she's great—Nate is officially moving in next month."

"Aw. I'm so happy for her!"

"Yeah, me too."

Silence.

Crap. I knew she was thinking about how she wished the exact same thing for me.

I took a deep breath and, for some godforsaken reason, decided to share. "So, listen. About tonight, I actually have a date so I won't be able to make it."

More silence.

"Mom?"

"You have a date," she stated more than asked.

"Yes. I have a date."

"With a man." Again, more statement than question.

"No, with a small child. Of course with a man!"

"I...I don't...you really have a date?" This time it was a definite question.

"Yes, Mother. You make it sound as if I have a giant goiter or an issue with body odor. I've actually been told I'm kind of adorable, you know. It's not outside the realm of possibility that a man would want to take me out and share a meal."

"Of course not! I was just so surprised. I mean, not surprised, just taken off guard. Of course someone would want to take you out—what man in his right mind wouldn't find you wonderful and precious?"

Oh lord, here we go.

"All right. You don't have to oversell it. Besides, it's just dinner. It's not a big deal."

At this point, I actually heard her whimper a little in her attempt to hold back her hopefulness. I had to cut this thing off—now.

"Anyway, I'm sorry I won't be able to make it, but tell Mrs. Rogers I'd be happy to talk to her grandson any other time about the regatta."

"Oh, right. Of course, the regatta. Don't worry yourself over it one bit. You focus on your evening out."

God, I hoped she wasn't drawing blood with how firmly she was biting her tongue. The call simply had to end before she injured herself.

"I'm going to run to the store and then get ready for dinner, but have a nice time tonight and I'll talk to you later, okay?"

"Okay, sweetheart. Have fun! I love you!"

"Love you too. Bye."

I was willing to wager she didn't even set the phone down before dialing my dad.

After my quick run to the drug store for my prescriptions, and a short but fruitful detour to a tiny boutique on the way home, I carefully chose an outfit for the night. Mark had said to dress however I wanted so I decided to go for casual to communicate that I wasn't trying too hard. I went with my D&G harem pants, a cotton tank, and my favorite True Religion denim jacket since it was a bit cooler tonight. I left my make-up as it was, threw my hair up into a top-knot and brushed my teeth.

Now, if you're not in the habit of saying a daily prayer, then might I suggest taking advantage of teeth-brushing time for any necessary spiritual connection. You are unable to engage in anything but free thought or self-contemplation, therefore making it a great time to chat with the man upstairs.

Hey God, how's it going? I'm feeling pretty okay but I'm a bit confused about the sexy man who seems to want to claim me or something. Also, my hair is weird this week—what's up with that? Oh, thanks for that awesome parking spot yesterday. And, lastly, as always, please let me live. Thanks, God!

Spit and rinse.

I know it's a bit untraditional but we all have to make it work any way we can, right?

Anyway, it didn't take me long to get ready so by the time 7:00 rolled around I was super restless and decided to throw on my wedges and meet Mark downstairs. I was just locking my door when my phone rang again.

"Hey, Mom, did you forget something?" I asked.

"No, not exactly," my mother replied. "It just occurred to me that you never said who this date was with."

Good God.

"That's because you don't know him. Did you think I was making up an imaginary date?" I decided teasing might do the trick and get her to stop snooping.

"Don't be silly." She forced a casual laugh. "So, it's not someone we know?"

I rolled my eyes as the elevator doors opened. "No, Mom, it's just this guy named Mark and, like I said, it's just a date—no big deal. I'm getting on the elevator now so I'm going to lose my signal. Have a great night!" I hung up the phone as the doors closed, freeing me from the painfully awkward conversation.

As I stepped from the building to wait on the sidewalk, my damn phone rang *again*. Dammit, woman, I love you dearly but stop calling me! I checked just to make sure it was indeed the woman who'd given birth to me whom I was sending to voicemail —and not, say, some friendly customer service rep from India— when I heard Mark's voice calling from his truck.

At the time, I'd been so relieved to have a distraction from Miss All-up-in-my-business that I'd let my guard down for a moment and had literally *gazed* at him. Luckily, I'd quickly remembered my mission to keep this shit casual and brought out the smirky face I reserve specifically for Mark.

Not that it had done any good. Here I was sitting across the table from the mouth-watering man who'd just thrown down and announced his "intentions" or something.

Eek!

I opened my mouth to say … something, when he beat me to it again.

"Okay with you if we order the Scotch eggs as an appetizer?" he asked.

Pride chimed in again, telling me what I already knew. *"Fiona, girl, you are in* fucking *trouble."*

Dinner was awesome, as was the whole freaking date if I'm being honest. In addition to the perfection of the aforementioned Scotch eggs, Mark was an outstanding dinner companion. Not only did he look hot in his casual button-down, but he was funny and smart and considerate without laying it on thick at all. He maintained the same sarcastic charm that was quickly catching me up in his web, and I almost forgot I was supposed to be resisting this dating thing.

Thinking about it, I was shocked to realize that not only had I never had a boyfriend, but I don't think I'd had an actual date—the kind that hadn't been planned as merely the precursor to a scheduled tumble in the sheets—since high school. This dinner with Mark was my first actual adult date, a fact that suddenly made me a bit sad.

"Don't be sad! We can still turn this around into great after-dinner sex!" said Vagina, who was then echoed by her pervy cohorts.

I needed Guilt back to remind me why having a boyfriend was a terrible idea and was totally unfair to a guy like Mark—a guy who, I was coming to realize, was quite wonderful.

But this kind of thinking was getting me nowhere, so I had to back this truck up and get back into the good time I'd been having. And what better way to accomplish this than to talk about his double-crossing dad who was about to get bitch-slapped by Karma? I don't know why everybody assumes I'm so sweet.

"So tomorrow's the day, huh?" I asked as I scooped up the last forkful of chocolate cake. He even let me have the last bite—what in the hell is a girl supposed to do with that?!

"Yeah," he said, scratching the little bit of scruff on his chin. "I think Jake and I are going to have to admit defeat and let my mom go in by herself. But we will definitely be listening outside that door in case he goes off on her."

"I think that's smart to let her go in alone."

"Oh you do, do you? What a surprise." He grinned at me. I wanted to kiss that grin right off his face.

"Yes, I do. She needs to finish this on her own terms," I said in all seriousness.

"Well, I'm so glad you approve, Shortcake." He gave a little bow.

"You sound so sincere," I responded with a tilt of my head.

"Then I didn't say it right." He flagged the waiter for our check with that damn grin still planted on his stupid hot face.

"Oh shut up." That was my brilliant come-back. Awesome. "What do you think he'll do?"

"There's not a whole lot he can do. That's the beauty of it."

"Well, I'm glad you'll be there to back your mom up in case there's trouble."

"I'd never let her get hurt." His tone was quiet and serious.

I had no response.

Chapter Twenty-Eight

CLEANUP IN ROOM 437

MARK

I was a little disappointed I let dinner end on such a sober note because up to that point it had been damn fun. Fiona loved her food, something I'd already known from her cooking and road trip binging, but it was great seeing her in her element. She fought me for the last egg and moaned her way through her main course so I had little option but to let her eat most of the dessert while I watched and tried not to get hard. What I didn't understand was how the girl stayed so tiny with the way she ate. I guess she somehow burned it off by running her mouth like she does—something I was now finding to be mostly charming as opposed to irritating, as I'd first thought.

I held her hand on the way outside and kept a firm grip when she tried to pry hers apart. After a huff and an accompanying eye roll, she relented and didn't try to pull away again until I helped her into the truck. She fidgeted for the entirety of the short ride back to her place.

"Shortcake, I can actually *hear* you thinking, you're doing it so hard," I said as I pulled into a parking spot a block away from her building.

She scoffed and released her seatbelt. "For your information, I was thinking about my mother," she lied—poorly.

"Oh?"

"Yes, as a matter of fact."

I let that sit for a minute while I went around and helped her out of the truck. Her hand wasn't shaking as it had been when we'd gotten to the restaurant, but she was definitely flustered.

"So, were you thinking about how to tell your mother about the guy you're about to invite up to your bed?"

That earned me an indignant gasp and an arm punch. Totally worth it.

While she was busy assaulting me, I cut in with, "Because if that's the case, you won't have much to say. You can, however, tell her about the guy who took you to dinner because he likes you and enjoys your company. The same guy who is going to walk you to your door and kiss you goodnight—and then, tomorrow, he'll call and ask for another date. That guy, you can tell her about."

I don't know that I've ever actually seen a person sputter, but that is the best way to describe the sounds that came out of Fiona's mouth at that moment. I may have done the impossible and rendered her speechless. I pulled her along the sidewalk while she tried to recover. This time she didn't even attempt pulling away.

I was as good as my word and after a hot fucking kiss that began to stray into groping territory, I unlocked her condo door and gently pushed her inside while she stared up at me with lust-glazed eyes. I'm sure mine were a mirror image.

* * *

Now I was headed home but figured a call to Jake was in order.

"Yo, dickhead!" he greeted as usual.

"Hey, shit-for-brains. I'm calling about tomorrow. You come to any conclusions?"

He sighed. "I don't know. Part of me wants to storm in there and let him have it and the other part of me would be happy to never lay eyes on him again. The only conclusion I've been able to come to is that we need to make sure Mom comes out of it unscathed."

"Ditto. I think we're gonna have to let her go in like she wants. But no matter what she says, you and I will be right outside the door, not waiting in the car like a pair of douchebags."

"Damn straight. You want to tell her or do you want me to?"

"You go ahead. I'm headed home and I need some shut-eye. What time are we going over?"

"I think she said 10:30."

"Sounds good. I'll meet you two there unless I hear differently before then."

"Sure thing. Later."

"Later."

The next morning, I rolled up to the medical building and parked my truck in the space next to my mom's car. My nerves were tight and I couldn't wait to get this over with. I'd had a hard time sleeping, despite my level of exhaustion from the week's activities. My mind had kept wandering to the various possible outcomes today could have held had we not recovered the money. My gut burned with fury over my father's intended plan to take the money and let my mom fall prey to whatever the goons had in mind.

The only thing that cheered me was knowing that even if he had gotten the money, his idiotic plan involved handing it right over to another group of con artists. In other words, he'd be eyeballs deep in shit regardless. I believe that was the thought that had finally let me drift off around two this morning.

I found Jake and our mom in the main lobby and I had to do a double-take. Was she wearing makeup? I took her in from head to toe and realized that not only had she done her face up, but she was wearing a stylish outfit that looked new and fit her perfectly. The blouse was a deep blue, and the black skirt hit just above the knee, showing off her legs and —holy shit, she was wearing heels. Not Shortcake-height heels, but heels nonetheless. What had happened to my mother?

She spotted me and gave me a nervous smile and a little wave. Jake was pacing beside her and only spared me a quick glance as I approached.

"You look pretty," I told my mother as I bent to kiss her cheek. "You ready for this? Jake and I can always—" I began, but she cut me off.

"Absolutely not. I'm as ready as I'll ever be."

"Let's get this over with then," grumbled Jake, and we all headed for the elevator with him leading the way.

Outside room 437, my mom gave our hands one last squeeze

and then she slipped through the door. This was really happening. Finally.

The sound of her heels clicking toward the far side of the room reverberated in my skull and I stopped breathing for a moment so I could hear everything.

"Jim." Okay, good strong voice—confident.

"Thank God! It's about time. I was starting to get—wow, look at you!" He sounded completely surprised. Ha! Eat your heart out, old man!

"I have some news." She plowed right on through.

"Please tell me you got the money." His voice came out weak and a bit whiney.

"I did," she replied.

"Thank God." I could hear his relieved exhale all the way out in the hallway. I glanced around to see if anybody else was paying attention to us. The hall was empty.

"I did..." she repeated, drawing out the words, "but then there was an unfortunate run-in with the guys you borrowed it from. They weren't too keen on me keeping it."

"What the fuck?! That's why I told you to come earlier this week before they had a chance to come to the house and take it!"

I moved to enter the room, but Jake held me back. "Give her another minute." Where he'd suddenly found his calm was beyond me. I was on fucking fire.

"Is that so?" my mother asked, as smooth as can be. "What made you think they were coming to my house? According to our last conversation they didn't even know about me."

"I don't know...they didn't!" he tried to cover. "Fuck! The fucking money! Did they take it all?"

"They took the money before it even made it across the state line, not at my house! And I'm afraid I have nothing to give you, so you'll just have to figure out something else."

"B…but," he began again, "what about your money—the money you're investing?"

"Oh, that? Well, I think I've changed my mind. I'm not too fond of the kind of people you associate with," she responded breezily.

"Well what in the fucking hell am I supposed to do now?!" the asshole shouted.

Jake had to hold me back again.

"I haven't the first idea, Jim. But I can tell you what you're *not* going to do." Her voice had suddenly turned icy, her words cutting the air in a tone I'd never heard from her before. "You are *not* going to contact me ever again, and you are *not* going to set foot in this city again.

"Then you are going to *forget* that you ever had a wife and two sons, something that should be habit by now anyway. And lastly, when you get served with divorce papers later today, you are going to sign those damn things as fast as possible so I can get on with *my life,*" she practically hissed at him.

What the fuck? I looked to Jake only to find that he was just as surprised as I was. He shook his head at me and we kept eavesdropping.

"Well then, I think I've said everything I need to say so I'm heading out. And if you want one more piece of advice, you should figure out how to walk soon because I know more than a few people who want you gone even more than I do. And a couple of them could bench press you with one hand tied behind their backs."

The sound of her clicking heels resumed, followed by our father's pathetic pleading.

"Kelly, wait! You can't just ditch me here!" This was followed by a thump and a cry of pain, but the heels never faltered.

Our mom came strutting out of the room and right past us toward the elevators. We were both struck stupid and it took us a moment to get our feet in gear. Still ahead of us, she passed by a nurse.

"You may want to check on the man in 437. I think he might have fallen out of bed." The nurse hurried by us and our mother turned around. "You coming or what?"

Who was this woman and what the hell had she done with my mother?

* * *

"Shit, my favorite part was when she said Lou and Terry weren't 'keen' on letting her keep the money," Jake said, slapping the table.

Our mom chuckled and I laughed before taking another pull on my beer. "I highly doubt that word has ever come from either of their mouths," I responded.

"Thankfully, I never met them so I'll just have to take your word for it." My mom tucked her hair behind her ear and took a sip of her champagne. "I can't believe you boys have me drinking champagne at one in the afternoon."

"I can't believe you managed to rip the old man to shreds without even technically lying. It's like you were a morally upstanding version of Nurse Ratched. God, I wish we'd recorded that." Jake sighed. Mom and I snickered.

"I don't mean this to come out wrong," I said, "but I didn't know you had that in you. You eviscerated him and stayed as cool as shit."

"I didn't know I did either." She gave me a small smile. "And watch your language." She smacked my hand. "Now, you boys may not have anything to do today but I've got a long to-do list and I'm working tonight." She stood from the table and took her glass to the sink.

Jake and I both stood and gave her hugs goodbye.

"Next time someone at works steps out of line I'm sending you in," I joked. "You were amazing."

And that was no joke.

Chapter Twenty-Nine

A CRASH COURSE IN GYM ETIQUETTE

FIONA

"This isn't exactly what I had in mind when you said 'date.'" I looked up a bit pitifully into Mark's handsome face.

"What do you mean? I love this place." He blinked those ridiculous lashes.

I watched him take a satisfied perusal of his surroundings. "I'm aware." I gestured to his biceps. "Although I should have known when you told me to wear a t-shirt and 'those stretchy pants.' For some reason, I just thought you wanted a better look at my ass."

"Well that's just a plus," he said with a naughty grin followed by a smack to said ass. "Come on, Shortcake, enough stalling."

I should have guessed our destination moments after he'd picked me up from my condo after work and handed me a Belk bag. The level of excitement that had subsequently coursed through my veins at the gesture was more than a little over the top. But when a man like him—one whose entire being screams that he is not now and never will be a shopper—gives you a department store bag, what's a girl to do other than swoon? I snatched the bag and kissed him on the cheek. My Spidey senses should have anticipated a bribe of some sort.

"I asked the sales lady to pick something that a girl with only heels in her closet would wear. This is what she came up with. I hope you like it."

He looked nervous so I tore into the bag to end his misery. Inside were a small pair of pristine white socks and a shoe box with "Madden Girl" on the lid. A shoe box! Dear sweet lord, remind me why I wasn't keeping this man forever? I lifted the lid and tissue paper to reveal the most sparkly sneakers I'd ever seen. They actually shimmered in the sunlight streaming through the truck window. I felt like crying, but I held myself in check as I turned to face Mark.

"I love them!" I said as I threw myself across the seat and onto his lap.

One PG make-out session and a quick drive later, we'd arrived at our destination where my enthusiasm had begun to wane a bit— but only for the location, not for the first pair of adult athletic shoes I'd ever owned (sparkles or not).

"Fine," I huffed and stepped up to the strange contraption that had been promised to provide me with tone and definition in my upper arms.

Mark ran his fingers deliberately down the entire length of my arms before moving my hands to grasp the handles of the machine. I shivered.

I wished I could blame it on this godforsaken den of torture he had lured me into. Known to some people as a gym, the establishment was loud and smelly and filled with sweaty people and machines that looked like robots on the precipice of taking over the earth. But, no, this horrid place was not the cause of my shiver.

It was the delectable man standing behind me. The very same one who had been slowly torturing me for the last two weeks with flirty touches, passionate kisses, and nights ending in complete sexual frustration.

The entire gaggle of bitches in my head and nether regions were all up in my face insisting I find some way to pin the sexy beast down and screw the living hell out of him. I suspected even Guilt was secretly booking some alone time with her vibrator at this point. We were all strung as tight as one of Mark's t-shirts and I was bound and determined to get this show on the road.

Unfortunately, the current environment was less than ideal for seduction. So "triceps pushdowns" it was. Ugh.

"Now, I've set it at the lowest weight since this is your first time and I don't want you to overdo it." He stepped back from the stack of black weights in the center of the machine and faced me, apparently assessing my position or something.

"Oh come on," I argued, totally offended. "You can add a little more. I *have* exercised before, you know." I didn't mention that the last time had been high school gym class.

He put his hands up in a defensive position. "All right, Short-cake. Point taken—just trying to look out for you." He added another couple weights.

Honestly, how hard could it be?

Hands on the bar, I slowly pushed downward.

Nothing.

Evidently, I'd have to invest a little effort. No big deal.

I pushed down with what I considered a generous amount of strength.

The goddamn bar didn't budge.

Was that snickering I heard? My gaze flashed to Mark who was unsuccessfully attempting to smother his laugh.

I cleared my throat in reproach and he assumed a neutral expression.

No more fooling around, I was going to rule this damn triceps thingy!

I pushed down with every ounce of effort I possessed and let out a very unladylike grunt as the bar descended and I felt the entirety of my upper body scream in protest. Once it reached its lowest position, I triumphantly released the bar and prepared to woot-woot in victory.

That was, until the weights crashed back down on their stack with a staggeringly loud boom and every single face in the entire sweaty, smelly, robot-filled joint swung in our direction.

Mark covered his eyes and shook his head slowly in what I assumed was either shame or disbelief.

I just did what twenty-four years of humiliating myself had taught me to do. I met the disapproving gazes, smiled, and shrugged my shoulders. "Oops."

After the weight machine debacle Mark decided cardio was the way to go, so he set me up on an elliptical machine and then he proceeded to run an entire marathon on a treadmill.

Surprising myself, I actually had fun. This particular robot was sort of like a self-powered carnival ride. I could go forward or backward and the thing was wired up to a TV which I could program to any channel. I ended up getting exercise while not even noticing because I was so engrossed in watching Ina Garten prepare the loveliest picnic for Jeffrey—although I always think to myself that a more apt spelling would be Geoffrey. Right?

Anyway, once Ina signed off, I was ready to do the same so I hopped off the elliptical, nearly falling on my face in the process. They should really post a warning to use caution when exiting the ride. I signaled to Mark that I was heading for the locker room and he nodded and smiled in return.

However, I did not go directly to the locker room. It seemed my feet had been nailed to the rubber coated floor. In the process of completing his world-record marathon, Mark had taken the liberty of removing his shirt, much to the delight of the female occupants of the room. But, damn, I could not blame them one bit.

Sweat glistened on his chest, face, and arms while his legs pumped furiously on the treadmill's speeding belt. There was not one jiggle in sight, just firm hard-earned muscle and gleaming skin. He noticed my pause and his eyes stayed glued to mine, his feet never missing a beat. When I still didn't move, his smile transitioned into shit-eating territory.

He knew exactly what he was doing to me. Damn that man.

I forced my body to turn and get a move on.

In addition to being frustrating, the last two weeks had also been thrilling, fun, and, dare I say *romantic*? Mark challenged me in all the right ways while also making me feel like I was the most beautiful woman on earth, something I knew for a fact wasn't true. That honor belongs to Penelope Cruz and no one will ever convince me otherwise.

The only thing missing was the actual sex, although all the making out we'd been doing was pretty stellar if I do say so myself. Still, I was acutely aware that this arrangement was like no other I'd ever had. Mark was kind of my boyfriend.

Eek!

One piece of evidence pointing me toward that conclusion was Mark's reaction to a situation the previous weekend.

On that Friday, my mother had called, but this time it had not been to grill me about my mystery man. I was still trying to keep Mark under wraps lest I unleash the mothership and she descend to take his tuxedo measurements. The purpose of the call was actually to tell me that Chandler Rogers, Barbara Rogers' grandson, was going to be in Greensboro the next day and would like to take me to lunch to talk about the fundraising regatta for leukemia research. This was the kind of thing I did all the time and I didn't think twice before agreeing.

Well, let me just say that someone else had some real specific second thoughts about that idea.

"You're going out on a date with this guy?" Mark asked in disbelief when I told him why I couldn't hang out on Saturday.

"It's not a date." I laughed, but inside I felt a pang of satisfaction at his jealousy.

"Then what would you call it? A man who is not related to you is taking you to lunch alone." I could *hear* his scowl over the phone.

"It's just a lunch meeting to talk about some fundraising for my parents' pet cause." I was very careful not to get too specific.

Go ahead and get your judgy pants on. I had not told Mark a single thing about my leukemia or any of its implications. He was supposed to be my fuck buddy and fuck buddies did not talk about cancer. The fact that we were not actually fucking did cast a bit of doubt on that reasoning, however.

"Don't you find it kind of odd that your parents are constantly calling *you* to help out with *their* charity?"

I inhaled sharply, ready to let him have it, but what could I really say without revealing too much?

He continued, "I mean, don't get me wrong. I think you're a very generous person for volunteering your free time, and I feel the same about your parents. But why are you better qualified than they are to inform this guy about some fundraising event? Especially when it sounds exactly like a date?"

Gah!

Well, Mark, the fact is I am the proverbial poster child for this charity, seeing as the entire reason for its existence is the woman you are currently not fucking. I am often brought out like a show pony to be admired and serve as an example of the possibilities that lie ahead. I'm actually quite similar to Harry Potter, but instead of being "The Boy Who Lived," I'm "The Girl Who Lived"—but the amount of staring and attention is pretty much the same. Sorry I haven't mentioned I'm a leukemia survivor, but if I told you then I'd have to tell you everything and you would treat me like a fragile piece of china and then I'd have no choice but to punch you in the dick.

No, I couldn't really say that.

"We're just...we're just really close, and they count on me. They've always helped me out so much, so I help them when I can." Oh, and because Guilt won't let me say no. "Look, it's just lunch. Then you and I can do something afterward." I tried to appease him.

He exhaled. "Fine."

"Good."

"Not 'good,' fine."

That made me grin. "We can go see a movie and I'll even let you choose," I tempted.

"You know I'm not seeing anybody else, right?" Mark said out of nowhere, or at least that's how it felt. We were not talking about this.

"Hmm," was all I could make myself say.

I heard a reluctant little chuckle from the other end of the line. "You're killing me, smalls. I'll see you tomorrow. You'd better be up for some hard-core action because I have plans for you, Shortcake."

Ooh! This sounded promising. Thank God he was finally coming to his senses. And I had the best La Perla thong for the occasion! The lady bits started to cheer, but then his voice cut in and all our sexy-time hopes were snuffed out like the slutty girl in every horror movie ever made.

"The new Bruce Willis movie opened today." His chuckle had intensified and become downright self-satisfied—and dare I say a bit mean-spirited. Jerk-face.

As I made my way into the locker room and away from his tempting bod, I recalled that smug, jerk-faced chuckle and cursed him for once again making me all hot and bothered while refusing to deliver.

I was in need of a cold shower, but since I had no fresh clothes to change into, I just used the facilities and splashed my face with water while I waited for Mark. I was reaching for a paper towel when a sugary sweet voice came from behind me.

"Don't get your hopes up, sweetie. He doesn't take call-backs so you'd best enjoy tonight. You may want to think about a shower, though."

I looked around, face dripping, and saw Sports Bra Barbie standing behind me, designer water bottle in hand and boobs hailing an enthusiastic salute. I may have stared. Okay, I totally stared. How did she fit those things in that bra? With the distraction presented by her mammary display, it took a moment for her words to register.

Wait.

What the fuck?

I pointed stupidly at myself. "Um, are you talking to me?"

She rolled her eyes and shifted to one hip. "Duh."

What were we, five?

"*Who does this bitch think she is?*" asked Vagina, who was already on edge from the particularly tough couple weeks.

I took a moment to wipe my face and calm everyone down, and then it suddenly occurred to me. This girl was one of Mark's one-nighters. And evidence suggested she was seeing all shades of green and did not like the sight of the competition on her turf.

I lifted myself to my full height—damn that sweet man for buying me athletic shoes that only afforded an extra inch! "And you are?" I asked, attempting a tone of complete confidence.

"Aubrey," she answered and inspected her flawless nails. "I'm just trying to look out for you, honey," she said with the utmost *in*sincerity, conveniently leaving off the unspoken portion that was most likely something along the lines of, "as I help you over this scenic cliff and down to the rocky waters below. Whoops, my bad."

I gave her a fake-ass smile in return. "Thanks, *sugar*, but I think I've got it covered." I started for the exit.

Her hands came up in defense. "Fine, but don't come crying to me when he forgets your number."

I continued on by at a measured pace, resisting the urge to throw an insult at her, and walked into the main gym area in search of Mark. Our minds must have been in sync because I practically ran straight into him. He grabbed my upper arms before I collided with his sweaty bare chest.

"Hey, Shortcake. You ready to head out?"

"Definitely," I said, upset with myself that I'd allowed Sports Bra Barbie to get under my skin.

And, speak of the devil. "Hi, Mark." I heard her voice come from behind me again. I was going to have to rename her Ambush Barbie.

I looked up at Mark and saw his eyes drift over my head to the big-boobed model behind me. Who was I kidding? I couldn't compare to her. I didn't even want to. I was only in this thing for the sex anyway and once I finally got that a few more times he would move on to another version of Aubrey.

"Oh, hi," Mark paused and I saw a flash of panic cross his face. Interesting. "Aubrey," he practically shouted.

He'd forgotten her name.

Is it bad that I wanted to laugh my ass off?

After that, the girl couldn't get away fast enough. Mark popped into the men's locker room for a quick shower and then we were off.

"Well," Mark said as we exited the wretched gym and made

our way to his truck. "That didn't really go exactly as I'd envisioned."

Not sure if he was talking about my less-than-stellar athletic prowess or the run-in with Aubrey, I decided to assume the former. "Hmm, then it seems you're not quite as bright as I thought you were. I will say, though, I did have some fun on that elliptical thing —it really has some potential."

"You were a great sport," he said, grabbing my hand and lifting it to his mouth for a quick kiss.

"I'm glad you think so. We'll see how you do when I take you shopping."

Was it my imagination or did his face pale a bit?

Chapter Thirty

DOG SWEATERS AND PANIC ATTACKS

FIONA

The following night was Jake's long-awaited welcome home dinner. And as far as I knew, I was still the only one aware that he was considering a permanent move.

As promised, I'd set up the meeting with Jax and by the laughing and clear camaraderie I'd witnessed, I assumed the meeting had gone exceptionally well. What would happen next was anyone's guess.

My main focus was still on getting Mark back into bed, hussy that I am, and the previous night had not born fruit as I had hoped. He'd, once again, extricated himself from the nice steamy clutch we'd had going on and had left me practically panting in his wake. Clit was no longer speaking to me, and all the other girls were beginning to curse Mark's name. He was now known universally by my nether regions as "That Fucking Clit Tease" and "Future

Bloodstain on Karma's Highway." What in God's name was he waiting for?!

Happy to have a distraction, I spent the morning grocery shopping with Laney and fielding phone calls from Kelly on what to bring, what to wear, what time to come over and about ten other things. I'd heard all about her stellar performance at the rehab center and was so looking forward to seeing her again and giving her a giant hug. I was so flipping proud of her.

Nate and Gavin agreed to take Rocco out for the afternoon so Laney and I could prepare for the dinner party. Well, it was really so Laney could frantically clean the house and I could prepare for the dinner party. I love that girl like a sister, but one of these days I may have to call an intervention. Although I did have to admit the house was much tidier in general since Nate appeared on the scene. Still, Laney had more junk drawers than anyone I'd ever met—yet I was constantly uncovering odd bits of things in every imaginable spot in her house. It was not unusual to pick up a throw pillow and find a pack of paperclips and a bottle of cough syrup hiding underneath. True story.

Anyway, while she stashed things away, I washed and cut various ingredients and prepared dips and bread dough. When I had done everything I could, I retrieved three large cardboard sheets from their hiding spot in the garage. I was just unwrapping them when Laney reappeared.

"Oh my God! I can't believe we actually did this!" She covered her mouth.

I ripped the first sheet of wrapping and uncovered a giant poster-sized image of a young Jake and Mark—the very one that had sent us into fits of laughter at our first lunch with Kelly. Mark's skinny little ass faced the camera and Jake's very naughty smile beamed as he held his brother in a headlock. See? I'd known he was trouble from the beginning.

Impatient to see the rest, Laney ripped open the next two—one taken on Jake's sixteenth birthday, and another of both brothers where Jake was acting like a jackass and Mark was smiling shyly at the camera.

Sweet Mark.

Gah!

We ran around like crazy people trying to finish all the last-minute preparations while leaving ourselves time to get pretty before everyone arrived. I had chosen a gold metallic flared dress with wedge booties, and I had invested considerable effort into convincing Laney to wear a halter style pin-up dress in a vibrant red. She was stunning and I just knew Nate would choke on his tongue. I was putting the finishing touches on Laney's make-up when the doorbell rang.

"I know we're early but I just figured you could use the help so I dragged Jake out the door and we hit the road—oh dear lord!" Kelly stopped in her tracks on the way into the main living area. Laney, having just answered the door, trailed behind her with Jake bringing up the rear. Kelly covered her face and I couldn't tell if she was holding back laughter or tears at the sight of the huge photos of her boys. I didn't have to wait long to find out because she began fanning her face. "Oh, you girls are gonna make me cry! Just look at my sweethearts."

But my eyes didn't go to the photos. Instead, they traveled

down Kelly's body, taking in her slim frame and the lovely floral wrap dress covering it. I also marveled at her styled hair (a layered bob!) and carefully applied makeup. This was one beautiful babe!

"Kelly, holy shit, you look hot!"

"Completely," echoed Laney.

Kelly colored slightly and drew her eyes away from the photos and down to her dress. "You think?" she asked hesitantly.

"I *know*. Damn, woman," I said, and all three of us girls giggled a bit.

"Jesus Christ, what the hell is that?!" Jake was now gaping at the photos, having just noticed them.

"Um, surprise?" said Laney as I simultaneously shouted, "Welcome home!"

* * *

By the time guests started arriving, Jake was pretty much over the shock and had actually started throwing out some self-deprecating jokes. Nate's parents arrived, bickering about something I couldn't quite hear, and soon after, Rocco burst through the door from the garage and practically sprinted into Riordan's arms. He was subsequently rewarded with a bear hug and a swing onto the older man's back. Erin, Nate's mom, smothered Rocco with kisses as he pretended to be offended. "Nana, I'm practically six!"

Moving at a more human pace, Gavin sauntered in and headed straight for the kitchen counter, stealing some mushroom crostini and a scallop skewer. I moved to smack him on the back of his stupid head when I heard a thump from the direction of the garage.

Turning around, I caught sight of Nate rubbing absently at the back of his head where the door had obviously just smacked him. He stood still in the doorway and his eyes were laser-focused on Laney, who was chatting with Erin. Laney hadn't seen him yet but Nate had apparently seen all he needed to because in the next moment he opened his mouth and said loudly, "Marry me."

Everyone, except Rocco of course, stood in stunned silence as Laney finally turned to Nate. "W…what?" She brought her right hand up to her cheek.

Nate drew himself up and said it again, just as loudly. "Marry me."

"Oh, dear sweet baby Jesus," Erin stage whispered and clutched her chest.

Laney took a hesitant step toward Nate. "Are you serious?" I could see her hands trembling as they held both of her cheeks.

"I've never been more serious in my entire life." Nate stepped toward her until only a foot separated them. "Well, what's your answer? Don't leave me hanging." Nate smiled his devastatingly handsome smile accompanied by his equally devastating dimple. How could a girl ever say no to that face?

"I may be mistaken but I don't think you even asked me a question. It sounded more like a demand," Laney said with a sassy little grin as her hands dropped to her hips.

Nate rolled his eyes and then took her hands in his and asked with appropriate sincerity, "Laney, will you please marry me?"

"Hell yes!" Laney exclaimed and threw her arms around him.

"Mommy said 'hell'!" yelled Rocco.

* * *

Fifteen minutes and a billion hugs later, I stood gazing at my best friend whose face was literally glowing with happiness. Or maybe it was just the reflection off the gorgeous diamond that now adorned her hand. It turned out Nate had not been planning a trip to Paris, he'd been planning a proposal instead. When he'd caught sight of her in that dress, though, instead of choking on his tongue he'd spontaneously proposed.

I was still admiring the ring when I suddenly felt a tingle run up my spine and I knew, I just knew, the cause of it. As unbelievable as it sounds, I actually felt his presence in the room. What the hell? At that moment, no force known to man—not even an invitation to cobble shoes with Jimmy Choo himself—could have kept me from turning to face Mark. My belly took a supersonic nosedive while my heart suddenly rocked out to heavy metal and I stared.

He was sheer perfection—black dress slacks, pressed moss green button-down with just the right number of buttons undone, clean-shaven face, and a look weighted in … *something*, directed firmly at me.

My mouth forgot how to produce saliva and my forehead suddenly felt damp, as did pretty much my entire body. I opened my mouth but had no words, and he was all the way across the room anyway, so it wasn't as if he could hear me. A very unfamiliar sensation swept over me, and in that moment I recognized I had real *feelings* for this man. Feelings that had little to do with my schemes to get him into bed or my admiration of his hot bod. These feelings made me want to keep him for myself—damn the consequences.

My face must have been an open book because Mark's eyes

swept over every inch of it and then he visibly exhaled and dipped his head, shoving his hands in his pockets. He seemed…relieved.

Wishing simultaneously that I could run away or I could pull him off to another room and figure this crazy thing out, I chose neither and focused on hostess and cooking duties instead. I withdrew to the kitchen, excusing myself from my conversation and ensuring a small bit of privacy for the panic attack I would be experiencing momentarily.

I gripped the counter, still feeling confused and hot. I didn't understand this emotion that rushed through me at the sight and thought of Mark. I took a few calming breaths and then let it settle in.

Maybe this was kind of how a dog feels when presented with her first doggie sweater. It's strange and foreign and a bit intimidating at first, and she thinks, *no, not for me, I'm good.* Then once it's on and she wears it around for a while she starts to feel the warm cuddliness of it, not to mention the awesome zebra print— *just deal with it because even if it's imaginary, no dog of mine is going to dress in anything less than designer wear.*

I took stock of my emotions and general state of mind when I was with Mark or when I thought of him, which I couldn't seem to stop doing lately. Yeah, it definitely felt like I was wrapped up in something warm and soft. It was a damn nice sweater and it felt really freaking comfy. I was thinking this sweater might be for me after all.

So, I guess I was the dog and my feelings were the sweater? Or Mark was the sweater and I was still the dog? Wait, that's not a very flattering analogy. Whatever. This was too confusing.

I vowed to put the thoughts aside for the moment and directed my attention to the soup simmering away in a large pot. Time to get down to business and ignore the giant elephant in the room—the one that may have been wearing a zebra-print sweater.

Chapter Thirty-One

ME AND MY BIG FAT FUCKING MOUTH

MARK

I stood next to Jake as he gave me shit about the ridiculous photos that someone, *ahem*, had decided to blow up in a clear effort to add just the right tone of humiliation to the evening. One point to the ladies. Well done.

I took my lumps and didn't even attempt to dish any back. I was too distracted by the thought of Fiona and that look she'd given me when I'd walked in tonight. There was no way I had misread it. She may have tried to hide it, but it was right there on her face before she fled to the kitchen.

She was falling for me.

Thank fuck.

No, seriously, this bullshit plan of mine to withhold sex until I was sure she was in just as deep as I was (Christ, even my choice of words was sexually driven)? Worst plan ever. My balls were so blue it was a wonder I could still walk.

Now that I had some confirmation of Fiona's feelings, it was *on*. This party couldn't be over fast enough. Shortcake had better watch out because I was coming for her. (Goddammit, I did it again—I really needed to get laid.)

I decided to give her a little space since it wasn't as if I could have my dirty way with her on Laney's kitchen counter. And besides, she was full-on deer-in-headlights, so it was only fair to give her a minute. Not to mention, the smells coming from the kitchen were nothing short of fan-fucking-tastic, so I wasn't about to mess that up either.

A strong hand gripped my shoulder and turned me around.

"Did you hear the good news?" Nate asked, a huge-ass grin on his face.

"What news? I just got here."

Laney popped up between us and shoved her hand in my face. For a second, I thought she was going to back-hand me—I'm sure I deserved it for something—but then I noticed the diamond that was about to jab a hole in my eye. Holy shit, he'd actually pulled it off!

"No shit?" I looked to Nate.

"No shit," he replied, still grinning like an idiot.

I wrapped Laney up in a hug. "You know, darlin', you could do better but I'm happy for you anyway."

She pulled back and punched my arm, but her grin was just as big as Nate's. "Thanks, I think."

I held out my hand to shake Nate's. "So you worked up the balls to do it, huh? Congrats, man." And I found I was genuinely happy and excited for them. Look at me being all mature.

"Thanks," he replied and then looked around. "Where's Bay? I thought you were picking her up on your way."

"She couldn't make it after all, but you should definitely call her with the good news—I know she'll be upset she missed it."

My plan had indeed been to pick Bailey up on my way, but when I'd gotten to her place I could tell something was up. If I didn't know better, I'd have sworn she'd been crying.

"Can you just make something up?" she'd asked when she'd opened her door and poked her head out.

"Like what? Why don't you want to go all of a sudden?"

"What's the big deal? I've never even met your brother," she'd countered, suddenly defensive.

I'd reluctantly agreed to drop it, knowing I was already running late, but I was still determined to get to the bottom of this. Just not right now. No, I had some awesome food to eat, some hands to shake, and my girl to take home. Not bad for a Saturday night.

* * *

"Have you ever thought about being a chef?" I asked a few hours later when we were on our way to my place. I was making my intentions crystal clear by not even asking if my place was okay. Fiona would have to speak up on her own if she wanted to call it a night. She'd willingly left her car at Laney's so I wasn't expecting any surprises.

"No way," Fiona said, shaking her head emphatically.

"Shortcake, everything you've cooked has tasted incredible. You'd kill it as a chef." I was genuinely puzzled at the vehemence of her dismissal. "What was that soup again?"

She smiled in my direction. "Zucchini with crème fraîche and cilantro."

"See! I don't even like zucchini and I had seconds—that's how good your food is. And don't even get me started on the chicken." I grabbed her hand and held it on my thigh.

She continued to grin at me. "Well, I'm glad you enjoyed it, and I really do love to cook. But I would never make it as a chef."

"Why the hell not?" I was feeling defensive on her behalf and I got that feeling again that there was something I was missing. Somebody had made her see herself negatively. I was hoping I wasn't going to have to kick anybody's ass.

She sighed. "Well, first of all, I don't have a degree. Second, being a chef takes lots of smarts and the ability to remain calm under pressure. Does that sound like me?"

I thought about it for a moment. Had she asked me that question a month ago, I probably would have laughed, but now I had seen first-hand how good she was at maneuvering her way through tough situations. And she was so far from the dumb blonde I'd pegged her as in the beginning. "I think you're selling yourself short."

"I believe that detail is pretty obvious, big man." She laughed at my unintentional joke.

"Let me ask you this. Do you like the job you have now as much as you like cooking?"

She squeezed my hand. "It's a lot more complicated than that, Mark. Trust me."

I could tell the subject was closed for the night but I wasn't going to give up. My girl deserved to be happy in every way, and damn anybody and anything that stood in the way.

* * *

"So, now that you have me here, what are you going to do with me?" Fiona sat perched on my couch with one slim leg crossed over the other, her gold dress riding up her thighs and showcasing some short leather boots that belonged behind my back.

"I'm going to ask you a question." I stood a few feet away from her with my hands on my hips.

Her saucy smile fell a little. "Oh."

"You want to be with me?"

Her brow furrowed. "Of course. I would think that was obvious. I've been trying to get you back into bed for weeks—you're the one who keeps pulling away."

"You know that's not what I meant." I should have expected she'd deliberately misunderstand.

She uncrossed her legs and shifted forward on the couch, hands clasped on her lap. "Mark, you know I really like you, and I find you incredibly attractive. I also like spending time with you. But I'm not cut out to be anybody's girlfriend if that's what you're asking."

"That *is* what I'm asking and you know it." I kept my tone gentle. "I think you're scared and you're making excuses. What are you scared of?" I sat down next to her and grabbed one of her hands, rubbing the back of it with my thumb. "Shortcake, what's scaring you about this?"

She groaned and dropped her forehead to our connected hands on her lap. "Ugh. This is so hard. I don't know anymore."

"What is your gut telling you right now?" I asked, hoping like hell I'd get the answer I wanted.

"Honestly?" She pulled her head back up and looked at me.

"Honestly."

"It's telling me I can trust you."

"You can."

"It's also telling me that I am so horny I might actually cause you bodily harm if I get another brush-off, Mark."

I laughed. "No more brush-offs. I promise." It seemed Q & A time was over so I leaned in and met her lips with mine.

Things quickly became intense—we were both so keyed up from the last few weeks I was starting to wonder if I'd even last long enough to let her come first. Knowing I had to keep myself in check I decided to change up my game plan. I pulled away for a moment when I realized she had already gotten my belt undone and was working on my button with one hand while her other gripped the back of my neck.

"Come on, Shortcake, we're taking this to the bedroom." Before she could protest, I flipped her over my shoulder in a fireman's hold and strode down the hall. She shrieked and smacked my ass, threatening to put her heel somewhere unpleasant if I didn't let her down. It was cute.

I plopped her down unceremoniously on the bed.

"Why do you do that to me?!"

"Because I can." I shrugged my shoulders and then knelt on the bed.

She huffed and pulled her dress down.

"Oh, no you don't." I pushed it right back up and kept going until it was gathered in a golden swath under her breasts. "Damn." I'd missed seeing her like this, silky bare skin and lacey panties.

My hands parted her legs at the knees and I leaned in for a kiss on both of her inner thighs. Goosebumps rose on her skin and she gave a little gasp, so I buried my nose in the lace of her panties, feeling her heat and reveling in her scent. "Your panties are already damp," I said.

She panted a little. "No shit. You've had me so hot and bothered I've never done so much laundry in my life." She grabbed onto my head, as if I had any intentions of moving from my favorite spot in the world.

My fingers hooked in the sides of her panties and pulled them down and off. I brought my hands back up to part her folds and then swiped my tongue up, circling it around her clit.

"Oh God," she moaned.

Loving the taste of her, I continued my exploration with my tongue and then added my index finger, slowly making my way inside. She was soaked. I was hard as a rock and hoping like hell I could hang in there.

"Mark," she moaned as I found the perfect spot. "I want you inside me."

Not wanting to ignore the lady's request, I took one for the team and decided to comply. I quickly applied a condom from my nightstand and settled over her with my elbows on the bed and my hands framing her face.

"God, you're incredible," I murmured as she squirmed under me. I pushed her hair from her face and traced her lips with my thumb. She opened her mouth and bit it.

Okay, that was it. The combination of the squirming, biting, and lingering taste of her on my tongue propelled me to action and I pressed into her center, pulling back only once before thrusting completely inside. I groaned and she mewled like a cat, with her nails in my back to make the comparison particularly apt.

"Don't stop," she said, and I continued a slow rhythm while we both worked to remove her dress the rest of the way. Her flimsy bra was next and then my teeth tugged at her pebbled nipples while she groaned her approval and gripped the back of my head.

Wanting desperately to see her ride me, I easily flipped us over, without losing our connection, and thrust up into her. She cried out and found her rhythm, one hand to my chest and the other to her own breast.

Shit, that was hot.

I gripped her hip with one hand and grasped her ass with the other as she rode me. She picked up speed and began whimpering as I thrust up to meet her each time.

"Holy shit, Mark," she gasped.

"Shortcake," I responded through clenched teeth. "I need you to come."

She was moving even faster now and I couldn't understand the words coming out of her mouth. The only thing I knew was that nothing in my life had ever felt better and I was about to come in the next few seconds. I brought my thumb down to her clit and circled it a couple times.

That did the trick. She exploded around me, writhing and squeezing my cock with her inner walls as she climaxed. Needless to say, I was right behind her.

She collapsed in a sweaty heap on my chest with my cock still inside her. I couldn't have moved if I'd tried. To be honest, I wanted to stay just like this for the rest of my life with Fiona on top of me sated, happy, and relaxed.

Once I worked up the energy I brought my hand up to stroke her hair. "Are you still alive?"

"Barely," she mumbled. "Actually, I might be dead after all. I'm not sure yet. I'll get back to you."

I chuckled and the movement of my chest caused her to move with it.

"Hey, some people are trying to sleep here so knock it off," she said.

"I hate to break it to you, but there is the matter of the condom to take care of at some point." I continued to stroke her hair and had as little enthusiasm to break our contact as she did.

"Bah," was all she said.

"Are you a sheep now?"

"Shhh, not a sheep, asleep." She sounded drunk.

I couldn't help but laugh again, finally causing her to roll off me and collapse on the bed.

"I'll be right back." I leaned over and kissed her lips before pulling myself up to go take care of the condom.

When I got back to bed she was in the same exact position, gloriously naked and resting on her back with her hands above her head. I climbed over her again, dropping kisses on her belly, breasts, chin, and lips. My eyes roamed her face and she opened her drowsy eyes and gave me a smile so sweet it practically knocked the wind out of me.

Without any thought, I went ahead and did the dumbest thing in the world. I opened my big fucking mouth and said the one thing sure to ruin everything.

"I'm falling in love with you, Shortcake."

Chapter Thirty-Two

SCENT OF A MAN (AL PACINO WILL NOT BE APPEARING IN THIS FEATURE)

IONA

No No No No No!

Why did he have to say that? I was basking so blissfully in my afterglow and mentally writing my Dear Diary entry on the best sex of my life. I was even going to include classic phrases like "swollen staff" and "glistening portal of womanhood" and "fiery culmination," and he had to go and ruin it by saying the most fucking wonderful thing anybody could say to another person.

Dammit!

I proceeded to flip the fuck out by squeaking—yes, I actually squeaked—and then retreating as quickly as possible to the bathroom.

I'd been in Mark's house a couple times before, but never for long lest I use my womanly wiles to lure him into the bedroom at a time that conflicted with his "trick Fiona into buying the cow" plan. Up until this evening, I had only seen the main living space and the kitchen. The house was nestled in a quiet street in an older neighborhood with beautiful mature trees and winding sidewalks. Mark kept the place very tidy and the furnishings were classic but simple—nothing fussy in the least, yet a step up from "single twenties guy" decor.

What I'd seen of the bedroom on my upside-down ride there seemed to be much of the same, and now I was getting my first look at his bathroom. It, too, was tidy, but that wasn't the first thing I noticed. As soon as I slammed the door behind me and leaned against it, that scent surrounded me. It was a little different—a little more sterile—than when it was combined with Mark's own personal scent, but this was definitely it.

Happy to focus on something other than the horrible/wonderful thing he had just said, I let my nose lead the way and blood-hounded it over to the bar of soap sitting unceremoniously in a plain soap dish next to the faucet.

Soap? Not possible.

Soap did not make you want to consume an entire person in one bite. Soap did not make butterflies invade your belly and have a rave. Soap did not make you want to throw caution to the wind and risk absolute heartbreak. Soap did not make you fall for a guy.

No! This was not happening!

I turned right around and flung the door open. Mark was standing directly in front of me with his hands braced on either side of the door. I jerked back, a bit startled, and then darted under one of his arms and raced for the living room, grabbing my dress off the floor in the process. Panties be damned.

Buck-ass naked, I found my purse and scrambled wildly for my phone. One quick emergency text to Laney and I was throwing my dress over my head, knowing that Mark wouldn't just let me walk out—and I couldn't have this conversation naked.

Seemingly in no hurry, Mark finally emerged from the bedroom in only a pair of boxer briefs. He folded his arms and leaned against the far wall while I tried to occupy my hands with tidying my dress and fussing with my purse.

He still didn't speak.

I really didn't want to do this.

Still no speaking.

Shit.

"How many times have I told you this is a bad idea?" I finally said, facing him with an entire room, an entire world, between us.

"I already agreed you can have our friends if things don't work out for some unforeseeable reason. I don't really even like Nate that much."

He was making fucking jokes?

"This isn't a joke, Mark."

"I know it's not. Do you know how many times in my life I've told a woman I have feelings for her? Once. You." He maintained his calm and his pose.

"This will not end well." My whole being begged him to just accept it.

"So you've said, but before this discussion circles around *yet again*, I just have to ask, did somebody hurt you? Did some guy treat you badly? Break your heart? Or worse?"

What? Where in the hell had that come from?

"What?! Why in the hell would you think that?"

His calm faded a bit. "Look at it from my perspective. You like me, you like spending time with me, you're attracted to me, the sex is great, we have fun together." He checked things off on his fingers. "There has to be a reason you don't even want to try!"

"There is!" I knew he had a point and I also knew I would have to tell him everything.

"Then tell me so I can fix it."

"Gah! That's the exact opposite of what I want!"

"Then what do you want?" His hand scrubbed over his hair in clear frustration.

I was doing this to him.

"I want my life to be simple, manageable," I started.

"Boring? Lonely?" he countered. He was hurt.

"Normal."

"What's more normal than having a boyfriend?"

"You don't understand." Jesus, I was a broken record.

"Then help me. For the love of God, Fiona, help me understand. What am I missing here?" He gesticulated with open hands.

"It can't last, Mark."

"Why? And I want the truth this time," he demanded.

I stood my ground but I knew my eyes turned tender. "Because good things are taken away all the time. I may trust you, but I don't trust a good thing and there's nothing you can do to change that."

"What was taken away from you? Tell me." He pushed off of the wall and his voice was gentle again as he stepped toward me.

"My childhood, my future," I whispered.

"What does that mean?"

I swallowed the lump in my throat, wishing with all my might that I could just erase everything.

But I couldn't. So, I let it all out.

"When I was nine, I was diagnosed with leukemia. We fought it for a long time using a lot of drugs that eventually got the leukemia but did other kinds of damage. I can't have kids. I have a good chance of developing other cancers. My brain doesn't work right. I am twenty-four years old and I have a cardiologist and a pulmonologist. My bones are weak. I constantly feel stupid and inadequate and I can't even hold down a job answering phones and making coffee. I am going to be a burden on everyone who loves me and I can't take on one more heart that will eventually break because of me."

He had stopped in his tracks at the word "leukemia."

"Shortcake. Fiona. W…what…why didn't you tell me? Are you sick? I mean, are you sick now? Shit, have I been hurting you? I can't believe I threw you around like that. And I made you lift weights!"

"This is exactly why I didn't tell you," I said, my voice choked with tears that were on their way.

"What do you mean?"

"The way you're looking at me right now. That's why I didn't tell you. I wanted to be sexy, fun, silly Fiona—not damaged, sick, breakable Fiona. I've always been that."

He closed the distance between us and grabbed my hands. "You're not damaged! You're beautiful and you *are* sexy and fun and absolutely nuts and I love that about you! But I can't just ignore what you're going through—what you've been through."

I tried to pull my hands away but he held on. "Look, Mark, you deserve a girl who is funny and smart and sexy and *healthy*. Not somebody you will probably have to take care of, who can't give you everything you want in life."

"What if *you're* what I want in life? What if I *want* to take care of you? Don't I get any choice in the matter?"

"No. You don't. I'm going to go. I texted Laney already and she's probably outside waiting by now."

"Don't do this, Shortcake." His eyes were wet.

"I have to." I pulled at my hands again and this time he let them go.

"You don't."

"You'll thank me later."

"I promise you I won't."

A horn honked outside and I kissed his cheek quickly, one last time. "Goodbye, Mark," I whispered and then, before I could change my mind, I dashed out the door.

Chapter Thirty-Three

LESSONS FROM KARMA AND HER MINIONS

MARK

"Well, this is even more pathetic than I imagined."

Maybe if I opened just one eye it wouldn't be so bad.

Nope, didn't work. Bailey stood at the end of my couch with her hands on her hips and a look on her face that suggested she'd just tasted something rotten.

"If you're not here to bring me more liquor then you can go away now," I mumbled.

"I mean, I knew it wasn't good when you didn't show up for work, but you haven't even been to the gym—this is serious."

The song playing on my phone ended and then started once again.

"Are you shitting me? You have this song on repeat? How many times have you listened to it?"

"I lost count after Sunday morning. Did you know Fiona lives on the fourteenth floor? That has to mean something, right?"

"Fuck. I'm going to need reinforcements. Hang in there, Buffy, I'll be right back."

She left the room for God knows where and I couldn't have cared less. All I wanted was to be left in peace to get drunk and listen to that fucking song. Too bad I was out of booze.

Every word of "Kiss Me Slowly" was burned into my brain, and with each verse and chorus I remembered every single moment with Fiona, even the ones where I'd wanted to murder her and hide the body. Her smile, her sexy-ass little outfits, her smart mouth, her laugh, her eyes, the way she fought me on everything, the way she felt in my arms, the way she changed everything.

It was official.

I had grown a vagina.

The irony was not lost on me. Fiona had ditched me immediately following mind-blowing sex that would never be repeated. How many times had I left a girl's bed happy in the knowledge I would never sleep with her again?

Karma had planted her boot firmly up my ass.

"Okay," Bailey began, once again interrupting my mental breakdown. "I am woman enough to admit that I'm not capable of handling this shit on my own. Help is on the way."

"I don't want help. Just go away." I put my arm over my eyes.

"Just go away," she mocked me using the tone of a nine-year-old. Resuming her normal voice, a.k.a. her jerk voice, she continued, "Not happening. Seeing you wallowing in misery seems like it would hold a lot of appeal, but in reality, it just makes me a bit ill." She fake gagged.

Why in the hell had I given her a key? I don't have a pet. I don't have plants. I could just have my mail held by the post office when I leave town. Idiot.

"So, first off, you need to put clothes on. I may be immune to you but the rest of the world's female population seems to find you pleasant-looking for some reason. At least put on a pair of pants—those boxer briefs are bordering on indecent and I can only avert my eyes so much."

I thought about just removing them entirely in an attempt to scare her off, but then I remembered we had to work together—and there is really no going back once your coworker and almost-sister sees your dick.

"Exactly who is coming over here?"

"Jennifer Lawrence. Who the fuck do you think? Laney."

"What the fuck?! Shit, get me some pants, will you?"

She stalked by me on her way to my bedroom and flicked my ear with her finger.

"Ow! Don't you have anybody else to torture?"

Her voice came from down the hall, "I do have a list, but you won today's drawing, asshat."

She came back with a pair of track pants and a blue t-shirt. I guess it was time to sit up. Ouch. I pushed past the head spins and got dressed.

Bailey turned my music off.

"Hey! I was listening to that!"

"No you weren't. You were torturing both of us with that."

"I like that song. It's really good."

"Oh my God. Are you pouting? I am half tempted to look inside those pants and make sure you still have your balls."

"You don't understand." I laid back on the couch and ignored her comment because it hit a little too close to home.

"Then tell me."

I lifted my head a bit and caught her eye. "Why do I always have to tell you stuff and you keep your shit tight as a duck's ass?"

"Because I'm not the one who hasn't showered in two days and who missed work so he could cuddle up with a sappy fucking song and a bottle of Jack."

She did have a point.

"Fine. Fiona dumped me."

"Duh. I already know all about that—leukemia, shitty fallout, thinks she's a bad bet—what else?"

I sat up. "Wait, how do you know that when I just found out—wait, what day is today?"

She moved my legs over, somewhat violently in my opinion, and sat down on the couch where she proceeded to flick my other ear. "Monday!"

"Ow! Stop doing that shit!" If she were a guy I could hit her back. This woman perfectly embodied the utter unfairness of a double standard.

"Oh, don't get your twat in a knot. I just found out last night. Emergency girls' night at Fiona's. I barely survived." Her head dropped back.

"So what am I supposed to do? I can't *make* her be with me."

The doorbell rang and Bailey put a finger up signaling me to wait while she let Laney in.

"Damn, he's worse than she is," said Laney when she saw me.

"This is nothing," said Bailey. "You missed the Thunder Down Under show I caught earlier. It was obscene."

Laney set her purse down and went to the kitchen before coming back with a sports drink and some ibuprofen she'd unearthed from her bag. She handed both to me and shrugged. "I'm a mom."

I took them from her and then couldn't resist asking, "How is she?"

"A fucking mess, just like you," said Bailey before Laney could answer. "I was just trying to get his drunken recollection of events. I feel like Derek Waters—but at least that dude gets to drink along."

"Well, I'm all out of booze, thank you very much, so you're shit out of luck," I said in what was probably a petulant tone. "But, like I said, I can't *make* her be with me so there is nothing you can do."

"I hate this so much for both of you," said Laney, the nice one. "She *wants* to be with you but you have to understand, all this stuff she's telling herself is so deeply ingrained in her mind she can't see past it. I'm her best friend and even I have to tread lightly where all of this is concerned."

"Well, if you want my two cents, I know one place you could start," said Bailey.

Was it possible she could actually have helpful input? Ha!

"You need to stop treating all the women in your life like they'll break if you don't constantly hover over them." She pointed accusingly.

What a crock.

"What are you talking about? I don't treat *you* that way," I protested.

"That's just because you think I'm half dude. I don't count."

"I don't treat Laney that way," I countered.

"That's because she and Nate would both kick your ass."

Laney stepped in. "I have to say I agree, Mark." She hesitated for a moment and went on, "Take your mom—I think it's really sweet you care about her so much, but have you seen her lately? For the first time in her life, she is kicking ass and taking names all on her own."

I stared at her.

It's always been my job to take care of my mom. She needs me.

Right?

Shit.

"Fiona did that," I finally said.

They both nodded.

"That's why she didn't tell me, isn't it? About the health stuff, I mean."

"I'm sure that's part of it," responded Laney. "But I think the bigger part is, despite all outward appearances, *she* sees herself as weak, and nothing we can do will change that."

I popped the ibuprofen in my mouth and chased them with the entire bottle of sports drink. "Well, ladies, if you can help me, I'd like to just see about that."

Chapter Thirty-Four

AND NOW, "THE AMAZING DISAPPEARING MAN!" PARTS ONE AND TWO

FIONA

"Thank you so much," I said as I forced my gazillionth smile of the evening. "Your support is truly appreciated."

The couple finished shaking my hand and filtered back into the crowd of attendees and donors. My mother leaned over to whisper in my ear.

"Are you sure you're okay, sweetheart? You seem pale. Are you coming down with something?"

I shook my head and shrugged my shoulders. "I'm fine—just a rough week."

It was Friday night and I was back at another function, but this time we were just guests, thank goodness. That didn't mean we could relax and fall back on our duties, though. Anytime we were in the presence of big money, we had a job to do.

"Well poor little you," Guilt chastised. *"I'm sorry to trouble you with all the kids out there who still need help."*

Okay, okay. She was totally right, but sometimes a girl just wants to take a night or ten to wallow in sadness when she gets her heart broken. Even if she's the one who broke it.

I vowed to do better and wallow tomorrow instead. I had been a complete zombie all week, and at this point Jax was probably ready to fire me. If it weren't for Ollie picking up the slack, I'm sure I would have gotten the ax already.

But tomorrow was Saturday and I had no commitments, so I planned on taking full advantage. I had Tina and Amy cued up, Kim waiting on the counter, and good old Ben and Jerry on standby. This time they would work in shifts, though. Fool me once, shame on you; fool me twice…

Shame on me.

Indeed.

I had done this to myself. What idiot turns down a guy who gets a look under the hood and still wants to be with you?

"It's for his own good and you know it," Guilt chimed in again.

You know, if you're going to make me take this damn high road the least you could do is pitch in for the wine!

This week had probably been the worst of my entire adult life.

When Laney had picked me up from Mark's, she'd behaved like the model best friend. I'm ashamed I ever considered trading her in for Rocco. She asked zero questions and drove like a bat out of hell to get me away from Mark's house. Once we were back at her place she gave me a huge comfy t-shirt, a blanket, and a bag of Cheetos. Then she settled us in on the couch and put her arms around me in a giant snuggle. I cried into her enormous boobs and she stroked my hair. Neither one of us had spoken a single word.

After my sobbing had subsided to the occasional hiccup, she released me and looked into my face. "Do you want to talk about it?"

I shook my head and hiccupped again.

"Okay, I'm going to change my shirt so I don't look like I'm competing in a wet t-shirt contest and then we're going to watch some crazy bitches on TV." She stood up but then looked back down at me. "But tomorrow we're talking, Fee."

An hour later we both fell asleep on the couch with orange fingers and the TV still on. It was only later that it dawned on me I had hijacked my best friend's engagement night with my own drama and neither she nor Nate had said a word about it. Damn, I have extraordinary friends.

The next day I still felt wretched, but I dragged myself home after promising Laney we'd have a girl gabfest at my place that night. She took it upon herself to invite Bailey and Charlotte, her neighbor, thinking that the more women we involved the better our chances of solving whatever problem had sent me into a tailspin. At that point, I was beyond caring who knew my business. I just needed this giant knot in my chest to go away. And, besides, Charlotte was Texas born and bred and tended to throw out wacky Southern phrases and call people "Sugar" and "Honey Pie." I figured that on its own might help.

So, I spent the evening spilling my guts and drinking wine with these awesome women. They were understandably a bit shocked by the breadth of my personal history share—Charlotte and Bailey hadn't even known about the leukemia, much less the rest of the shitstorm.

They all tried to reassure me that Mark was a grown man and could make his own decisions about what he did and didn't want. And I had to endure the lectures about how I deserved to be happy and I needed to stop worrying so much.

Still, at the end of the night I was right back where I started—broken heart and aching chest. But at least I had people to share it with. The problem was that as hard as they tried, they couldn't know what it was like to stand in my shoes, even if they were kick-ass Manolos.

The rest of the week was the same. Laney called and texted constantly and sometimes tried offering more advice, but we both knew it wasn't making a dent. I was useless at work, and on Thursday morning, when I absentmindedly poured a bag of sugar into the coffee filter, Jax finally told me to just go home and rest.

But resting meant lying around thinking about Mark, so that was the last thing I wanted to do. I decided to go shopping and take myself out to lunch instead. Going with the fake-it-'til-you-make-it theory, I dressed up to the nines and headed for Friendly Center where a girl could always find good fashion, food, and hopefully some perspective.

I stopped at a couple cute boutiques and picked up some good-ies. I was about to head into Soma for some sexy underthings when I remembered there was nobody to see such things, so I quickly moved on with only the briefest sniffle.

In need of distraction and caffeine, I headed to Caribou and pulled open the glass door—only to run smack into the last person on earth I expected to see.

"Terrence?!"

His face brightened at the sight of me, and out came that perfectly imperfect smile. It immediately warmed me, but not in the same way it once had.

"Fiona! Holy crap!" He wrapped me up in a hug while balancing two takeaway cups. I hugged him back tightly. "It's so good to see you," he said to the top of my head. Why was everybody so freaking tall?

He pulled back and we stepped out of the doorway to keep from blocking traffic. "You're looking beautiful as always," he said with a smile.

I had to laugh. "You're not looking too bad yourself. What are you doing here? I thought you were based out of Raleigh now?"

He looked a little sheepish. "Well, I am, but my…my girlfriend is here in Greensboro."

I didn't know what reaction he'd expected, but despite the miserable state of my own love life I was so pleased for him. "Really?" I put a hand to my chest and drawled dramatically.

That relaxed him immediately and he smiled again. "Yeah. She's an intern at the hospital." He gestured down the road. "I'm actually on my way to bring her a caffeine fix," he said, raising one of the cups in his hands. "You know, I'm happy I ran into you. I've been meaning to call."

Huh? "Oh?"

"Do you have a minute?" He set the cups down on the nearest table and indicated I should sit.

"Sure," I responded, completely *un*sure.

We settled and he dove right in. "So, I feel like I owe you an apology."

I jerked my head back. "Why in the world would you think that? I'm the one who went all Hulk on you when you told me you wanted a relationship."

He looked suddenly uncomfortable. "Yeah, about that…I have a confession."

In the history of mankind, nothing good has ever followed that opening. I braced.

"Remember that time when I was in town and you had to run over to pick Rocco up?"

"Yeeaahh…" Where was this going?

"Well, you'd left some papers on the counter. Some medical paperwork."

Shit.

"I know it was a total invasion of your privacy, but I saw the first page and once I read that I couldn't seem to stop. I read the whole damn packet—your entire medical history was summarized."

I knew exactly what packet he was talking about and I suddenly remembered that weekend like it was yesterday. "That was the weekend you had to leave early."

He looked right into my eyes. "I didn't have to leave early. I panicked."

"But the next time you came to town you told me your feelings had evolved into something more and you wanted a relationship."

"Yeah," he said, shifting in his seat. "This is why I owe you an apology. I invaded your privacy, then lied to you and bolted. Once I got home, I felt like such an asshole for ditching you and for running like a scared kid when I found out the girl I was hanging out with had baggage."

"Why do you think I only wanted casual in the first place? I mean, yeah, it was kind of douchey to read my private stuff, but I don't blame you for running. What I don't understand is why you came back and why you suddenly wanted more." I was completely perplexed.

"This is where I owe you another apology," he said and then took a deep breath. "I felt so guilty about what I'd done and I thought about how you needed someone to take care of you, not ditch you. So, I told myself I should man up and be that someone."

What. The. Fuck?

"So, let me get this straight. You felt guilty. Then you pitied me so much you decided to take one for the team?! That's…that's…awful…crazy…and really fucking embarrassing, Terrence!"

"I know!" He covered his eyes with his hand.

I was getting pissed. "Why exactly did you feel you had to share this with me? Especially now that it's in the past? You never struck me as the type who would need to get something off your chest knowing it would only hurt the other person." I started gathering my things so I could get the hell out of there.

"No—that's not why I had to tell you," he said imploringly. "Please, just give me one more minute."

I dropped my bags and crossed my arms. "Then why?"

"Because when I met Carly—I don't know. When I met her it hit me like a lightning bolt and I knew right then I had been a fool to be content with always keeping women at arm's length." He ran a hand over his face, clearly frustrated.

"You and I are similar, Fiona, whether you can see it or not. I was afraid of letting anyone in, and I assumed my career that had me absent half the time was unfair to put on someone else."

He put his hands on the table. "Look, I understand that your situation is definitely more serious, but I think the fear is the same. You're afraid to pursue your future. And you're afraid to let someone in because you don't want to hurt them. But, honey, *nobody's* future is guaranteed—I don't care if they're on their deathbed or healthy as a horse. When opportunity comes, you have to grab onto it, and when love comes, you have to hold tight and just take it one fucking day at a time."

He grabbed my hand and squeezed it. "Fiona, I know you and I weren't meant to be together, but I'll never regret having you in my life. I just really want you to get out of your own way and be happy."

Well, shit. Now I'd gone and lost my mad.

I couldn't really say anything. This was too much information to process all at once.

Terrence stood. "I'm sorry I ambushed you, so feel free to call me later and yell at me," he teased. "I have to run, but I mean it—call me anytime." He dropped a kiss on the top of my head. "One day at a time, honey. I promise it works." And he was gone.

He'd been like a strange messenger of shock and awe, here one minute, gone the next. After that, I'd had to upgrade my order to a grande and ask if they happened to carry any liquor behind the counter.

That had been yesterday and I still hadn't fully processed everything Terrence had said, but I had a niggling feeling it was important. Putting those thoughts aside and re-focusing on the party, I smoothed my dress—my *black* dress—and attempted a reassuring smile for my mother. But she wasn't looking at me.

"Fiona?"

Holy baby Jesus and all his baby friends—I knew that voice.

"I don't believe we've met," my mother spoke up as I attempted to hide in open space. "I'm Johanna Pierce," she greeted the only man on earth capable of simultaneously breaking me into little pieces and making me whole. Fuck!

"Mark Beckett." I heard him say and then I couldn't keep my eyes averted any longer.

I may have whimpered.

His voice addressed my mother but his brown eyes never left me for a second. He stood there in a perfectly tailored dark gray suit and an *orange* tie—the leukemia awareness color—and I thought I might faint. If I'd thought he looked good in cargo pants and a henley, that had nothing on this man in a suit. It was on par with naked Mark, and that was saying something.

"Oh my," I heard my mother whisper.

Oh my, indeed. Was it really fucking hot in here all of a sudden?

I could not make my mouth function properly so I proceeded to speak in tongues and let out a combination of about ten words at once. "WhButIwhoHoMy." Then I tried to end the awkwardness for all of us by clamping my hand over my stupid mouth.

I saw one corner of Mark's lips twitch. "Good to see you too, Shortcake."

There was no ignoring the intense stare coming from my mom, so I had to remove my hand and get my shit together. "Um…so… Mom, this is my friend Mark." His eyebrows rose at that and I ignored it. "Mark, this is my mother, Johanna."

"Yes, we've just met, Fiona," my mother said deliberately. Turning to Mark she said, "It's lovely to meet you, Mark. It's not often we get to meet Fiona's *friends*." Her glance shifted back to me oh-so-subtly.

"Um, what are you doing here?" I asked, trying not to sound panicked or rude or absolutely fucking crazy.

"Just came to make a donation and to give you this." He held out his hand, palm up, revealing a small pink flash drive with rhinestones on it.

I couldn't help the smile that came to my lips as I plucked the little device from his outstretched hand with trembling fingers. "How very secure you must be in your masculinity," I teased. What the hell was I doing?! "What is this?"

"Just something I wanted you to see," he said, telling me absolutely nothing helpful. Then he turned back to my mom with an outstretched hand and said, "It was a pleasure to meet you, Mrs. Pierce." To me, he just said, "Shortcake, I'll be seeing you." And then he was gone.

What was it with men dropping bombs on me and then disappearing in a puff of smoke?

Good grief.

Chapter Thirty-Five

FYI – THE APOCALYPSE IS NIGH

FIONA

I shut the door to my old bedroom, my dad's laptop tucked under my arm. I had no earthly idea what was on that flash drive but there was no way I was going to let my parents see it.

The rest of the event had flown by, mostly because I'd been so completely and utterly distracted. As I'd known she would, my mother pulled me aside and grilled me about our mystery visitor. I finally had to admit to her that he was, in fact, *the* Mark I'd been seeing, but I made certain she knew things were finished.

"Well it didn't seem like *he* was finished," she felt the need to point out.

"Mom, we have friends in common. We'll have to see each other on occasion but, trust me, it's not going to work out."

"I don't understand. Don't you like him?" She smoothed her

flawless hair which was arranged in a side bun this evening. She looked beautiful.

I more than liked him. I was afraid I might be in love with him.

"It's not that."

"Then what? He seemed nice and even I could see that he's a hottie." She smiled wickedly.

"Ew—just ew. That is more than I needed to know. I'm going to run to the restroom." I had to avoid having the exact same conversation I'd been having with everyone for the last week. I didn't need my mother repeating the "give love a chance" mantra, so I managed to avoid her until the drive back to their place. And even my mother had known better than to bring this subject up in front of my dad. I was relatively certain that my mom's level of desire to marry me off was rivaled only by my dad's level of desire to shoot the balls off any man who came near his innocent baby girl.

Now safely ensconced in my bedroom, I'd reached the moment of truth. I pushed the power button and waited for the computer to start up. Meanwhile, I changed into one of my silk nighties and brushed my teeth.

Hey, God. It's me again. So, as you probably know, I've had quite a week. Any idea if the next one will be better? Mark came to the fundraiser tonight. I realize you already know that—you didn't have anything to do with that, did you? Please make him happy—you did a good job with him and he deserves it. Okay, that's about it. Oh, wait, one more thing. The peep-toe sling-backs I tried to buy were on backorder—I don't suppose you could...never mind. Thanks for letting me live. Later.

Rinse and spit.

It was time. I took the laptop to my bed and laid down on my stomach before inserting the flash drive. A video file popped up. It was titled, "Dear Fiona." I took a deep breath and double-clicked.

I almost gasped when Mark's handsome face appeared on the screen, although I don't know what else I expected to pop up. I could see his living room in the background.

"Hey Shortcake," he said with a sad smile. I wanted to reach out and touch him. "So, I know you probably don't want to hear from me but I've got a few things to say and then a couple other people want to talk to you."

Say what?

"I think I understand a little better now, and I don't blame you, but you still need to know something." He took a deep breath and peered intensely into the camera. "You, Fiona Pierce, are the strongest person I've ever met in my life. Yeah, you're tiny and you have the muscle mass of a two-year-old." He smiled and that about undid me. "But you have strength where it counts. Your character, your determination, your independence, your drive to help people, your willingness to go it alone without putting your problems on other people. All of that and more." My eyes began to tear up but I willed them to stop so my view of his perfect face wouldn't be impaired.

"And that isn't even counting the kind of strength you bring out in everyone around you. You single-handedly let my mom see just how strong she could be—I've been taking care of her for years and you come along and she suddenly has 'lady balls' as you so eloquently put it." He covered his eyes with his hand for a moment at that comment. "The point is, she always had it in her, but you brought it out. *You* did that, Shortcake." He pointed at me through the screen.

"Then there's me. Before you came along, I was kind of an asshole. Shocking, I know." He grinned and my heart flipped over in my chest. I released a sputtering laugh against my will.

"I'm sure you're having a good laugh over that."

How did he know that?

"I know now that I was scared of opening up to anyone. I figured that caring about another person only made you a target—it was easier just to be by myself. But you changed that—you made me brave enough to risk it. And even if things never work out between us, I'll never regret it. You changed me for the better." He was going to make me cry for sure.

"Now, before I officially lose my man card and get in touch with too many emotions, I need to ask you a question." He shifted and I felt like his eyes were burning into me. "What if I got into a terrible car accident and was paralyzed or injured in some traumatic way? Would you wish I had let you go before anything like that could happen? Think about it and stay tuned." The screen turned black.

I sat there in shock, but had no time to process what he'd asked.

The screen suddenly lit again with Laney's face. To say her smile was strained was an understatement.

"Hi, Fee. Don't kill me. Damn that man—he is so convincing when he's determined. Sorry." She shrugged her shoulders. "But since I'm here I do have something to say and I'm kind of happy I'm talking to a camera so you can't change the subject."

Grrr.

"You know I couldn't love you more if you were my own sister, but I haven't been the friend I should have been. I guess I didn't realize how much of your own pain and guilt you were holding back until we really started talking about it this week. You were always my fearless and crazy and lovable Fiona." She smiled, but there were tears in her eyes.

And mine too.

"I hate that you put on a brave face when you're hurting inside." She swiped a finger under one eye and let out a breath.

"So, here's the deal. You gave me the courage to give Nate a chance and now look at us—we're getting married." She couldn't help but smile and I did as well. "So I am going to do the same for you because I want you to be as happy as I am—and it's not because I think I'm Marcia. I'm happy to be Jan as long as you get to be happy too, whatever that means.

"Having said that, though, I will kick Mark's ass so hard he won't be able to do butt presses—or whatever the hell he does—if he hurts you even a little. I love you, Fee. And give the guy a chance—I don't think I've ever seen anybody so pathetic." She giggled and gave me a little wave before shutting off the camera.

Next up was Jake of all people. "Hey, future wife. I don't know why Mark asked me to talk to you since any woman given the choice between the two of us would obviously pick me, but that's his mistake." He laughed a bit maniacally.

"I do want to thank you, though, for your help on my little project." He winked into the camera, his naughty smile on full display. "Things are shaping up really well, thanks to you. And, if I'm being completely honest, I'll admit my little brother is a pretty good bet, faults and all. The one thing I can tell you is that he's never let me down a single time in my life, which is more than I can say for myself. Looking forward to the next dinner! See ya."

Short and sweet. The exact *opposite* of how I'd describe Jake.

Before I could do more than smile over Jake's little speech, Jax appeared on the screen.

WTF?

His spiky blond hair was its usual mess and his wicked grin lit up the computer.

"I thought it would be funny to start this video by telling you you're fired, but your man here didn't agree." He laughed at his own joke and then got on with it. "So, I'll be quick."

He took on a serious tone I didn't see very often. "Miss Fiona, do you know why I hired you?" He paused as if I could actually answer him. "I hired you because from the moment you opened your mouth during your interview you made me fucking happy. When you left that day, I was so damn cheerful Ollie was about to call a doctor.

"And that's what you do for every customer you talk to. I should have shown you this before now, but do you see this?" He held the camera up to his computer screen. I could make out a little but not much. "All these customer reviews mention you. Sure, they love me because I'm brilliant and I treat them right, but every review since you started working here raves about how awesome you are too."

He brought the camera back around to himself. "So I don't give two shits if you misfile a document, break the copier, or pour cocaine into the coffee maker. You are fucking brilliant at your job and don't ever doubt that. So, that's all I've got for now but I'll see you Monday." He reached for the button to shut the video off and then paused and brought the wicked grin back. "Oh, and I'll make the coffee."

The screen switched and my heart flipped in my chest again. It was Mark.

"So, it's me again. I'll let you go and you can decide what to do next. But I can tell you with one hundred percent certainty that I want to be with you, and I want us to take care of *each other*. Hopefully, that will mean bringing out the best in one another and being happy, but even if it doesn't and bad shit happens, it's still what I want. Later, Shortcake." He winked and shut off the camera. The video ended.

I was in a bit of shock.

I was equal parts embarrassed, confused, and bowled over by the outpouring of affection from the people in my life and the effort Mark had gone to in order to fight for me.

I bawled my eyes out and fell asleep knowing that I would look like Sloth from *The Goonies* when I woke in the morning.

✶ ✶ ✶

"Rise and shine, beautiful." I heard my father's voice beside me. I opened my eyes a crack and saw him standing at the side of my bed dressed in his navy-blue robe. It was still dark out.

"Sorry to wake you so early, sweetheart, but I couldn't sleep—I had too much on my mind," he said.

"What time is it?" I managed to mumble. My face was tight and my eyes were practically swollen shut from all the crying I'd done last night.

"Six-thirty—I know, it's early, but I want to talk to you."

What was this, confession time before the apocalypse? Since when did everybody have so fucking much to say to me?!

"Dad," I whined, "I need sleep. You can talk to me later."

"I want to talk before your mother wakes up."

That got my attention. He never kept anything from her. I made myself sit up and piled the covers around me. He took the opening.

"Your friend called me."

I was wide awake now. "Laney? When? Is something wrong?"

He shook his head. "Not Laney—Mark. He called me earlier this week."

"You're joking." It wasn't enough that he had rallied my friends to give me motivational speeches—he had to enlist my dad as well? Couldn't they all find a celebrity charity to focus on instead? I'm sure there are plenty of homeless cats in need of a good catnip supplier.

"Before you jump to any conclusions I want to tell you why he called."

"I know why he called. I broke up with him and he's using extortion to get me back for some unknown reason!" I huffed.

"He called to ask me about your health, not about anything having to do with a relationship. That's between the two of you."

Ha! If only. "But my health is open to public discussion?"

He gave me the "Dad" look. I guess when half of Raleigh knows all about your medical history it's kind of public already.

"What did you tell him?"

"Nothing at first," he said and then settled on the edge of my bed. "But then the more I talked to him the more I realized how much he cares for you and how worried he is."

I didn't know what to say.

"Fiona, why is it that this young man you've only known for a short while had to be the one to tell me that my baby girl is living scared?"

"He had no right—" I began, but my dad cut me off.

"Maybe not, but *I* have the right. Your *mother* has the right. You've always been such a cheerful, positive young woman. Your smile brightens the room—you take everything in stride. How is it I didn't know you've been living each day waiting for the other shoe to drop?"

Well, he had me there. I looked at my dad and was reminded again of my reasons. But I guess the jig was up.

"I didn't want you to worry about me anymore. I saw what a toll the leukemia took on you guys and I wanted you to think my life was perfect again."

"But clearly it hasn't been."

"Not so much," I admitted with a pathetic little shrug.

He pulled me in for a hug. "Baby girl," he whispered, and I cried a little into his shirt. At this rate, I was approaching the dehydration level of a stick of beef jerky dressed in cute pajamas. Lovely. No wonder Mark was so hot for me.

Following our conversation, my dad made pancakes while I sat at the kitchen island and drank a regimen of juice, water, and coffee while holding a cool cloth over my eyes so I could hopefully regain my full vision one day. He set my plate in front of me and then went to wake my mother so we could have a family meeting.

Yay. Cue sarcasm.

But it actually didn't turn out to be so bad. Knowing my love of lists, my father proceeded to line the island with list after list.

First came the statistics on someone in my situation developing another cancer. Then came lists regarding the health of my heart, lungs, and bones. And lastly, he produced a list of therapists, and both of my parents encouraged me to focus on that list in particular.

Our little meeting ended and lots of hugs and promises to check in with each other followed before I gathered my things and headed back to Greensboro. At the last moment, though, my dad pulled me aside and reminded me exactly who he was. "By the way, in the event you do decide to date this Mark guy, please remind him that I know where to find him if I ever have cause to."

Good God.

My brain buzzed on overload the whole way home—I had a lot of thinking to do.

But first, I owed somebody a response.

Fiona: Thanks for the video. I think.

Mark: Yeah, I figured it could go either way.

Fiona: Can I have some time to think?

Mark: As much as you need, Shortcake. You know where to find me.

Chapter Thirty-Six

THE FUTURE

MARK

Six Weeks Later

"For the one-hundredth time, yes, I am coming to the engagement party."

"Don't bite *my* head off. *I'm* just the messenger. Laney was afraid to call you again. Wimp," Bailey said on the other end of the line.

"I'm a grown-ass man. I can be in the same room as Fiona and not lose my shit. And, besides, I'm actually looking forward to seeing her," I admitted as I leaned back in my desk chair.

"So you're still holding out hope? Pardon me for saying this, but you're a glutton for punishment, Beckett."

"I think that's the first time I've ever heard you say something in a remotely polite way," I baited her.

"Shove it up your ass, Romeo," she growled.

"And, yes, I'm still holding out. She's gonna come around —you'll see."

"Well, I hope for all our sakes she does because I don't know if I can handle any more of these GNOs she keeps organizing. I mean, it's bad enough with all the wedding stuff."

"What in the fuck is a GNO? It sounds like a lady-doctor problem."

"I know—they actually have an acronym for it. It's supposed to stand for 'Girls' Night Out' but I secretly refer to it as 'Got No Orgasms.' It's just a bunch of girls drinking and talking shit about guys. I mean, sometimes I guess it's not so bad, but with all the girly wedding crap? I'm maxing out on all things 'girl.'" She made a lovely gagging sound. "Laney's going to make me wear a dress to the wedding," she whined.

"Bailey, you're one of her bridesmaids. Of course you have to wear a dress. In fact, I think you're required to wear the exact same dress as the rest of the bridesmaids."

"What? That's just idiotic."

"I don't make the rules. Anyway, I gotta run but I'll see you tonight. And don't wear jeans and a t-shirt! This party is the kind you dress up for." I stood from my chair.

"Motherf—" She began, but I hung up, laughing to myself.

I grabbed my hard hat and headed toward the trailer door to go check in with the crew. Before I got there, however, there was a knock on the door. I turned the knob and swung it open, expecting to see one of the guys. Instead, Fiona stood on the top step looking like a fucking dream. Hell, maybe she was.

"Hi, Mark," she said quietly.

Nope, not a dream.

"Hey, Shortcake," I responded and couldn't help the dopey smile I'm sure was plastered across my face. Her returning smile told me it looked as stupid as it felt.

"I'm sorry to barge in on you like this but I finally worked up the courage so I just had to go with it." She looked down at her designer-shod feet before bringing her eyes back to mine and scrunching her face up in the cutest fucking way.

"You can barge in on me anytime you want—you know that." I was starting to get a bit nervous. For all the waiting and forced confidence I'd had, now that the moment was here I was afraid she was going to end things once and for all. "Come on in," I stepped aside and held the door for her. If I was going to get dumped at least I could ensure a little privacy.

She stepped in and walked toward my desk before turning around. "You've been so patient and I really wanted to thank you for that. Um…a lot has happened." She ran her hands down the skirt of her sexy little sundress. Girls don't wear sexy outfits when they're going to dump a guy, do they? Oh, who was I kidding—she looked sexy in anything so it was a moot point.

"Oh?" was all I could manage.

"Yeah," she began again. "I've started seeing a therapist my oncologist recommended. It's been helping me gain a new… perspective…on things. I'm taking a break from my parents' foundation—from all the charity stuff, really. My therapist thinks that in order for me to stop fearing the worst around every corner I need to shed the past as much as possible and focus more on the future."

"That sounds pretty smart," I said and then forced myself to ask, "So, which part do I fall in—the past or the future?"

She turned and plucked a stapler off the desk, playing with it to occupy her hands. "I'm also considering starting a small catering business—a *very* small one." It was as if she hadn't heard my question.

"That sounds like a great idea," I responded, genuinely pleased, but not understanding where she was going with this.

"Yeah, it's funny. Your mom was the one to come up with the idea."

Now that was a surprise. "My mom?"

She let out a small laugh. "Yeah. With all her waitressing experience she has a lot of great ideas. I don't know, it's just a kernel of an idea at this point."

"Wow. I never thought of that—of course she would be a huge help in that area." I scratched my chin.

"The future," she said suddenly, her eyes meeting mine in earnest.

My heart may have stopped. "What?"

"The answer is, you're part of the future—if you want to be, knowing what that could mean."

She'd hardly finished her sentence before I scooped her up and kissed the fucking hell out of her. She started laughing halfway through the kiss and that got me laughing too. "We sound like complete idiots," I managed to say between laughs and kisses.

"No, *I'm* the idiot. I almost let you go," she said, grabbing my face in her hands.

I pulled back and looked at her. "Nah, I never would have let that happen, Shortcake."

She scoffed. "Cocky bastard." But she was smiling.

"You know it," I replied and pulled her in again.

* * *

The party was in full swing by the time we got to the restaurant. A small detour to Fiona's condo ended up in a furious round of what I suppose qualified as make-up sex. Whatever it was, I was looking forward to a whole lot more of it.

"Oh, thank God you're here!" Laney accosted Fiona the moment we walked into the private room. It took her a moment to realize Fiona and I had come in together. She pointed back and forth between us, her mouth agape. "You…you…really?" She was beaming at us. We both nodded our heads and then she Lost. Her. Shit.

There was squealing that I probably only heard part of—the rest being audible only to neighborhood dogs—and some weird references to the Brady Bunch. When the squealing started again, I managed to still Fiona long enough to kiss her quickly before I went in search of testosterone.

I found Nate, Gavin, and some of the other guys gathered near the makeshift bar in the corner. After a round of handshakes and some razzing about my date, Nate cut in.

"Hey, why am I just finding out now that your brother is moving back to Greensboro?"

I put my hands up defensively. "Don't ask me—I just found out the other day when he called to tell me." Truthfully, I'd missed Jake since he'd left a few weeks back, but I wasn't ever going to tell him that.

"What's that all about? I mean, not that I'm not happy to have him around, but I thought he loved Florida."

"Who the hell knows," I replied. "All he said was that he was sorting shit out and he'd be moving here within a couple months, hopefully. I don't know what he has in mind." I left out the part where he'd said he was moving back to steal Fiona. Why did I miss him again?

"Must have to do with his future wife's cooking," Gavin taunted, as if he'd read my mind.

"You'd best watch yourself, Junior, or you're gonna end up with a broken nose," I told the little douchebag. Okay, so maybe he wasn't little, but he was definitely a douchebag.

"Calm your tits, Beckett. All of you sappy lovesick assholes are such easy targets," he threw back at me and then wisely backed up a few steps. "I'll grab some beers."

I refocused my attention on Nate, considering that he and Laney were the actual guests of honor at this party. "Congrats, man. I'm really happy for you guys. Laney's got her work cut out for her, though." It was my job to give him a hard time.

"Speaking of," he replied. "I hope you don't mind that I volunteered your new girlfriend to save the day and get me off the hook."

I just looked at him quizzically.

"The chef was supposed to prepare some healthy shit for my dad, but now he's saying it's a set menu with no exceptions so Laney is panicked."

Nate's dad had a heart attack last summer and his mom had been vigilant about Riordan's diet ever since then. She'd gotten Laney on board as well so I knew this had the potential to mess with the evening. Let's just say Riordan was not one to acquiesce quietly. And neither was Erin.

"Well, if anyone can sweet talk her way into a professional kitchen it's Fiona," I said.

"My thoughts exactly," said Nate.

Gavin approached and handed us each a fresh beer—probably as an apology for being a douchebag. Or not.

"To crazy-ass women," Nate said, raising his beer.

"To the man brave enough to take on my crazy-ass sister," Gavin chimed in, raising his.

"To the ladies brave enough to take on…anything," I finished as we clinked bottles and took a healthy swallow of our beers.

Yeah, I was a total fuckmuppet.

You got something to say about that?

EPILOGUE

MARK
Three Months Later

"Hurry up, Shortcake! The ceremony starts in fifteen minutes."

"I just had to make sure Kelly has everything under control!" she yelled as she rushed up the front steps of the church where I was waiting.

I held out my hand and she sighed dramatically before handing over her cell phone. She was adorable when she pouted. It also usually made me want to bite her bottom lip.

I turned the phone off and tucked it into the pocket of my tux. "You know everything is going to run perfectly. The two of you have been over this a hundred times, everything is already prepped, and you yourself said the recipes are simple."

She sighed again. "You're right. I don't know why I'm worrying about this. I should be focusing on Laney—I'm a terrible Maid of Honor."

"Ducking out to make one phone call does not make you terrible. You girls spent the entire morning together and she's all ready to go."

"I hate that Kelly can't be here, though," she said quietly as I opened the front door of the church and ushered her inside.

"We'll all see her at the reception, and Jake promised to take lots of pictures. Now kiss me quick because I have to go keep Nate from passing out."

She did, letting her lips linger a little too long for a church setting—not that I was complaining. Then she shot me her gorgeous bright smile and strutted off in her tan heels and blue dress, looking as stunning as ever. Oh, right—a few weeks ago I'd been scolded for using the words "tan" and "blue" and had been informed that the wedding colors were to be referred to only as the very elegant "parchment" and "pale cerulean." That had been the moment I'd decided Nate was more pussy-whipped than I was.

It was hard to believe Nate and Laney's wedding was already upon us. The last three months since their engagement party and the "official" beginning of Fiona and me as a couple had flown by.

In the beginning, I'd vowed to tread lightly and try not to overwhelm Fiona, but she'd put the kibosh on that pretty much immediately and we'd spent every night together since. Although we still maintained two residences, we were basically living together.

Fast? Hell yes.

Scary? A bit, especially when I got my first real look at her closet and realized that if we were ever to get a place together we'd have to dedicate an entire room to her wardrobe. The shoes could possibly require a small addition.

But we made sure to communicate openly with each other, and

her therapist was helping her work through things and focus on her strengths. Her mantra was to take things one day at a time and I was totally on board with that.

And that kernel of an idea my mom had had about doing some catering had actually turned into a great little side business for the two of them. They were only doing small events, but word was getting out and I was sure the wedding reception today would result in new business.

Fiona hadn't wanted to do the reception at first because she wanted to be able to focus all her attention on Laney. But when Nate and Laney decided to just do hors d'oeuvres and drinks and save their money for a kick-ass honeymoon, Fiona had finally relented.

The business was doing wonders for her self-confidence, and she and my mom worked together like a dream. My mom never let Fiona freak out about forgetting things or losing track of her thoughts, and she was always the one in charge of any waitstaff and set-up. That allowed Fiona to delve into her favorite parts of the business, which included creating menus, cooking, and schmoozing with clients. It was a wonderful partnership, and I was relatively certain they could turn this into a full-time business and hire a manager if they wanted to. We'd just have to wait and see— one day at a time.

I made my way up the center aisle of the church, which was about half-full, and sought out Nate, hoping to find him still upright. He was exactly where I'd left him, standing with Gavin in the sacristy just off the altar. Gavin tucked a flask into the inside pocket of his tux jacket as I walked in, and Nate was looking a bit calmer but still kind of pale.

"Well, man, everything's under control. The moms, Bailey, and Fiona are with Laney; Rocco and Laney's dad are waiting to walk her down the aisle; and your dad is gonna walk the moms down in just a few. All you've got to do is hang in there a few more minutes, say your 'I do's, and we can all go have a drink." I had no idea how I'd gotten so involved in my friends' wedding, but there are certainly worse things than standing up with a good friend when he gets hitched to the right girl.

Nate took a breath. "Okay, I can do this."

"Did you remember to break the news to Fiona about the reception speech?" Gavin asked.

Shit.

"Shit. I forgot," I said and then gestured for him to bring the flask back out so I could partake.

I knew I'd forgotten something.

You see, back at the engagement party, Fiona had insisted on giving a little toast to the crowd where she had, in her traditional style, said something that really struck a chord. I believe the exact phrase that had sent the crowd sniggering was, "To Laney and Nate, as they enter into this union, may they only have happy endings." While it had certainly been a memorable toast, it was not one that Laney and Nate wanted repeated at their wedding reception. As the boyfriend, I had been tasked with breaking it to Fiona that there would only be Gavin's Best Man speech this evening, although I wasn't sure how that could possibly turn out much better. Their wedding, their rules, though.

"I'll catch her afterward and tell her."

Just then, the priest walked in and I quickly hid the flask behind my back.

He just laughed. "Son, you think Jesus didn't drink?" Then he turned to Nate. "You ready?"

Nate nodded once and then stiffly exited the small room to go meet his bride.

* * *

"I still don't understand why I'm not giving a speech. The food is all set and the servers and assistants have things covered. I'm just here to party," Fiona said, giving a little shimmy.

I pulled her to me and wrapped her up in my arms so I could feel her against me. "Then party away, Shortcake," I said into her ear before giving the lobe a little nip. She shivered and I smiled.

The small band Laney hired had just begun their first set, so I swayed with Fiona a little as we stood beside the dance floor. The newlyweds were about to have their first dance and I intended to spend the rest of the evening with my girl in my arms, both here and upstairs in the hotel room I'd booked for the night.

Nate and Laney had chosen to dance to "The One" by Kodaline, and as the song started even I had to admit they looked pretty damn perfect dancing out there with eyes only for each other. That was, until Rocco decided to join in. Nate bent down and easily hoisted him up to join in the dance.

"Awww," Fiona said into my shoulder and I could swear I heard her sniffle. Apart from Laney and Nate, I don't think there was a happier person in the room than my Shortcake. That's just who she is.

When the song was over and everyone clapped uproariously, the band's lead singer invited everyone to join the couple on the dance floor and enjoy the music. Fiona and Laney performed a shockingly sexy dance that had me almost sweeping Fiona away to our room that minute. I managed to resist, but I made sure every man in the room knew she was spoken for. I was less than subtle in my claim and caused Fiona to smack my chest at one point and call me a caveman.

I was just about to suggest we take a break and get another drink when the lead singer addressed the crowd again. "This one is a special request for Mark, one of tonight's groomsmen. Enjoy." I pulled my head back in confusion and then looked down at Fiona, sure she had to be the one behind this. But she looked just as clueless as I was.

Then the first chords of a song I knew better than any other in the world rang out over the room. I swiveled my head in search of the culprit and, sure enough, Bailey stood leaning into a high table across the room. She was wearing a strapless dress identical to Fiona's, and I had to admit the girl cleaned up good. When I caught her eye, she smiled her smartass smile and lifted her drink to me in a silent toast. I laughed out loud and ushered a confused Fiona back onto the floor where we proceeded to dance to "Kiss Me Slowly."

Fiona burrowed into me and then, partway through the song, she drew back and looked up at me, her eyes alight. "I live on the fourteenth floor! That's got to mean something!"

I smiled and said, "Yeah, I think it does."

The song was just winding down when I heard Nate's voice come from my right. "What in the hell does he think he's doing?"

I turned in his direction and Fiona and I moved closer. "Who?"

"Your asshole brother," he said, gesturing to the other side of the room with his chin.

I'm allowed to call Jake all sorts of filthy names because he's my brother and he usually deserves it, but I was taken aback by the uncharacteristic acid in Nate's tone. That was, until I looked over and saw that my brother was indeed the asshole who happened to be kissing Bailey in the corner of the room, his hand halfway up her thigh.

Fuck!

Laney and Fiona both gasped and then for some reason known only to the female population of this planet, they both sighed and said, "Aww."

"This shit is not happening," Nate spat out and started to remove his jacket.

"Whoa there, Mayweather, I got this. Stick with your bride and go cut some cake or something." I eyed both women and they ushered his ass away.

By the time I got across the room, the slutty little slutbags were nowhere to be seen. I made a token effort to search the adjoining hallway and the men's room (I wouldn't put much past Jake) but came up empty.

Back in the reception hall, I found the rest of the wedding party gathered together watching Rocco show off some hilarious dance moves.

"He totally gets that from me," Laney said, and I actually think she was being serious.

I put a hand on Nate's shoulder and gave him a thumbs-up when he turned to me. No use spoiling his big night. Bailey and

Jake were both adults and nothing I could say would have made a difference anyway.

Rocco finished his performance by giving a little bow to hoots and cheers from his family, and then Gavin spoke up.

"Well, I guess it's about that time," he said and then walked toward the band to take the mic and start his Best Man speech. We all turned our attention to him and he ran a nervous hand through his messy brown hair.

"Um, hi everybody. For those of you who don't know me, I'm Gavin, Laney's brother. I wanted to say a few words to the happy couple." He gestured in our general direction and someone in the crowd hooted.

"Nate, I've never had a brother but I'm proud to call you one now. You make my big sis and the little dude happy, and that's what counts in my book."

Laney and Fiona both awwed again.

"Laney, you've been a great sister and a better friend than I probably deserve, and I'm really happy for you that you found the right guy to make your family complete."

Nate looked at his shoes and Laney tucked her arm around his waist while she beamed at her brother.

"Now, I was going to end my speech there, but I think something else needs to be said, so everyone please raise your glasses for a toast." We all obeyed and Gavin smiled. "To Laney and Nate, as they enter into this union, may they only have happy endings!"

Fiona squealed and fist pumped the air.

Laney buried her face in Nate's shoulder.

Nate dropped his head in defeat.

And I threw my head back and laughed my fucking ass off.

~THE END ~

Continue the series with **The Lucky One**, Bailey and Jake's story. Read on for an excerpt.

Stay up to date on Sylvie's upcoming books and projects by subscribing to her newsletter! http://bit.ly/NewsSylvie

www.sylviestewartauthor.com

* * *

BONUS SCENE and DOWNLOAD!

Here are two exclusive extras for this latest edition of *The Spark*:

- Print and complete this fun word search based on *The Spark* for your chance to win a signed paperback! http://bit.ly/TheSparkWS
- Want to read what happens next for Kelly? Read the exclusive **Bonus Scene!** http://bit.ly/TheSparkBonus

ABOUT THE AUTHOR

USA Today bestselling author Sylvie Stewart is addicted to Romantic Comedy and Contemporary Romance, and she's not looking for a cure. She hails from the great state of North Carolina, so it's no surprise that most of her books are set in the Tar Heel state. She's a wife to a hilarious dude and mommy to ten-year-old twin boys who tend to take after their father in every way. Sylvie often wonders if they're actually hers, but then she remembers being a human incubator for a gazillion months. Ah, good times.

Sylvie began publishing when her kids started elementary school, and she loves sharing her stories with readers and hopefully making them laugh and swoon a bit along the way. If she's not in her comfy green writing chair, she's probably camping or kayaking with her family or having a glass of wine while binge-watching Hulu. Or she's been kidnapped—so what are you doing just sitting there?!!

**Winner of the 2017 National Indie Excellence Award for Romantic Comedy

**Winner of the 2017 Readers' Favorite Silver Medal for Romantic Comedy

* * *

Thank you so much for reading *The Spark* – I hope you enjoyed it. If you did, a **review** on your favorite book site is always appreciated!

* * *

Want to stay updated on new releases, promotions and giveaways?
Subscribe to my newsletter! http://bit.ly/NewsSylvie

Want to hang out with me and my other readers?
Join my reader group on Facebook: **Sylvie's Spot - for the Sexy, Sassy, and Smartassy!** http://facebook.com/groups/SylviesSpot

Thanks! XOXO,
Sylvie

Keep up to date and keep in touch!
www.sylviestewartauthor.com
sylvie@sylviestewartauthor.com
Follow me on BookBub for sales and new releases!

facebook.com/SylvieStewartAuthor

twitter.com/sylvie_stewart_

instagram.com/sylvie.stewart.romance

I would like to apologize to the great state of New Jersey. It's not me, it's Fiona. I swear.

Also, if you're wondering what makes Mark smell so good, it's Hudson Made *Worker's Soap*. Makes hard-working men smell yummy!

Chapter One: Hello, My Name Is Satan

BAILEY

"I swear his eyes are following me."

"It *is* a little creepy, I'm not gonna lie," said Mark, glancing over my shoulder.

A shiver ran down my spine and the hairs on the back of my neck stood at attention.

Mark took in my expression—which I'm sure was one of intense revulsion—and laughed right in my face, his straight white teeth not even attempting to bite his tongue. This was entirely unsurprising.

Mark's day is not complete unless he has tortured me in some way. He's the twin brother I never had and certainly never wanted. I already have an older brother, but Mark somehow worked his way into my life and I can't seem to get rid of him and his ridiculously bulky bod no matter how hard I try.

Still smiling at my pain, Mark shook his head and asked, "If he freaks you out so much, why the hell did you say yes?"

I glared at him, hands on my hips. "What in the hell was I supposed to do?! There were tears! Wet, sloppy tears!"

This did nothing to tame his smile. "You are such a fucking pushover," he whispered in my ear before skirting around me and approaching the creepy son-of-a-bitch.

"Ha!" I declared as I turned around, completely forgetting to keep my gaze averted. "Shows how much you know. I talked the kid down from a puppy!" I was actually quite proud of myself, despite my lack of forethought.

Turns out I can't stand lizards. Who knew? But the joyous expression on my nephew's face and the complete cessation of all waterworks was my prize to revel in.

Totally worth it.

I'm sure I broke every babysitting rule in the book, but desperate times call for desperate measures. It looked like my brother and his new wife just got themselves a pet gecko.

Whoops.

"Okay, little man. Everything is all set up," Mark said to a nearly-vibrating Rocco. "The light will keep him nice and warm, he's got a good place to hide in that log, and your Aunt Bailey will show you how to feed him the crickets." Mark's smile turned evil as his eyes found me again.

What in God's name had I been thinking? To be fair, I had assumed these crickets would be dead when the twelve-year-old sales associate had pushed his glasses up on his nose and mentioned we'd need to stock up. By the time I realized we would instead be bringing home a plastic container teeming with live insects, it was too late. Rocco, my adorable nephew, had fallen in love.

"Fist bump," Mark requested of Rocco, whose attention was completely captured by his new pet. Rocco extended his little fist without letting his eyes stray from the tank. "Thanks, Mark."

"Sure thing," Mark replied, ruffling the kid's dark hair. Then to me, "I gotta get back to Fiona."

"Is she feeling any better?" I asked, leaning against Rocco's dresser.

"Eh, hard to say."

Mark looked slightly distressed at the thought, and I marveled for the umpteenth time at the transformation my once-slutty friend had undergone since meeting his girlfriend, Fiona. Gone was the arrogant manwhore and in his place was an arrogant, pussy-whipped little douchebag. Ah, it warms the heart.

"I picked up an antibiotic for her, so hopefully that will start working soon," he said as he gathered his things.

I felt a sympathy pain in my throat just thinking about Fiona and her bout of strep throat. I cursed the damn virus for forcing me to step in and babysit Rocco while my brother, Nate, and his new wife, Laney, were off on their honeymoon. The same virus that, today, revealed just how ill-equipped I was to care for a child without becoming the biggest sucker known to man. "Well, tell her I hope she feels better and not to worry about Rocco—I got this."

Mark stopped in his tracks on his way to the door. He cocked his head, his eyebrows arching and his mouth sporting that damn smirk I wanted to knock off his stupid face. "Oh, I can see that."

I flipped him off, confident that Rocco's attention was elsewhere.

Mark's smug cackle echoed in the hallway outside Rocco's bedroom. "I'll let myself out!"

"You do that, Buffy!" Asshole.

Damn. It was just me and the kid again.

It's not that I don't like kids—I love my new nephew. I'm just not all that comfortable around tiny humans. I think I'm always waiting for them to judge me and find me inadequate somehow.

I'm the youngest of two kids, and I was never the babysitting type. My teen years had been spent sketching, reading, and plotting to get Nate in trouble whenever possible. And I'm a total daddy's girl, so I never pursued anything Riordan Murphy would consider "girly," much to my mom's disappointment. Babysitting, makeup lessons, and trips to the mall were eschewed in favor of hanging out at building sites with my dad and rocking out to heavy metal while painting and drawing. And, although my taste in music evolved as I reached adulthood, the rest pretty much stayed the same.

Everything I knew about taking care of a child consisted of lessons learned through trial and error over the last twenty-four hours.

I had been minding my own damn business last night, scarfing down cold pizza and channel surfing, when my phone had rung. I'd been ready to let it go to voicemail when I saw it was my brother. I hit the accept button; I should have let it go to voicemail.

* * *

Get your copy of ***The Lucky One*** today!

ALSO BY SYLVIE STEWART

The Carolina Connection Series:

The Lucky One *(Carolina Connections Book 3)*

The Game *(Carolina Connections Book 4)*

The Way You Are *(Carolina Connections Book 5)*

The Runaround *(Carolina Connections Book 6)*

* * *

The Nerd Next Door *(Carolina Kisses, Book 1)*

Then Again

Happy New You

Game Changer

About That

Full-On Clinger

* * *

Between a Rock and a Royal *(Kings of Carolina, Book 1*

Blue Bloods and Backroads *(Kings of Carolina,* Book 2)